**SHE HUNGERED FOR A MAN
SHE COULD TRUST AND LOVE
WHERE MEN LUSTED ONLY FOR
FLESH AND GOLD.**

Raised by Indians after her own westward-bound parents are massacred, Dawn Carlyle is left wandering naked and alone when the tribe that raised her is wiped out.

Nevada Jones, the man who finds her, saves her from his own partner's lust, defends her to the wagon boss who fears her, and protects her innocence with his very life . . . until they reach the Lost Chinaman.

But in the raw violence of the mining camp, Nevada's fortunes take a bitter turn. Again Dawn is on her own. Barely a woman, but growing in candor, soaring in courage and spirit, she faces a savage world where women are few, where men lust and kill for the two things they want most—women and gold!

THIS FEVER
IN MY BLOOD

MARY LOUISE MANNING

A DELL/BRYANS BOOK

Published by
Dell Publishing Co., Inc.
1 Dag Hammarskjold Plaza
New York, New York 10017

Dell ® TM 681510, Dell Publishing Co., Inc.

ISBN: 0-440-18684-6

Printed in the United States of America

First printing—February 1980

Hungry Moon had chosen to meet the Great Sleep, and she was naked under her warm robe of braided rabbitskins. The coming night had the smell of mountain snow on its breath.

Hungry Moon stared dully at the baskets of provisions the others had left her as she'd sat, silent and stubborn, with her back to the bole of an ancient juniper near the crest of the hill. Her eldest son, Runs Down Antelope, had left too much food, but he'd always been a foolishly generous person, even for a Paiute. Runs Down Antelope had not wanted to leave his mother behind when she announced she was no longer able to keep up with the band. He had even offered to carry her, as if she'd been a child, but in the end, Medicine Dreamer and the other older and wiser men had persuaded her weeping son to follow the way of the Real People.

At last she was alone.

She wondered how long it would take her to die. It was a thing nobody knew. Sometimes, as the bands wandered, they came upon the remains of some old person left behind the winter before, but there was no way of guessing how long they'd lived after being abandoned to the Long Sleep.

A chill gust swept over the hill from the distant

Sierra Nevada to the west as the sun sank low, and despite her warm robe, Hungry Moon shuddered. She was used to hunger. Her name had been given her by the women of her clan because of her coming into the world during the awful late summer of the Great Basin, when the hunting was at its poorest. She had no memory of the famine she'd been born into, but in sixty-odd summers a Paiute woman became very aware of what it felt like to go days or even weeks without so much as a grasshopper to eat.

Now there was plenty to eat in the covered baskets her sons and daughters had given her. Any Paiute could live for months on the piñon nuts and jerked rabbit they'd thrust on her. It was the wolf wind from the north that would kill her. Her son had insisted on leaving a fire drill and had even gathered dry cones and bark in case she changed her mind, but Hungry Moon had decided not to build a fire. And winter was upon the Great Basin.

She wondered if she'd see the fire of her son's camp through the coming night. Paiute bands wandered constantly over the basin-and-range country in search of such meagre fare as the semidesert provided those keen of eye and cunning of wit. So Runs Down Antelope and his people would not be far for the first few days, and . . . Hungry Moon bade the thought be gone. Of course she could catch up with them, if she made any effort at all, but she was old and tired and her mind was made up.

She didn't know what arthritis was, but she knew its agony. Each long march was getting more painful than the last, and the snow would lie deep in the passes where her band intended to winter through. Hunting was good in the winter. No Paiute ever went hungry when the freshly fallen snow betrayed every passing beast's tracks, but it hurt her so much to live through the colder moons—and what was the point of it all?

Her few surviving children were grown, with children of their own to provide for. Once she had loved a man, but he no longer smiled across the evening fire at her. How long had it been since the Horse Utes had killed him, over near the Humboldt River? Could it really have been more than ten summers ago? Hungry Moon frowned, counting rabbit drives and the births and deaths of infants in her mind until, in the end, ten summers seemed about right.

"Damn the Horse Utes!" she swore bitterly. "They had no reason to kill our Rabbit Boss. The Mexicans no longer pay for scalps, even when the Horse Utes lie and say they came from Apache heads. Medicine Dreamer used to say the Horse Utes sold scalps to those funny-looking people over by the Great Salt Lake, but that's not true, either. Horse Utes are just wicked people!"

Inside her robe, Hungry Moon absently began to fondle her genitals as she thought about her long-dead husband. There was no reason not to masturbate and it had been a long time since she'd done it last, but she stopped and decided to think about something else. It was only self-torture to stimulate oneself when the sun and winds had made one an object no man ever smiled upon. Besides, she had plenty of time before the Long Sleep claimed her. Maybe later, when it was dark, she could throw off the robe and work up a sweat masturbating in the night winds. Yes, that would surely hasten the end, and thinking about her long-dead lover would keep her mind off the cold.

The hillside where Hungry Moon awaited death was covered with a ragged growth of piñon and juniper brush, and when she first heard the odd sounds she couldn't see what was making them. They sounded like a crying child, but Runs Down Antelope and his band had left hours ago and there were no other Real People within a day's hunt. Perhaps it was a bird. The canyon jays made all sorts of odd sounds for reasons only a bird could understand. If she simply sat still, the source of the noises would doubtless appear.

For at least five minutes as the White Eyes counted time, there was silence. Then, farther off, the weird sound was repeated. The birdcall, if that was what it was, sounded very much like a child calling out to someone, though in words no Real Person's child had ever been heard to utter.

"It's going away." Hungry Moon shrugged as if that settled the matter, but of course it did not. Hungry Moon had spent her life as a food-gatherer, and curiosity formed a large part of her survival instincts. If the creature making the funny noises went away, she'd never know what it was.

On the other hand, her hip was bothering her again and the damned noises were coming from at least three minutes' walk away. What did it matter to a dying person? Even if she learned a new thing, she'd be dead in a few days, anyway, and . . .

"Mamma, where are you?" called the distant voice. This time, despite her ignorance of the meaning of the words, Hungry Moon sensed that the sounds were made by a human child.

"Well, what of it?" she grumbled aloud. "I am a dead person. There's nothing I can do if some idiot of a young mother has let her child stray from the gathering line. They'll miss the child in a little while and somebody will find it. People have no right to lose children near a person trying to die with dignity."

"Mamma! I can't see you!" The sobbing wail echoed through the scrub and Hungry Moon grimaced and leaned forward. She moved her bare heels under her center of balance and, bracing her back against the juniper trunk, forced her aching body erect as the distant child wailed again.

"I'm coming, you inconsiderate brat!" grumbled the old woman, making her way through the scrub toward the sounds. Her hip ached as if red ants were gnawing at her bones, and she was cursing savagely as she searched for the source of her annoyance. Later she would always insist she'd been about to give up, but in truth her mind welcomed any diversion after hours of cramped boredom. Despite her age and arthritis, Hungry Moon was a healthy woman with an active mind and had found waiting for the Big Sleep a very tedious business.

No native of the Great Basin could survive a month without a keen set of senses and the ability to use them well. Hence, once she'd decided to locate the source of those ridiculous noises, Hungry Moon had only to limp a short distance to intercept their wandering path through the brush.

Hungry Moon saw the lost child and stopped. The child was now coming her way, and no Paiute likes to waste energy on useless movement.

The lost child was a little girl of perhaps five, dressed in the printed calico of the White Eyes, with hair the color of bunch grass in the dry season. Her exposed skin was pinkly sunburned, and Hungry Moon remembered that the funny-looking people with the big wagons burned easily in the desert sun. The Paiute woman slipped off her robe and limped, naked,

toward the lost child, calling out, "Here, wrap yourself
up. You look like you have been boiled with camas
roots."

The child stared open-mouthed at the apparition of
a naked brown lady draped to the waist in greasy
iron-gray hair. For a moment she seemed poised to
run. But to Hungry Moon she looked as if she'd been
running and running all day and couldn't find the
White Eyes' wagons.

"Have you seen my mamma?" asked the child, cautiously.

Hungry Moon had no idea what the words meant,
but she saw that the child was frightened and managed to smile, hiding her annoyance as she held out
the rabbitskin robe. "Get out of that sun, you silly
little thing. I was getting ready to die, but I have
some food and maybe we'll stay alive until your people
come looking for you."

The lost white child stared soberly up at the smiling Indian woman for a long moment. Then, responding to the exposed yellow teeth of Hungry Moon, she
smiled shyly back. "How do, ma'am. My name is
Ruth Jean and we is trying to catch up with our wagon
party. We busted a wheel and got left a-hind and
Dad says we gotta hurry and catch up, for there's
snow on the mountains coming and a heap of bad
Injuns hereabouts."

The woman didn't answer and the child asked,
"Are you an Injun, ma'am?"

Hungry Moon came over, wrapped the child in the
robe, and picked her up, grimacing silently as a sharp
pain lanced through her hip. Then she started walking
back to where she'd chosen to die, crooning a Paiute
lullaby half under her breath as she sought to gather
her thoughts. This unexpected event was very con-

fusing, and the babble of strange words in Hungry Moon's ear didn't help as she carried the foundling. Hungry Moon knew a few words of other Indian dialects, and could ask for salt and tobacco in Spanish. This awful little girl wasn't saying one word Hungry Moon had ever heard before.

Halfway to the juniper where she'd left her provisions, she told the child to shut up, but the effort was wasted, for the mysterious thing the White Eyes had lost in the desert simply prattled on. "I mind they didn't know I'd woke up early and got out of the wagon to play with my migs. Mamma says it ain't right for a girl child to play with migs like boys do, but Dad allowed it don't do any harm. What do you think?"

With a last gasp of tortured effort, Hungry Moon reached the juniper trunk and slid down it, the child squirming around into her lap and throwing aside the rabbitskin robe. "Oh, my," she chortled, "it's so nice and shady under these trees, but I'm pure thirsty just the same, ma'am."

Hungry Moon didn't understand the words, but she didn't have to be told to know the lost child would be thirsty. Shoving the little girl off her lap, she reached for a gourd of drinking water and pulled the rag stopper with her teeth. She offered it to the child, who drank much faster than any Paiute child would have. Hungry Moon pulled the gourd away and said firmly, "That's enough. You waste water if you drink enough to throw up."

Then, grudgingly, she uncovered a flat basket of shelled pine nuts. "Eat. You are very fat for such a young girl—but I was about to die anyway, and the food is of no use to me."

The girl calling herself Ruth Jean gingerly tasted

a single pine nut. Then, as she chewed and swallowed, she grinned and said, "Oh, my, these are better than popcorn, ain't they?"

Despite herself, Hungry Moon smiled back. The freakishly blonde little thing was sort of pretty when she smiled like that. The Paiute woman said, "If you were a Real Person, your name would be Dawn. When you smile with your whole face like that, it's like the dawn breaking over the desert in the good hunting moons. Once I had a child about your age and she smiled well, too. We named her Laughing Bird, but I think Dawn would have been a better name. I didn't think of it then, though, and she died before I thought to give her a better name."

"Would you like to see my migs, lady?"

"Many of the children died on that march. Our medicine was bad, and the waterholes were empty when we reached them. What are you doing with those funny little beads?"

The lostling had taken four glass marbles from a pocket sewn into her tattered gingham dress and spread them out on the dust between them. "These are my migs. One of the boys in our train gave 'em to me and I know how to shoot 'em. You want to see?"

Suiting action to words, the child the Paiute would know as Dawn brushed a space near her knees clear of pine and juniper needles and drew a circle in the dust with a twig. She put three marbles in the circle. "This clearie is my best shooter. I've been learning and learning, and when I get to California I'll bet I can beat any durned old boy at migs, so there!"

Hungry Moon watched with detached amusement as the child played with the marbles near her knees. It was a silly game, but harmless. The object seemed to be to knock one bead out of the ring with the bigger clear glass one. After a time, with meaningless words but obvious enough gestures, the child asked the old woman if she wanted to play migs. Hungry Moon shrugged and decided to try.

The game was not without its points of interest, after all. It was more difficult than it looked to make the little glass ball go the way one wanted it to. It took Hungry Moon almost an hour to get the hang of it, and by this time it was getting dark.

Hungry Moon had planned no night fire, of course, since a dying person needs no night fire, but there was only one robe, and this funny little stranger might not be used to the desert nights of early winter.

So Hungry Moon took her fire bow and started a modest blaze as the child scampered among the trees, gathering brushwood. When she threw too much on the fire, Hungry Moon warned, "Don't make a fire like a damned Mexican, child. Too big a campfire means you cook on one side and freeze on the other. You see, we make a small fire and we can sit close to it, the way Real People do."

Then, noting that the child seemed hurt by the scolding tone of her words, Hungry Moon sighed. "Oh, damn, as long as we have a fire I suppose I may as well cook something."

The Paiute people had neither pots nor pans, but they made do with ingenuity. Hungry Moon filled a watertight basket with water and grated jerked meat and dried roots while waiting for the rocks she'd thrown on her fire to glow red hot. Then she took a rock from the fire with moist twigs held like chopsticks, blew the ash from the rock, and dropped it, sizzling, into the water-filled basket. She removed the rock as it cooled, replacing it on the fire, and dropped another white-hot sliver of granite in the now somewhat warmer liquid. By the time she'd repeated the process a few times, the water was boiling.

The soup she prepared would have been passable in a white woman's kitchen. To the hungry child it was manna. Years later, as the belle of San Francisco society, Dawn Carlyle would be famed for her occasional servings of "that goddam Injun slop of hers!"

By then she would have forgotten her first night under the stars with Hungry Moon, as well as her real name and the fate of her real parents. But she would never forget the fragrance of Paiute camp cookery, nor, try as she might, recapture it on a white woman's kitchen range.

In truth, the first meal she was to share with a Paiute was meager, even by Indian standards, for Hungry Moon was worried about how long this nonsense was liable to last. Runs Down Antelope had left her enough provisions to last a few months at her own rate of consumption. A growing child who kept asking for more was another thing entirely.

At last the ravenous little girl had eaten enough to keep her quiet and make her sleepy, so as the night fire burned low, the two of them dozed the cold night away. Or rather, Hungry Moon dozed while the child slept soundly in her arms under the soft fluffy robe. Hungry Moon had been afraid the sunburn would make the child fretful, but Dawn, as the woman now thought of her, was too exhausted by her ordeal to be kept awake by mere discomfort. By morning the fire had died out completely and it was starting to snow.

Gingerly, so as not to wake the child, Hungry Moon slipped from under the robe and, squatting naked in the gently falling first flakes of winter, began to spin her first stick with the bow. She frowned at her strong brown hands as she worked, for while there was plenty of wood, she knew she was doing a foolish thing. If she kept them warm, they'd slowly starve. Everyone knew freezing was a faster and easier way to die. Why was she doing this? Damn that child! Why had her crazy parents abandoned her on a Real Person's mountain, anyway?

Behind Hungry Moon, Dawn sat up and stared out sleepily from under the rabbitskin robe. Then she laughed. "Oh, it's snowing!"

She came over to the Indian woman and hugged her. "Good morning, Injun lady. Ain't you cold without no shimmy or nothing?"

The fire tools in Hungry Moon's hands blurred, and she stopped what she was doing to place one hand on one smooth little arm the child had wrapped around her neck. Dawn leaned her own blonde head against Hungry Moon's gray strands and said, "You're a nice lady and I love you."

The words meant nothing to a Paiute, but somehow Hungry Moon understood. Not looking at the child, Hungry Moon stared up at the low-hanging winter clouds and muttered, "Ka!"

Then she got stiffly to her feet, picked up the rabbitskin robe, and wrapped the child in it before lifting her to one shoulder and starting down the slope.

The trek took all morning and much of the afternoon, and Hungry Moon's hip was a raging inferno of shooting pains as she reached the circle of brush shelters hastily erected around a council fire in a sheltered draw. But Hungry Moon was hardly limping as she put the child down, wrapped herself once more in her robe, and, leading Dawn by one hand, walked over to the group of Indians.

One of the five men warming their hands over the

central campfire glanced up and gasped. Then Runs
Down Antelope leaped to his feet and called out joy-
ously, "Mother! I never thought we'd see you again!
What has happened? Why do you have that child
with you? She looks like a Saltu!"

Hungry Moon answered calmly. "She used to be a
Saltu. Now she is mine. Her name, Dawn, was given
to me in a sudden vision, and I shall not have her
called anything else."

The chief of the Sage Grouse clan smiled down at
the little white girl. "I welcome you to my full sharing, little sister," he said.

Then, as other Paiute came out to circle the newcomers with happy but uncertain smiles, Runs Down
Antelope shot his mother a cautious look. "If you have
a new child, you will have to take care of her, Mother.
I know you had other plans, but—forgive me if I seem
rude—my women have their own children to care
for."

"I have changed my mind," said Hungry Moon,
simply. Then, holding the hand of her new reason for
existence, she added, "I don't think this would be a
good day to die."

The child called Dawn was twice favored by fate
in joining the band of Runs Down Antelope when she
did. The snows came early that winter of 1843, and her
real parents would die in a nightmare disaster of the
High Sierra. Fate's second favor to the lost child
was that the Indians were going into their winter
encampment; no white child, even one as healthy as
Dawn, could have lasted a month with Paiute on the
move without the hardening Dawn received under
Hungry Moon's care.

Runs Down Antelope would never appear on any

white man's list of warrior chiefs. His twenty-odd years had been spent in simply keeping himself and his people alive. Yet Runs Down Antelope was a great leader in his own right. He led the Sage Grouse clan that winter into a sheltered valley in the rolling foothills claimed by fearsome warriors, knowing that his mounted enemies would not be patrolling their hunting grounds in the deepening snows. The same blizzards that decimated white travelers in the Sierras were a blessing to those native Americans who knew how to live with nature instead of fighting her.

The Sage Grouse clan was part of the great ethnic stock the white men classified as Uzo-Aztec and, as the name indicates, shared a common ancestry and language with the semicivilized, bloody-minded Aztecs of Mexico, the peace-loving Hopi farmers of the Black Mesa, and less civilized "tribes" of the semidesert Great Basin. The tribal names given them by white men meant nothing to the people labeled with them. They called themselves Ho (people). Indians who spoke other dialects were Saltu (stranger). The strangers who crossed their lands in big wagons were Saltu with White Eyes.

The white men made snap judgments and divided the Real People into "tribes" based on the way various bands lived. One group of Ho, living near the well-watered grasslands of the Humboldt River valley, had obtained horses from their Shoshoni cousins to the north and learned to live as desert raiders. These bands were called Horse Utes, or Bannock, by the white men who'd learned to fear and hence respect them. Those related bands who clung to the old food-gathering life, afoot, were dismissed as "Diggers" by the white man and treated with the contempt he felt they deserved.

The Sage Grouse people were Diggers, not because they didn't have enough sense to break and ride horses, but because the lands they wandered were too dry and barren for horses to survive in. A horse must drink water every day. A human being can last up to four without it. A horse, while swifter by far than a man afoot, must rest after a thirty- to fifty-mile journey. A Paiute huntsman often covered a hundred miles without a break. Runs Down Antelope had earned his name through his ability to do just that. A pronghorn antelope can run sixty miles an hour for a short distance. A determined hungry man can simply jog along after it until sooner or later he catches up with the exhausted frightened animal. A white man would have frozen or starved in the valley Runs Down Antelope chose for that winter's quarters. To Real People, it was a welcome change from their endless wanderings.

The Innuit—white men called them Eskimos—were not alone in their knowledge of the igloo. The Diggers built theirs in an easier way. Brush was gathered from the hillsides and piled up into what might have seemed flimsy shelters until drifting snows covered them with an insulating blanket. The same hillsides produced firewood in abundance and even a lazy younger wife had little trouble keeping her snug lodge warm with a tiny Indian fire sunk in its earthen floor.

A few boiling stones and a supply of tightly woven waterproof baskets were all she needed for cooking, and the snow provided endless water for the often thirsty wanderers.

The People went nearly naked, of course, and white men could never fathom how naked Diggers survived the knife-edged cold of a Great Basin winter. Yet here again appearances were deceptive.

Dawn's rescuers would have laughed at the thought of any man's going outside when the wolf winds blew. It seemed only common sense to know that every blizzard must end sooner or later, so the Real People simply sat in their snug lodges, wrapped in loose, warm rabbitskin robes, until the storms blew themselves out.

Between blizzards, the sunny snow-covered slopes were as comfortable to move about on as anyone with a reasonably tough skin could ask. Dawn's dangerously damp cotton clothes were removed and discarded by Hungry Moon, lest the child grow chilled. Then, naked like the other children, she was sent out to play on milder days.

"Play" to Indian children consisted of trying to behave as much like their elders as their size and skills allowed. Boys helped their fathers set rabbit snares along the game trails through the brush. Girls were given little digging sticks and probed for food the way they'd watched their mothers do. When a boy snared a quail or rabbit, or a girl found a horde of nuts stored between the rocks by an outraged ground squirrel, they were praised and petted for their cleverness. If they failed in these efforts, or simply wasted time running boisterously about, nothing was said. Striking a child, or anyone smaller than oneself, was considered a cowardly act of mindless cruelty in most Indian cultures. Children were expected to learn by example. Those few who never learned to be Real People were punished, in time, simply by failing to survive as adults.

Dawn's naked skin toughened and tanned as her legs grew strong on the slopes and her hair bleached to silver-blonde. At an age when her white contemporaries were learning the alphabet, Dawn was learning that the underground tuber the white man called bitterroot could be scraped free of its astringent outer coating and baked like a potato. She was ignorant of the well-known "fact" that the bitter acorns of the scrub oak were inedible, for she'd helped Hungry Moon leach the tannin out of acorns by tedious rinsings until the sweet, starchy stone-ground paste could be baked into unleavened bread in the hot ashes of her foster mother's hearth.

White settlers often suffered a deficiency disease they called rabbit hunger, and many marveled at the ability of the Diggers to live on the tough lean flesh of the desert hare. Dawn would never forget that rabbit flesh, alone, lacks carbohydrates and must be basted with internal organ fat and eaten with roots or nuts to make a filling meal.

She learned to weave baskets. Never, it's true, with the skill she'd always admire in future years, but baskets good enough for grudging acceptance by Hungry Moon. It was Hungry Moon who taught her how, in the future, to tell a Real Woman's basket from the mass-produced fakes the West would one day be cluttered with. For no Real Woman ever produced a *perfect* basket, no matter how skilled she might be. The spirits were liable to be offended by perfection. Hence, most Indian weavers made one deliberate mistake to show Spider Woman they meant no arrogance. In later years Dawn would look for the break in the design, or perhaps a clumsy splice in an otherwise perfect spiral weave, and when she failed to find it, smile and say, "Made in Japan, I'd guess."

She learned stories. Stores her own children and grandchildren would hear in delighted wonder. For there were many days she could not leave Hungry Moon's lodge and the old woman told her of Changing

Woman and Laughing Girl, or the terrible Spirit Bear, who often walked at sunset, disguised as a Real Person. When you met a stranger, you had to sneak a quick glance at his footprints in the dust behind him, for though Spirit Bear looked like a Real Person, his footprints were always backward. Hungry Moon had never seen Spirit Bear, but then, she'd always been very careful to look at a stranger's feet. Spirit Bear avoids Real People who are wise.

By the time the first avalanche lilies were pushing up through the melting spring snows, Dawn was leaner and stronger than most white boys her own age. Runs Down Antelope noted the lilies as a source of edible bulbs, and a warning that the snow-choked passes were once again open to his mounted enemies.

As the band left winter quarters, Dawn's sturdy young legs carried her with a spring few adult whites could have matched, and her tongue had mastered the difficult sounds of the Ho language.

Later in life she would read the often foolish things written in the white man's books. She spoke Ho with the Paiute accent but called it Shoshoni, as most whites termed the common language of the Great Basin, although her knowledge of Indian culture would allow her to enjoy privately the Indian jokes about some of the other silly things white men said.

Springtime is pleasant in the Great Basin. The open playas between the endless ridges of rimrock are green in the spring, and purling brooks run down from the high country to form lakes and ponds as cool and blue as they are insubstantial. Ghostly transparent shrimp and tiny singing toads magically appear in temporary desert ponds, to be gathered in open-weave baskets and eaten with relish. Shrubs that stand as dead-looking bundles of twigs through most of the year put out leaves and berries for a few short weeks, and the dunes are covered with carpets of tiny flowers that go to seed, wither, and vanish within days.

Deer come down from the high country to share the lush grazing with tougher desert hare and antelope. Vast marshlands form in low-lying desert flats to be crowded for short periods by migrating water fowl. To the Ho, it was a good time to be alive.

By late June the grass was the color of Dawn's hair. By July the game had retreated to the high country, where Runs Down Antelope dared not follow. By August, Dawn had discovered what it was to live with hunger as a constant companion.

The hunger of a food-gathering band is not the hunger of an occasional missed meal. It is a constant preoccupation. Skilled by a thousand years of wandering the Great Basin, the Diggers seldom starved to death. Yet there was never quite enough to eat.

Dawn and her friends ate grass seed. They ate lizards, snakes, and insects. Sometimes they managed to catch a rabbit. Sometimes they were lucky enough to net a swarm of Mormon crickets, and such days were remembered as feast days, for the wingless Mormon cricket tastes very much like shrimp and was eaten with the same relish.

There was salt to be gathered in the bitter desert flats, and dried bodies of red ants made a fine spice when added to a stew of desert roots, reptile, or other meat knocked down by the cleverly thrown digging stick of an alert Indian.

The Sage Grouse clan had never heard of the term "Indian file" and would have considered it a silly way to travel, in any case. The band moved abreast, sweeping the land with the fine-tooth comb of a hundred hungry eyes as they traveled. Dawn stalked the desert at the side of the limping Hungry Moon, learning to find food in barren dunes even a Bannock would have scorned as empty.

Along with an ability at food gathering, the child learned what it was to be a Real Person. One morning as they moved out, Dawn caught a lizard still sluggish from the cold night air. She grabbed it above the hind legs, well aware how the crafty lizard can shed its tail to a carelesss hand. She bit its head off as she'd seen the others do. The lizard's blood was delicious, for she hadn't eaten the day before, and Dawn was pleased with herself until she heard Hungry Moon's voice snap, "Are *you* going to eat that lizard, child?"

Abashed, Dawn turned to face her foster mother. "It's mine!" she stammered. "I *caught* it!"

Hungry Moon shook her head sternly. "Bear Woman is nursing a child. Her need is greater than yours."

The little girl licked her lips. The meaty taste was so very nice and, damn it, it was *her* lizard!

Dawn knew Hungry Moon wouldn't punish her. Her half-forgotten white mother had spanked, but these new friends were different. Dawn stared soberly up at the old woman for a time, the still-quivering ounces of fresh red meat in her hand as she gauged her alternatives. Then she sighed and turned away, spotting the distant figure of a woman carrying a baby on her back. Bear Woman had seen her catch the lizard, of course, but Bear Woman wasn't looking at her. Bear Woman was probing an anthill with her stick, looking for possible food and moisture.

Dawn turned back to Hungry Moon and asked, "Can I offer her half?"

"You do what you want to, child."

Dawn nodded, turned, and trotted toward Bear Woman. "I have something for you, Aunt Bear

Woman!" she called out as the young mother gave up digging in the dead and deserted anthill.

As Dawn ran toward Bear Woman with her gift, another woman drifted closer to Hungry Moon, who stood proudly watching, and murmured, "Her hair is strange, but you have a real daughter, Hungry Moon."

Hungry Moon didn't answer. Of course she had a real daughter. Had anyone ever doubted this for an instant?

Inspired by her neighbors to the north, Mexico had declared her independence in 1821, then fallen into a series of civil wars and petty dictatorships. Her vast holdings in what is now the American Southwest were neglected as a motley crew of political adventurers fought for control of the rich central mining and ranchlands around Mexico City. The Hispanic pioneers to the north of the Gila Rio Grande line were left to fend for themselves against Apache, Texan, and other interlopers.

The Spanish-speaking Californians were clinging to a handful of small towns along the Pacific shore as British, American, and Russian traders crowded in from the north and east. By the 1840s there were more Americans in northern California than there were Indians or Mexicans, for while Mexican rancheros held vast land grants on paper, the land was for the most part simply empty.

Some of the newcomers had gone through the formality of taking out Mexican citizenship and filing claims in Monterey for the lands they'd seized along what was even then known as the American river on the western slope of the Sierra Nevada. Others had simply carved out vast timber and grazing empires without so much as a by-your-leave, openly defying anyone to take an inch from them.

By 1846 the Americans had driven Russian traders away from the California shoreline and were presenting a problem to both governments. So they decided to go to war.

The Mexican War lasted from 1846 to 1848, and as wars go, it wasn't too bad. Few people were killed on either side, and the fighting in California was rather comic-opera. A Mexican militia leader named Pico shot up some truculent Americans just to the north of present-day Hollywood, and another "general" named Vallejo taught Frémont's Volunteers not to take a California ranchero's fighting ability for granted. Then, not wanting to get into serious trouble, the two sides avoided one another until a peace treaty could be worked out between Washington and Mexico City.

Few pioneers paid attention to any of this, and the Indians were unaware that anything unusual was going on among the White Eyes. Dawn and her Indian friends were too busy staying alive to worry about the occasional rumors of "Blue Sleeves" marching across the desert in force.

Runs Down Antelope had a war of his own to contend with.

His old enemies, the Horse Utes, had learned a new and dirty trick from the soldiers they alternately fought and traded with. It was called a water well.

The Horse Utes, or Bannock, pressed back from the pastures along the Humboldt by the rifles of the White Eyes, had learned to create water holes in hitherto barren desert with iron tools traded or stolen from the wagon trains. The Bannock adopted another white man's device called a feedbag, and a horse with canteen water and grain could move where no horse had ever moved before. Hence, the Digger clans were now faced with a new threat to their lives as once-safe desert flats were invaded by their fearsome cousins.

Just why the Bannock liked to murder Diggers has never been explained to anyone's satisfaction. The Diggers had nothing worth taking, even their lives. Yet the Bannock took them at every opportunity.

Perhaps the Bannock had learned to share the contempt felt by White Eyes for the wandering Digger bands. Perhaps, since the White Eyes were fearsome in their own right, it behooved a Bannock warrior to prove his manhood by attacking someone less apt to be armed with a Sharps rifle. Perhaps, as Hungry Moon observed, the Horse Utes were just wicked people. For whatever reason, the Bannock took to hunting down Diggers as if they were small game.

The way one survived was, as always, to keep moving. Even with water and grain, there were places where Runs Down Antelope knew a mounted enemy couldn't follow. The drifting sand dunes and cruel lava flats he chose, however, were not good places to find food, and the Sage Grouse clan suffered terribly. Old ones were left behind and children died in the years Dawn spent with her foster mother. And then, one morning, she lost Hungry Moon herself.

By this time Dawn was nine or ten and barely remembered any other life than the harsh one she'd been forced to lead. Hence, she knew that morning that Hungry Moon meant it when the old woman refused to rise from her seat near the hastily extinguished campfire.

Bannock had been spotted moments before on a distant rise, and Runs Down Antelope had said, simply, "We must run into those sand dunes to our south. They have seen us, but people can run faster in soft sand than any horse."

Catching his mother's eye, he'd looked away and muttered, "We cannot carry anyone. I have spoken."

Hungry Moon nodded. "Go. I shall meet Changing Woman in this place." And though she'd said this before, the others knew this time she meant it.

As the others started moving out, Dawn started to take the carrying basket from her tanned young shoulder. "I have some roots here, Mother," she began. But Hungry Moon shook her head. "Run, you silly child. The others can't wait if you fall behind."

"Are you sure you have spoken, Mother? I can help you, if your hip is bad this day."

"My hip is bad every day. I shall meet Changing Woman here, but you must go, Dawn. I ask you to save yourself in return for the few small favors I might have done for you in the past."

The girl swallowed hard. "I can't do it. I won't. I'll stay and help you fight the Bannock, as Laughing Girl fought the Na-Déné in the grandfather times."

The old woman's eyes misted, but her face was wooden. "You must run because I have spoken, Dawn. You must save yourself if your heart holds any love for me."

Dawn dropped to the sand near Hungry Moon and hugged the old woman, sobbing. "Oh, I do love you, Mother. Please try, just one more time!"

"You know of Changing Woman, and what she does when an old person elects to stay behind, Dawn?"

"Yes, Mother. They say, just before one dies a beautiful woman comes, smiling, and changes the dead person into someone or something lovely."

"Then listen to me, child. When Changing Woman

asks me what I would like to be in the next life, I shall tell her I wish to be reborn with hair the color of summer grass and a smile that makes one think of a beautiful day about to begin. In the meantime, your brother and the others are almost to the dunes and you had better run for it."

"Mother, I don't understand your words, but . . ."

"Someday you shall. Turn and run and don't look back. I shall be watching, with pride, as you overtake the others!"

Dawn started to say something. Then she saw a mounted Bannock on the rimrock less than a mile away and, without another word, turned and ran for her life.

They escaped the Bannock that time and the next, and it's possible the Bannock might never have caught Dawn's band. They were caught, however, by something far more deadly than their mounted enemies.

The white men called it measles.

Somewhere in the desert a white child with measles, moving west in a wagon train, coughed. The infection spread to the Sage Grouse clan, and the results, while ghastly, were all too predictable.

Although Dawn didn't remember it, she'd had measles when she was two. For members of her own race it was a childhood disease that seldom killed. To the American Indian it was a deadly plague they'd never been exposed to. Among healthy well-fed Indians the mortality rate from measles ran as high as 75 percent. The half-starved Diggers were in no condition to fight off even a white child's head cold. Runs Down Antelope, a whipcord-strong youth in his prime, was the first to die. He died quietly, shivering in agony, two days after the first warning flush of fever.

The others followed rapidly as Dream Singer prayed, shook a gourd rattle, and broke out in pustulant running sores to die in turn.

Dawn, frightened but untouched by the mysterious plague, did what little she could in the way of fetching water in her basket. She had to run a mile out on the moonlit flats to scoop it from a brackish pond, but no matter how much water she brought back to their hiding place in the rocky outcropping, there was never enough. In the end she was openly daring the Bannock by lugging water in broad daylight, but it did no good. And then, one morning, she shook Bear Woman's shoulder, gasped, and knew she was alone.

For the rest of that day she sat among the dead, keening softly as she'd heard the other Indian women mourn their dead. Overhead, vultures circled, waiting for her to go away.

Dawn knew the vultures would give her position away to any distant horseman, and so, as the sun went down, she gathered as much food as she could find among the carrying baskets of the others and headed north by moonlight, crying softly.

Hungry Moon had taught her it wasn't womanly to cry, but she just couldn't help it, this once.

Nevada Jones was riding point a mile out front of Captain Fannon's wagon train. He'd never seen the Sierra Nevada they were headed for and his name wasn't Jones, but the wagon master hadn't seen fit to question this when he'd joined the train at Salt Lake City. The Shoshoni had hit another wagon train near Carson Sink and the lean young man with a Colt .36 slung low on one hip had been a welcome addition to the party headed west.

They were crossing another sage flat after swinging

away from the Humboldt River's marshy inland delta, and Nevada was scouting sharp as he walked his chestnut gelding at a pace the slow-moving wagons could match. A buffalo rifle rested across his thighs and his gray eyes swept the gray-green sage on all sides from under the brim of his dusty black sombrero. It was seven times hotter than it ought to be and he was thirsty as hell, but Captain Fannon said the next water hole was forty miles ahead, so he'd wait a spell before he took another sip from the warm canteen hanging from his saddle horn.

The scout spotted a slim, small figure on the trail ahead and reined in his horse, raising a hand to signal the wagon teamsters behind him. The mounted youth sat his horse in silence for a time as be studied the stranger in the middle distance. Behind him there was the sound of hoofbeats and a voice called out, "What is it, Nevada?"

Jones waited until Wabash Brown reined in abreast of him before he answered. "Beats all hell out of me. Looks like a kid. Naked as a jaybird and wearing some kind of yaller headgear."

"Hell, it's a Digger," said the fat-bellied Brown reaching for his saddle gun.

"Hold your fire, old son. I said it's a *kid*, and he don't look like he's fixing to do nothing but stand there staring at us like an owl-bird."

"I'd best shoot him anyways, Nevada. You gotta let them Digger rascals know who's boss hereabouts, or they'll be all over you, begging for tobacco and red-eye."

Nevada's voice took on a slight edge. "I said not to shoot him and I meant it, Wabash."

"You partial to Injuns or somethin'?"

"I ain't partial to shooting down nobody like a dog,

less he gives me a reason. You cover me and I'll mosey on over and see what he wants."

"Hell, I told you what he wants. He wants a smoke and a drink. And shootin' a Digger ain't the same as shootin' a dog. Dogs has feelings."

"You stay here and cover me. I won't take it kindly does a rifle ball pass my ear without no good reason, Wabash."

Nevada kneed his mount forward, moving at a slow walk as he sized up the small stranger. Dawn's knees were shaking as the big frightening man on the big frightening horse approached. Every instinct told her to run, but she was alone in Bannock country and her mother had told her she'd once been a Saltu.

The fierce-looking man stopped his horse a few paces away and smiled in surprise. "Great balls of fire! You're a bitty girl-child with yaller hair! What are you doing out here in your birthday suit, missy? You are a *white* gal, ain't you?"

Some of what he said got through to her. Dawn searched her memory for the half-forgotten language of her real parents and stammered, "They are dead— all of them—I am alone."

Nevada swung down from his saddle and unbuttoned his hickory shirt. "Well, put some clothes on, for God's sake. I know you be just a kid, but you ought to be ashamed of yourself. What happened? Injuns hit your party? How'd you get away?"

Dawn allowed him to drape the big shirt over her naked shoulders as she puzzled over his words. He stepped back and frowned. "Button up, damn it! Your privates is still showing." Then, as Dawn fumbled with the unfamiliar fastenings, he snorted and reached out to button the shirt down her front, being careful to keep his fingers from her flesh. "Spooked, I reckon," he muttered. "Kid must be half loco after whatever she just went through."

Wabash Brown rode up, calling out, "What in thunder are you giving your shirt away for, Nevada? Has the sun ball cooked the few brains the good Lord gave you?"

Nevada called back, "It's a bitty white gal. Looks like the Shoshoni run over her train. She's too spooked to talk much."

Wabash Brown's voice took on a new tone as he swung out of his own saddle and ran over with a canteen. "Do Jesus! Are you all right, missy? Here, take a drink of this here water. How long you been out in this gol-durned desert, anyways?"

Dawn didn't answer but took the canteen and gulped thirstily away.

"Easy, honey," Nevada said, gently removing the canteen from her lips.

It was going to be all right, she thought. Their words were strange, but they were good people, after all. Dawn reached out and hugged Wabash, pressing her cheek against his chest as she tried not to cry. Wabash put a gentle hand on her sun-bleached hair. "Aw, shoot, honey." He looked bleakly at Nevada. "What we gonna do with her?"

"Carry her back to the wagons, of course. Kid needs clothes and some mothering, most likely. Captain Fannon will likely want to ask her about the Injuns, too. You want to take her back or shall I? One of us oughta stay out here on point."

"I'll do it," Wabash said, scooping Dawn lightly from the ground and placing her atop his own mount.

Dawn gasped as she stared down from the great height. The big fat man swung up behind her and Dawn closed her eyes in terror as the horse suddenly moved to one side, nearly making her fall. Then Wabash braced her with his arms. "Steady, little gal. What's the matter? You must have rode a horse afore this."

Dawn said, "No. We had no . . . horses. Others had horses. They were bad."

"Come west with oxen, did you? Well, no matter, honey. I ain't about to drop a pretty bitty thing like your ownself. We'll just walk him back slow, hear?"

Nevada was staring thoughtfully after them as they rode away. He didn't like the way Wabash had looked at that kid. What was the matter with Wabash, anyway? She was a pretty little gal, but Jesus, she couldn't be twelve years old!

"You got a dirty mind," he told himself, mounting his own horse to resume position as lead scout. Hell, it wasn't as if old Wabash had trifled with the kid. She'd be all right with Captain Fannon's wife in the lead wagon. Wabash was all right. Just sort of stupid. None of the single men in the party had been with a woman for over a month, but a man would have to be crazy to have country thoughts about a bitty girl-child.

Hell, Wabash hadn't even seen her naked like that, and them bitty little tits hardly showed under that shirt.

He was suddenly aware that he was sweating under his red flannel undershirt and wondered if it had gotten even hotter or if he was coming down with some ague. Nevada shrugged and walked his horse west. His palm was sweating, too, as it rested on the stock of his rifle. No doubt about it. He was catching some damned ague.

Well, he'd just keep going 'til he died or got better. Wasn't no doctor worth mention this side of the High

Sierra. He scanned the shimmering horizon for smoke signs. The kid hadn't made much sense, but if Injuns had hit her train, they couldn't be far away. She'd been sunburnt fierce—but how many miles could a naked child walk, out here in these sage flats?

Nevada pictured Dawn as he'd first seen her, a tawny nude form with the first bloom of approaching womanhood rounding out her firm young body. The peachfuzz just beginning to form in the V of her thighs had been sun-bleached, too. How long had she been out in this damned sun without clothes?

"Think about something else," he warned himself, aloud. Jesus, what was the matter with him? He'd had that squaw up in South Pass only a month or so ago and she'd pleasured him enough to last any sensible man all summer. That little lost gal was too blamed young for any decent fellow to think about, naked or dressed in a Saratoga trunk full of shimmy shirts!

"I'd kill him if—" Nevada muttered, not looking back as Wabash and the girl reached the wagons. Nevada knew the kid was safe from *him,* but some old boys just had no sense.

A few minutes later he heard a shot from the wagons and turned in the saddle with a frown. The lead wagon had swung off the trail and . . . why in God's name were they circling up this early?

Nevada shot an anxious glance around the entire horizon. There was nothing where the sky bowl met the sage tops that he could see. A signal was a signal, though, so Nevada loped back to the wagons as the flank scouts moved in from either side of the wagon ring. Nevada dismounted near Captain Fannon's ox-team and tied his reins to a sagebrush before walking stiffly over to the wagonmaster and some others who were gathered around the very confused child he'd sent back to them. Catching Fannon's eye, he asked, "What's up, Cap? Why are we stopping?"

Captain Fannon, a bearded man of thirty with a steel-trap mouth, pointed at Dawn. "This kid just told us she remembers being lost from a wagon party when she was about five."

Nevada shrugged. "So what, Cap? She had to be lost. Never come west on her lonesome. What's this all about?"

"What it's about is that she ain't no five. She might have been a *while* ago, afore the war with Mexico. As far as me and my old woman can put it together, this here kid's been living with the *Injuns* all this time!"

Nevada stared soberly down at Dawn for a time. "That makes sense. She had to be living with somebody all these years, Cap."

Fannon said, "They sent her in to us. It's some sort of Shoshoni trick. We're taking a vote on what's to be done with her."

"A vote? What the hell for? She's a *white* girl, Captain Fannon!"

"Well, mebbe she is and mebbe she ain't. She hardly talks English, and if she's lived with Shoshoni this long, she's likely in on it with 'em."

"Aw, hell, Cap. She's just a bitty kid, and like I said, she's white. I don't see what we can do, save carry her along with us to California and maybe find some kin of hers who got through."

There was a low murmur of disagreement from the others crowded around. A woman shouted, "Hang her from a wagon tongue and teach them redskins a good lesson!"

Dawn didn't understand what was happening, but the tall man who'd given her his shirt seemed to be her friend and the fat man who'd ridden to these huge wagons with her wasn't saying anything. She stepped over to Nevada and waited to see what was going to happen next.

Captain Fannon raised a hand for silence. "There'll be no killing in this company. I think the best thing to do is simply send her back to her Injun friends."

Nevada sighed. "I don't think I cotton to that much, Cap."

"Nobody hereabouts cares all that much what you cotton to, Nevada. You be just a scout. I'm captain, and I say she goes."

Nevada stared thoughtfully at the surly faces all around. "Well, if she has to go, I 'spect I'll just have to go along with her. I won't leave no kid alone in this here desert."

He reached down for Dawn's hand. "We'd best move on out, missy. Folks hereabouts don't seem to remember they be Christians."

"Your guns and possibles are yours, Nevada. The chestnut is mine."

"I'll give it back to you if we ever meet in the gold fields, Cap. Next to deserting children in the wilderness, there's nothing riles me more than walking."

"You try to take my horse and I'll order you hanged as a thief."

"Well, now, you might order it, Cap, but I don't hang easy. If you folks be spooked by an unarmed child, you don't want to see *me* in an ugly mood. Come on, kid. We're off to California."

Captain Fannon made the mistake of placing a careless hand on the grips of the pistol slung from his belt. An eyeblink later he found himself staring into the unwinking eye of a Colt .36 as Nevada said, softly, "Let's keep this neighborly, now."

Fannon blanched, "Why, you damn fool! You're outnumbered thirty to one!"

"Yeah, I know. I'll likely go down if we push it much further, but five or six men figures to go down with me. And Cap, I aim to shoot you first, so . . ." He saw Wabash moving toward him, and without moving the muzzle of the pistol trained on Fannon's heart, he said, "You'd best stay put, Wabash. I don't figure to say it again."

"I'm just getting out of the line of fire, Nevada. If it was up to me, the little gal could stay, but this ain't my fight."

A youth named Red called out, "I'll pass on this deal, too, gents. If you be watching my hands, Nevada, you'll see. I'm keeping them far out and sociable."

Captain Fannon became uncomfortably aware that the men in position to catch a stray bullet fired in his direction were moving to his right and left with desperately neutral expression. He licked his lips. "Oh, hell, if it means that much to you, she can stay, Nevada."

But Nevada said, "Nope. Sooner or later I have to sleep, and I figure to sleep somewhere out in the sage where I've a better chance of waking up in the morning." Still holding Dawn's hand, he back them both to his horse, let of her moist palm, and reached behind him to slip the knotted reins free. Then, still facing the wagons, they backed off, afoot, until out of pistol range. He suddenly holstered the gun, swung Dawn up in the saddle, and started dogtrotting away, leading the horse by its reins.

Back at the wagons Fannon yelled to his wife, "Fetch my rifle, woman!" But Wabash warned, "Leave it lay, Cap, I think I know who that old boy was afore he started calling hisself Jones." The woman didn't move. Captain Fannon swore softly, but didn't insist. He'd proven his manhood by making the offer, and he, too, had heard the rumor about that shootout at Bent's Fort.

Fannon said, "I'm going to swear out a warrant on that horse, do we ever get to California."

Wabash nodded. "That's your best move, Cap. They say that army officer had the drop on Nevada when they had it out at Bent's Fort. You just saw how fast he moves a gun, and we got enough to worry about with them blamed Shoshoni all about!"

By this time Nevada was far enough away to feel safe about mounting behind Dawn and, riding double, they headed into the afternoon sun at a slow trot, not looking back.

The girl clung to the saddle horn in terror as the saddle bounced under her naked thighs, and even though the man behind her had his rein arm braced under one of her elbows, she was sure she was going to fall off. But after a time she felt secure enough to say in halting English, "Going wrong way. Salt pans ahead. Horse can't run on crusted salt. We got away—from Bannock—by crossing salt pans."

"Do tell? Well, which way to do you think we ought to aim, kid?"

She pointed to the rimrocks to their left. "Water there, and cleft. Can hide horse. We sleep."

Nevada gazed at the rock outcropping she'd indicated on the horizon. "Sun ball's still high, missy. We'll get some water, but I want to put a few more miles betwixt us and them wagons."

"Be dark soon. No moon before midnight. We sleep Can make next waterhole before sun go down again."

Nevada snorted, "Hell, kid, we're covering six miles

an hour and that ridge can't be more than two hours from here at the rate we're going!"

"Don't know what mile is. Will take rest of day reach rocks, so slow."

"Well, we'll see if you're right. I make them rocks to be ten or twelve country miles from here. Things do have a way of being further off than sensible, hereabouts. You've rode this range afore, have you?"

"Walked. Took longer. We stop here—wait before move to rocks after dark."

Nevada started to ask why. Then, since he wasn't totally ignorant of the rules of survival west of the Mississippi, he nodded. "We scout for unwanted company afore we light and set a spell, eh? You figure them Shoshoni know about the waterhole, too?"

"Horse Indians—this side of Humboldt—Bannock. Shoshoni stay far side, between salt sinks and High Sierra."

"Come on, kid, we been brushin' with Shoshoni all the way along Humboldt headwaters above the Great Salt Desert."

"On north bank. Horse Utes south and east of big river—Bannock."

"Is it all that important to know the difference?"

"No. If meet Bannock or Shoshoni, alone, with horse and guns, they kill us. "

The cleft in the rocks Dawn led the way to after sundown was a demiparadise after a long hot afternoon on the burning dusty sage flats. The fault-block range of volcanic rock had been split by some ancient upheaval of the earth to form a deep narrow oasis with a tree-shaded pool of cool clear water in its hidden heart. Slopes of grass-covered sand ran from the pool

to the sheer rock walls on either side, and as Nevada
tied the horse to a black willow and made camp,
Dawn scouted in the dim light for edibles. Nevada
had said he had plenty of grub in his saddle bags, but
they had a long way to go if he meant to cross the
High Sierra. Dawn had never been west of the Sierra
foothills, but if her new big brother wanted to go
over the snow-covered peaks to the mysterious lands
beyond, she assumed they must be good lands. It was
the man's task to lead the way to new hunting grounds,
the woman's task to follow and keep them eating.

Nevada built a white man's fire, much larger and
brighter than fires Real People built, but Dawn didn't
say anything. They were hidden well by the rocks—
and maybe he had some reason for his strange habits.

As she approached the campfire with a handful of
edible roots, the youth glanced around and gasped,
"Good God, you're naked as a jaybird again! What
in tarnation's wrong with you, kid?"

Dawn knelt at his side and shoved the roots into
the hot coals. "Shirt is sticky," she said. "Will wash
it in pool. Put on when dry."

"You can't run about naked in front of folks, kid."

"Why not? You think my body—ugly? Breasts are
small but not my fault. Girl must wait until Changing
Woman make her pleasing in men's eyes."

"Damn it, you're pretty enough to eat without salt
and pepper, and you know it! You're too old to run
about naked, kid. I'm not a man who trifles with kids,
but you're gettin' to where any man's likely to have
country thoughts about you, so put some damn duds
on. Wrap yourself in a blanket or something."

Dawn stood up as Nevada looked away from her
across the dancing flames, and when she returned to
the fire, she'd draped one of the blankets from his

bedroll over her shoulders. She squatted down and poked at the roots with a willow stick. "You like better?"

"No, your damn privates is still showing, and damn it, we're headed into the gold fields, honey!"

"I know. You told me. What difference whether cover body or not?"

"Jesus, didn't them Injuns teach you nothing about the facts of life?"

"Of course. I knew good parsnip growing where water seeps from rocks. You be careful not pick bad parsnip with double roots. Look and taste same, but Dream Singer said make person fall asleep and never wake up, so . . ."

"I'm talking about the ways of men and women, damn it!"

"Oh, I know. Man puts body inside woman and they make baby. You want to do?"

"God, no! You're just a kid!"

She nodded, laughing. "Hungry Moon said almost old enough, but time not right to make babies. She said Striking Snake make good husband for me, in another summer. But Striking Snake died with others, so never found out."

Nevada studied the flames for a time before he asked, quietly, "Were you in love with this Injun boy?"

"Yes, I loved him. He was good person. Wasn't as pretty as you, but he was loved because never spoke in anger, even when very hungry."

"Sounds like a decent enough cuss, for an Injun, but I wasn't talking on that kind of love, kid."

"Oh? How many kinds are there, Nevada?"

"Don't rightly know. Hundred, mebbe."

"You love me?"

"Hell, no! You're just a pesky kid!"

"I don't understand. When people back at wagons talk bad about me, you pointed gun at them. Why do that if don't love me?"

He grinned. "I must be loco, most likely."

Neither spoke for a time. Then Nevada mused aloud, "I growed up in the Cumberlands on a hog-scrabble hillside farm my granddaddy fought the Shawnee for, back in Dan'l Boone's time. Had me this kid sister named Clara Sue and we used to play a fool game in the corn patch. We called it honky donky and it was sort of like hide-and-seek, only we laughed a lot more when we played honky donky."

"Did you love sister, Nevada?"

"Well, sure I did. She was my sister, damn it. She used to jump out at me and yell honky donky and then we'd both laugh fit to die. Clara Sue was a good little gal."

"Will we meet her in California?"

Nevada's eyes grew hard in the firelight, and he didn't answer for a time. "Not hardly. The Stuarts killed her."

"Oh, I'm sorry. What is Stuart? Like Bannock or Shoshoni?"

"Worse. My folks feuding with them pesky Stuarts since we got to America from the old country. Nobody remembers what the feud was all about in the first place, but there's been a heap of killing betwixt Stuart and Campbell just the same."

"Are you Campbell? Thought your name Jones."

"I say a lot of things, don't I? Anyway, one night the Stuarts got the drop on us and burnt our cabin. Clara Sue was one of them as got hit whilst we ran outside to get away. But then, that was a long time ago. Let's talk on something else."

"You talk." She looked at Nevada in despair, muttering to herself in Ho.

Nevada leaned over and patted her hand. "Beats me how you can talk English at all. You're doing fine, kid. Let's eat!'

"Roots almost ready. Like meat to go with them?"

"Sure. I'll get us some jerked beef from the possibles and . . ."

"No. Must save dried food for desert. I catch fresh meat—you watch parsnips don't burn."

As Nevada watched with a puzzled frown, Dawn sprang to her feet, threw off the dusty blanket, and stepped naked into the pond beyond the fire.

"You sure picked one hell of a time to go swimmin', kid," he said, as Dawn dropped to her hands and knees in the shallow water and splashed about for a time. "Loco. She's gone plumb out of her head," he muttered.

A few moments later Dawn returned to the fire, her nude body red in the firelight. "I have meat," she said happily.

Nevada gagged at the sight of the wriggling olive-green amphibians in Dawn's hand. "Mud puppies? You expect me to eat mud puppies like some damn furriner? I hear tell the Franchies eat frogs, but mud puppies is ridiculous!"

Dawn impaled the fat salamanders on willow sticks and squatted at his side to toast them over the flames. Don't taste as good as snake, but more fat than frogs. I think need salt, don't you?"

"I think you should put some clothes on, girl. You know, young as you are, you figure to be a heap of trouble in the gold fields. I reckon we'd best say you're my sister. I mean, my real sister. You're gonna get us in a lot of trouble if you don't learn not to shuck your duds like that, sister or no."

"You want me to· be Clara Sue?"

"No, Dawn is your name, so Dawn we'll call you. Just make sure you don't let on we're not related, hear?"

"If you say so, Nevada. But—why?"

"Well, hell, a man can't hardly traipse about with a female he ain't married up or related to, can he?"

"Don't understand, but I'll say we're married, if you want."

"That's loco. How old are you—eleven, twelve?"

"Don't know. Hungry Moon said four or five when she found me. I lived with the Sage Grouse clan about five or six years. I guess I'm between ten and twelve. Does it matter?"

"It makes you too young to marry up with. I suspect we'll get by with saying you're my baby sister. We're gonna have to make up some sort of story afore we get to the gold fields. The thing is, we can't have you comin' down off the trail with no menfolks of your own."

"Why?"

"Why? Hell, kid, the gold fields are rough. Half the world's headed for the gold fields since Marshall found that nugget at Sutter's Mill last year. There's thousands of men away from home panning the creeks running into the Sacramento, and not enough women worth mention. Even do I get you dressed right, we figure to have trouble with some of 'em."

"Then why are we going there?"

"Why are we going there? For the *gold*, of course!"

"Oh. What is gold?"

Nevada started to say that everybody knew what gold was, then he reconsidered and reached in his pocket, taking out a twenty-dollar gold piece. He handed it to Dawn, who studied it in the firelight. "It looks like a bird," she said. "Are we going to the gold field to hunt birds?"

"That's the durned old American eagle. Gold is what the coin is *made* of. Jesus you don't have enough sense to mention!"

"You mean yellow iron this bird thing made of? Very heavy. You make gold guns and tools? Yellow gun be very pretty."

"Never mind. We'll get that through to you later. The thing I'm most worried about is the way you run about bare-ass. You're gonna get us in a lot of trouble unless I can break you of that habit. I figure we can whip up a skirt from blanket cloth, and with the shirt and all, we can keep you from getting raped until I can buy you some decent duds, if you behave yourself like a well-brung-up young gal."

"What is rape?"

"Oh, shit, let's eat. Them mud puppies smell right nice, a-cooking on the stick like that. You sure you ain't gonna kill me with them parsnips?"

"Your face red. Why your face red, Nevada?"

"Beats the hell out of me. We'll study on it a mite betwixt here and California, kid."

Neither would have made it alone. Together, the ignorant deadly young man and his tiny trail-wise companion were in better shape to brave the California Trail than many a large and well-armed wagon train.

They complemented each other in their weaknesses and strengths. The youth was a crack shot, while Dawn had no idea how one fired a gun until Nevada had grudgingly shown her, and she would never be a really skilled markswoman. On the other hand, she saved him precious rounds of their limited ammunition by teaching him to knock delicious porcupine out of juniper and piñon trees with a well-thrown rock. She showed him how to catch desert pupfish from green-scummed ponds he'd have never thought to fish in. One morning she saved him from pulling on a scorpion-infested boot when, sniffing the morning air and knowing the hiding habits of the venomous creatures, she detected the hint of vinegar near his bedroll.

In turn, Nevada's horsemanship and sharpshooting made their travels far more comfortable than any she'd experienced with the wandering diggers. Even after she'd learned to shoot the rifle, Dawn found it hard to grasp that a game bird too distant for a Paiute to consider as possible prey could be knocked from its perch by a well-placed ball.

Thus each learned from the other, and together they formed a team most Indian raiders or casual outlaws would have been well-advised to avoid.

They encountered neither, for Dawn knew the ways one avoided encounter in the basin and range country, and warned her companion of likely points Shoshoni or Bannocks might choose for ambush. She knew the hidden waterholes and campsites of her timid Digger friends, and they ghosted by moonlight or in the late afternoons when the shimmering desert air made it difficult to spot a moving dot on the mirage-haunted flats.

Once she grasped how much water their horse needed, Dawn found water where Nevada would have sworn there was none. On more than one occasion she saved him and the chestnut from drinking limpid-looking but deadly water that gathered in low

places filled with metallic salts leached from the surrounding mountains. Nevada gave her credit for some
Indian sixth sense at times like these. In truth, it was
a knowledge of botany few white college professors
of the time possessed. Hungry Moon had taught her
how the harmless salt bush, safe for any grazing animal to eat, thrived with its roots in water poisoned
by arsenic and borax.

Her ability to cook delicious meals from scruffy-
looking vegetation and small darting creatures her
quick fingers caught among the rocks of any campsite
never ceased to amaze Nevada. Sometimes she made
him eat things he wasn't too sure about, but once
he'd gotten used to the idea of "livin' Injun" he took
a secret delight in allowing as how roasted rattlesnake
tasted much like chicken, admitting he'd never eaten
better in his own ma's kitchen.

As they reached the rolling foothills of the Sierra
the hunting grew better, but Dawn may have saved
Nevada from an illness that had destroyed many a
mountain man when she explained they could eat
every part of a young grizzly he shot except its liver.
Dawn had no idea what trichinosis was, but she
knew no Indian ate the often-infected liver of any
carnivore.

Neither knew the way over the High Sierra, but
summer was upon the mountains and the pass they
chose in their innocence—one avoided by experienced
mountain men—spared them its July blizzards.

As they wended their way down the gentler slopes
to the west of the alpine heights, Nevada grew more
concerned about the girl's seminudity. He fashioned
a crude dress for her by cutting a hole in one of their
blankets and drawing in the poncholike garment
around her waist with a belt of latigo strap cut from

his saddle. The maroon split skirt hung down to her naked ankles when she was afoot. Nevada insisted she start riding sidesaddle behind him, for it was considered indecent for young ladies of those mid-Victorian times to be seen astride a horse. Dawn found it uncomfortable and considered it a silly way to sit a horse, but complied; they'd learned to trust each other's often mysterious notions.

Nevada had a Bible in his gear and a fair knowledge of reading, so that when they'd sit by the fire after a day's journey, he'd teach her words and then sentences. She was a quick learner and soon caught up with Nevada.

As they moved down out of the trackless conifer forests of the upper slopes, the land grew gentler. Soon they were riding through a parklike land of sensuous rounded hills covered with knee-high grass, chest-high wild mustard, and the appletree forms of California oaks. Dawn was well pleased with the smiling empty landscape they'd come to, for the oaks afforded endless acorns to be pounded and leached to Indian bread flour. A purling brook wound its way through every valley. Nevada's wide-set gray eyes grew more thoughtful with every mile, however, for the country matched the descriptions he'd heard about the gold fields and he knew they'd be meeting up with white men far from home. And womankind.

The first camp they came to was called Middle Fork City. As they rode in a little before sundown on a Thursday afternoon, their appearance caused a sensation.

Despite its name, Middle Fork City was a motley collection of canvas tents and hastily erected brush shelters lining both sides of the small stream that occasioned its site. The population consisted of about forty hard-looking men who'd been panning the Middle Fork without much luck.

Before they'd reached the center of the camp, word had spread that a stranger was coming in with a white gal and every man jack in Middle Fork City dropped what he was doing to investigate this welcome change from the monotony of mucking about in wet gravel for any trace of the bright gleaming gold they'd hoped, and failed, to find.

Young men who hadn't bathed in months suddenly decided they needed a shave, and hoarded bars of naphtha soap were hastily dug from possibles bags as a delegation made the newcomers welcome.

Nevada sat his horse warily, with Dawn behind him, bare feet dangling. A jovial-looking giant with a black beard roared out, "Welcome to Middle Fork City! I'm Bully Dalton and you-all are bunking with me!"

Nevada smiled thinly and said, "My name's Jones. This here is my kid sister, Dawn. We was figuring on trying for Calaveras County afore we set down anywhere for more'n a cup of coffee."

The camp boss snorted, "Shoot, you're *in* Calaveras County, old son, and you can't ride into them ornery camps further down with no white gal. Why, they got Chinee and Mexicans betwixt here and Angel's Camp. It wouldn't be safe."

"Chinee? How in tarnation did Chinee get to Angel's Camp?"

"Beats me. Swum, most likely," Dalton said. "The whole blamed world has come to Californee since Marshall found that nugget at Sutter's Mill. We don't allow nobody but white folks here in Middle Fork City and as for the coffee, we'uns got all the coffee you and that purty little gal can ever drink. My tent's the biggest in the gulch, and like I said, you'll be bunkin' with me."

Nevada shifted in his saddle as he eyed the others crowding around, and as one of the men reached for the rein of their mount, he snapped, "Keep your hands to your ownselves, gents. I told Ma I'd look out for this kid, and in case you're wondering, she ain't more'n ten years old!"

Bully Dalton laughed. "Hell, we ain't that sort of gents, Jones. I told you we'uns was all white hereabouts. Why, iffen any man here says a thing to make your little sister blush, I'll cut his heart out with my barlow knife!"

"Well, I can see you're a gent, Bully. We'll maybe stop for some coffee and a smoke, but we'll be bunking further down the trail tonight."

"Shoot, we'll study on that part later, old son. Right now we're gonna have us a real shivaree in honor of ... Dawn did you say her name was? How do, Miss Dawn. You're the first white gal who's ever been to Middle Fork City and we're gonna fill you with food and likker fit to bust! You foller me on that horse, Jones. That big tent yonder is mine."

He turned to a small older man with a limp and added, "Gimpy, you put their horse with mine and make sure he gets rubbed down and fed some grain afore you jine the party."

Nevada allowed them to be led over to the camp boss's oversized gray tent as he murmured to Dawn, "You stay close to me, girl. I mean, close as a dog tick, hear?"

"Are they bad people, Nevada?" she whispered.

He shrugged. "Don't know. You just stick tight and don't make a move without I say so. Go easy on the coffee, too. If you got to pee, you'll just have to hold it for a spell whilst I get the lay of the land."

When they reached the tent, Nevada dismounted first before helping the girl down. The old man called Gimpy took the reins, and as his head neared Nevada's he whispered, "Watch yourself, mister. Bully's one ornery son of a bitch, even sober."

Nevada's face was blank as he answered softly, "Thanks. You siding me, Gimpy?"

"Nope. Just telling you. Nobody hereabouts figures to side nobody."

"You mean it's between me and him, fair and square?"

"I'll tend your horse. You just worry 'bout yourself and the girl."

Then he was gone and they were on their own.

The fly of Bully Dalton's tent was up, forming a porchlike canopy in front of the messy dark interior. Bully had a cask of corn squeezings atop an improvised table of packing crates and was already pouring drinks into tin cups. "Wet your whistles with this, folks," he called out. "How long you been on the trail, anyways?"

Nevada took a cup. "Couple of months. The kid don't drink red-eye."

"Hell, one drink won't hurt her. We'll get her some coffee later on. Ain't that right, boys?"

There was a murmur of agreement from the men all around. Nevada saw he was hemmed in and noted a certain determination in the eyes of the camp boss holding out another cup to Dawn. He sighed and slapped the cup from Bully Dalton's hand, spilling its contents in the dust. "She don't drink, gents," he said softly.

Bully Dalton frowned down at Nevada as it suddenly got very quiet in Middle Fork City. After a long dangerous pause, Bully said, "You sure have piss-poor manners, friend."

"I know. You want me to drink my own likker first, or do you aim to have it out with me right off?"

"Don't talk like a damn fool. Nobody said nothin' about having nothin' out with nobody. You sure are a proddy son of a bitch, and that's—"

"I don't allow cussin' in front of my kid sister, neither. You want to keep this sociable or do you want to fight?"

Bully Dalton's jaw dropped in surprise as the others waited to see what was going to happen. They'd expected Bully to hoorah the newcomer, once he'd had time to size him up. Bully hoorahed everybody in camp, sooner or later. Nevada's surly manners had thrown the camp boss off stride by coming so soon in the feel-out.

Dalton shook his head mournfully, put his own cup down untasted, and stepped out into the sunset light. "I can see I'll have to teach you some manners, son. It ain't nothing personal, but I told you I'm the boss of this here camp, so . . ."

Nevada fired from the hip, pulled Dawn with him as he crawfished backwards into the darkness of the tent, and as another man went for his gun, fired a second time.

Then, for a very long time, nobody moved or said a word.

Finally, one of the miners bent over to study Bully Dalton's form in the dust. "He's dead. Ball took him right under the heart."

Another man said, "Ryan's dead, too. That was a

damn foolish move he made, tryin' to cross-draw agin' a man with his own gun out already.".

There was a murmur of agreement, and Nevada asked quietly, "Do we ride out peaceable, gents? Or did them two have friends who aim to speak up about what just happened?"

The older man called Gimpy walked over to the tent, leading Nevada's horse. He said, "I'd take her outten here afore dark, son. Don't reckon anybody hereabouts would try to stop you, cold sober."

Nevada nudged Dawn. "Get on the horse and wait for me on the other side of the creek, kid. I'll sort of mosey out after you, walking backwards."

Another man said, "Hell, you'uns can stay, Jones. Ryan was the only real friend Bully had in this camp —and I just shaved and put on a clean shirt."

But Nevada shook his head. "We'd be obliged if everybody just sort of kept their hands where I could see them until I'm out of range."

Dawn mounted the horse, astride, and trotted it around the tent and across the ankle-deep water until she'd reached a grove of oak on the far side. She reined in and waited as Nevada followed, walking slowly backward with his pistol trained on the knot of confused miners. He spoke without turning. "Keep moving until we're out of sight. I'll mount when it's safe."

Dawn urged the horse on, ducking her head as she rode it under the low branches of an oak, A moment later, Nevada holstered his pistol and swung up behind her, spurring the horse into a dead run. Somewhere behind them a rifle coughed a .44 ball through the leaves out to one side.

Nevada took the reins and swung the running

horse into a breakneck lope at right angles to the camp they could no longer see, as other guns took up the refrain. He rode them between some jagged boulders, changed course again, and slowed to a walk, moving upslope as he doubled back on their trail to throw off possible pursuit.

They kept going until it was quite dark, and finally Dawn asked, "What were you fighting about, back there? It all happened so fast!"

"I'll explain it later, kid. We'd best stop and wait for the moon ball to rise. This ain't no time to risk a fall in the dark."

"Are we going to make camp here?"

"No. Just get down and rest the chestnut. He's going to have to make forty miles betwixt here and sun-up."

"If you say so, Nevada. I didn't know those were bad people. I thought they wanted to be our friends. Some of them were smiling at me before you started shooting at them."

"I know, kid. You see, there's smiles and then there's smiles."

"Are we going to have to shoot everybody who smiles at me like that, Nevada?"

"Jesus, kid. I purely hope not."

Dawn dismounted, finding a rock to sit on with her bare feet drawn up under her wool skirts as the air around them grew chill in the mountain darkness. As Nevada rubbed down the horse, she thought a time before she asked, "Would they have wanted to fight with you if I hadn't been with you?"

Nevada gave the horse a brisk pat. "I don't know. The thing is, you was."

"Maybe you should have left me on the other side

of the mountains, then. Didn't you know I'd cause trouble for you, here in the gold fields?"

"I knowed it, kid. I just didn't know know what else I could do."

Their reception at the next camp was friendlier. It took them two days to reach Lost Chinaman, a camp much bigger and offering more comforts. Gold had been panned from Lost Chinaman wash, and where there was gold, there were women—of a sort.

In later years Dawn would scandalize sedate matrons of Nob Hill by repeating the uncouth ditty: "The miners came in forty-nine, the whores in fifty-one, and when they got together, they produced the Native Son." But in truth, the whores hadn't waited until 1851 before following the gold rush to California. They'd come in the wagon trains and around the Horn in clipper ships, or simply left the Mexican fields and missions to join their less dusky sisters at the world's oldest profession as soon as word got around that a girl could make hundreds of dollars a night along any of a hundred mountain streams where lonely men spent every hour of daylight panning for signs of "color."

The community was nearly six months old and beginning to take on the appearance of a small town as the first appalling conditions were slowly amended by the elected miner's committee charged with bringing order from chaos. Most of the lean-tos and tents along the creek were little more than hovels, but a grid of pathways and open sewers had been laid out, and new construction was supposed to be oriented more or less in line with the surveyed city plan. A stout corral and oak log livery stable formed the solid core on which the business center was being built of rough-hewn timber and adobe brick. The small log jail of the vigilance committee boasted one of the few formal gallows trees of the gold fields.

Piggy O'Day's combination hotel, restaurant, saloon, and bordello was the only two-story building in Lost Chinaman. It was hoped the stage coaches would stop there if ever a stage road was punched through the wilderness to the open lowlands of central California. A lean-to tacked onto one wall of Piggy O'Day's served as the only general store in town, for there was little that could be bought in the way of manufactured goods in Lost Chinaman. In an uncontrolled economy on the very rim of civilization, prices were insane in both directions.

Speculators had shipped anything and everything they could think of by lumbering overland wagon freight or by clipper around the Horn, to be packed into the back country by mule or man. Nobody had known in advance what would be needed in the gold fields. Hence there was glut and scarcity, side by side. Nails were selling at a dollar a piece and were needed in quantity, while picks and shovels, shipped in expectation of a killing, sold for little more to men who, after all, needed only one or two of either. Guns cost less than the cheaply stamped flat pans that wore out so quickly when filled with a mixture of sand and water and swished from dawn to dusk in hopes of a few grains of gold. Leather goods, obtained locally from the Mexican California craftsmen, were cheap. Textiles were nearly irreplaceable, as clothing wore out rapidly under the harsh frontier conditions. Nevada discovered this when his attempt to buy a dress for Dawn at the general store was met with incredulous laughter.

On the other hand, while material goods were expensive on the new frontier, human labor, as well as life, could be surprisingly cheap. The storekeeper suggested a Mexican seamstress who survived in a nearby hovel by patching together such rags as anyone might bring her. Rosalita's man had been killed by a falling tree during the timber-clearing along the creek. Nevada took Dawn to the haggard Mexican girl and a bargain was struck. Rosalita would make a serviceable wool dress from Dawn's poncho and throw in a pair of braided leather sandals for one of Nevada's twenty-dollar gold pieces.

As Dawn sat nearly naked on the Mexican woman's narrow bunk with the rifle across her slender thighs, Nevada left her for the moment to get his bearings.

Their arrival in the camp, while not as obviously welcomed, had not gone unreported. As Nevada handed the reins of their chestnut to the Indian lad at the livery stable, a trio of hard-looking men greeted him. "How do. We're from the vigilance committee, and we sort of run things hereabouts. You got any objections to voice about it, Mister . . . ah?"

Jones. Nevada Jones. Me and my kid sister is peaceable folks and we try to get along with them as'll let us."

One of the men said, "We'll let the name stand, Jones. That's a tie-down holster you're wearing. Be you a miner or a gunslinger?"

"I'm aiming to pan for color. Any gunslinging I've done in the past has generally been forced on me."

"You got papers out on you?"

"I ain't wanted by no legal lawman, far as I know. You look like sensible gents, so I'll tell you the truth. I shot a man over on the other side of the Rockies. Shot another in Salt Lake City. Shot two more up at another camp called Middle Fork City couple or three days back. I figured all five needed shooting."

"We don't like shooting in Lost Chinaman, Jones. We'd like to hear your reasons."

"Man at Bent's Fort drawed first. Mormon over to Salt Lake called me in a card game. The two I shot up the slope a few days back was aiming to rape my kid sister. I don't like shooting all that much, neither, but I can only be pushed so far."

The three vigilantes exchanged glances. Then their spokesman said, "We know them jaspers up at Middle Fork, so we'll allow as you likely had good cause in Bully Dalton's camp. On the other hand, Bully might be looking for you and we don't want no trouble, neither, so—"

"Bully Dalton's one of the two I shot," Nevada cut in. "The other one was named Ryan. He horned in whilst me and Bully was discussing my kid sister's honor."

The spokesman's frown was replaced by a grin. "You gunned down Bully Dalton? Why didn't you say so, Nevada? Hell, what are we doin' out in this hot sun? Let's go inside and belly up to the bar!"

"It's jake with you gents if me and the kid stay awhile?"

"Hell, son, you stay as long as you like. My name's Clampet, this here is Scars Wilson and we call this other jasper Blue Tooth. The first round of drinks is on me. You won't be able to buy your own, once word gets around how you civilized Middle Fork a mite!"

By the time Nevada got back to the shack of the Mexican seamstress, Dawn was wearing a serviceable

maroon wool dress and her first pair of shoes. Nevada
was only slightly drunk, for despite his wellwishers
he held his liquor well.

At the suggestion of his new friends, Nevada had
sold the horse and saddle for a handful of condor
quills filled with gold dust, one of the more trusted
forms of currency in the gold fields, where the rate
of exchange was as wild as everything else. He explained to Dawn that the cost of keeping a horse a
few days was more than the horse was worth and
that he'd been made a member of the vigilance committee and invited to stay and stake a claim.

Dawn understood little of this. She was even more
puzzled when Nevada asked the Mexican girl how
safe his young charge would be in her shack for the
night. When Rosalita explained how a few judicious
hangings had reduced the incidence of rape in Lost
Chinaman to reasonable proportions, Nevada gave
her another coin for Dawn's room and board overnight.

"Aren't you staying, too?" Dawn asked. "Where are
you going to sleep?"

Nevada shifted his feet. "Over at Piggy's, Piggy's
real name is Peggy. She ain't all that much to look
at, but we seemed to hit it off, and hell, kid, I been on
the *trail* a spell!"

"Are you going to sleep with her?"

"Her or one of the others. There's this one French
gal, come all the way from Paris on a clipper and
she's got a right nice pair of . . . never you mind.
You'll be safe enough, here with Rosalita."

"Damn it, I don't want you to sleep with that French
lady. I want you to sleep with me!"

Nevada caught the surprise on the Mexican seamstress's face and shook his head at her. "She's too young to understand, Miss Rosalita. You'll know where to fetch me if there's any trouble, eh?"

Rosalita nodded, not looking at him. "Be careful. The one called Piggy has been known to steal an unwary miner's poke, and they say the French girl has the disease."

"Hmm, maybe I'd best hide my loose change. There ain't no bank in camp, is there?"

"Your gold would be as safe as your sister, here. But of course, we are strangers. If I were you, I would bury it somewhere and tell nobody where it was."

"Shoot, if I can trust Dawn with you, I can likely leave my possibles bag and poke, Miss Rosalita. I mean, you're an understanding woman and all, but you ain't like them others."

"I don't want you to leave your money with me. Go with God and do what men do at Piggy O'Day's. The child will be safe with me for the night."

"Yeah. Well, you'll feed her, right?"

"I have some tortillas and beans to heat up. We shall have them, with coffee, before we go to sleep."

Nevada hesitated in the doorway, staring at the barely visible pair in the gathering darkness. "Hell, I ain't in all that much of a hurry. Maybe I'll eat here, if that's all right with you, Miss Rosalita."

Silently, the Mexican girl struck a light and placed a flickering candle on the plank table that served as her workbench, dining table, and only solid piece of furniture. "I'll heat up the coffee and such food as we have to share," she said. As Dawn caught the look that passed between Nevada and Miss Rosalita, she wondered what they were really trying to say. The Mexican girl wasn't really pretty, but Nevada was running his eyes over her high cheekbones and big sad eyes as if he'd just spotted a quail in the brush. What was the matter with Nevada? That Mexican girl had to be at least twenty-five!

Nevada eased over to a seat near the table. Rosalita knelt in the dust near the adobe fire niche built into the low corner of the brushwood shack and started to build a fire. She fanned the sticks to make a bed of coals while Nevada made small talk about men and women that Dawn had trouble following. She'd never heard that oddly purring quality in Nevada's voice before, and she wondered why Rosalita, instead of concentrating on the cooking, kept running a hand through her hair like that. Why was she combing it back with her fingers and tying it behind her with that red ribbon bow? Hadn't she just said they were fixing to go to bed, once they ate?

As Rosalita flattened the tortillas on the hot hearth near the pot of boiling beans, Nevada said something that made her giggle. Without turning around, Rosalita said in an oddly gay tone, "You'd better be off to Piggy O'Day's. I'm not that sort of woman."

Nevada laughed. "Never said you was, Rosie. Just asked if you had a man or two courting serious."

"There are some who look at me. I am a woman alone, and not deformed."

"Hell, you're dramn near pretty, Rosie! Don't seem right a gal like you is all alone like this, if you catch my meaning."

"I am alone by choice. My parents did not approve the young man I followed up here to the diggings. He was, as you know, killed in an accident, but I can't go back to Yerba Buena as a shamed woman."

"What have you got to be ashamed about? It ain't as if you was one of Piggy O'Day's gals. You need a horse to get home? Had I known before I sold the chestnut—"

"I can never return to Yerba Buena. I live here the only way I know how. It is a lonely life, but it is not a bad life. My needle and thread serves to keep a roof over my head and food upon my table," she said stiffly.

"Yeah, but an empty bed gets tedious, don't it?"

Rosalita suddenly rose on her bare feet and, not looking at either of her guests, spread three tin plates and three mugs of coffee on the bare planks of the table. She placed a tortilla on each plate and began to spoon beans on them. Nevada insisted, "You didn't answer my question."

"Go to your Piggy O'Day," Rosalita said. "If she rips your pants, I will mend them. I have no other services to offer a man just in off the trail!"

Nevada chuckled and began to wolf down his food as Dawn tried to understand what they were talking about. She'd had beans before, but the soft tortilla bread was new to her and she liked it.

After a time Nevada put his coffee mug down and rolled himself a smoke. "You got a mighty small bunk, Rosie. Think you and the kid'll both fit?"

Rosalita shrugged. "I shall make a pallet for myself on the floor. I have more room than furniture."

"I can see that. How do you figure to lock the door? It ain't much more'n a rawhide stretched on sticks, is it?"

"I have little to steal, and the vigilance committee frowns on burglary in Lost Chinaman. The child and I will be safe enough until you return."

She lowered her eyes and flushed as she added in a low aside, "You will be in greater danger if you spend the night with that French slut!"

"Well, maybe I'll just go over to Piggy's and jaw with the boys for a spell. Old Blue Tooth was telling me there's a stretch of the wash as ain't been panned yet, and he says he'll show me how to build me a sluice box, if I can come by some nails and then . . ."

Rosalita's voice was teasing. "And then you will drink, and then you will remember how long it's been since you've had a woman, and then . . ."

"Hold on, now, damn it! It was you as just told me to leave them gals over there alone! Do Jesus, I wish you'd make up your mind, Rosie!"

Dawn piped up brightly. "Why don't you sleep here with us, Nevada?" Nevada laughed and asked, "How 'bout it, Rosie?"

Then Rosalita got up from the table and started puttering aimlessly with her pots and pans. "I am not that kind of woman."

Dawn finished the last of her tortilla and beans and wiped a hand across her mouth. "What in tarnation are you two talking about, Nevada? I mean, first you say one thing and then you say another, and Jesus damn it, what's so complicated about folks going to sleep once the sun ball's down?"

Nevada smiled sheepishly at Rosalita's stiffly held back as he answered. "Drink your coffee, kid. It's something us growed folks have trouble understanding, too."

"Oh—you want to rape her?"

"Goddammit, kid, that's no way to talk!"

"Why not? It's the way you've been talking, isn't it?"

Nevada pushed away from the table and got to his feet. "I swear to God," he muttered. "One of these days I aim to give you a good lickin'!"

Then he ducked outside as Rosalita turned with a

stricken look on her face. Dawn smiled up at her. "Ain't he a caution? My, don't you ever look pretty with your hair fixed back like that!"

Rosalita started clearing the table, cursing softly to herself in Spanish as Dawn prattled on about their trip west together. After a time, the Mexican girl frowned. "Just a minute, Dawn. Are you trying to say he's *not* your brother?"

"Oh, no, we just say that 'cause men keep trying to rape me."

"I see. And has he—ah—done such things to you?"

"Of course not. He says I'm too young."

"You mean, all those nights alone with you on the trail? He never used you as a woman?"

"No. I told him he could, but he just got mad and said I shouldn't talk like that. He says he's a gentleman and that gents don't do bad things. I'm not sure what he's talking about, sometimes."

"I see, yet you are not really without female—uh— endowments. Have you had your first period yet?"

Dawn looked blank, so Rosalita explained and she brightened. "Oh, once a month for almost a year, now. Hungry Moon said I was becoming a woman, but if you ask me, it's sort of messy."

"Yet this Nevada never touched you? *En verdad,* he must be a gentleman, or a fool."

"I don't think he's a fool. He told me he used to have a real sister he loved and that I was a lot of trouble but . . ."

"Never mind, I see what sort of man he is now. You did a foolish thing in telling me you are not related to him by blood, Dawn. I am a woman who can keep a secret, but you must never tell anyone else here in Lost Chinaman that you are not his sister. Will you promise me this?"

Dawn nodded soberly. "It's sort of hard to understand, though."

"In time you will understand, and thank God you were taken in by such a man. But now I think we should turn in. You take the bunk and I'll make up my pallet here by the fire."

Dawn did as she was told, taking off her new dress and crawling in between the clean but ragged blankets of the Mexican girl's narrow bunk. By the time Rosalita had finished making up a wider sleeping place on the earthen floor across the shack, Dawn had fallen fast asleep.

She had no idea what time it was when the sound of movement in the dark shack awakened her. She whispered, "Nevada?" and heard his husky answer. "Yeah, go back to sleep, kid."

Dawn rolled her face to the brushwood wall, wondering where Nevada was going to spread his roll in the tiny room. After a time she heard Rosalita gasp, "Oh, *me toro!*" "Are you all right, Miss Rosalita?"

There was a stifled giggle and Nevada husked, "Goddammit, shut up and go to sleep!" So Dawn didn't say another word as she listened in the dark to the odd sounds of panting and murmured endearments. She knew what they were doing, of course. She'd spent the last five or six years in a close-knit band of Indians, who huddled together for warmth under the desert stars. But they sure were making a lot more noise on that pallet than any Paiute couple would have thought discreet with other people trying to sleep nearby.

As Rosalita gasped in stifled orgasm, Dawn felt a little twinge of envious curiosity. She liked Miss Rosalita and apparently Nevada thought *she* was old enough, but Dawn couldn't help wondering what it felt like and why Nevada wouldn't show her.

Nobody remembered exactly who the lost China-man had been, or how he got lost, or even if he'd ever existed. Like many of the streams running into the great Sacramento-San Joaquin valley, the wash was not a running stream in midsummer. Water lay in pockets under the smooth dry bed of hard-packed sand. Theory held that water stood above pockets in the bedrock and that gold, if it was there, should be under the water. Placers, or pockets of gold dust, tended to accumulate near the bedrock under the lighter quartz sand. Mucking down through the soggy overburden was hard work and all too often failed to pay off.

It was Dawn who told Nevada where to start dig-ging, once they'd made camp along the stretch of bank the miner's committee had allowed him to claim. He'd started to dig in the dead center of their claim with the same lack of imagination he'd shown in picking the name Jones for an alias. Dawn watched for a time as she built a small Indian fire near the tent he'd bought from a failed prospector. Then she walked out on the damp sand, pointed to some willows growing near a slight bend in the bank, and said, "You'll find water over there. The bedrock lies near the surface where you're digging."

Nevada looked up from his knee-deep hole. "What are you, a water dowser?"

"I don't know what a water dowser is. But a run-ning stream digs deeper on the outside of a bend, and those willows have their roots in standing water. Don't you know anything about digging for water?"

He laughed. "Well, you likely know digging, see-ing as you're a Digger at heart. We'll give your notion a try."

Nevada climbed out of his dry shallow hole and walked over to the spot she'd indicated Dawn fol-lowed, waiting until he'd sunk the blade of his shovel into the crust a few times before she asked, "Is digger a bad word?"

Nevada looked puzzled. "A bad word?"

"You say some words are bad and that only men are allowed to say them. When you say Digger, you curl your lips like you do when you say son of a bitch. If Digger's a bad word, what am I supposed to call Hungry Moon and my other friends?"

"Hell, I don't know. I ain't got nothing against Diggers. From what you told me, they sound like tolerable heathens. I reckon a Digger's as good as a Chinaman, and either one's better than a Mex."

"Don't you like Mexicans?"

"Ain't mad at 'em. Just don't trust 'em."

"Rosalita's a Mexican. Is she a bad person?"

"Hell, no, that's different."

"Why? Because you sleep with her?"

"Now, listen—I told you what happened the other night ain't none of your never mind. Hey, you know what? The sand over here *is* a mite wetter. I'll mind what you said about willow trees."

"Are you going to sleep with Rosalita tonight?"

"I don't know. I might. I asked her to come out here and tent with us, but she said it wouldn't look right."

"Why wouldn't it look right? You ought to take off your boots."

"I don't aim to stomp about in my bare feet like

some damn Chinese. And I ain't got time to explain about the way things look. You womenfolk get the damnedest notions, anyways."

"You'll rot your boots. They're wet already."

"Yep, I can feel it. Sand's wetter than hell and I'm only down a couple of feet. You'd best fetch that pan I bought and we'll try for some color."

"Pooh, you won't hit bedrock for another three feet, but I'll fetch the pan."

Dawn walked back to the tent and rummaged in their gear for the worn but still serviceable flat pan the bankrupt prospector had thrown in with the tent for enough to get him back to the Coast. As she came out of the tent she spied a tall dark man sitting a spotted pony on the edge of their clearing. Dawn smiled uncertainly and the man smiled back. "Top of the morning to you, Miss, I'm Brian Carlyle and I'll pay for coffee, if you have some."

Nevada had heard the exchange and walked over from the wash, one hand hovering like a lazy hawk near the butt of his holstered revolver. The stranger saw him, nodded pleasantly, and repeated, "My name's Carlyle and it's a peaceful man I am. I was just asking the lass if you'd sell me some coffee."

"We've no supplies to sell," Nevada said, "but we'll give you a cup for nothing if you'll get down off that pony and keep your hands where I can see 'em. You ride out from the camp?"

"I did, and if you're a committee man, you'll know I'm not a man to be watched. Shorty Grogan is a friend of mine and he'll vouch for me, if you know him."

"I know Shorty. Kid, put some coffee on the fire."

Dawn filled a cracked enamel pot with canteen water and a handful of grounds and placed it on the fire as the tall stranger dismounted and came over to hunker down across from her. Nevada remained on his feet with the friendly but thoughtful expression of any reasonable frontiersman meeting a man he didn't know.

"Panning the wash?" Carlyle asked.

"Maybe," Nevada said. "Ain't found color. You a prospector?"

"No. Engineer. Just graduated from Yale and came west when I heard about the opportunities out here. You may have guessed it's Irish I am, and there's not much work for a man with Paddy in his speech around Boston."

"Engineer, huh? There ain't no railroads out here."

"I'm not that kind of an engineer. It's roads and bridges I'd be after building. Coming up from the coast, I noticed a terrible need for both. Mines, too. Once the mother's lode's located, there'll be heavy construction needed in this country, and that's how I'll make me fortune, if I don't starve first."

Nevada gingerly hunkered down across the fire from Carlyle, a casual hand on his holstered gun. "Nobody figures to find the mother lode for years. Better men than you and me has tried."

"It's there, though. All this placer gold you lads have been mucking from the creeks has to come from somewhere. I'd say it's washing out of a band of salmon-colored quartz. I've noticed the sand around most rich placers is redder than the country rock around us."

"Well, likely you've as good a chance of striking the mother lode as anyone else."

"Oh, that's not me game, lad. I told you where I hope to make me fortune. Have you heard of Levi Strauss?"

"Can't say as I have. Where's his claim?"

"In a San Francisco sail loft. Levi came around the Horn to look for gold and found another fortune waiting for him in his own two hands. It's a tailor he was back east, and a tailor he is in San Francisco. You see, Levi makes pants."

"Pants? You mean pants like these I got on?"

"Better. Levi makes them out of canvas sailcloth. There's all these abandoned ships rotting on the San Francisco flats with devil a crew to sail them back where they came from. Levi buys the sails for a song and works them up into the stout sort of pants a man needs in this rough country. "It's famous he's become for his pants. They call them Levi's and he's selling them faster than he can turn them out."

Nevada thought for a moment. Then he nodded. "I can see where a tailor could make out without looking for gold, but I'm just an old country boy with ten thumbs and no education worth mention."

Carlyle laughed shrewdly. "I noticed the tie-down holster and the way you move them clumsy hands of yours. You are Nevada Jones, aren't you?"

"I could be. What else did they tell you about me in camp?"

"Nothing bad. You're said to be a decent cuss with a fast draw and a kid sister, who'd be herself, here. I suppose gunmen will be needed, too. We're not in competition, Nevada."

"Maybe. I notice you carry that Walker in a cross-draw rig that looks a mite worn-in by practice. I don't favor a cross-draw, but you don't size up as a man who backs down easy."

"Well, since it's sensible men we both are, we'll never know who's faster with a gun. I was talking about roads and bridges. I'm a builder, not a fighter."

Dawn murmured, "Coffee's ready," and started to pour a tin cup for the stranger. He took it with a gracious smile and a gallant bow. "Thank you, me darling."

"She's only twelve years old," Nevada grunted.

Carlyle laughed. "I heard about Bully Dalton, too. Your sister would be safe from me if she was twenty-seven. Though, in God's own name, I might be after courting her decent if she was, for it's a beautiful lass she'll be in a few years."

Nevada took his own cup from Dawn and muttered, "Yeah, well, let's not worry about that 'til the time comes for any kind of courting. Where did you say you was headed, Carlyle?"

"Oh, it's a road I'm surveying. Mostly in me own head, for the detail of grades and fills can wait until I've money to build with. You see, a road along the side of this wash and down the valley of the Middle Fork would mean cheap freight up from the Coast. Boats can bring supplies up to the village of Sacramento, and there's a railroad from there to the Folsom foothills already. It's the backpacking through this brush that makes a nail worth a dollar up here on the slopes. Bring the stuff in by wagon and the prices would come down within reason. There'll be no civilization here until we have some decent roads."

"Maybe so. There's talk of a stage line, someday, stopping at Piggy O'Day's."

"There will be, and a man who invests in the line will make a killing. I'll leave the placers and even the mines of the mother lode to you buckos. For I can see more gold in the building of California than you'll ever dig from her bones."

Nevada drained his cup with a bored expression and stood up. "I'm going back to dig a mite, anyways.

You're welcome to set a spell, but do I hear the kid holler, you'd best have that Walker out when I come running."

"You've said how you feel about the lass, Nevada. Let me finish this cup, and I'll spell you on the shovel for a few feet before I go."

"Why? I told you there's no color and this is our claim."

"Jasus, it's a suspicious one you are, and that's a fact. I'm a good man with pick or spade, and I owe you a favor for the cup of hospitality."

"Aw, shoot. The grounds is half roots the kid dug out of the mud, and the water's free. But I'd be obliged, if you don't mind getting your boots wet. Mosey on over when you've a mind to."

Nevada left them to return to the wash, not looking back. He knew Dawn would warn him if the stranger did anything foolish, and sometimes it paid to give a stranger a little rope.

When they were alone, Dawn asked Carlyle, "Would you like another cup, mister?"

"No, thank you, darling, for your brother's right about the taste, and me name's Brian to me friends. If you'll keep an eye on me pony, I'll give Nevada a hand and be off."

"Are you really going to build your road, or is it a someday thing?"

"Jasus, you do look through a man, don't you, Dawn? It's not all dreams I'm made of, but—yes, it is a someday thing, for the moment. I've been trying to get the others interested, but they'd rather pay a dollar a nail and hope for El Dorado in the bottom of some wash."

"I think you'll build your road. I think you're pretty, too."

"Do you, now? Well, that makes the two of us pretty, lass. But we'd best leave off that sort of talk until you're a wee bit older. Is it twelve your brother said you was?"

"We don't know, for sure. You see, he's not really my brother and—"

"Whist! Not another word, lass! Who you are and what you are to Nevada Jones are none of my business, and I'll hear no more about it. I thank you for the coffee, and if I was you, I'd keep family secrets in the family. Do you understand?"

"No. I keep asking Nevada to explain things but he says I'm too young. Do you know why he wants everyone to think I'm his baby sister?"

"Maybe I do and maybe I don't. Just do as he says and keep your pretty lip buttoned on the subject of relations."

"Pooh, you're as bad as Nevada! Honestly, I don't understand grown men at all!"

Carlyle got to his feet and turned away, not daring to ask the question that was on his mind as he went to give Nevada a hand. It didn't seem possible that the odd pair were living in sin, yet she was a pretty little thing and . . . Jasus! he warned himself. The thoughts you're thinking could get a man killed, and that's not what we came west to be after!

The first hole Nevada dug to bedrock held no placer gold. Neither did the second or third. On the fourth try, there was color in the pan. Dawn couldn't see why he was so excited when he ran over to the tent with what seemed to be a few pinpoints of yellow light in the black grit he'd washed from the lighter sand. It was a small pocket of low-grade washings, but Nevada was beside himself with joy and celebrated the event with a trip into Lost Chinaman Camp with his ward. He bought Dawn a length of pink ribbon for her hair and himself a bottle of Maryland rye, which he passed around to everyone he met. When the bottle was empty, Piggy O'Day gave them another, on the house.

Despite her horrendous name, Piggy O'Day was a little more attractive than a pig. In her younger days she'd been quite pretty, and the name had been Peggy. Now she was a frowzy blonde of perhaps forty summers, give or take a few years and a hard life.

Dawn had expected to stay in town with Rosalita, but as the afternoon wore into evening and the evening turned to a noisy night of celebration at Piggy's log "hotel," the Mexican seamstress didn't seem to be included and Nevada was rapidly getting drunker than Dawn had ever seen him.

The interior of Piggy O'Day's was a far cry from the plush Victorian saloon and parlor houses that would one day form a feature of the West. The barn-like room with a beaten earth floor was furnished with odds and ends, the so-called bar simply some boards atop a row of barrels. Tables and chairs had been improvised from crates and lengths of split logs. An oil lamp hanging over the bar and some candle-ends stuck in empty bottles dimly illuminated the windowless room, which was blue with tobacco smoke. Half the people in Lost Chinaman Camp were there, counting the miners and a handful of painted women who needed a change of clothes and a bath.

The whores smiled at Dawn as Nevada placed her in a corner with a bowl of chili and a mug of what passed for coffee, but nobody seemed much interested in Nevada's kid sister. They all wanted to hear about his strike.

"I figure to take out over a hundred a day, Lord willing and the creek don't rise." Nevada laughed as Shorty Grogan questioned him on the color in his pan. A man offered to sell Nevada a sluice box, pointing out the advantages of his homemade contraption. Another man snorted, "You need runnin' water for a sluice, damn it! What Nevada needs is a rocker box. That feller who shot hisself the other day has a rocker box in his possibles. It's busted, but ten, twenty dollars worth of nails should hold her together and you can't beat a rocker box for gittin' out the dust with bucket water!"

Dawn ate her beans, not really following what the older men were so excited about. After a time she found herself watching a dapper little man in a snuff-colored frock coat and pearl-gray sombrero. He was at the next table, dealing cards to three miners who didn't seem at all interested in Nevada, either. The small man had pretty hands, and it was fun to watch the way he made the cards dance on the rough planks of the table.

When the French girl, Yvette, came over with some tortillas to go with the beans, Dawn asked her who the man in the gray sombrero was. "That's Ace Purvis," Yvette murmured. "Your brother wouldn't want you to talk to him, *chérie*."

"Why? Is he bad?"

"He is a gambler and most bad indeed. They say he killed a man in Angel's Camp. Do you wish some more coffee?"

"I have enough for now. Why did he kill that man in Angel's Camp?"

"Who can say? Perhaps the man was cheating Ace.

Perhaps Ace was cheating the man. It is not a thing to worry one's pretty little head about, *non?*"

The whore returned to the celebration, leaving Dawn to study the dapper gambler. Once he looked up from the hand he was holding and for a moment their eyes met. Ace Purvis looked surprised as he took in the age of the child in the corner. Then he nodded at Dawn with a thin smile and dropped his eyes to his cards again. Dawn noticed that the men at the table were playing with condor quills full of gold dust in place of chips, and that Ace Purvis seemed to have most of the quills on the table in front of him.

After a time, the gambler caught the eye of one of the whores and beckoned her over. The powdered girl leaned near the gambler, looked at Dawn with a nod, then came to Dawn's table. "We're moving you to another corner, honey. I'll carry your dish."

Dawn eased out from behind the table and followed the older woman, puzzled. Why had the gambler ordered her away from his part of the room? Was he angry with her for some reason?

Nevada, despite his drinking at the bar, had caught the play and came over as the whore placed Dawn at a table on the far side of the room. He asked what was up and the girl murmured, "There's a showdown brewing. Ace has been trying to let that Greek win back some of his dust, but the man's a fool and he's talking ugly. Ace allowed as how your kid sister shouldn't be in his neck of the woods, when and if."

Nevada nodded, turned, and raised his bottle in a silent toast to the gambler in the corner, who merely shrugged. The Greek who'd been losing turned and shot Nevada a dirty look before turning back to the game.

A little while later, Piggy O'Day herself came over to Dawn and beckoned. "Come with me, honey."

"Where are we going, Miss O'Day?"

"Upstairs. Your brother feels you'll be safer there."

"Is something going to happen?"

"I hope not. You'll be all right in my room."

Dawn followed the madam as Piggy led her up a narrow log stairway to what would have been the loft in a more respectable barn. Piggy's room consisted of a partitioned-off crib with a roughly hewn bedstead and a packing-crate dresser. A cracked mirror hung over the dresser and there was a small window made of bottle bottoms set in clay. The room smelled strongly of powder, perfume, and a musky smell Dawn couldn't identify. Piggy O'Day rummaged around in a corner for some newspapers and handed one to her. "Set yourself down and read or something. I've got to get back to the party."

Before Dawn could answer, there was muffled sound of gunfire downstairs and Piggy O'Day said, "Oh, shit!"

"What's going on?"

"You just sit tight and I'll come back and tell you, honey. Mind you don't leave this room 'til me or Nevada comes for you, hear?"

Dawn agreed and would have obeyed, but she was alone some time and the noises from downstairs were terribly confusing. After a while she went out to the loft floor and tried to make sense of the voices coming up the stairwell. Hearing a footstep behind her, she turned to see a bearded man approaching from one of the cribs, buttoning his pants.

He frowned at Dawn. "Ain't you a little young for this business, sis? What's goin' on down there?"

"I don't know. It sounded like a fight."

A woman's head appeared from below, and as the whore and her trailing customer joined them on the landing, the bearded man repeated the question. The whore shrugged. "Some Greek got shot. The vigilance committee's deciding whether or not to hang Ace Purvis."

"That who shot the Greek?"

"Yeah. Looks like they'll vote it self defense. Nevada Jones saw it and allowed as how the Greek went first for his gun."

"Nevada's my brother," said Dawn.

The whore frowned and pulled her to one side. "This ain't no place for you, child. What the hell are you doing upstairs? Don't you know what goes on up here?"

"Miss Piggy brought me here. Is my brother all right?"

"Who, Nevada? Shoot, he wasn't in the damn fight. You'd best go back in Piggy's room, if that's where you belong."

Then the whore turned to her customer and added, archly, "My room's down this way, handsome."

The bearded man waited until the couple had passed, then told Dawn, "You do like they say, sis. I'll tell Nevada where you're at when they finish holding the trial."

"I don't see why I can't watch, if the trouble is over."

"You ever see a man hang, sis?"

She shuddered. "No, have you?"

"Yep. You go along now and play with your dollies or something. It won't take long now, one way or t'other."

Dawn went back to the madam's crib and sat on the bed, thumbing through the out-of-date newspapers she couldn't read in any case as she thought about the little man in the pearl-gray sombrero. He'd been thoughtful of her and she hoped they weren't going to kill him. He had friendly eyes and his hands were pretty. If Nevada was on his side, they'd probably have to let him go.

After a time, another whore came up to get her. "You can come down, now, honey. It's all over."

"Did they hang him?"

"Who, Ace? Naw, the vote was seventeen to five in his favor and he agreed to pay for the burial. Piggy wants her room back. She's, uh, gonna be using it for a spell."

Dawn followed the woman down to the riotous scene in the main room. Ace Purvis was sitting on the bar, grinning at the others as they sang "For he's a jolly good fellow!" and it wasn't too clear whether this had been occasioned by his ridding the camp of an unpopular newcomer or because he'd invested some of his recent winnings in drinks all around. Nevada was sprawled on a box against the wall with his back to the logs, grinning owlishly at everyone. Dawn shook her head at him and said. "You're drunk!"

Nevada nodded, grinning insanely. "We found us some color and we're rich. You're my little sister, right?"

"Nevada, I've never seen you like this."

"That's true. Ain't it a bitch?"

"It's getting late. We ought to go home."

"Shoot, kid, we ain't got no home. The Stuarts burned it, but I kilt me a mess of Stuarts on the way out of the county, didn't I?"

"Nevada, you're talking crazy. You stop that this instant, hear?"

Nevada didn't answer. His eyes rolled up in his

head and he suddenly fell sideways to the floor. Dawn looked about her at the boisterous men and women in the dimly lit saloon. She suddenly felt very alone in the crowd of noisy elders.

As she bent over her fallen guardian, trying to shake him awake, a familiar voice asked, "Is it drunk he is, lass?"

Dawn looked up at Brian Carlyle, the tall engineer, and shook her head. "I think he's sick. I've seen Nevada drink before, but he was never like this!"

Carlyle bent over and reached down to lift one of Nevada's eyelids. Then he grunted mysteriously and straightened up. "I'll be right back, lass. Stay with him and watch his pockets."

Dawn squatted on her heels near Nevada's unconscious form, a study in misery. In a moment the big Irishman was back with Shorty Grogan. Grogan dropped to one knee, studied Nevada for a moment, and muttered, "You're right, Carlyle. The lad's been drugged."

"I didn't think a man that size could get so drunk on the little he'd had. Miss Dawn, we're going to look in his pockets and you'll be after watching, for we mean no harm. We just want to know if he's been robbed."

Grogan searched Nevada, and shook his head. "He's still got a few coins and the poke of dust he came in with. Do you think Piggy did it?"

"Piggy or one of the others, but why? Why put sleeping powders in a man's liquor if you've no intention to . . . ahhh, *Jasus!*"

Grogan nodded grimly. "Ay, that's the way I see it. Who do you know who'll back us? I'm taking it you're a friend of Nevada's too?"

"Don't ask foolish questions. I'm trying to see how

many of the others are here and who's missing. Nevada voted to let Ace Purvis off and the man's still over at the bar. Do you think he'll help?"

"He's a damned Scotsman, but good with a gun and he does owe the lad a favor. I see Scars is still drinking with him, so he's neutral at the least and not worth asking."

Dawn tugged at Carlyle's sleeve. "What's going on? What are the two of you talking about?"

"Your brother's strike has attracted the attention of false friends, lass. Is there anyone here in camp you'd be safe with for the night?"

"I think Rosalita would let me sleep with her. She lets Nevada sleep with her."

"Rosalita it'll have to be, then. Grogan, see the lass over to the Mexican girl's shack while I talk to Ace and see how many others we can get."

Grogan took Dawn's hand and led her through the crowd to a rear exit. She repeated her questions and Shorty Grogan said, "We're not certain, lass. It looks like claim jumpers. Let's get you over there on the quick step ,eh?"

As Dawn trotted alongside the little man who was only a few inches taller than herself, she gasped, "What's a claim jumper?" But Grogan merely grunted, "Whist, you're to say nothing to the Mexican lass or anyone else until we get back. Do you mind what I'm saying?"

"Can I tell the men on the miner's committee and the vigilantes? Nevada's a member, and—"

"Not a word to anyone, lass. Your brother's enemies would be members, too, or they'd never be trying such a raw deal on a man who's known to have friends in camp and a fast draw!"

They were within sight of Rosalita's now, and

Grogan let go her hand. "Scoot, and mum's the word. I've got to get back to Carlyle."

"You'll come soon and tell us what's happened at our claim?"

Grogan smiled grimly and promised, "I'll come back if I'm still breathing, lass. You have the word of Grogan on that."

As it turned out, the showdown was anticlimactic. There was, in fact, no real showdown at all. The matter was settled in a silent power play after Carlyle, Shorty, Ace Purvis, and a dozen of Nevada's friends rode out to the claim and found it deserted, save for some wooden stakes marked CALAVERAS MINING COMPANY 20/7/50.

Carlyle pulled one of the stakes, remounted, and led the grim little party back to Lost Chinaman Camp just before midnight.

Nevada had been put to bed in one of the rooms overhead by the solicitous Piggy ODay. Dawn was huddled with Rosalita in the frightened seamstress's shack, so neither witnessed the short drama that followed Carlyle's slamming the stake down on the bar and bellowing "All right, out with it, who's the son of a bitch who left this in Nevada's turf?"

Morgan Sears, a morose Texan who was nominal head of the vigilance committee, peered thoughtfully at the claim stake. "Who wants to know?"

Carlyle snapped, "Myself and some other friends of Nevada and the girl. I'm willing to back me brag that I'm his friend as far as any man here wants to take it. I know for a fact that Nevada was the lad who made the strike, and by God, his claim will be taken from him over me own dead body!"

Sears shrugged. "It's not for me to say. Nevada

never recorded his claim, though. The law says a man don't own nothing until he's recorded and registered it with stakes and paper."

Carlyle brushed the rival claim stake from the bar and ground it under a booted heel. "The claim belongs to Nevada. Does any man here say different?"

Nobody answered.

Ace Purvis smiled thinly out from under his gray hat brim.

"Let's all have a drink on it, then. I'm willing to allow it was all an honest mistake by someone who didn't know the claim was Nevada's in the first place."

Morgan Sears hesitated before he nodded at the gambler. "These things happen," he muttered. "I take it you're backing Carlyle here?"

"I am, if there's need to. I'd rather buy drinks all around and forget it."

Shorty Grogan blurted, "Just a minute. Who's the son of a bitch who calls himself the Calaveras Mining Company? I'll not drink with the bastard before he shows his face!"

Again there was no answer. Carlyle laughed and said, "Let it lay, lad. Ace is on the right course, and we're all friends here. Ain't that right, me buckos?"

There was a chorus of eager agreement and Ace put a quill of gold dust on the bar. "Drinks are on me. Oh, and by the way, I'm sure Nevada will wake up in the morning with nothing missing from his pockets. You see, Grogan took inventory before Miss Piggy took him up to her room."

The bargirl nodded, pale-lipped, and murmured, "I'll mention it to Piggy, Ace. This first round is on the house."

As the boys bellied up to the bar, Ace and Carlyle raised their cups but only went through the motions of drinking. They'd learned to have seconds thoughts on Piggy O'Day's red-eye. Shorty Grogan drank his, though, and after he'd remained on his feet for a time the two older and wiser hands exchanged glances and thin smiles. Apparently the matter had been settled for the moment. Carlyle motioned with his head toward the door and Ace nodded, following him outside, where they were shortly joined by Grogan.

Grogan asked, "Shall I fetch the lass?" and Carlyle said, "Go and tell her it's over and that her brother's safe, but leave her with Rosalita. We'll get the two of them back to their claim in the morning."

As Grogan left, Ace Purvis rolled a smoke musingly. "No way of finding out just who the Calaveras Mining Company might be, I suppose?"

Carlyle leaned against a post and said, "Oh, we could find out, but I'm not sure we want to know. I'd say they went out of business even faster than they incorporated, wouldn't you?"

"Looks that way. Guess the old-timers didn't know Nevada had so many friends. Think they'll try again?"

"Doubt it. It's a matter of public record that they backed out of a fair fight. You going to be around for a while?"

"I was fixing to mosey on down to Angel's or Murphy's. They just made a strike at Murphy's—and the pickings have been slim in this camp. You figure you're going to need me?"

"Might be dangerous, Ace. The Greek might have friends you don't know about, and some of the vigilantes did vote to hang you, you know."

"Hell, a lot of folks have voted to hang me. And if the Greek has friends, they'll find me just as sudden in any camp in the gold fields. What's the play? Do we set up camp near Nevada or just stand by, looking big and ugly?'"

"I don't think they'll need a guard of honor out there at their tent. We'll just go about our business as usual, letting it be known we're Nevada's friends. I'm thinking it's over."

"Hope so. The boy's a trusting fool and that kid sister of his is too pretty to be this close to the sort of men who'd rob a man with sleeping powders. How old would you say Dawn was, Carlyle?"

"I don't know. Nevada says twelve."

"She looks older to me. Gonna be a looker in a year or so."

"Ay, but right now she's too young."

"No argument, partner. I like my olives green, but she's got a bit of ripening to do before I'd come courting."

Carlyle's voice was cautious as he said, "Oh? Is it courting you'd be thinking of?"

Ace laughed and kicked idly at a stone. "Come on, you said yourself she was only twelve. I'm just talking to hear myself talk. A man does get tired of whores and Injun gals, don't he?"

"Maybe, but he lives longer that way. I don't think Nevada would want a gambler courting his sister, even if she was old enough."

"Not many men would. What's the matter with you, Brian? *You're* not sweet on the girl, are you?"

"Aw, Jasus! That wee thing?"

Ace took a thoughtful drag on his smoke before he muttered. "Who are we joshing, Irish? She's as pretty as a picture and we both know it. But you're right about her not being for either of us, even when she blossoms the way she figures to. You do much reading, Irish?"

"Read? Of course I read! It's a Yale man I'm after being, for all me Paddy brogue!"

"I read this book one time when I was a kid. It was all about knights in armor and ladies pure and all that muck. I suppose it was a lot of nonsense, but I don't know, I always wanted to be a knight in armor when I grew up. You may have noticed I didn't grow all that big."

"You were big enough, backing me just now."

"Hell, Mister Colt made all men equal when he invented the six-gun. I guess you might call my way of living the closest thing to a knight in armor that's left. They lived by their wits and gun hand, too, you know."

"What's this got to do with here and now, for God's sake?"

"Nothing I should even be trying to explain to a damned engineer with a slide rule for a heart. But sometimes a man feels like talking—and so far, you've never hit me."

"It's the California sun or some of Piggy's red-eye that's been after hitting you, Ace. I've done me share of dreaming with me slide-rule heart and I've read of errant knights and ladies fair, but we've saved the lady from the dragon and it's time we got some sleep. Where's your bedroll—up in Piggy's?"

"Do I look like a man dumb enough to leave his roll where whores can get at it? I'm camped with a Mex and his woman, up the slope. They don't know where my poke is buried, either."

"Well, I'll be off to my own lean-to, then. If you're back here by ten in the morning I'll buy you a drink."

"That sounds reasonable. How late are we going to let Nevada sleep?"

"Oh, I'll get him and the girl home a little after

sunup and see she puts some breakfast in him. He's going to be sick as a dog for days, but the powders wear off faster if a man has something in his belly worth throwing up."

"You don't need any help?"

"You gave us help when we needed it, Ace. I won't forget it. I don't think Nevada will, either."

"It was nothing. I told you I always wanted to grow up to be a knight in armor. See you around ten?"

As the dapper little gambler started to walk away, Carlyle called, "Hey, Ace?"

"Yeah?"

"I know this is none of my business, but it *was* because Nevada voted for you at the vigilance meeting, wasn't it?"

"You must be joking. I don't even know the clod."

"Damn it, he saved your life, didn't he?"

"Maybe he did. Maybe he didn't. My life's not worth a hell of a lot to anyone."

"Then you did do it for the lass?"

"Of course I did. Didn't you?"

The plot to steal Nevada's claim, having fizzled in the face of his surprise support in the community, was never repeated in Lost Chinaman Camp. This may have been because of simple fear, or the fact that the claim, in the end, wasn't the bonanza Nevada had thought.

The gold was there, but it was mixed with an awful lot of sand, and the labor of extracting it taxed a strong man's effort. Nevada bought the rocker box and repaired it. Dawn helped by pouring bucket after bucket of water on top of the sand as Nevada rocked it back and forth with weary arms. At the end of each day they'd accumulated barely enough gold dust to keep them in food and supplies. Like many a miner of the so-called gold rush, Nevada was making barely more than any hard-working farmer could have made with a few acres of bottomland and a good milch cow. It was the *idea* of gold that kept him going. Any fool could be a farmer.

The summer wore into fall and the early snows of winter made the work nearly impossible, but they kept at it. They had no choice. It was keep going or pack it in, and many, that winter, did pack it in.

Brian Carlyle made a killing when he left the camp just before the Middle Fork froze for the winter. He built a raft, announcing his plan to float down to Sacramento with such passengers and freight as he could carry. The fare was five hundred dollars for passengers and a thousand dollars a ton for freight. Passengers would be fed, and were expected to help pole the raft through stretches of slack water. It was a preposterous proposition, but he had to turn away prospective customers who'd struck pay dirt and wanted to travel in relative comfort and safety back to civilization. So Carlyle left, promising to return with supplies in the spring, carrying more than ten thousand dollars' worth of gold dust in his poke.

Ace Purvis announced no intentions. He merely vanished one day for points unknown after another shooting incident at Piggy O'Day's. The wounded miner lingered on for several days, so the vigilance committee didn't vote on the matter, and Piggy used the contents of the dead man's poke to bury him decently with a modest profit to herself and her girls. The girls, by now, were barely making enough to pay the room and board Piggy demanded.

It was too cold, now, for a tent. At Dawn's direction, Nevada thatched and braced the tent into something that resembled a cross between a peasant cottage and an Indian wickiup. She taught him the wisdom of holing up during the blizzards, and working the rocker box during mild spells. Her skill at foraging eked out their supplies, and though Nevada grumbled at her acorn "Injun bread," they saved on flour, which was selling for the price of beef at the general store. Her ability with a fire drill saved on nearly priceless matches, and they bought little more than salt and ammunition once they'd paid for winter clothing at the scandalous going price.

By January the hills were nearly deserted and the game in the area had been shot or frightened away by hungry white men who hunted with more enthusiasm than skill. One morning as Dawn went outside to rebuild the cooking fire, she spotted the Indian watching her from the tree line near the snow-filled wash. She didn't call to Nevada, still dozing in the tent-shack. Nevada was too prone to shoot first and ask questions later, and Dawn sensed something in the shy stillness of the watching Indian that told her he meant no immediate attack. Just what he did want was something hé would indicate in his own good time.

Dawn kept her eyes away from him as she fanned up the fire and placed a kettle on to boil. She knew the Indian realized he'd been seen. Had he not intended to be seen, he'd have been better hidden.

After a time, in a conversational tone, Dawn spoke in Ho. "We have some White Eyes brown-water, if any friends would care to share it with us."

There was a long silence. Then, cautiously, the watching Indian asked, "Are you a Person? You look like a White-Eyed Saltu."

"I am both Ho and Saltu. My White-Eyed mother

died in a blizzard when I was little. My Ho mother was Hungry Moon of the Sage Grouse clan."

"I don't know your people. My people are called Was-Ho. This used to be our land. My name is Crippled Deer. When this was our land, I was the chief of my band."

"My band is dead. They were killed by a fever on the other side of the mountains. Are you hungry?"

"I ate yesterday. My woman and children are less brave. They are up the slope in a cave the White Eyes don't know about. I have been hunting. The hunting is not good this winter."

"Why doesn't your woman gather acorns? There are many around here. I found some camas bulbs the other day, too. A bed of them grows just up this wash, not far from here."

"We know. My woman is afraid. One day, two moons ago, some men with hair on their face and white eyes shot at her when she was picking camas. I have been hunting at night. They seldom shoot at Real People they can't see."

"My brother and I are not like that. Do you have a carrying basket?"

"Not with me. Why do you ask?"

"I want to give you some food. We are not wealthy with food, but we can spare some acorn cakes and camas. I have some salted meat for you, too. Tell your woman to boil and leach it or it will make you sick. The White Eyes use much salt in their food."

The Indian approached suspiciously as Dawn got up to rummage among the snow-covered food cache over the fly of her shelter. She started putting supplies in a metal bucket. "I would like this container back," she said. "If you are afraid of my brother, leave it near the edge of the clearing and I will find it."

Crippled Deer asked, "Why are you doing this? Are you not afraid I'll steal your container?"

"Why should I think that? Are the Was-Ho thieves?"

Inside the shelter, Nevada's voice called sleepily, "Who are you jawin' with, kid? Who's out there?"

Dawn said, "Be still, Nevada. Don't come out until I tell you, hear?"

"What the hell's going on?"

"Nothing I can't handle if you'll just be still. Are you awake?"

"'Course I'm awake, damn it. Just let me git my boots and—"

"Nevada, listen to me. I'm talking to an Indian and he's all right, but you'll spook him if you come busting out, so just you hush!"

She turned with the bucket of supplies to find the Indian had backed off a few paces at the sound of Nevada's voice. Dawn held out the bucket and walked toward Crippled Deer. "It's just my White-Eyed brother," she said gently. "He doesn't understand our speech, but I told him you were our friend."

Crippled Deer's hunger overcame his fear enough for him to stand his ground as the girl reached him with the bucket. He suddenly snatched it from her and without a word ran for the trees.

Behind her, Nevada stuck his head out of the shelter.

"What in thunder's going on?"

"I just gave some vittles to a digger. You can come out now. He's gone."

Nevada stepped out into the snow, rifle in hand. "You gave to a beggin' Injun? What in hell did you do that for?"

"He was hungry. He said he hadn't eaten in days and that he has a wife and kids of his own, upslope."

"Damn it, that's no reason to give away our grub! Don't you know we'll have every beggin' Injun on the western slope hangin' about for tobacco and salt, now?"

"He didn't say he wanted tobacco or salt. He said he was hungry."

"Child, you are purely a fool! Nobody gives nothin' to Diggers, unless it's a rifle ball. Why, Piggy O'Day told me they had a lot of trouble with Diggers hereabouts, until they run them off a couple of winters back."

"You helped me—and I was a Digger when you found me."

"That ain't the same. For one thing, you was white. For another, I was a greenhorn who didn't know no better, then."

"Would you help another white kid like me, now?"

"Well, of course I would. Jesus, can't you tell the difference between white folks and Injuns, kid?"

"I know most of the ones you call Diggers are friendlier than most of the men in Lost Chinaman Camp. Was it Diggers who doped you and tried to steal this claim?"

"Hell, we got that settled peaceable, kid. I don't want you handing out supplies to begging Injuns anymore. Do you understand?"

"No. Half our supplies are mine. I'll give them to any blamed person I aim to, Nevada."

"You'll what?"

"You heard me. I've worked this claim just as hard as you have and I've kept you warm and fed, besides. If you want to spend our gold dust on Rosalita and Piggy's whores, I'll spend mine any way I want to!"

Nevada's jaw dropped. "Why, you sassy little thing! I've a good mind to turn you over my own

knee and give you the spankin' you been askin' for
since the first day I found you on the other side of
the Sierra!"

"Pooh, you've been saying that a long time and I've
never been spanked yet!"

Nevada leaned his rifle against the shelter and took
a deep breath. "Well, we'd best get to it, then. You've
been gettin' too damned big for your britches, kid.
It's time you learned who's boss hereabouts."

He advanced on Dawn, expecting her to run, but
she stood her ground. Nevada hesitated, towering
over her. "I really mean it this time. You say you'll
mind your manners and I'll let you off."

"My manners suit me just fine, Nevada. You're the
one who drinks and whores our gold away, so there!"

Nevada grabbed her, seated himself on a box, and
tried to put her over his knees. Dawn didn't go along
with the idea at all, and fought back with a strength
that surprised him. He held her around the waist, and
as he tried to pin an arm behind her, she twisted free
and his palm slid over one of her small firm breasts.
Nevada gasped and let go as if he'd picked up a hot
coal. Dawn pulled away to stand above him, facing
him with a confused expression on her own face. Why
were her legs so watery all of a sudden? Why did
she went to run and sink to her knees all at the
same time?

Nevada looked away, flushing. "Let's leave it be for
now. You're too old to spank, I reckon."

"What do you want to do to me, then?"

"Damn it, I don't want to do nothing. Is there any
coffee, or did you give it all to your damned Injuns?"

"There's coffee. What's the matter? Why won't you
look at me?"

Nevada frowned up at her. "Who won't look at you?

I ain't afeared to look at nobody kid."

"Your face is all red. I feel sort of funny, too. Something just happened, Nevada. Something I don't understand."

"Nothin' happened. We was just funnin' about and got us both out of breath, is all. Don't you go gettin' no foolish notions about the way my hand done slipped. I didn't mean nothin' country, hear?"

"If you say so. You know what I thought? I thought you were going to kiss me. How come you never kiss me, Nevada?"

"Are you loco, girl? Why in hell would I want to kiss a skinny bitty girl-child like you?"

"You kiss Rosalita and Piggy O'Day. I've seen you do it."

"That ain't the same. Fetch the coffee."

Dawn went over to the fire and poured him a cup. As she handed it to him he refused to meet her eyes. She asked, "Why isn't it the same, Nevada? Don't you like me?"

"Well, of course I like you. I've been taking care of you all these months, ain't I?"

"What's it like, Nevada? What does it feel like to kiss the way you kiss Rosalita?'

"You hadn't ought to talk that way, kid. It ain't right for us to talk this way."

"I just want to know what it feels like. I know I'm too young to fuck, but—"

And then Nevada's fist shot out to catch Dawn full in the face, sending her flying across the fire to land, sprawled on her back, in the snow.

An instant later he was on his knees at her side, holding her dazed head against his chest. "Jesus, honey baby! I'm sorry, so sorry, but you never should have said *that word!*"

Dawn shook her head to clear it as she muttered, "What's the matter? What's wrong with fucking? You do it all the time, and—"

"Don't *say* that! It sounds plumb awful comin' from your bitty mouth! Where in thunder did you ever learn such a word?"

"Fuck? Everybody in Lost Chinaman's Camp says it all the time."

"Not *you*, kid. Promise me you'll never say that word again."

"I will if you won't hit me, but you sure are acting funny this morning, Nevada."

"You caught me by surprise, using that dirty word."

Dawn started to repeat the word, remembered, and asked, "Why is the word so dirty if *doing* it isn't?"

"Hell, the whole thing's dirty. The saying and the doing."

"Then why does everyone want to do it to Rosalita and Piggy and the other grownup ladies?"

"It ain't *right*, kid. It's just a thing a man has to do. It's sort of like eating, or drinking. It's what you call a—a appetite. Yeah, that's what it is, a appetite."

"Then why is it wrong? You'd save an awful lot of gold dust if you taught me how to do it instead of going into town to pay those other girls all the time."

"Don't talk like that. You're a *good* girl."

"Don't good girls have appetites?"

"Not if they've been brung up proper. Good girls never let a man do nothin' to 'em 'less they's married up with him proper."

"Oh. Then I can find out what it's like if I can get some man to marry me, right?"

"You're jumpin' the gun, kid. You ain't old enough to be talkin' on gettin' hitched. This whole damn line of talk is plumb foolish on both our accounts. So I'd best be goin' in to . . . Damn! I can't leave you out here alone with them Injuns skulkin' about!"

"I'm in less danger from Crippled Deer than you are from Piggy O'Day. You run along and take care of that appetite of yours, which is still just a polite word for what I can't say out loud without getting killed, around here!"

"Look here, kid, what goes on betwixt me and them gals at Piggy's is my own business."

"Everybody else seems to be minding it, then. I heard some men at the corral joshing about Piggy taking more gold out of our rocker box than the two of us put together and—oh, by the way, whats a Cumberland virgin?"

"Cumberland virgin? Never heard of one. Why?"

"One of the men said a Cumberland virgin was a gal who could run faster than her brothers. I didn't get the joke."

Nevada reached for the rifle he'd leaned against the shelter and said quietly, "I did. Which one of the men in town said it to you, kid?"

"Nobody said it to me. They didn't know I was listening."

"It's still a killing thing to say. So once again, who said it?"

Dawn stared soberly at the worn rifle in Nevada's hands and shook her head. "I don't aim to tell you. Not this morning. You've been on the prod since you woke up, and I think you ought to work it off on the rocker box."

"Damn it, that remark was aimed at *us*. You know I'm from the Cumberland!"

"I know. Rosalita says there's been a lot of dirty talk

about you and me, but she warned me not to tell you no names. Rosalita is a nice girl. Why don't you spend more time with her instead of those mean-mouthed whores at Piggy's?"

"I don't aim to get too tight with no Mex gal. It's a thing you ain't old enough to talk about. What sort of dirty talk did she pass on to you, with names or without?"

"She said it was usual. She said I was either wrong about my age or growing up faster than most white girls. She said a lot of men were looking at me funny, but when I asked her what she meant she said she'd tell me about it later. You grownups sure keep lots of secrets from us kids."

Nevada shook his head and muttered, "I thought sayin' you was my kid sister would hold it off, but you are startin' to fill out faster than I ever figured. If only I could strike it rich we could maybe put you in a boarding school or something, down in San Francisco."

He put the rifle down. "You're right about it being a good day for the rocker box. We ain't gonna get the gold out, dreaming about it."

"I'll fix you some breakfast, first. You can't just work on coffee."

"I ain't hungry. Not for food, leastways. You get the shovel and keep the slush coming whilst I rock. We got to git us rich afore the way you're sproutin' gets me killed."

The next morning Dawn found the bucket she'd given Crippled Deer at the edge of their clearing. A few days later she found a butchered and dressed side of venison tied to a willow above the reach of prowling beasts. When she commented on this to Nevada, he shrugged and said some Injuns were likely more honest than others.

As the snows clung to the west slope of the Sierra, Nevada spent more time than ever working his crude extracting device. This was partly because he was worried about the Indians skulking in the nearby woods and partly because he'd developed a bad taste in his mouth for the half-deserted mining town. The gold accumulated a grain at a time, at the cost of back-breaking work and feet that never seemed to be dry and warm from one day to the next. Nevada had no idea of the prices down in the San Francisco area, but he was determined to get all the dust the limited deposit held and to move them on before some fool said to his face what he knew they were saying behind his back.

One morning, as Dawn prepared breakfast in front of the tent-shelter, Crippled Deer broke cover with a small, shy Was-Ho squaw who carried a basket. The couple approached gingerly, and the squaw placed the basket down near Dawn and ran back to the trees. Dawn thought the basket would contain a gift of nuts or roots and was amazed to see the handful of gleaming yellow nuggets in its coiled bottom.

Crippled Deer said, "We have watched you and your brother. Is it yellow iron like this you are taking from the sand with that big funny box he keeps rocking back and forth?"

Dawn nodded. "Yes, but we've only been getting dust. Where did you get these grains? There is more yellow iron there than we can find in a month!"

"A White Eyes died in the hills above us last summer. The coyotes ate most of him. He had these grains of yellow iron in a little leather bag. The bag had rotted open, so I told my daughter to put them in this basket for you. Are you pleased?"

"I am pleased, but you must let us pay you for them. Don't you know what you could buy from the White Eyes with so much yellow iron?"

"No. I don't understand why you other people attach so much importance to the stuff. It's too soft to work up into a cutting blade. What do they use it for? Is it a medicine? I have heard that the White Eyes suffer a sickness that can only be cured by yellow iron. Do you and your brother have it?"

Dawn smiled and started to shake her head. Then she reconsidered and said, "Perhaps my brother does. I will buy you things at the general store with this. What do you need?"

Crippled Deer considered, then asked, "Will it buy our land back?"

"No. I don't think so," Dawn said. "I can get salt and matches for you. If you know how to shoot a gun, I will buy one for you. How about blankets or some clothing? It is cold this winter."

"We make better blankets from our own rabbit skins than the ones of the White Eyes. We need no other clothes. We need no guns. If the White Eyes would only go away and leave us alone, we would need nothing else they might give us."

"There must be something. I can't pay you back for your lands, but it would be wrong to take this gift without returning something very nice for it."

Crippled Deer said slowly, "Do you think you could offer me friendship?"

"You have that already, Crippled Deer."

"Your brother is not our friend. How much yellow iron would I have to find for him before he would think of me as a man?"

Dawn thought for a moment. "Wait here. Don't run away as you usually do when my brother comes outside."

She scooped up a couple of nuggets and ducked inside the tent fly, shaking the sleep-drugged Nevada awake as she spoke swiftly and earnestly in the semi-darkness. Nevada took the nuggets and tested them with his teeth as she explained about the Indian's finding them and offering them for friendship—a thing so easy to give any person of good will.

Nevada muttered, "By God, it's real gold! You say all this Injun wants is to be friends? Hell, what's the fuss? I never shot at them when you fed 'em ,did I?"

"Nevada, you've got to go out there and smoke some tobacco with Crippled Deer."

"That's all? Hell, I know they keep beggin' tobacco, but there's enough gold in this one nugget to buy him all the cigars his tribe could smoke in a year!"

"You're missing the point. They haven't been begging tobacco. They've been begging and pleading for some white man to sit down and *smoke* with them!"

"You mean, like a peace pipe?"

"The calumet ceremony is an eastern Indian tradition. The Ho just share a smoke and pass the time of day around a friend's fire. Will you do it?"

"Hell, for nuggets this size I'd smoke a hundred cgiars with the devil his ownself. But what am I to *say* to the jasper? I don't talk no Injun lingo."

"Just wipe that frown off and come outside and let me do the talking, all right?"

Not waiting until he'd pulled on his damp boots,

Dawn stepped out to find Crippled Deer still in place. She took a blanket from the drying rack near the entrance and spread it on the snow near the small smoldering fire. "Sit down. My brother is coming out as soon as he finds some tobacco."

The nearly nude Was-Ho asked soberly, "Are we going to smoke?"

"Doesn't one man smoke with another, if they wish to be friends?"

Crippled Deer smiled for the first time since Dawn had seen him, and sank cross-legged to the blanket. He ran a cautious hand over the red wool and observed, "It is thin, but well made."

Nevada came outside, his face wooden with hidden confusion, and as Dawn pointed to the blanket, eased himself down beside the Indian, holding out his right hand. Crippled Deer regarded the outstretched hand with mild curiosity. Dawn said, "They don't shake, Nevada. Roll a smoke, light it, and pass it to him."

Nevada withdrew his hand, and as Crippled Deer watched like a curious child, he rolled a thick smoke from crumb tobacco and Mexican corn paper. He leaned forward, took a burning twig from the fire and lit one end, inhaling deeply to get the crude cigarette going. Then he blew a smoke ring and handed it to Crippled Deer. "Your turn, old son."

Crippled Deer puffed on the cigarette, handed it back, and said to Dawn, "Will you tell him to do that again?"

"Do what, Crippled Deer?"

"Draw a circle in the sky with smoke. I have never seen a man do that before."

Dawn explained, and Nevada, relieved to be doing something he understood, blew a series of smoke rings as the Indian watched in delight. With Dawn's help, Nevada showed the Indian how to blow a smoke ring, and after a dozen aborted attempts, Crippled Deer managed a ring and laughed out loud. Nevada too, and slapped Crippled Deer on the back. "There you go, you unwashed heathen bastard!"

The pat on the back, though confusing to Crippled Deer, seemed friendly enough. So he hit Nevada behind the nape of the neck and laughed again.

Nevada flinched and looked at Dawn. "He's got a mean wallop, ain't he? Tell him you ain't supposed to hit so hard."

Dawn did so, and Crippled Deer repeated his well-meant backslapping with a gentler blow. Mollified, Nevada said, "That's better. What do we do now?"

Dawn said, "We wait. He'll go away when he feels like it."

The two men passed the smoke back and forth until it was gone, and when Nevada asked Dawn if Crippled Deer wanted him to roll another, the Indian said, "No. Good medicine should not be wasted. I would like to understand why the two of you rock that box in the dry river bed."

Dawn tried to explain the workings of a rocker box, searching for Ho words to show how the heavier gold was trapped in the riffles of the box as the sloshing water washed the lighter sand on through at the bottom.

Crippled Deer held up a hand for silence. "Your words are beyond me. If some of us helped you rock the box, would the thing work as well?"

"Of course," Dawn said. "You don't have to understand a tool to use it." In English she added to Nevada, "I think he's offering to work for us." Nevada said, "Ask him what sort of a share he had in mind."

Dawn tried, but the idea of stock in a white man's mining venture was harder for Crippled Deer to grasp than the workings of a rocker box.

He said, "We are friends. Friends help one another."

"True, but you have hunting and other tasks to keep you busy enough."

"The hunting is bad. My women have dug all the roots we can reach where no White Eyes claim the land. It is my thought we could find food enough near this place, if your brother would not shoot us."

Dawn translated and Nevada laughed. "Hell, I can do better than that. I'm a member of the Vigilance Committee. I'll have me a talk with the rest of the boys and maybe see if we can work out some sort of peace treaty. We leave them be with their roots and acorns, and they promise not to steal or pester folks."

"That's all he really wants. How many hours of work shall we ask him for?"

Nevada shook his head and said, "Wouldn't be right to ask so much work for so little in return. I don't hold much with slavery, and it seems to me that making a man work for you just 'cause you ain't killin' him is perilous close to slaving."

Dawn smiled warmly and would have kissed Nevada, had she not known how upset it made him. She repeated his words in Ho to Crippled Deer, who looked down at the ground for a moment in silence, wiped a hand across his face, and said huskily, "You are good people."

"Have you spoken?"

"No, hear me, and say my words to your White-Eyed brother. I am Crippled Deer, and I am weak. My people are few. They are weak, too. I know your brother's White-Eyed friends are many and powerful, but if either of you ever need a handful of small weak men to stand at your side against Lord Grizzly or all four hundred devils of the spirit world, you have my word we shall be there. That, I have spoken."

Crippled Deer got to his feet and walked away, not looking back, as Dawn translated his words to Nevada. Nevada shrugged and followed the Indian with his eyes. "I'd rather have any man for me than agin' me. He's a puny cross-grained cuss, and that's a fact, but I reckon it's our Christian duty not to hurt a pore old man who don't want nothin' from us but his heathen life."

And so, with Nevada's grudging consent, Dawn became "The White-Eyed Ho Woman With A Good Heart" and her fame spread, unknown to her, through the brush-tangled canyons and coyate-haunted ridges of the Western Slope.

It became known that the young woman with yellow hair admired good basketwork, so shy proud women of a dozen tribes searched among their meagre belongings for examples they were proud of. The younger digger squaws no longer wove the beautiful baskets of their mothers' time, for life had become hard and the old traditions seemed senseless in the face of tin buckets and glass bottles rummaged from deserted prospectors' camps. But they brought Dawn the best they had to offer, approaching shyly to squat by the fire with the white girl who spoke their tongue, however oddly and with a Great Basin dialect.

Others never overcame their fear enough to venture openly into the clearing, but left a gift of acorn mush in a basket woven by their grandmothers, then watched, sometimes for hours, until the distant blonde figure, half-hidden by the intervening trees, found the gift. Dawn would wave once to all four points of the compass and go back to her tent-shelter for a moment to return with some trifle such as a spool of bright thread, some needles stuck in a slip of paper, or a handful of salt wrapped in a knotted rag. The value of the exchanged gifts was not important, at first, to either side. It was amazing to the diggers that a white person showed them any sign of unselfish friendship.

The diggers had been worried from the beginning. Crippled Deer had told them, and the others that Dawn and her brother were good people, but they had heard this before about other whites, for there *was* some contact between whites and Indians in those first years of the gold rush. Generally, White Eyes wanted Digger men to show them where gold could be found. They wanted the Digger women to sleep with them. They paid little or nothing for either service and often would hit or shoot a Real Person for no reason at all. Thus came the first suspicion, and thus Dawn's fame—once it became known that her heart spoke with but one tongue and that her heart was good, despite her weird hair.

One day Dawn spied an avalanche lily peeking up from the apron of a snowdrift. Nevada was in town at the time, so Dawn began moving their gear herself. She knew that the guns, tools, and ammunition were most important. So she half-dragged, half-carried them to a nearby knoll first. As she returned to the tent-shelter and began to roll a barrel of flour uphill, a shadow appeared at her side and a voice, speaking Ho, asked, "What are you doing?"

Without looking at the young Was-Ho who'd appeared from nowhere. Dawn said, "I am moving

our camp to high ground. I think there is going
to be a thaw soon."

The Indian stepped around in front of her and
hefted the barrel to one thin but wiry shoulder. "I
think you are right. My name is Coyote Singer. I am
going to help you. My brothers are watching from
the trees. It is said you are a good person. If nobody
shoots me, they may come out and help you, too."

"Are you from Crippled Deer's band?"

"No. We are Was-Ho, but our valley used to be a
day's hunt to the north. Some White Eyes are digging
holes in the ground over there now, and they told us
to go away. So we went. Crippled Deer says it is
safe in this watershed. Is this true?"

"It is true from the bend in the wash below us to
the dead spruce with the hawk's nest in it, upstream.
My brother has no control beyond those points, but
he has spoken to the others who seek yellow iron
and most have agreed to leave the Real People alone.
We can't speak for them, however. Keep your women
out of sight and avoid White Eyes who yell a lot and
walk funny. When they have been drinking firewater, they can be bad."

Coyote Singer put the barrel down where Dawn indicated and fell in step with her as she returned to
the tent-shelter. "This part I understand," he said. "I
have tasted firewater and it made me feel very funny
before it put me to sleep. What I don't understand
is why the White Eyes treat us as enemies before
we have done anything to them."

When Dawn started to pick up a box the Indian
snatched it from her, so she contented herself with a
lighter bundle of baskets. "The seekers of yellow iron
are afraid of Real People. They don't know how to
tell a Was-Ho from a Shoshoni or a Bannock. Far to

the south there are people called Apache who have killed many White Eyes. I don't know who started it, but much blood has been spilled and my brother's people are inclined to fight anyone who doesn't look like them."

Coyote Singer shook his head. "Forgive me, but your brother's people must be stupid. I can tell a Maidu from a Miwok as soon as he opens his mouth. I know a Yana on sight, as I do a Mono, or the flatland Wintun or Yokut. There are great differences in the way Real People braid their hair or weave carrying baskets. There are no Shoshoni raiders on this side of the mountains."

"I have explained this to my brother. He is a good man and willing to listen, but he and the others met bad clans coming to this land from their hunting grounds to the east of the shining mountains. They call all of you 'Injun' and mix Ho with Apache, Shoshoni, or Blackfoot. Please try to understand they are not really bad men. Only ignorant."

"That's what I just said. Stupid. I'll admit the Bannock and Shoshoni speak a dialect we can understand. I don't know these Apache, but I have heard of the Blackfoot, and they are not even People. They speak some strange language nobody understands." He put the box down and added, "You are dumb, too. The flood waters of the thaw will reach the things you put here. We should take them higher up the slope."

"We can't. Our claimed land extends no farther from the wash. Besides, I came here in summer and know its moods better than yourself. It has no spring at its head, so it runs much drier than the streams to either side. I have read its past floods from the boulders it has rolled down from the hills above us. I don't think the waters will come this high."

"You may be right." The Indian glanced at the loaded baskets in the shelter. "You people carry a great deal of trash around with you, don't you? How do people who are so afraid of harmless strangers move their camp in a hurry?"

"They don't. They stay and fight."

"Ah, that may explain some of their odd behavior. People only fight when they can't move their belongings quickly. Once the Yana had a war with the Atsugewi over a valley where camas bulbs grew thickly. I think they were fools, too. Camas grows almost everywhere and today there are very few Yana or Atsugewi left. It was trying to hang on to things they couldn't move that made them act so foolish."

"People are like that. Even Real People. Who won in the end, the Yana or the Atsugewi?"

"Neither. Some White Eyes came along and took the valley from them for their cattle. Now even the camas bulbs are gone. The cattle ate them too fast for them to grow back. The war was for nothing, as most wars are. My people know better. We travel light and move away from trouble. That is the way Changing Woman intended it to be for everyone. Nothing ever stays the same, so why fight about it? Even our lives slip through the fingers of our hands like grains of dust. Do you know who will own this stretch of the wash, in time?"

"I'm not sure. My brother says we have taken out most of the yellow iron. I supppose we'll move on to another place like it. Maybe then your people will have it again."

"If we do, it will only be a few breaths to the mountains or a heartbeat to the sun. In time, Changing Woman will turn the mountains to a plain, or fish will swim where we are standing now. High on the ridges there are places where fish once swam. Their shells and bones may still be seen in the creek bottoms after a rain. Perhaps, when fish swam here before, they fought over whose sea it was."

Coyote Singer suddenly stiffened and quickly muttered, "I must leave you, now. I left a gift for you at the edge of the wash. Look for it when your other guests leave!"

As the Indian slipped away toward the nearest brush, Dawn turned and saw two mounted men down near the tent-shelter. She recognized them as members of the Vigilance Committee and waved, moving down to meet them.

One of them said, soberly, "Your brother wants you to come with us to Piggy's, Miss Dawn. This camp'll be crawlin' with soldiers in a minute or two. Give me your hand and I'll boost you up to ride pillion behind me."

"What's happened? Is Nevada all right?"

The rider took her hand in his to help her mount. "You jest come in to town with us and I'll explain it on the way. We got to get you out of here and you'll be safe at Miss Piggy's. Nevada left some color and instructions with her."

Dawn sat sideways behind the rider as one of his companions muttered, "We'd best circle in. Them bluebellies may be staked out along the trail, hoping Nevada will be foolish about this kid sister of his'n."

Once more Dawn demanded an explanation and this time the rider said, "You must have knowed your brother was wanted by the U.S. Army, ma'am. A whole mess of cavalry just rode up from Sacramento to arrest him." He chuckled wryly and added, "Nevada don't arrest worth mention, though. Best shoot out we've seed since Ace Purvis left town."

"Some soldiers came to arrest Nevada and he shot it out with them?"

"That's what I just said, missy. He put three of the rascals on the ground afore he fit clear. One of the troopers is dead and Nevada was last seed bleeding some and heading into the high country with half the U.S. Army after him, mad as hell."

Piggy O'Day was waiting for Dawn at the saloon, along with her whores and almost half the men in town. The other half were said to be off with the soldiers, combing the hills for the wounded Nevada. As the girl called Yvette filled a tin cup with beer for Dawn, a jovial miner suggested the men helping the army might be funning the bluebellies. The panning had been poor in Lost Chinaman of late and the War Department paid well for the services of civilian scouts.

Ignoring the offered drink, Dawn insisted, "I don't understand all this! Nevada never told me he was wanted by the army!"

A miner shrugged and said, "You must have knowed you and him wasn't really named Jones. Army warrant allowed his name was Campbell. Said he shot an officer who tried to arrest him one time for desertion."

Piggy O'Day shushed the miner with a warning look. "What Nevada done during the Mexican War ain't our worry. It's betwixt Nevada and the soldiers, and up to now, he's ahead."

Another man laughed. "That's for sure," he said. "I have never seed a man handle a gun so sweet, and I've seed some gunplay in my day. Do Jesus, I like to laughed myself sober when that sassy lieutenant

went down, still reading the warrant in his hands."
He spat and added, "They likely never figured Nevada
to draw with a whole cavalry troop surrounding him."

Dawn demanded, "What was that about Nevada
being hurt in the fight?"

Another witness explained, "Some of the soldiers
come unstuck afore he was clear. It 'peared as if
Nevada got hit once or twice as he made his exit
in a cloud of gunsmoke. Miss Piggy, here, seen him
last, after the fight."

Yvette said, "He ran in here right after he had it
out with those soldiers near the corral. He was not
hurt too badly."

Piggy O'Day put a plump arm around Dawn's
shoulder. "She's right, hon. He was hit in the thigh
and left side but still thinking straight and moving
sudden. He told us we was to look out for you 'til
things cooled off and he could come back to get you."

A miner broke in. "That's what he done, all right. I
was here and heard it all. He gave Miss Piggy some
dust to pay her for her trouble and she has the rest
of his poke locked up where the soldiers can't find it."

"Damn it!" Piggy snapped. "Hesh your face about
where Nevada's gold might or might not be. There's
men from this camp hunting Nevada for the reward
and this bitty gal is underage."

There was an abashed, worried murmur and the
madam went on. "That's right. That's why Nevada
put me in charge of his baby sister! Under the law,
she can't own property and the army figures Nevada
owes 'em. So we'll all have to forget he had a placer
claim or a next of kin, savvy?"

There was a mutter of agreement, but Dawn shook
her head as if to clear the cobwebs of a bad dream.
Then she looked around and asked, "Where is Ros-

alita? Nevada said if anything bad ever happened
to him I was to go get Rosalita and—"

Miss Peggy patted Dawn's arm protectively. "He
did say something about his Mex gal, Dawn. Now
that you mention it, I sent one of the boys to fetch
her as he was leaving. But she wasn't in her shack.
She might have rode off with him, though. You likely
know they was sweet on one another."

Dawn pulled away angrily. "That's crazy! Nevada
would never light out with another gal if there wasn't
time to get me!"

The people around her made soothing noises and
insisted she have a drink, but Dawn pushed through
the crowd and ran outside, calling out to Rosalita as
she dashed the few yards to the Mexican girl's shanty.
But Rosalita wasn't there. The shack was empty and
messed up, as if there'd been a struggle, or at any
rate as if Rosalita had packed to leave in a hurry.

The man who played the piano for Miss Piggy
joined Dawn as she came out. He spat and said, "She's
gone, Miss Dawn. We've looked high and low for the
gal, but you can see for your ownself she ain't here.
Why don't you come back to Piggy's and we'll see
about some vittles for you?"

Dawn shook her head. "I'm going back to our
claim. Nevada may circle back to pick me up."

"Honey, he lit out with a whole troop of U.S.
Cavalry on his tail and two pistols balls in his hide!"

"I'm going back anyway. The water's about to rise
and I have to move our camp to higher ground."

The piano player looked uncomfortable. "We'll
bring your stuff into town, Miss Dawn. You can't stay
out there no more."

"Why not? I'll be safe there as anywhere and there's
work to do on our claim."

The man looked away and said, "Uh—it ain't your claim no more, Miss Dawn. Just afore he lit out, Nevada sold out to Morgan Sears. I reckon he needed cash in a hurry."

Dawn stared up at the piano player in dismay. "He sold—our claim—without telling *me?*"

"Hell, missy, he had a whole posse chasing him! How in thunder was he to tell you? Besides, as I understands it, the whole plot was to save the claim for you all. As an outlaw, Nevada can't hold a mining claim. As a minor and a gal, you don't own nothing, legal, neither. I figure Old Morg aims to just hold the claim 'til he sees how it all turns out. If Nevada gets away, he'll likely sell it back to you someday."

"I see. But if it's all just to fool the law, why can't I go on living there?"

"Because it wouldn't look right. Morgan has the bill of sale and you ain't kin to him. You're kin to a man wanted on ever' charge from desertion to murder. So you'd best do as Piggy says and hope for the best."

Dawn stood her ground, shaking her head. "I don't want to stay at Piggy O'Day's old whorehouse!" she insisted. "I don't understand what's happened! It's all falling in on me so sudden and—"

"Miss Dawn, we're trying to help you. I know what they say about Old Piggy being no saint, but you have to face facts. You're a half-growed gal with no rights worth mention. You need all the friends you can get and you'd do best to throw in with Piggy. For she's about the only grownup in Lost Chinaman who figures to do a thing for you without putting a hand up your skirt!"

"I'm going to find Rosalita and ask her what she thinks I should do."

"You do what you've a mind to, honey. When you gits hungry, or the sun ball starts to set, you just come on home to Piggy's and she'll tell you what to do." He spat and added, "That Mex gal has had enough work keeping her ownself from starvin' to death hereabouts. Don't know where she's run off to, but when you find her, you won't get nothin' but a lot of Spanish hoorah. She can't do a blamed thing for you."

"Rosalita is my friend. She'll let me stay with her, and I still have Nevada's gold, so I can feed us both until the trails are clear."

"Well, that might be your best play, if you're too high falutin to bunk with Piggy. You do as you like. I gotta git back indoors afore I freeze my fool-self."

He walked away, not looking back, and Dawn was aware for the first time how cold it was getting as the late afternoon sun dropped below the treetops of the valley. She went inside Rosalita's shack, poking at the fire in the corner to see if there were any glowing coals. The fire was dead. Where on earth could Rosalita have vanished to in the dead of winter?

More to keep moving than anything else, Dawn went outside and started walking back to the claim up the wash. As she was passing through a stretch of oak a totally strange Indian emerged from the shadows and fell in at her side, speaking Ho as he asked, "Were you looking for the Mexican woman who used to live back there in that shelter?"

Dawn said, "Yes, she is a friend of mine and my brother's."

"We know what happened and who you are. Some White Eyes came to the Mexican woman's shelter and took her away. She tried to scream, but one of the men put his hand over her mouth. They went toward the sunset. When they came back, the Mexican woman was not with them."

Dawn stopped with a gasp and turned to face her Indian friend. "Do you think they hurt her?"

"There is a deep ravine down that way. It is filled with brush, and this time of the year, snow lies there higher than the head of one man standing on another's shoulders. I think they threw her down there. When the snow melts in a moon or less, the waters will carry her body far before the condors find it."

"Oh, dear God! Could you recognize the men who did it, if I took you to the others and asked you to point them out?"

"I would know them. I would not go into the White Eyes' camp even with such a friend as you. Do you seek vengeance?"

"Of course! If they murdered Rosalita, they ought to be hanged!"

The Indian shrugged and said, "I don't know how to hang a man. It seems like a lot of trouble to go to, just to kill a man."

"Hear me, you have to help me bring the men who killed my friend to justice."

"If you want them dead, just say so. My arrows fly true and the Real People say you are a good person."

Dawn nodded, grimly. Then she thought again. "No. The murderers must not be killed by Ho. It would mean destruction to your own families if any of the seekers of yellow iron were to be found with Was-Ho arrows in them."

"I am a Miwok, but your point is well taken. Tell me, what would happen if the men who killed your friend simply vanished?"

"Could you manage that?"

"Of course. A man who can carry a deer to camp can carry a dead man anywhere. I think it would be a fine joke if we threw them down in the same ravine with the woman they killed, don't you?"

"It's far better than they deserve. Is there any way to get my friend's body up out of the ravine for a proper burial?"

"It would be very difficult. I think it would be foolish, too. How would you explain her to the others, unless you accused someone of killing her?"

"I could say I just found her and . . ."

"*Think*, little White-Eyed Ho! The men who killed her would know their crime had been discovered, no matter what you said. Right now they feel safe, and a safe deer makes an easy target. Do you follow my words?"

Dawn nodded. "Yes, you have spoken well. I shall leave the matter in your hands and say nothing. May I know your visiting name?"

"I am Spotted Elk. That is my medicine name, too. I tell it to my friends. My visiting name is Walks Alone."

"You honor me with your openness, Spotted Elk. May I ask why? I know you are a good person, but I have done nothing for the Miwok Ho."

"Yes you have, Dawn of the Paiute. I call myself Walks Alone because the lands where I hunted elk in my boyhood have been taken from us. I know some Spanish and a few words of the American White Eye's speech. I know what "Digger" means, as it is spoken by the newcomers to these lands. I know you are not as the others, Heya, it is said among the Real People you have a better heart than many of our own hungry people, for hunger does bad things to anyone's heart. I know . . . Never mind, as long as I

walk this earth, alone or in the company of my few
remaining brothers, you are my sister. If you wish, you
may come and live with us in the hills to the south-
east. We have little, but what we have we will share
with you."

Deeply touched, Dawn reached out to grasp the
Indian's forearms as he in turn grasped hers. Then she
shook her head slowly. "I must remain here to guard
my dead brother's property. I must see what has
happened to our campground. And he has yellow
iron locked in the lodge of a woman I hope is a friend.
When the trails are dry, I shall leave this place, but I
shall never forget either Walks Alone or Spotted Elk.
They are both my brothers."

Spotted Elk said, "Be careful, then. The men who
killed your Mexican friend are as good as dead, but
there may be others. Do you know why they killed
her, by the way? We were puzzled by their actions.
They didn't want to use her as a woman and they
took nothing from her shelter."

"They were afraid she'd help or advise me. Rosalita
could read and write."

"What could she have told you—that condors circle in around every death? If they were afraid she'd
tell you something, why didn't they kill you at the
same time?"

"I'm not certain. My brother had many friends in
these parts and I am American White-Eyed. Rosalita
was Mexican and had few friends. I think they mean
to take advantage of my years, thinking I am too
young to know they are not my friends."

"Heya, that reminds me of the story of Sage Grouse
and Coyote. Do you know it?"

"Of course, and that's what I must be, helpless
Sage Grouse with a broken wing, fluttering weakly

just ahead of Coyote until he forgets where I placed my eggs."

The Indian faded away into the low-hanging oaks with a chuckle, and Dawn continued on to the camp she and Nevada had shared. Her mind was in a whirl.

As she arrived at the shelter, she found three men poking about among her belongings. She recognized one as a red-bearded loafer called Jigger. "What are you doing here? Those things belong to me."

Jigger smiled at her and ticked the brim of his hat with a finger. "No argument on that, missy. We're jest seein' how much gear there is. Mister Sears is gittin' a couple of Mex to tote it into Piggy's for you."

Dawn noticed a fresh claim stake driven into the snow-covered earth nearby. "What does that writing say? Calaveras Mining Company?" she asked.

"Shoot, Miss Dawn, we don't know who them ornery jaspers was. Morgan Sears bought this claim fair and square and has a bill of sale to prove it. I'll tell you true, there was some ugly talk when Morgan first said so, but he showed the paper your brother signed to the miner's committee and they're satisfied it's legal. Likely they can read as good or better than you or me."

Dawn tried to hide the bitterness she felt. "The placer's not that important. The wash will be too flooded to work in a few days, anyway. I'll just finish moving my things to high ground and tent up there on the rise until . . ."

"Miss Dawn, this land is posted. We've orders to run ever'body off on sight, with these guns iffen we has to. Only, seein' as it's you, we're tryin' to be polite. You just go on back to Piggy's and we'll see to your gear. You got our word we won't steal nothing as is your'n."

Again Dawn bit back the obvious angry retort that Morgan Sears had already stolen the only thing of value within a country mile. That Sears had been too cowardly to back his last attempt at claim jumping while Nevada and his friends were ready for a showdown. But what could an unarmed, friendless girl do against the bully? She'd be in danger of sharing poor Rosalita's fate if she were to be out here alone after sundown.

Rosalita's deserted shack would be less safe than the claim, she knew. Besides, if Nevada had intended to leave her in the charge of Miss Piggy, he'd likely try to get word to her there if he was still alive.

Pasting an innocent smile across her numb lips, she nodded at Jigger and the other man. "I'll head back before it gets dark, then."

"You do that, Miss Dawn. These woods is crawlin' with Injuns, bears, and worse. Morgan Sears said we was to make sure nothing bad happened to you or Nevada's other stuff."

Dawn retraced her steps to the settlement, burning with resentment. The cowardly claim jumpers were playing it safe, aware Nevada had friends in Lost Chinaman even if the army caught him. But how long could this game last, and more important, what was her next move?

At least it was warm in the saloon. The barmaid greeted Dawn warmly. "We got your room fixed up for you, sis. Miss Piggy said to feed you and put you to bed like a good little gal."

"You mean, up—*there?*"

"Hell, honey, we don't screw in all the cribs. You

want a drink?" Somewhere a loud female voice was shouting, "Goddammit, I've said it before and I'll say it again! This is a high-toned house and I'll not have any of you sonsabitches getting in my beds with your goddam boots on!"

The barmaid chuckled. "That'll be Piggy. She's entertaining a miner who just come in from the diggings with a full poke. You ever taste a boilermaker, kid?"

"I don't know. What's a boilermaker?"

"Maryland rye with a beer chaser. It'll grow hair on your chest."

"What if I don't want hair on my chest?"

The whore's eyes misted slightly as she said, "It'll make you forget, honey. This whiskey deadens the pain and the beer kills the rawness of the whiskey."

Dawn was about to refuse when a man came in, stomping his boots dry as he announced loudly, "Well, it's over, folks. Old Nevada never made her past Angel's Camp!"

As Dawn froze by the bar in numb horror, another man asked, "Army caught up with him at Angel's, then?"

"Nope. It was the town marshal down there. Some fellar Nevada come west with recognized him and pointed him out to the law. Likely for the reward."

"Jesus! Town law beat *Nevada* to the draw?"

"Not hardly. Marshal has a wife and kids. When this fellar pointed Nevada out in the saloon, the marshal just drawed and fired. Took Nevada betwixt the shoulder blades with two .44 rounds, and that was all there was to it."

The man with the wet boots suddenly spied Dawn near the bar and stammered, "Ôh, I'm pure sorry, missy. Didn't expect to find you here."

Dawn's voice was colder than the snowswept hills

outside as she asked quietly, "Was the man who informed on Nevada called Captain Fannon by any chance?"

The miner shook his head and said, "No, ma'am. His name was Brown. Wabash Brown. He said him and Nevada come west together. You know him?"

"I thought I did. I'd better have that drink, after all."

The barmaid handed her the battered cup. "There you go, honey. You're learning. All men are bastards, but it ain't as noticeable when a gal stays drunk."

A few days later, as Dawn was sweeping the back porch of Piggy O'Day's, the morose-looking man she remembered as Morgan Sears came over from the corral and touched his hat to her. He ignored the broom in her hand. They both knew she was a mite young for the other chores about the premises. He said, "You were out to my claim the other day, weren't you, sis?"

"I went out to my brother's claim, Mister Sears. Your hired guns ran me off."

"That's been settled with the miner's committee and I'll have no more sassy remarks about it, missy. You did see Jigger, Luke, and Andy out there, right?"

"I spoke to the one called Jigger. I don't know what the others used for names."

"But there were three men there, right? I sent them to tidy up and fetch your gear to Piggy's, here."

"I told you I saw them and that they ran me off. What's this all about, Morgan Sears?"

"The three of them never come back from your—I mean my—claim. Piggy says the Verdugo brothers brung your gear here to her place."

"They did, and for that much I thank you. I have to sweep these planks."

"Hold on, sis. There's something odd about all this. The Verdugo brothers said the place was deserted when they drove out there with a team to fetch your gear. My three men ain't been heard from since. They ain't in camp and the trails is snowed over. It's a thing to make a man wonder a mite."

Dawn forced her face to remain blank as his words sank in. So Jigger was one of the men who'd murdered Rosalita, as her Indian friends had suggested. The man who'd ordered it was standing at her side this very moment!

Morgan Sears was casual as he mused, "Nevada had some Injuns workin' for him, didn't he?"

"Not working," Dawn said. "Just gathering roots and acorns on our claim. Why do you ask?"

"Three men missing is reason enough, I 'spect."

"The Diggers have gone up to their winter camp," Dawn lied, adding, "I can ask if they saw or heard anything, next time I meet Crippled Deer. The Indians we had visiting us were friendlies."

"Mebbe. But I'm still missing three men, and a Digger is a Digger."

"You say the Mexicans saw nothing?"

"That's right. What of it?"

"Jigger and those other men were armed to the teeth. The Verdugo brothers didn't have a gun between them when they brought my things to Piggy's."

"Now what's that supposed . . . Oh, I see what you mean."

"Hostile Indians would hardly jump three armed white men, leave the camp unlooted, and then allow a couple of unarmed boys to pass through in the dark, would they?"

"Hmmm, that still don't explain where them three old boys went, though."

"I had a poke hidden in my bedroll, Mister Sears. It was missing, too, when the Verdugos brought my things to me. I didn't want to mention it, but it might explain everything."

"A poke, you say? Are you accusing us of robbing you, Miss Dawn?"

"The thought had crossed my mind, but I didn't want to make a fuss over a few ounces of dust, so . . ."

"A few *ounces?*" Sears cut in. "Do Jesus! I see it all, now! Just wait until I get my hands on them three!"

Dawn made her voice innocent as she asked, "You don't think Jigger took my poke, do you? He seemed so friendly and there wasn't all that much gold dust in it."

"That scoundrel would rob his mother's grave—and as for the other two . . . Well, never you mind, Miss Dawn. How much, exactly, was in that poke?"

"Gee, I don't know. Not more than a couple of ounces, like I said. It was the last gleaning of the rocker box before Nevada lit out. Would two or three ounces of gold be worth much?"

Morgan Sears started to say one or two hundred dollars at the least, but he caught himself in time. "Oh, it's likely half grit, but Jigger and them other rascals would steal spit. I'll tell you what I'll do. I'll order you a new dress from San Francisco and we'll call it square. Is that jake with you?"

"Gee, Mister Sears, you're being awfully generous, aren't you?"

He bristled. "Just how do you want me to take that, young miss?"

Dawn stared up at him, wide-eyed. "Whatever do

you mean, Mister Sears? I think you're being very nice about everything, considering it's not your fault those men stole a few things from my bedroll."

Mollified, Sears said, "Well, I aim to be your friend, Miss Dawn. I know you and me had some black thoughts, right after your brother died, but you just leave ever'thing to me and you'll learn I'm a friend you can trust."

"I know how you can be trusted, Mister Sears," said Dawn, looking away.

One day Dawn would tell her children and grand-children how Snow Burner killed Morgan Sears and avenged the death of Rosalita. It would be put down, in the end, as one of the old woman's notions. For Snow Burner was not an Indian. He was an Indian god, the son of Changing Woman, or perhaps more sensibly, Snow Burner was what the Ho termed the wind that whites would call the Santa Ana.

Dawn would always prefer to think of that hot, unseasonable blast from the south as her Indian friendly spirit, however, and in truth, Snow Burner swept up the Sierra far north of his usual haunts that early spring, as if in answer to her anguished prayers.

Dawn had been afraid to ask her Indian friends to take further revenge on the men who'd robbed her, not because of what their friends might do to her but because of the "Injun hunt" she knew could result from yet another mysterious vanishing. Hence she'd nursed her hate, smiling at the smug Morgan Sears whenever they chanced to meet, and praying in her heart for some revelation. There had to be a way, yet none had come to her.

And then, one day, it got warm.

The warmth changed to muggy heat as Snow Burner

swept over the snow-covered slopes with cactus and greasewood on his breath. The snows of winter melted quickly and the hundreds of little ravines draining into the Lost Chinaman wash gushed waist-deep torrents of melted water. In the wash itself, water rose higher than a mounted man's head and swept down and through and over the gold fields in a churning mass of muddy water, uprooting trees, rolling boulders and anything else it could catch between its flood terraces.

The flood caught Morgan Sears and a handful of his miners as they were just rolling out of their sleeping bags to investigate the thunderous roar that had awakened them that morning. The little camp where Dawn and Nevada had stayed had been moved to apparent safety up the slope. But this spring, Snow Burner had pounced with more strength than even the oldest Indians could remember, and the camp, Sears, and his henchmen were spun away like screaming twigs in the roiling water.

The flood killed Scars Wilson, old Blue Tooth, and some of the others Dawn had come to know and possibly trust, for Snow Burner is a mighty god whose wrath falls on innocent and guilty alike. The wash itself was swept clean of man's puny works as the flood waters redeposited sand and gravel bars, and any gold they might contain, in a brand-new pattern.

In the town, well back from the steep side of the wash, the waters rose gently to a foot or more, and while the ground floor of Piggy O'Day's was flooded, Lost Chinaman Camp received a good cleaning as the accumulated trash and filth of its untidy inhabitants joined timbers, rocker boxes, and bodies on their way to the sea.

Dawn watched all morning from an upstairs window, and when Yvette asked her what she was muttering in "Injun," Dawn smiled softly and said, "It's just as Spotted Elk said it would be. In time, everything changes. They say he's Changing Woman's son, you see."

The whore shrugged. "*Merde alors,* you talk so crazy, *chérie.* When the water she go down, you will see everything is as before, *non?*"

Dawn shrugged, idly watching a man wading toward Piggy's through the knee-deep water in the main street. He glanced up and saw the two faces watching him from the open window. He waved and called out, "You gals all right in there? They jest fished another old boy outten the flood. Can't say who he be. The water rolled him up with some timbers afore it spit him out."

Yvette called down, "We are all safe, *mon brave.* Come inside and dry yourself with my sheets, *non?*"

"Can't stop fer pleasure, Miss Yvette. Miner's committee's holdin' a meeting on high ground, directly. Damn flood's washed out all the claim stakes and God knows what else we'uns gotta put to rights. Kilt a mess of people, too, looks like. We've accounted fer eight or ten old boys but there's twice that many missing."

"What about Morgan Sears?" Dawn called down, hardly daring to hope.

The wading miner shook his head and said, "That knoll he was camped on is swept bald as an egg, Miss Dawn. Water's gone down some, but it must have been eight feet deep when it sloshed over the high ground, further up. I 'spect you'll just have to ferget that dress from San Francisco old Morg promised you, 'lessen he grew gills sudden."

Dawn didn't answer. She couldn't answer. She'd managed, with a mighty effort, to draw a breath, and the pinwheeling stars were just beginning to fade. If only she could stay on her feet long enough to make her lungs work one more time . . .

Piggy's voice seemed far away. "You go on back to Yvette's room and rest a spell, honey. We'll talk about your future when you're feeling better, hear?"

With a silent nod, Dawn staggered down the corridor to the cramped quarters she shared with the French girl, and Yvette helped her to the bed. "There, it is over, *chérie*. Next time, you will listen to Yvette, *non?*"

It seemed to take forever, but in time, as Dawn lay in a ball on her side with Yvette stroking her hair, she recovered enough to sob, "What am I to do? I've been robbed. I'm penniless, without a friend to turn to!"

"*Merde!* Yvette, she is your friend. Piggy, too, will take ze care of you, once you get over zis foolishness about *la virginité*. Tell me, *chérie*, have you ever, how you say, make ze masturbate?"

"I don't know. What are you talking about?"

"The business with the hand, to make *l'orgasme*. It is the ignorance of such things that makes the young girl afraid of men, yes?"

"Oh, you mean do I play with my privates? Some of the boys used to do that when I was with the Indians. Dream Singer said it was silly, so I never tried it."

"This Dream Singer was the big fool, too. Myself, Yvette, could never live this way if she did not have *l'orgasme* from time to time and, truly, few men know how to make love properly. After a busy night, before I go to sleep. I must help myself. *Merde*. I have

"That's too bad," Dawn murmured. "I did so want my new dress, too. This thaw will open the trails, so maybe I'll just go on down and buy it myself."

Yvette suddenly drew her away from the window and murmured, "Listen, *chérie*, I know you think Yvette is bad woman, but she would be your friend, if you would listen, *non?*"

"What are you talking about, Yvette? What's so secret?"

"This business of leaving us, *chérie*. If Piggy, she hear you, she will be most cross. She has, how you say, invest in you, yes?"

"What are you saying? Nevada paid Piggy to board me. The trails will be a sea of mud for a few days, but if this wind keeps up . . ."

"*Mais non*, for you there will be no trail to San Francisco, *chérie*. You are, how you say, worth your weight in the gold for Piggy. And she is, forgive me, a most *pratique* businesswoman. I, Yvette, have heard her discuss your, ah, *virginité!*"

"*Virginité?* What does that mean, Yvette?"

"You have never make *la zig-zig* with the man, eh? That is *virginité*. Here in California, most rare. More than one man has ask Piggy about you, but the price she set is *très formidable!* You think Piggy will let you go from this place without selling you for such a price? *Mais non*, such opportunities are rare in zis business!"

Dawn frowned and stammered, "That's crazy. I'm not a whore. Why, poor Nevada killed men trying to protect me until I was old enough, and he paid Piggy and she said . . ."

"*Merde!* I know what was done and what was promise, *chérie*. But your Nevada, he is dead, and

Piggy is a woman who sells other women, so . . ."

"But I'm not a woman, either. I'm only eleven or twelve years old!"

"Bah! Yvette, she was in this business at nine. And you look at least fourteen, even without the paint and corseting, *non*? Your Nevada, he was the fool, or perhaps, as he kept telling us, your brother. Yvette, she feel for you, *chérie*. It is not a life she would choose for her own daughter, but there are worse lives for a woman than ours. What would you do in San Francisco if you got there uneaten by ze bear or unscalped by ze Indian—take in the washing? Scrub the floor? Sell the matches on the street corner?"

"Nevada said when I was old enough I could get married."

"*Merde alors*, you think that is some improvement on our life? *Eh bien*, how does one go about zis business? Will you run up and down ze Embarcadero shouting, '*Alors*, I wish to get marry'?"

"Well, I have the money Nevada left me. I could move into a hotel—"

"If you value your life, forget about ze gold Piggy said she'd keep for you, *chérie*! Madam Piggy is not without generosity. She feeds us, she clothes us, she allows us a few coins for the gambling, but when it comes to real money, what can I say? She is inclined to become *très furieux*!"

Dawn looked at Yvette silently. "I'm going to have it out with her, then. I was right there when she promised Nevada to look out for me."

She left the crib and started for Piggy's room as, behind her, Yvette called softly, "You will be sorry!"

Dawn soon was. She found Piggy O'Day sitting on her own bed, listlessly thumbing through a fashion magazine a year out of date. Dawn smiled in at her

from the doorway and said, "I was just about the gold Nevada left with you for me,

Without looking up, Piggy asked, "Wh child? I don't remember hearing nothing ab gold."

"Why, yes you do, Madam Piggy."

The older woman got to her feet, an ominous on her features, as she asked quietly. "Are you ca me a liar, girl?"

Dawn stared in disbelief at the whore. "It's in yo strongbox! Nevada was banking it with you! He tol you . . ."

And then Piggy struck. She swung her large bony fist with the skill of a hundred whorehouse brawls and caught Dawn just under the ribs, knocking the wind out of her as the blow sent her staggering out the door. In fright and agony, Dawn tried to draw breath, any breath, into her knotted middle as she slumped against the far wall. Her lungs refused to respond and her eyes were filled with little pinwheeling stars as Piggy moved in on her, slapping open-handed so as not to damage her merchandise. "Don't you never call me a liar to my face again, girl! Do you understand me?

Dawn couldn't answer. The stronger woman slapped her again and repeated, "I asked, did you understand me, girl?" And this time Dawn managed a weak nod.

Satisfied, the whore stepped back a pace as Dawn fought to recover her breath. Down the hall, a head appeared from a crib, saw what was happening, and vanished as Piggy said, "I do mind Nevada gave me some dust to look after you for a spell, child. It's a long since spent and I've been meaning to talk to you about how you're gonna pay for the food and board you owe me."

made *la zig-zig* with as many as thirty men in the row
and you know what Yvette she feel? She feel not ze
thing. Just—how you say—*très* tense."

"Does it . . . hurt, when they put those things in
you?"

"Hurt? Bah, I spit on their hurt. Not one man in ze
hundred has the thing to make a girl like Yvette feel
it is in her."

Yvette reconsidered and, still stroking Dawn's hair,
mused, "Your Nevada was nicely made. One time,
when he and Yvette make *le zig-zig*, she is feeling
something, almost."

"Did he fuck good, then? I know Rosalita liked it
when he did it to her."

"Bah, Rosalita was amateur, almost. Any man could
have satisfy that Mexican slut. To be just, however,
Nevada was *formidable* in bed."

Partly curious, and partly flushed with an odd sensation of emptiness, Dawn sighed and said, "We
never made love. I was willing, but . . . What's it
really like, Yvette? I mean, what's it like when it's . . .
right?"

The French girl's face softened as she thought back
to a long-ago moment in back of a Normandy hedge-
row, then she shrugged and said, *"Merde, l'orgasme,
c'est l'orgasme.* Would you like to have one?"

"I don't know. I'm curious, but scared. Besides,
there's no men here today. They're all working to
clean up after the flood."

"Take off your clothes," Yvette said, getting to her
feet and suiting her own actions to her words as she
stripped with the practiced skill of a worldly prostitute. Dawn lay on the bed, watching wordlessly as
Yvette's lush white flesh was revealed above the black
knit stockings she hadn't removed within living mem-

ory. Nude, save for her legs, the French girl sat back down on the bed beside Dawn with an inviting smile. "What are you waiting for? There is no business today and we shall have the party, *non?*"

"I don't understand. Aren't we supposed to have a boy with us if we're going to fuck?"

"To be *pratique, chérie,* a woman can do anything to another woman a man can do, and often much better. Now, off with ze clothes, eh?"

Dawn allowed Yvette to help her as she undressed, muttering, "This is silly. We can't do it. Neither of us has a *thing!*"

And then Yvette was pressing her back against the pillows, the larger breasts of the older woman against the virgin's smaller ones as she kissed Dawn's throat and crooned, "Passive, my sweet. Just lie still and let Yvette break you in, yes?"

Before Dawn could answer, Yvette was kissing her on the lips. It felt oddly exciting, and Dawn was surprised as the older woman's tongue entered her mouth with a darting motion. She was drawn and repelled at the same time. Maybe if Yvette would only give her time to think . . . But Yvette's hand was between Dawn's thighs now, and though the girl tried to cross her legs, an odd frightening thrill ran through her flesh as she felt moist fingers massaging her aroused clitoris. Moving her head to one side, she gagged, "Stop it! I feel all funny! I'm going to pee on your hand if you don't stop, Yvette!"

Yvette laughed huskily, and whispered, "Open the legs, *chérie!* I will make you come *avec* my mouth!"

Numbly, Dawn lay on the bed, in trembling confusion and mingled desire and disgust as Yvette started kissing her way down across Dawn's breasts and abdomen. Dawn knew what Yvette was going to do.

She'd heard the men jesting about "French love," and from what they'd said, it sounded like something amazingly wonderful. Dawn closed her eyes, trying to picture Nevada crouched over her like this as moist lips trailed a chain of kisses toward her tingling groin. Lips were lips, after all, and it would have felt like this if Nevada . . . And then Yvette's long perfumed hair trailed across Dawn's nipples, and suddenly she wanted to vomit.

Rolling into a ball, Dawn wrenched free of Yvette's caressing hands and turned to face the wall, knees drawn up to her chest. Yvette placed a hand on her naked hip, tried to roll her back, and then, at the unexpected but firm resistance, laughed.

"You like it," Yvette insisted mockingly, leaving her hand in place but not forcing the issue for the moment.

Dawn shook her head, face to the wall. "Please, Yvette, I don't want to. I can't."

"Poof, it is all ze same to Yvette. *Regardez,* she can take care of herself. Yvette does not need you. Yvette needs no one but herself!"

The two girls lay on the bed together, Dawn against the wall and not daring to move as beside her, Yvette masturbated for a time, made one attempt at lesbianism near her own climax, then subsided with a contented moan. "Little fool, you shall have to be broken in by one of Piggy's customers. It would have been easier on you, my way."

The snow was gone, but the trails were running quagmires of ankle-deep mud as the men of Lost Chinaman Camp put their affairs in order. It was back-breaking work, with little gold to show for it by the time claims were restaked and the gravel was once more being sifted from sunrise to sundown. Less than a week after the flood, however, the men were drifting in to Piggy's from the scattered placers to drink her awesome rotgut and taste the dubious pleasures of her girls.

Dawn was spared casual rape at the hands of a regular only by Piggy O'Day's greed. She'd dressed Dawn in a tight pink satin dress, her tiny waist drawn in even further by a stiff whalebone corset, and Yvette had helped powder and paint the virgin's innocent young face to what Piggy and the others considered a madonnalike visage. The long blonde hair was curled with hot irons and piled atop Dawn's head. By all in congress assembled, the girl was pronounced a vision of loveliness.

Piggy let it be known that Dawn's cherry would cost the lucky buyer one thousand dollars in dust on the barrelhead.

The best offer the first night was eight hundred dollars in gold and an unproved claim a mile up the wash.

Piggy put Dawn behind the bar to help with the drinks and said she'd pass on the first bidding. The Santa Ana was drying the trails fast, and she could afford to wait. Sooner or later a real gent would arrive who knew the value of real merchandise and had the wherewithal to pay for it.

The evening Ace Purvis returned to Lost Chinaman, Dawn was tending bar alone as her erstwhile mentor entertained a paying customer upstairs with her less expensive charms.

Dawn was not awaiting her pending debut as a prostitute with the detachment her expressionless face might have indicated. Snow Burner was drying the land and the camas bulbs were sprouting. She intended to run off to her Indian friends at the first opportunity, but the few times she'd escaped Piggy's watchful eyes to explore the nearby oaks, there'd been no sign of Ho. The Real People were in the high country on the spring hunt, she knew. As the game moved up to the green pastures of the timberline, her friends, Crippled Deer, Coyote Singer, or Spotted Elk, would be waiting on the rimrocks to intercept them. Heya, the spring migration, was still a good time to be a Real Person, but how was she to last until the late summer seed-gathering brought her secret allies back down the western slope?

Dawn hadn't looked up as Ace Purvis entered the saloon. He, in turn, barely glanced at the painted apparition behind the improvised bar as he placed a silver dollar on it and said, "I'll have anything wet."

Dawn knew a dollar bought little more than beer in Piggy's, and the liquid they called beer was really Mexican pulque. So she filled a tin cup with pulque, slid it across the bar, and pocketed the dollar.

Their eyes met in a mingled shock of recognition, and for a moment neither said anything. Then Ace murmured, "What in thunder are you doing here, Dawn? Where's Nevada?"

"Dead," Dawn replied bleakly, "He was shot in the back before the thaw. They killed Rosalita, too."

Ace glanced about to see they weren't being overheard as he asked, casually, "You need any killing hereabouts, kitten?"

Dawn smiled bitterly and said, "I wouldn't know where to start. Besides, it's not your fight, Ace."

"Oh, I don't know," the gambler mused, sipping his pulque before he added, shyly, "you look like you've been drug through the keyhole, backwards, and a knight in armor I once knew told me to start with the biggest dragon and work my way down. What happened, kid?"

In short sentences, interrupted by having to serve other customers, Dawn brought the dapper little Ace Purvis up to date on her misfortunes. His sardonic face remained calm, but the muscles of his blue jaw were bulging dangerously long before she'd finished. Once, he interrupted to ask, "This thing about selling you, Dawn. Have they done it yet?"

She drew a deep breath. "No. The asking price is a thousand dollars. The mule train you rode in with is the first up from the low country, so . . ."

"Wait here!" he cut in grimly, moving away from the bar.

Dawn called out to stop him, but the catlike little man was moving through the crowd toward the stairs, unbuttoning his frock coat. Was he really going to face Piggy and her hired bullyboys with what she'd told him, without considering the odds? He couldn't be that crazy. Ace Purvis was a notorious gunfighter, but so were at least half the men Piggy had on her payroll.

Her mind in a whirl, Dawn swabbed the bar with a damp rag, wondering whether she should just run outside and take her chances in the woods. They'd track her, she knew. Her Indians friends were a good ten days away, and while she knew more of woodcraft than Piggy's henchmen, she'd be taking a terrible risk in committing herself to open defiance once and for all. Maybe, if she didn't do anything, Piggy would just beat her again. She now knew Piggy beat with some skill. They wouldn't kill her, or even leave marks on her, if she could only . . . What could she *say* to Piggy? That Ace had just been crazy? No, she'd told him too much, and if they got it out of him before they killed him . . .

"Let's have a drink, honey," a miner was saying, and wordlessly Dawn went through the motions of obeying him. It was very important in Piggy O'Day's for a girl to be obedient.

Upstairs, Ace Purvis found Piggy saying good-bye to a customer. Standing politely to one side, he waited until the man had left, then took off his hat, nodded to Piggy, and said, "I've got something we ought to talk about, madam."

Piggy waved him inside but said, "I'm too tired to screw right now, Ace, but Yvette ain't had a customer for at least an hour and she knows the way you like it. Where the hell you been?"

"Up near Colima. Hit pretty good in a game of three-card monte I was running for a spell. Had to leave, though."

"Shoot anybody on your way out of camp?"

"Now, you know me better than that, Madam Piggy. I'm a peace-loving man, given the choice."

"Vigilantes run you out, huh? Well, we drowned half our Vigilance Committee in the spring thaw, and them as is left are scared skinny of you. So how long do you figure to stay this time?"

"I'm leaving for Poker Flat directly. Wanted to pick something up here in Lost Chinaman first, though."

"Oh, that's right, you took some IOU's afore you left last winter, didn't you? Don't know as you'll collect from Shorty Grogan. He was swept away in the flood."

"Madam, I'll come right to the point. I'm taking Dawn Jones with me. I heard about Nevada . . . So let's talk about that thousand dollars you think she's worth on the hoof."

"You got a thousand dollars, Ace?"

"Yep. Told you I hit pretty good in Colima. I got over half in dust and the rest in hard cash. How about it?"

"You want to buy her cherry, Ace?"

"Nope. Want to buy all of her, lock, stock, and barrel. I'll pay you your asking price, so you won't be out nothing. Once she'd been broke in, she's just another whore and . . ."

"Now hold on, damn it! I figured to sell her as cherry more than once, in the first place. And she's still the best looker in the place, in the second. Why, I reckon I could make thousands and thousands on that kid, Ace! I ain't gonna let her go, permanent, for what you got in your poke with your hat throwed in."

Ace Purvis smiled wolfishly and said, "There was another four or five thousand in gold you were supposed to be holding for her, madam. I figure that about evens us out, don't you?"

"Has that sassy wench been lying to you, Ace? I swear to God I never laid eyes on more'n a few ounces of Nevada's gold, and the kid like to et me outten house and home. I'm giving that girl a good lickin' for telling them lies about me and—"

"You ever lay a hand on Dawn again and you're a dead woman!" said Purvis, flatly. Then, noting the stricken look on Piggy's face, he added in a nicer tone, "It ain't worth it, Piggy. I know about Hanlon and McGuire and your other hired guns and do we push it to shove, I'll likely go down in the fighting, but once we get out that hand, its likely a bad deal for everybody."

"Damn it, I don't scare all that easy, Ace."

"I know that. That's why I'm talking instead of just bragging my way out with the girl *and* my gold. You think a bit before you answer and you'll see I'm offering you a fair shake. You get your asking price for her virginity, the gold you robbed her of, and we part friends. I can think of worse ways we could work it out."

"What if I tell you to go to hell?"

"Don't. I promise you'll reach hell at least six shots ahead of me."

"Hey, come on, Ace. You wouldn't shoot a *woman*, would you?"

"Don't see why not. I never shoot nobody unless I have to, but if you don't want to part friends . . . What the hell, Piggy, you're twice the man that damned Greek I shot last fall was."

Despite herself, Piggy O'Day laughed. Ace joined in, but his dark eyes were hard as jet as he urged, "Do we have a deal?"

Piggy said, "I don't know." But the gambler reached in his frock coat, took out a couple of well-filled pokes, and threw them on the bed. "Yes, you do. You'll find over a thousand in there. I'm going downstairs and get the girl. If anybody tries to stop us from riding out friendly, they'd better do it right, or I'll be back—and I'll kill you."

Then, not waiting for a reply, he turned on his heel and left the speechless Piggy ODay to her own devices. If she was planning any.

The conversation hadn't taken long, but downstairs it seemed to Dawn as if it had been hours since she'd started waiting for the dreaded sounds of gunfire overhead. Then Ace appeared on the stairs, walked over to the bar, and said, "Let's go. From what you told me, you haven't anything worth pack-ing, and you can wear my extra coat. We'll get you some decent duds in Murphy's Camp."

The girl gasped. "Piggy's letting me go?"

Ace shrugged and said, "She ain't made up her mind yet. I reckon we'd best be on our way before she does!"

Wordlessly, Dawn moved down to the end of the bar and joined her rescuer near the front entrance. A miner just coming in shouted at Ace. "Where you been, pardner? Ain't that Piggy's cherry you got by the arm?"

"Just bought her," said Ace, quietly. And then he shoved past and they were outside in the gathering dusk. Ace said, "My horse is in the corral. We'll ride double and . . ."

"No," Dawn objected. "Not if you meant what you said about getting me away from here."

"Of course I meant it, Dawn. What's eating you?"

"They'll expect us to ride out. If Piggy means to stop us, she'll send her gun fighters after us down each trail, and we can't beat them riding double."

"All right, I'll steal us another horse, then."

"And have the vigilantes after you as a horse thief? Follow me."

"Follow you? Where the hell do you think you're going, girl?"

"Into the oaks. I know a game trail where the brush is so low that even a tall man on foot has to walk bent over. I don't know where it leads but . . ."

"You noticed my size, huh? Well, lead on, Macduff. Your plan makes sense for the next five minutes, and that's more time than I've been allowing for."

With Ace at her heels, Dawn skirted the deserted shack of the dead Rosalita and led them up what seemed, in the darkness, a brush-choked ravine. Once they'd forced their way in a few yards, the shade of the overhanging oak, having cut off the underbrush from sunlight, provided a narrow but clear sandy pathway. Dawn broke into a jog, calling back, "Hurry, our feet are leaving marks and we have to put some distance between us and Lost Chinaman before daylight."

Ace jogged after her, clumsy in his high-heeled boots, and once, as a low branch whipped his hat off, scooped it up with a laugh. "Hell, I'm a mite taller than you after all, ain't I?"

Not looking back, but in dead earnest, Dawn answered, "You're as tall as you need to be, Ace. I'll thank you proper when we've a chance to stop and catch our wind."

The wiry little gambler smiled, watching her bobbing form in the semidarkness ahead as they half-jogged, half-stumbled up the steepening slope of the winding ravine.

God damn! he thought. "Who'd have dreamed a few short months could fill a girl out like that? Why, save for that kid face, she's a full-growed woman!

A small woman, he amended wryly, but then, he himself was a small man. He'd gotten used to looking up at any woman he kissed. What would it be like to hold a girl against you who only came to your nose? Wonderful, most likely. Of course, there was that problem about her being a virgin, so he'd have to move in a mite slow . . . but, oh, sweet Jesus, he was going to have her! He was going to have her if it cost him his worthless life!

The rising sun found them camped, or rather, resting in the mouth of a rock shelter high above the river valley. Having left his horse in the corral for Piggy's bullyboys to find, Ace had nothing on him but his guns and a few items of survival gear in his pockets. One of the items happened to be a deck of marked cards, and so he played with them in the dust of the shallow cave's entrance as the girl prattled on about knowing there was an Indian shelter up here, somewhere, because her friends had told her so.

Ace dealt himself an ace of spades, turned the point away from himself for luck, and asked, "Did your Injuns tell you how we get ourselves over the ridge and out of here? We haven't either food or water, and I can see the damned camp from here!"

"Oh, we dasn't show ourselves against the skyline before dark," Dawn cautioned. "No white folks know about this cave. I'll see about water and something to eat once I shuck this durned old corset."

Ace stared, bemused, as Dawn hiked the satin skirt up around her breasts and proceeded to unlace the corset Piggy had made her wear. Ace flushed, looked away, and said, "You, ah, ain't wearing no drawers, Dawn."

"Oh, I'd best turn my back, then. I keep forgetting white folks aren't used to seeing one another's privates. I'm sorry if I upset you."

"Upset me?" Ace croaked, not looking, but still seeing the triangle of golden pubic hair between the fading suntan of her thighs. There was a rustle of satin and Dawn said, "You can look, now. I promise to go behind something the next time I pee."

"You're, uh, sure you're still a virgin, Dawn?"

"I think I am. Yvette tried to break me in, but she never, and I don't think it counts with a girl, do you?"

"Not hardly. What did she do, go down on you?"

"She acted silly. I think she wanted to lick me between the legs, but I made her stop. It was making me feel all wet and funny, you know?"

"Then you've never, ah, come?"

"Oh, I came a lot of places. I came over the Sierra with Nevada and I came up here with you and I . . ."

"Never mind, I reckon I savvy you better than you savvy me. You said something about water. Maybe we better study on eats and drinks before we delve into your peculiar upbringing."

Dawn brightened and said, "Wait right here." Then she stepped from the shadows of the overhanging rocks, crouching so as not to display a flash of pink satin to any watcher of the hills in the valley below, and vanished like a rabbit into the chaparral.

Ace watched the distant specks in the valley for a time, saw there was no change in apparent activity, and went back to his solitary card game. He played like an automaton, without enjoyment, or, indeed, conscious thought of what he was doing. Ace riffled, shuffled, and dealt the way a nervous boy might crack his knuckles in school, just to be doing something. He'd been doing so since his tall puritanical father had caught him with a deck of cards at the age of fourteen and broken two bones of his hand with a cane. The caning had been administered, it was said, to teach a lazy good-for-nothing boy that cards were the devil's bible. Ace had run away as soon as his hand was out of the sling and his father seemed to be recovering from his short-lived repentance. He'd played with the devil's bible ever since, and despite a tendency to ache above the knuckles in damp weather, his small graceful hand and the one that went with it were worthy of a stage magician's envy. Ace had learned not to let his fingers betray him as he dealt, for nature abhors a straight line. It was uncanny and disquieting to see a row of cards hit the table in a ruler-straight line, overlapping with microscopic precision. Ace had learned to deal every third card exactly one-eighth of an inch out of line. While this varied no more than the ticking of a clock with one missing gear tooth, the irregularity seemed to lull suspicion well enough for most mining camps.

Ace finished the deal, scooped up the cards in one smooth movement, and shuffled the deck with one hand before dealing himself a royal flush without looking down. It was only for practice, of course. A royal flush on the first deal was a suicidal proposition in any frontier card game. Ace considered himself a discreet businessman who won only a modest profit in every game. It was winning every game that kept him moving one jump ahead of the vigilantes, however. Nobody was more familiar with Lady Luck than the harder-working members of the gold rush community, and sooner or later a man who won every time was bound to cause comment.

Dawn returned to the cave with the front of her skirt hiked up but her thighs covered with the cotton petticoat, to the mingled relief and wry regret of her rescuer.

She knelt at the man's side and dumped the contents of her improvised gathering basket in a pile between them. "The small green things are to drink," she said. "Those bulbs are camas."

Ace had heard about Dawn's "Injun notions" from the late Nevada Jones, so he assumed she knew what she was talking about. He bit into a camas bulb, commented that it tasted like an onion with no hair on its chest, and nibbled one of the small scallionlike shoots of sourgrass for a time before spitting out the pulp. "Nothing much to it, is there? I mean, it's all taste and no substance."

Dawn laughed and said, "It's mostly water. Nevada called it Injun lemonade. If we had time and running water, I could pound us some acorn flour. I found a big cache of canyon oak nuts down the slope in a rock pocket just now."

"I'll pass on acorns. These nothing-much onions ought to get me through the morning. You say we can't leave until dark? What's on the other side of the ridge above us?"

"I have no idea. From the lay of the land I'd say there'll be a valley like the one below. Only, since Lost Chinaman is the only white camp in these parts, and my Indian friends couldn't live there, it'll have to be a dry one. You notice all the chaparral up here on this slope?"

Ace glanced out at the mixture of stunted canyon oak and waist high blue-gray brush and nodded. "So what?"

Dawn said, "The other slope is heavily wooded. There's something wrong with the soil of this ridge. It's probably shallow, over the bedrock. That'll mean no oak, no manzanita, no springs or running water. There shouldn't be anybody at all on the other side of the ridge."

"That suits me just fine, kitten. Only where do we go from there?"

"Oh, all the valleys on this slope head down into the Middle Fork, and the Middle Fork will take us down to Murphy's, Angel's Camp, or even San Francisco."

"You mean on *foot*?"

"Well, we don't have any horses, do we? I don't think it's more than forty miles or so to Murphy's. Do you have any money left?"

"Not enough to buy two horses, but enough to get in a card game. You say forty miles like you've walked it, kitten."

"Heavens, I've walked hundreds of miles, and your legs are longer than mine."

Ace frowned and muttered, "You have to keep bringing it up, don't you?"

"Bringing what up, Ace?"

"My size. My old man never got tired of the subject. He allowed a puny child was the Lord's punishment for him having missed a Sunday go-to-meeting just before I was born."

"I don't see anything wrong with your size, Ace."

"You don't, huh? Well, you're still growing. Meanwhile, I got me a brace of Colts, and they do say Sam Colt created all men equal.

Dawn chewed a shoot of sourgrass thoughtfully for a time as she considered his bitter little turned-away smile. Then she said, gently, "Don't play bad arrow with me, Ace. We're friends."

The little gambler glanced back at her with a puzzled frown. "Bad Arrow? What in thunder is that supposed to mean?"

"It's an Indian joke. Sometimes a boy doesn't shoot too straight, and to cover up he says one of his arrows must have been crooked, or out of balance, or maybe just filled with bad medicine. Dream Singer said you could tell that a boy had grown to be a man when he no longer shot bad arrows but apologized for a bad shot. Boys blame their luck on bad arrows. Men work at improving their aim."

Ace sighed and said, "Well, my aim is tolerable enough, I reckon. There's nothing I can do about being the runt of the litter."

"You can stop beating yourself with it. Dream Singer had another saying. He said a man could argue with the cold wolf wind from the north and freeze, or he could wrap himself in a rabbit robe and be comfortable. You can't grow any taller, but you can stop fretting about it. I hadn't noticed you were short until you kept whining about it."

"Now look, missy. Ace Purvis never whines about anything!"

"Not with your mouth. It's in your eyes when you make those little jokes about your size. Last night I told you I thought you were as big a man as I needed when you faced down Piggy and her bullyboys and got me out of that awful place. I've just said it one more time, and I'm getting pretty tired of burping you, Mister Ace Purvis!"

An angry retort formed on the man's lips, to fade and die as he smiled boyishly. "By God, I think she means it. Consider the subject closed, kitten. I do talk too much about myself, don't I?"

"No. You've only been talking about how short you are. That's not what I'm interested in. Why don't you tell me about *yourself*, Ace?"

"Myself? Hell, there's nothing you don't know, kitten. I'm a drifter, a gambler, a worthless little . . . oops, I promised, didn't I?"

"I know you're very brave. I know you stood by Nevada and me against those claim jumpers last fall, too. The girls at Piggy's told me about the fights you've had and the gold you've won and lost. But who *are* you? For instance, you talk funny. One minute you twang like some old country boy off a farm. The next you quote some book you've read like an educated man. Which voice is funning me, Ace?"

Ace considered for a moment. Then, in the more educated tone he used when off his guard, he said, "I suppose you could say I'm neither fish nor fowl. My father was a country minister, back in Virginia. He was not a very loving man, but he'd been to school, and in our house we spoke passable English. I learned at an early age not to talk that way in front of the good old boys I played with down at the swimming hole. I won't blame it on the bad arrow of my size. They'd have joshed me black and blue if I'd been seven feet tall and talked like a preacher."

"I know. We do pick up the way the people around us are speaking, don't we? You know, sometimes after I'd been at Rosalita's for dinner I used to come back to Nevada with a slight Mexican accent? And the funny thing is, I don't speak Spanish!"

Ace laughed. "I do. It's not hard, once you know a little Latin. Your own accent would be a bitch to place. You speak English with just a hint of Big Chief Injun and some of Nevada's Cumberland twang."

"Could you teach me to talk right, Ace?"

"I guess I could, given time."

"Do you know how to read and write?"

"Of course. Don't you?"

"No. You'll have to teach me that, too. I'm sc glad you're smart. I'll bet our babies will be smart, too."

Ace's jaw dropped as he stared at her and gasped. "Our what?"

"Babies. Aren't we going to have any children? I mean, after we marry up and all?"

"Sweet Jesus! Are you asking me to *marry* you?"

"Well, don't you want to? I thought, when you saved me from Piggy O'Day, you loved me and wanted to marry up with me."

"Hey, kid, you don't understand what you're talking about!"

"I know. Likely I've a lot to learn, but you can teach me. I must be old enough to marry up with, if Piggy thought I was old enough to be a whore. I was going to marry Nevada when I grew up, but you know what happened to him, and damn it, I've just got to marry somebody!"

She suddenly wiped the back of one hand across her face and turned away as Ace continued to stare at her with a puzzled little smile on his fine-boned face. After a time he said, "You're green as an emerald and twice as pretty. Nevada meant a lot to you, didn't he, kitten?"

"I loved him and wanted to have him love me, but he never did."

"You're wrong, kitten. I never knew Nevada that well, but I know men well enough to tell you he loved you. Loved you better than most men would have."

"Do you love me, Ace?"

Ace started to make a joke. Then he nodded and said soberly, "I think I do, in my own fashion. Dealing with a straight deck, I'm not as decent a man as Nevada was, but yes, as far as I understand the word, I guess it's true."

Neither spoke for a time as Ace stared down at his cards, his nervous hands, for the moment, stilled in his lap. Then he cleared his throat and asked, in a desperately casual tone, "What about you, Dawn?"

"What do you mean?"

"Do you love me?"

"I reckon I do. I don't know you like I knew Nevada, but you're brave and pretty and smart, so I 'spect I ought to love you."

"Damn it, girl. I don't want you to love me the way a child loves a favorite uncle. I'm talking about the way a woman's supposed to love a man."

"I don't know about that kind of loving, Ace. I 'spect you'll have to teach me."

Ace suddenly reached out, took both Dawn's shoulders in his hands, and pulled her over to him, twisting her unresisting form so that she lay with her shoulders against his knees. He slowly lowered his face to hers and, his heart beating wildly, kissed her gently but full on the lips. Then, as he saw she didn't struggle or laugh the way so many women had in the past, he hugged her closer and kissed harder, wondering if he was dreaming or really about to faint.

After a long lingering kiss, Ace drew his lips from hers just far enough for them to breathe as he continued to hold her against his aching chest. Dawn smiled up at him and said, "Oh, that was nice."

"Nice?" He sighed, "That was like opening the door to heaven a crack and peeking inside. Let's stand up. I want to try something."

Wordlessly, Dawn allowed him to help her to her feet. She wondered what he was going to do next. He kissed ever so much nicer than Yvette, or even Nevada, that one time. It didn't make her feel all funny inside like before. Maybe that was because they were fixing to marry up and so it wasn't bad.

Ace faced the girl at arm's length. "There's something I've always wanted to do." Miracle of miracles, he found her fresh young face smiling *up* at him.

Then he drew her against him, kissed her long and

lovingly, and drew back with a laugh. "Why, that was lovely, Miss Sarah May. I hope I may presume it was more than the moonlight, here on the veranda, that occasioned such bliss?"

Dawn frowned up at him. "What moonlight, Ace? It's not half noon and the sun ball's shining in on us!"

Ace chuckled. "Just letting an old dream come true, kitten. You'd be surprised how hard it is to dream with a camp-following Mex in one's arms and . . ."

"Can we kiss some more? I really like it."

Ace kissed her again, and this time, remembering how Yvette did it, she ran the tip of her tongue between his lips. He flinched but continued to hold his lips to hers as one hand ran down her spine to the cleft between her firm young buttocks and forced her pubis hard against his erection. Dawn felt his virile member through the clothes between them and wondered if he was going to rape her or fuck her. The two words were mixed up in her head, and she wasn't sure which was which anymore. Nevada had said it was rape when the woman didn't want it, and just bad when she did but they weren't married. She moved her body away slightly and twisted her lips aside to whisper, "We're supposed to get married first."

Ace started to pull her back, reconsidered, and let her go, taking in a deep gasping breath before muttering, "Jehosaphat! I *am* going to save it for our wedding night!"

"Are we going to marry up, then?"

"You're damned right we are, kitten. I'm going to marry you and take you to San Francisco and smother you in jewelry and furs! I'll buy you a coach and four, and a fine brick mansion, and by God, if the moon's for sale, I'll buy that for you, too!"

"First I want you to teach me to read and write. Who was Sarah May?"

"Sarah who? Oh, just some girl I knew a million years ago in Virginia. She lived in a big house up the hill, and I was never invited to her birthday parties."

"Were you in love with her, too?"

Ace kissed Dawn again, gently, and said, "I might have been. It was a long time ago and I seem to have grown up a mite since last night."

They waited until dark, taking turns at watching the valley below and catnapping through the long warm day. Then Dawn tied her trailing skirts into a bloomerlike fold between her legs and led her newfound fiancé up the slope and over the ridge into the unknown canyonlike valley beyond.

Partway down the brush-covered far slope, Dawn stopped and sniffed the night air suspiciously. Ace asked her what was wrong and she said, "Smoke. If there's a campfire down there it's an Indian one. I don't see it."

Ace inhaled, smelling only the vaguely medicinal chaparral odor of the California hills as Dawn led them down a rabbit trail at a slower pace. After a time, Ace whispered, "I smell it now. You think we'd better go back?"

Dawn said, "We can't. If they're Diggers, it's all right."

"What if it's somebody else?"

"We'll work our way along midslope and get around them. From the drift of the wind, the fire I smell is down in the bottom of the canyon. It's probably a small Digger band camped near a water hole in the deepest draw of this dry valley, but we can't take the chance. I'd have sworn there'd be no water over on this side, but we did have all that melt water a few weeks ago and . . ."

"*Quien es?*" snapped a gruff male voice from the darkness above them, and the fugitive pair froze in place.

There was the ominous sound of a musket being cocked, and the voice repeated its question. Ace put a hand on his holstered revolver and called out, "*Que pasa, amigo mio?*"

The unseen Mexican laughed and said, in passable English, "Ju are no friend of mine, gringo. And take jour hand from jour pistol before I blow jour face off."

Wordlessly, Ace raised his hands to shoulder height with a bitter little smile. The unknown had the drop on him and was hidden by the darkness of the slope behind. How *he* could see in this light was a mystery they could only hope to live long enough to fathom.

"*Bueno,*" the picket said. "I see you are people of good sense, after all. Now, ju will move slowly and drop jour gunbelt to the earth. Then ju will move slowly down the hillside. I do not repeat my orders, gringo."

Ace unbuckled his gunbelt and let the brace of Colts slide down his legs. If the greaser didn't know about the derringer in his vest pocket, Ace had no intention of bringing it up. A man with a hidden weapon was still, by God, a man, and he'd been in tighter fixes than this one.

A short downhill walk took them to the dry sandy bottom of the canyon. Their captor directed them up, and moving around a boulder, they found themselves in a small circle of firelight around a tiny Indian campfire.

But while a couple of the dozen-odd men squatting on their booted heels around the fire might have had Indian features, all were dressed like Mexican vaqueros. A man in a black silver-trimmed outfit and flat Spanish hat got to his feet as the picket behind them called out in Spanish. He removed his hat with a flourish and said, "Welcome to the humble estate of Murrietta. La Señorita shall sit over here. Would El Señor like a drink of wine before we kill him?"

Ace licked his lips and said, "I could use a drink. You'd be Joaquín Murrietta, right?"

"*Es verdad.* My fame has spread more than I deserve, I fear. But why are you both standing on ceremony? Did I not invite you both to sit down for a few moments?"

Dawn looked over at Ace, and when he nodded, she stepped around the fire to sink gingerly to the sand near the spurred and booted heels of the notorious bandit leader. One of the others handed Ace a leather drinking bottle, and he hunkered down in place with a nod of thanks. He'd nail the big greaser in the black and silver with his one derringer shot, once it started to get ugly. After that . . .? Well, there wasn't going to be all that much, afterward.

Ace took a swig of wine and smiled. "It's good stuff. My handle is Ace Purvis, and I'm an outlaw, too."

Murrietta returned the smile. "Is there any other kind of gringo? If one speaks of law, this land was ours before you and your kind stole it from us at the point of a gun. But drink, my friend, this is not the time to bring up past grievances. You have, oh, perhaps five minutes to live, so why not enjoy them, eh?"

Murrietta resumed his seat in the sand at Dawn's side. She could now see by the dim light that he was a dashingly handsome man with a smooth-shaven chin and a narrow moustache. He turned, smiling at her, and said, "You have nothing to fear, *palomina mia*. Once, I had a wife as pretty as you. Gringos mistreated her and she died of mingled shame and injuries. I do not, however, seek revenge in such a cowardly fashion."

"Are you going to rape me?"

Murrietta raised an eyebrow. "I just told you I am not. Behave yourself and all will go well with you. May I ask how you are called?"

"I'm Dawn Jones. . . . I mean, Dawn Purvis. Ace, over there, just married up with me."

Murrietta sighed gallantly. "Ah, honeymooners. How most unfortunate for El Señor. For my part, I would be inclined to let your bridegroom live to taste your sweet charms, *señora mia*. But you see that glowering giant over there, the one who keeps giving me the dirty looks? He is Three Fingers Jack. He hates gringos worse than I do and is ever accusing me of softness, so . . ."

The half-breed spat in the fire and said, "You play the cat and mouse, Joaquín. Kill them both and let's eat!"

Murrietta smiled. "You see how it is?"

Dawn said, "We have the vigilantes hunting us, too. Let us go and we won't be able to tell anyone where you're hiding out."

"In God's name, I wish I believed you, señora. Once I believed gringos who said they were my friends. Of late, somehow, I seem to have grown suspicious."

Ace took another sip, trying to make his drink

last, and asked, "Is Murrietta your real name, or is it a joke?"

"Ah? You are familiar with our language, señor?"

"Enough to know Murrietta means sullen or sulky and that Joaquín means Jack. It comes out Sulky Jack in English. Mexican gal I know told me onetime you were from an old Spanish land grant family and that the part about you being a poor peon who was robbed was a lot of bull."

Murrietta laughed. "Ask any two Californianos about me and I can promise you three stories. Suffice to say I was robbed, by any name, and now I rob in turn. This Mexican girl would be the one called Rosalita, in the valley you just came from?"

"Rosalita Vasques is dead," Dawn said. "Three miners killed her and hid her body in a ravine."

"*Es verdad?*" Murrietta frowned, adding in a cat-like purr, "And would you know the names of these three men, Señora Purvis?"

"They're all three dead. I had them killed. Rosalita was my friend."

Murrietta snorted, "You did such a mighty deed, *palomina mia?* In truth, none of my people know what happened to Rosalita. A brother in Yerba Buena asked me to inquire about her, and forgive me, we heard no such a tale. Our local informants only can say she is no longer in the Lost Chinaman area."

Dawn insisted she was telling the truth, and as the bandit leader listened with a bored, disinterested smile, told him the whole story of how her Indian friends had seen and avenged the murder of the Mexican seamstress. She was almost finished when one of the men, who'd been listening in apparent sullen silence, suddenly asked her in Was-Ho, "Are you the White-Eyed Ho called Dawn of the Paiutes?"

Dawn replied in the same language, "Yes. Are you a Person?"

The Indian dressed in rough Mexican ranch garb nodded and got to his feet. He walked over to where Ace was squatting and stood silently until Murrietta asked, in Spanish, "What is wrong with you, Indio? What was that all about?"

The Digger-turned-bandit shrugged and said, "This is the man of a friend to my people. I stand with him. I have spoken."

"Are you drunk, Indio? We're going to kill the bastard. The girl will be set free, whether she's your friend or not."

The bandit called Indio shook his head and said, "I have spoken."

Ace understood just enough Spanish to ask the Indian, quietly, "Are you sure you know what you're doing, friend?"

Indio didn't answer.

Murrietta muttered something under his breath as another man with Indian features got slowly to his feet. "I stand with my brother and these two White Eyes," he said. "I have heard the stories they tell in the hills about this woman. She has a good heart. If you want to kill her man, you will have to kill all three of us. I, too, have spoken."

Across the fire, Three-Fingered Jack swore and rose. "That's no problem at all!" But Murrietta snapped, "*Silencio!* I must think about this most grotesque turn of events!"

Then he turned to Dawn. "I think I begin to believe that you might have been the friend of a Mexican woman. It is most obvious you are a friend to my Indian guides, and I need them in this strange country. How do you explain this strange habit of yours for making friends in the most unlikely places, *palomina mia?*"

"It's nothing special. I reckon I just *like* most folks."

The bandit's face softened in the firelight as he murmured, "It is more special than you might think, little one. Tell me truthfully, how do you feel about me, the terrible Joaquín Murrietta?"

Dawn studied his face for a time before she said, "I think you're a man who's suffered. I think you're more cruel than you really want to be because you're afraid."

Three-Fingered Jack laughed gruffly and spat. "Hey, *gringa linda,* our leader is afraid of neither man nor devil!" But Murrietta held up a hand for silence and stared into the fire. "From the mouths of babes, it is written, eh? The two of you shall go with God, señora. We shall give you two fine horses no vigilante's nag can match. Oh, we shall give you a couple of rifles, too, and provisions to take you to the next settlement."

Ace said, "That's right neighborly of you, Joaquín."

Murrietta snapped, "Shut your mouth! I was not speaking to you. You are nothing to me. The gifts I offer your wife are little more, for I steal what I need as I pass. Go up the draw with Indio there, and he will give you the horses and other things. I don't wish to discuss it further with you, gringo."

As Ace left the campfire with the Indian who'd helped save his life, Murrietta turned back to Dawn. "Does he treat you with respect, *palomina mia?*"

"Oh my, yes. Ace is a very nice person."

"He is lucky, at the least, for by my God, you are lovely. Tell me, little reader of souls, what else do you see in me or for me? This habit you have of gentle witchcraft is disquieting, but we have only a moment to speak and I have never met a witch before."

Dawn put a hand on his sleeve and said, "Go home, Joaquín Murrietta. That's what you really want to do. That's all you really want."

"I have no home, *palomina mia*. That part of my tale is true. They burned us out and stole our lands. The name I have taken is but to protect those relatives who have not the stomach for the life I lead in the hills these days."

"They're going to kill you if you keep on this way, you know."

"*Es verdad?* Truly, I need no witch to tell me this, but I may lead them a merry chase before they get me. Do your gifts foretell my date with death?"

"No. I just see a hurt, frightened man who's doing his best to find some way out of the grave he dug for himself. Couldn't you change your name another time?"

"My name is unimportant. My face is too well known. They tell me the government has sent for Texas Rangers to track me down. In the end, I suppose they will catch us. We do not intend to be taken alive."

Ace and Indio came back, leading a pair of fine Spanish barbs with silver-mounted saddles. Murrietta got to his feet and held out a hand to assist Dawn. She noticed, as he pulled her to her feet with gentle strength, that his palms were cold and damp. He led her gallantly to the mount he'd chosen for her and helped her up to the saddle. The spirited horse pranced a few paces away before Dawn got it under control and reined in, smiling back at him and the not-yet-mounted Ace. Murrietta nodded at the gambler and said, "Take good care of her. You are a lucky man. Do you mind if I ask you a question, though?"

"What's that, Joaquín?"

"How do you live with a woman like that? Doesn't she frighten you with those eyes of hers?"

Ace started to deny it. Then he nodded and replied with a wry grin, "She scares the hell out of me, but I think she's an angel."

Murrietta waited until the gambler had mounted and joined Dawn with a farewell wave before he muttered, "Angel, witch, or whatever she may be, she'll be more than you can handle, little friend."

Three-Fingered Jack limped over to him, scowling at the vanishing mounted figures as they rode away. "What's the matter with you, Joaquín? You know they'll betray our position as soon as they reach Murphy's. Have you forgotten the reward they posted on you down in Sacramento?"

"She will not betray us, and we are moving out in any case."

"Moving out? Where to? They know about our old hideout in the Tule marshes to the south. Do you think we should try to make it over the Sierra to the east, or go north into the redwood country?"

Murrietta shrugged and said, "North, south, to the High Sierra or the devil, what does it matter?"

"It matters that we get away from those Texas Rangers. What's wrong with you, amigo? You look like a man who's just found a fly in his soup."

"Perhaps a fly, perhaps the truth, perhaps a forgotten dream. Let me sleep on the matter before I make up my mind."

The fugitive pair didn't go to Murphy's or Angel's Camp that spring. Mounted well and armed with Dawn's foraging skills as well as the fine hunting rifles the bandits had given them, Ace and the girl skirted the gold fields and made for the great interior valley between the coast ranges and the Sierra. In Sacramento, the capital of the new Bear Flag State and the biggest city Dawn had ever seen, Ace sold the horses and silver-mounted saddles for steamboat passage down the river to San Francisco. Before they boarded, however, he took Dawn to a justice of the peace and married her.

The long nights on the trail had been sheer hell for Ace, but he'd made up his mind to make an honest woman of her first, and stuck to it. Not so much from gallantry as an almost maniacal insistence that their wedding night be spent in a proper bed with a roof over their heads and a lock on the door. The worldly Ace had had his fill of rutting with some squaw in the brush or a short flaccid interlude with some blowsy whore in a flea-infested bordello. Almost as if it were some odd parody of a maiden's dream, Ace Purvis had always wanted to spend his honeymoon with a chaste, beautiful virgin, and come hell, high water, or furtive masturbation, he meant to have one of his tattered little dreams come out right!

The *Sacramento Queen* was a ramshackle sternwheeler slapped together from California lumber and machine parts carried by clipper around the Horn. Yet to Dawn it was a floating palace and their stateroom, a tiny cubicle over the dangerous boiler room, as grand a bridal suite as she'd ever imagined.

The news had spread among the other passengers that there were newlyweds aboard, and despite his hunger for Dawn's body, Ace took her to the grand salon for a sedate meal as the steamboat pulled away from the Sacramento docks with a long blast of its tinny little whistle.

They'd left after sunset, Ace having planned the trip down to the bay with a night aboard in mind, and Dawn watched every move of her clever little husband's hands as they dined on the first tablecloth she could remember. She knew how to use a knife and fork, but the way Ace did it was so dainty that she had a time matching his movements. If her table manners left anything to be desired, however, nobody commented. The captain, in fact, sent a complimentary bottle of Madeira to their table.

Ace knew the others were watching. Watching and possibly sniggering at what he suspected they thought of as "that darling little couple." So after a long, leisurely meal he helped Dawn to her feet, gave her his arm, and suggested a stroll around the deck before turning in.

They were moving through the marshy delta now, and the moon rose above the tule reeds to a chorus of piping little frogs as they leaned against the rail, holding hands. Dawn leaned her head against her husband's shoulder and murmured, "Oh, my, it's all so pretty. I'm glad I married up with you, Ace."

"Are you tired, darling? Our, um, stateroom's made up, and it's been a long day."

"I could just stand out here forever and watch the moon ball rise, Ace, but if you and me aim to make babies, I 'spect we'd better get cracking."

He laughed, tucking her arm in his. "That's not the way we'd have said it in Virginia, but I want you so bad I can taste it. Let's go to bed. I promise I'll be gentle."

"Shoot, you're always gentle, Ace. I'm not scared if you're not."

They turned from the rail as a tall, familiar figure taking a constitutional stroll approached from around the swell of the bows. The man almost passed, then with a shock of recognition, Brian Carlyle stopped, swept off his sombrero, and gasped, "Bejasus, it's Ace Purvis in the flesh and if me senses don't damn me for a blind fool, herelf would be Dawn Jones!"

Ace's tone was wary as he said, "It's Dawn Purvis now, Irish. We just got hitched, back in Sacramento."

"Did yez, now? Well, let me be the first to congratulate yez! I heard about what happened to Nevada, Miz Purvis. Will you be after accepting me condolences with me congratulations? Bejasus, this calls for a drink all around on Carlyle, and that's a fact!"

Ace said, "We just finished dining, Irish. We, uh, were thinking of retiring for the night."

Carlyle started to object. Then he suddenly grinned and said, "Och, it's a fool I was born and a fool I'll probably die. There'll be time for a morning drink and the telling of tales before the steamer ties up in Frisco, eh?"

"That's the way I see it. Any objections?"

"Objections? What in God's name do I have to object to, you lucky wee dog? It's goodnight I'll be saying and goodnight I'll be meaning, but—do I get to kiss the bride?"

"No," said Ace, flatly. "You don't."

There was an awkward silence. Then Brian Carlyle said, "Right. God's blessings on yez both and I'll just be after saying goodnight."

He left, and Ace took Dawn to their tiny stateroom, not attempting to light the one oil lamp, as the moonlight streamed in the porthole with light enough for any honeymooners.

Dawn had waited until they were alone before she asked, "What was the matter with you back there, Ace? Brian Carlyle is a nice man and our friend."

"He's too big and he smiles too much. I suppose I was a bit curt, but damn it, I'm jealous of him. How's that for a straight arrow?"

"Are you afraid he'll hurt you?"

"I'll kill him if he tries, and he knows it. I'm not afraid of him. I'm not afraid of any man. It was, well, the way he looked at us."

"At us? He just seemed glad to see us, Ace."

"Glad, or amused. You know, I'll bet that big Irishman outweighs the two of us. I'll bet I know the picture he's forming in his mind about us right this very minute, the son of a bitch!"

"You mean about us making love?"

"Not just that. You wouldn't understand."

"Aren't we supposed to take our clothes off?"

"Uh, yes," he stammered, turning his back to her as he started to unbutton his clothing. Ace had bought Dawn a more seemly dark blue dress in Sacramento, but she'd balked at the corsets and petticoats a woman of her generation was expected to burden herself with and it only took her a few moments to shuck out of her clothing, hang them on a nail, and climb into bed, nude. She noticed Ace was still wearing his shirt and trousers. "What's the matter?" she teased. "Are you afraid?"

Not looking at her, Ace said, "I think I must be. My damned hands are all thumbs. The place where my father hit me hurts like hell, too. Must be the damp from the river."

"Why are you lying, dear? What's really the matter?"

With a savage oath Ace tore off his shirt, dropped his pants and underdrawers to the floor, and kicked off his socks before turning around, a small ivory figurine with the body of a fourteen-year-old boy. He stood stock-still in the moonlight. "That's what's the matter. Look at me. Go ahead and laugh if you want to. I'm used to it."

Dawn stared up at him soberly. "I think you're pretty."

And then Ace was in bed with her and atop her, sobbing mindlessly as, all thoughts of slow promised foreplay forgotten, he forced her thighs apart and entered her savagely, or at any rate, as savagely as a man endowed with the genitals of an immature youth was capable of. Dawn gasped in surprise as she felt his flesh melting into hers, and then, responding to the sensuous movements of her desperate little mate, she gave herself willingly. "Oh, my, it does feel nice, doesn't it?" she whispered.

"I'm not hurting you, darling?" he croaked, trying to control himself. Dawn sensed he wanted to get deeper inside her and opened her thighs as wide as she could. "No, it's nice. I'm starting to feel all funny and wet again, but this time I like it."

Ace laughed triumphantly and, raising his chest from her small breasts, hooked an elbow under each of Dawn's knees, forcing her thighs apart and opening her vagina to its fullest possible width. "Bottom," he grunted. "I want to hit bottom with every stroke. Am I hitting the bottom of your pussy, darling?"

Dawn considered that. "I think so. It sure feels good."

Then she felt a warm wet flushing inside her and Ace rolled off with a satisfied moan. "Oh, Jesus, that was it. That was what I've always wanted and never had. Jesus Christ, you fuck like an angel!"

"I do?" Dawn frowned, wondering why he'd stopped just as it was getting interesting. She lowered her legs to the mattress and waited to see what he'd do next, but she'd become familiar on the trail with the sounds of his breathing, and she knew he was asleep.

For a time Dawn lay there, staring up at the dappled light patterns reflected by the moonlight on the passing river water outside.

Then she murmured to herself, "Is that all there is to it? For God's sake, I don't see what in thunder all the *fuss* is about!"

Absently, she fondled her moist genitals, wondering if she should wash or something. Ace had filled her slit with some sort of slippery goo and she supposed that was the stuff that made babies. So she decided not to wash it out. Her moist fingers found her most sensitive spot—her unsatisfied clitoris, aroused and turgid. It felt almost as nice to finger it like this as it had when Ace had been doing it with his thing. She remembered how Yvette used to play with herself, and while it seemed silly, it still felt good. For some reason, she wasn't sleepy at all.

As her new husband slept at her side, Dawn experimented with casual masturbation until, after a time, she felt her first orgasm welling up.

Frightened, Dawn stopped. Then, as the spasms subsided, she gingerly resumed her stroking, wondering what it would be like if Ace could have kept moving over it like this whether she wanted him to stop or not. Then, quite suddenly, she came.

"Oh, Jesus Christ!" she marvelled, staring up at the dappled ceiling as she tried to decide whether that wild feeling had been good or just frightening. So that was what Yvette had meant about *l'orgasme*, was it?

Gently, Dawn started to repeat her experiment, picturing Ace doing it to her. Then, as her second orgasm approached her more experienced fingers, she sobbed aloud, "Damn you, Nevada, why'd you have to go and get your fool self killed? This would have been heaven, with you!"

Brian Carlyle didn't greet them at breakfast in the morning. The big engineer, who knew more than Ace suspected about truculent little men, stayed in his stateroom until the boat docked in San Francisco and contented himself with a friendly distant wave as the honeymooners disembarked.

Dawn was having second thoughts about little men, too, by this time. Ace had awakened her at sunrise for another attempt at lovemaking, but while he'd managed to excite her even more, now that she knew what was supposed to happen, Ace was just too tiny and too easily serviced to satisfy even an immature girl of Dawn's probable age.

They'd told the dubious justice of the peace who married them she was sixteen. She was thirteen at most and still growing, but save for a few sparse pubic hairs, Ace, while nearly thirty, was no more developed than many a fourteen-year-old boy. By some glandular quirk, his mature face and thin beard had left the rest of him stranded in everlasting childhood. His small body was muscular, but it was the smooth, almost feminine body of an active youth. Except for Indians, Dawn had seen few naked male bodies, so Ace was spared her having a complete grasp of his inadequacies. Once dressed in his double-breasted frock coat and dashing sombrero, Ace could pass muster as simply any other wiry short man. He, of course, knew better and, despite his delight with his new bride, swaggered more than Dawn could remember as they strolled the streets of San Francisco.

The town in the early fifties was not the San Francisco of song and legend. A squalid collection of slapped-together dwellings and warehouses, it squatted on the mudflats of the bay beneath the brushy empty hills. From a crude wooden semiphore erected on one isolated hill near the north beach, a lookout, having a view of the Golden Gate around the bend, could signal the arrival of clipper ships. People were starting to call the small rounded peak Telegraph Hill. To the west of Telegraph Hill a long steep ridge of chaparral-covered waste sprawled like a sleeping beaver with its nose to the north beach and its high rump dominating the mission road. Merchants had begun to call it Market Street. Near the beaver's shoulder hump, Russian seamen from the Fort Ross trading post to the north lay buried. Nobody was sure why or when they died, but they called it Russian Hill.

Such civilized comforts as existed in San Francisco at the moment were near the crossing of Market and Montgomery streets. Sprawling north-northwest around a gentle curve to the north beach lay a nondescript and evil-smelling shantytown made from ships' timbers, canvas, and stolen hardware from the many ships that lay abandoned on the mudflats. The shantytown was divided into two sections. Whites and Mexicans had set up camp on the more desirable flatland nearer the bay. Up the slope to the west rose a rabbit warren of tumbledown shacks inhabited by Chinese contract laborers imported to do the dirty work of a town where no white man would work for less than ten dollars a day. It was, of course, called

Chinatown. The squatters' sprawling settlement along the waterfront had been nicknamed Barbary Coast, in dubious honor of the pirates of North Africa whom Louis Napoleon was at the moment said to be cleaning out. Ace warned Dawn never to enter either Chinatown or the Barbary Coast. It was said the Barbary Coasters would cut your throat for your shoes, and the Good Lord only knew what a Chinee would do to a white woman, given the chance.

Ace checked them into the Deluxe Hotel. The first of many Deluxes that would rise along Market Street, it was only a slight improvement on Piggy O'Day's, but Dawn liked the wooden floors and real glass windows.

It was well she did, for once they were quartered, she saw little enough of her new husband. Ace was, as she'd known when she married him, a gambling man, and the gambling of Gold Rush San Francisco was a round-the-clock business.

Unlike the greenhorns of the gold field, gamblers of San Francisco knew their game, and Ace was hard pressed to win enough to keep them in room and board as Dawn waited, bored and listless in their shabby little room, for him to come home.

When he returned as a loser, it was often drunk, for Ace Purvis was not a man who liked to lose. He was not an ugly drunk, for in his own way he loved his little wife, and once the liquor had lulled the dull ache of losing to some bigger mocking man, Ace contented himself with sleeping until it was time to go back and try his luck again.

The best times were when he'd won. Cashing in a winning pot, Ace Purvis was a charming boy who couldn't wait to show Dawn the newest gift he'd bought her.

He bought her ribbons and combs and outrageous hats. He bought her Swiss chocolates shipped around the Horn at great risk and considerable cost, and perfumed French soap to go with the brocaded kimono from far-off mysterious Japan. When he was on a winning streak, they dined on antelope steak, bay oysters, and imported European wines. Madeira was the wine that shipped around the Horn best, but Ace insisted on delicate white wines that cost the earth, and tasted, after a few months in the hold of a clipper, like vinegar. The taste didn't matter; it was having the best that counted.

Slowly, grudgingly, Ace was persuaded to teach Dawn to read. He'd put it off as long as he could, for a child bride who could read was that much less a child. Yet he loved her, in his fashion, and wanted her to be pleased with him. And so he taught her to read, then went out and bought a set of expensive books bound in red morocco and gold. The fact that the books were in French seemed irrelevant at the time.

They made love when he was winning, and while he lacked virility, Ace was an imaginative and experienced lover. He taught her every position of the Karma Sutra and a few he'd made up himself during lonely nights on the trail. They tried cunnilingus, and thanks to his small size, sodomy was not without mild interest once in a while. With time, Dawn managed to reach orgasm with her fervid little husband. Yet there was always a sense of loss, as if, somehow, she were missing something. She tried not to think of it, but often in the night, as Ace lay sleeping at her side, Dawn remembered how big and muscular Nevada had been, and the way Rosalita had called him *"toro mio."*

Eventually, Ace might have made her happy for Dawn was not a demanding woman and, when he was in his boyish winning mood, found herself quite fond of him. It was the loneliness, or perhaps the pointlessness of their existence, that wore her down.

One evening, knowing Ace would not be home before one or two in the morning and restless at having nothing to do, Dawn found herself wandering down Montgomery Street. Window shopping was out of the question, as there were few shop windows in the first place and they were down on their luck at the moment in the second. Yet it was better to be outside, seeing people, even strangers, than to sit alone in a darkening room, waiting for her husband to come home, dead tired, in the wee small hours.

As she crossed a muddy side street, a garish hand-painted sign caught her eye. Her lips moved as she formed the words with her newfound reading skill: SEE THE HEAD OF JOAQUÍN MURRIETTA, TAKEN BY CAPTAIN LOVE OF THE TEXAS RANGERS AT TULE LAKE LAST MONTH. ADMISSION ONE DOLLAR!

"Oh, dear God!" she gasped, lowering her gaze as she hurried by the crowd around the illuminated false front of the so-called museum. So they'd caught him, as she'd warned him, had they? But his *head* . . .? On exhibition like a stuffed trophy?

A man coming out said to his companion, "That's him, all right. Ain't it funny how he's still smiling? Smiling with his haid in a jar of spirits. Ain't that a bitch?"

Dawn grimaced, then, despite herself, edged into the waiting line. What was the matter with her! She didn't want to see a man's head pickled in a glass jar! Why was she doing this?

"That'll be a dollar, miss," said the man at the door,

and even as she fished a coin from her purse and handed it to him, she wondered why she was doing it.

Inside, the "museum" was illuminated by whale oil lamps and smelled of Formalin and decay. A large lithograph of a seedy-looking fat man with a grizzled beard proclaimed, "Captain Love, Captor and Slayer of the notorious Mexican Bandit, Joaquín Murrietta!" Dawn grimaced in distaste and passed on. There were stuffed animals, a two-headed calf, and a grisly mummified thing said to be a mermaid. It looked like the body of a monkey badly stitched to the tail of a smoked codfish. And then, as a man in front of her suddenly stepped to one side, she found herself staring at the head of a faintly smiling young man floating in a jar of alcohol.

Dawn gagged and turned her eyes away, but the ghastly dead face remained in her mind's eye, and with a puzzled frown she forced herself to look again.

It wasn't the man she and Ace had met in the mountains a few months ago! It was someone else. A total stranger with a handsome, rather puffy face. Although the features were Hispanic and the severed head wore a moustache, the resemblance ended there. The famous Texan, Captain Love, had apparently shot the wrong Mexican, or if the poor young man in the glass jar had indeed needed shooting, he'd been palmed off as the real Murrietta for the reward. In either case, the desperate young man she'd befriended in the hills was still alive—and all California thought he was dead!

"Go with God, Joaquín," she murmured, nodding at the head in the jar. "And you too, sir, whoever you were."

Delighted with her secret, Dawn hurried back to

the hotel. Wait until she told Ace! The whole thing
was just too delicious. That paunchy Texan, Captain
Love, had bilked the government out of all that reward money and Joaquín Murrietta was still at large
and . . . No, they'd have to keep it a secret. She knew
Murrietta's raids had ceased with the announcement
of his death, and if he'd meant what he'd said about
his dreams, he deserved a chance. She'd share it with
Ace, but he'd have to promise not to tell . . .

Wearily, Dawn threw her hat and purse on the bed
and started to unhook her dress. She wasn't going to
tell Ace. She wasn't going to tell anybody. She knew
that now. Yet, as she stared at her dim reflection in
the tarnished mirror of their furnished room, Dawn
wasn't at all sure why this had to be so.

The hill was terribly steep, but Dawn's legs were
strong and it was a fine crisp day for walking, even
in a long skirt. She'd walked up through the houses
above Market Street to the south and, when the
housing ended against a brushy slope, kept walking.
Between the clumps of sage and chamis, little orange
poppies smiled up at her from their beds of frosty
green, as if they knew she wouldn't pick them.

Dawn reached the very top and paused to get her
breath and bearings, gasping in pleasure at the pan-
orama all around her. Oh, my, she thought, it was a
very good idea to walk up this way, after all. Off to the
north and east shimmered the deep-blue island-
spangled waters of San Francisco Bay and the tawny
hills beyond. The sky overhead was a bowl of cobalt
blue, and turning to the northwest she could make
out a sailing brig just entering between the steep
wooded hills on either side of the Golden Gate. Below, the brawling town filled a shallow slot between

this unnamed rise and other hills beyond. The western horizon was a jagged line of yet more hills, the cloven crest of Twin Peaks dominating. If there was one thing San Francisco didn't seem to need, it was hills. But they were lovely, nonetheless.

Suddenly, Dawn spied the figure of a man moving up along the ridge that led from what she now thought of as *her* hill to the lower one to the north called Russian Hill. Dawn frowned in mingled annoyance and uneasiness. She was alone, and who would hear a cry for help shouted to the winds up here above the city?

Dawn prepared to move down the slope she'd just climbed, but there was something vaguely familiar about the approaching man that made her pause. As he drew nearer, he glanced up, saw her, and waved.

Dawn waved back, smiling. It was all right. The man was that big Irish engineer, Brian Carlyle.

Carlyle trudged up the remaining distance between them, smiling as he said, "Oh me eyebrow! Ain't it a climb, though? What are you doing up here, Miz Purvis?"

"I was about to ask you the same thing. I went out for a walk, and well, I guess I kept walking. Isn't it lovely up here?"

Brian looked around and nodded. "Bejasus, what a fine place for a man to build a house! Why, he'd feel like king of the world looking down on everything of an evening."

"Pooh, the hill's too steep to think of living on. Besides, I like it better the way it is. If the people of San Francisco have any sense, they'll leave these big brown hills the way they are, for children to roam and for lovers to get away to."

"Ay, it would be nice to set some of it aside. There's

talk of saving the rocky heart of Manhattan Island for a great park, back east, but I doubt they'll do it. There's too much money to be made in the selling of lots and the taxing of the same."

"Even land as steep as this?"

"Och, they'll grade it a bit and terrace shelves for the houses to sit on. Getting water up here's no problem, now that we have steam pumps to do the fetching. Ay, you can see how the flats below make up less than a third of this peninsula and half of that's built on already. If Frisco's to grow, it'll have to grow up its hillsides. Bejasus, if a man had the money to invest in this steep land right now, he'd die as rich as Croesus!"

"Is that what you're doing up here, surveying building lots? I thought you were going to build a road to the gold fields, Mister Carlyle."

"*Mister* Carlyle, is it? Ay, I noticed how you've toned up your speech since your marriage. Where is himself, by the way?"

Dawn looked away and said, "Ace had business to attend to. We were talking about your road."

"Were we now? Ay, there will be a road up there, one day. Who's to have the building of it is the devil's own guess, with the prices of tools and labor what they are these days. If I could only afford to bring in a shipload of Chinamen and another of blasting powder . . . Och, you said it was a dream."

"You've given up the idea, then?"

"No, just set it aside. I've been making a fair living packing in supplies and bringing out dust on consignment. I'll be taking a mule train up to Lost Chinaman in a few days, by the way. Is there anyone up there ye've a message for?"

Dawn smiled wryly and said, "Hardly." Then, as

Carlyle rolled a smoke, she filled him in on her rescue from Piggy O'Day's, adding with a sigh, "I even had to leave my baskets behind."

"Baskets?" He frowned, striking a light with his thumbnail and lighting his well-made smoke.

Dawn explained how she'd collected basketwork from her Indian friends, and Brian nodded. "I'll have a word with old Piggy when I get there," he said. "She's probably cooled off by now, and if she isn't after burning them, I'll fetch them back to Frisco for yez. Where are you and himself staying these days?"

"We're at the Deluxe. But I don't want you to quarrel with Piggy on my account."

"Och, there'll be no quarrel. Piggy needs me services, for I get me mules in and out alive with what's been loaded on their packs. You know, I was wrong with my first road survey, now that I've come to know the lay of the land up there. I've learned to think like a Mexican mule skinner instead of like a Roman."

"A Roman? What have Romans to do with packing supplies into the hills?"

"Not much. They went most everywhere on foot. That's why they taught us to build roads with a straightedge. You can't build straight roads in the mountains. Or you'll be after killing your mules and coach teams on the grades. You have to sort of wind up and around, with the land. That's how me and me mules make it up to Lost Chinaman in good health and only a little slower than them who bull their way over hill and dale like Roman infantry."

"That's the way Indians travel. I mean, the easy way around. This is a fine country, for those who bother to learn her ways instead of trying to turn

California into . . . What *are* they trying to turn her into, Mister Carlyle?"

"Rome. The Romans started our idea of civilization, you see, so we've been cutting the world into squares and plastering her with gridiron cities ever since. That's how they taught me to do it in school. It's taken me some time to see how much meself has left in the learning of real engineering."

He took the smoke from his mouth, waving it in a semicircle aorund them. "Look at the way the bay and hills were made by God and tell me how to make it fit a gridiron. Do you know how I'd do it? I'd build a fine broad road all around the bay in a grand ragged circle, following the contour line all the way so that no wheels would have a grade to climb. Jasus, can ye see it, lass? A circle of homes and lights all around us in a great ring city bigger than the Romans dreamed of when they were drunk?"

"You'd have to end your boulevard at both sides of the Golden Gate, wouldn't you?"

"Och, why should we? It's only a mile or so across over there. We'll build a bridge someday. That'd complete the circle and . . ."

"A bridge across the Golden Gate? You must be joking."

"Och, it'd have to be a big one. Most likely a hanging bridge, like the Incas built in Peru. I'd use steel instead of rope, and a lot of steel it would take, but there's a fellow named Bessemer in England and a foin Irish lad named Kelly in Pittsburgh who've been smelting ore as easy as brewing ale. Steel is the coming thing in engineering and . . . Och, forgive me, Miz Purvis. I do blather on about me mad dreams, don't I?"

Dawn smiled in agreement. Then, glancing at the sun, she said, "I have to be getting back. Ace and I were planning to dine early tonight."

"I'll see ye to your hotel, then."

Dawn hesitated, then said, "I'd rather you wouldn't, Mister Carlyle. My husband is, um, a bit possessive and . . ."

"Say no more," he cut in. "If you'll forgive me bringing it up, me intentions to ye have ever been honorable, Miz Purvis, but I can understand how a man could take me blarney the wrong way. So, once again, I'll say good day to ye, but I'll watch from up here until I see ye safe down yon slope, if ye won't mistake me meaning."

Dawn nodded and, awkwardly, held out her hand to say good-bye. She expected him to shake hands with her. Instead, he took her fingertips in his hamlike paw and raised her hand to his lips, kissing the back of her hand. Dawn snatched her hand away, flustered, and Carlyle said, "It's a gintleman I'd be after acting, if the lady would let me. There was nought but respect in that, either, Dawn Purvis."

Dawn gave him a nod of forgiveness and turned away. She went down the slope at what she hoped was a dignified walk, mindful of his eyes watching her from above. Damn, she thought, why had she acted so skittish back there? She knew it was the fashion for a gentleman to kiss a lady's hand, even in front of her husband. Why had she felt so . . . so *excited* when his warm smiling lips had merely brushed her hand?

By the time she reached the hotel she'd managed to put the big Irishman out of her mind. Ace, to her pleased surprise, was waiting for her in the lobby.

She smiled at him and said, "You're home early, dear."

Ace nodded briskly. "We have to pack. We're moving."

"Oh? Have you found us other lodgings?"

Ace grinned and said breathlessly, "The word just came in—there's a new stampede. It's El Dorado all over again. It's not *one* mother lode. It's a whole damned band of gold-bearing quartz that runs for miles. You see, they were looking for the wrong stuff. The gold-bearing bedrock's the color of sandstone and the greenhorns have been walking right across it all this time, looking for white rock flecked with gold, higher up. This town'll be half empty by sundown. I've already booked passage on the steamboat."

"I'll start packing our things, then. Are we going to stake a claim?"

Ace laughed bitterly. "Not hardly. I'm a gambling man, not a big ape with hands made for a pick or shovel. We'll get the gold *my* way, after bigger and dumber men dig it out of the rock for us!"

The new camp was called El Dorado, even though another Camp El Dorado lay just across the county line. The one they'd reached was in the county of Calaveras and, unlike earlier ones, was not located on a placer stream. There was, in fact, little running water worth mention. The first rush of '49 had ignored the drier valley and others like it. The gold of the new El Dorado wasn't to be panned from wet sand, but pried from the salmon-colored quartz veins of the surrounding hills, where it lay in wirelike threads.

The men who sank the shafts of the second stampede were a more substantial breed than the '49ers.

It took hard work—and money—to wrest gold from the roots of a mountain. El Dorado was financed by a mining company. The workers, for the most part, were members of an immigrant party of sons of Italy who, arriving in New York to find the streets not paved with gold after all, had stubbornly set out to find it farther west.

A few miles up, another wagon train of European immigrants was sinking a shaft for a young man named Hearst on an erstwhile Mexican sheep ranch. The new frontiersmen were hard-working peasants who built substantial adobe houses instead of shacks, and El Dorado was rapidly taking on the appearance of a Mexican village rather than a shantytown. The one saloon-hotel-bordello, on one leg of the T-shaped street layout, was a substantial two-story building of thick adobe brick with a massive timbered roof and a cut-glass fanlight over the swinging doors. The whores used the upstairs cribs to the right of the staircase, while more respectable guests occupied larger rooms to the left, above the barroom.

Ace Purvis cased the new town while Dawn unpacked. Neither took long, for the town was small and Ace had made Dawn leave many of their heavier belongings behind, selling a few items of value for what he called his stake. Ace walked the dirt roads of El Dorado with a puzzled frown, trying to understand some of the things he saw in passing. Many of the Italians had brought their wives along, and tomatoes sprouted in stony dooryards. It was late afternoon, and the men were coming back from the mines, but they didn't seem interested in having a good time. Or at least, a good time as Ace understood the term. He passed a husky man sitting on a doorstep with a child on his knee, and when Ace nodded a greeting, the man merely stared. Italians were funny hairpins, all right.

Ace returned to the hotel to find Dawn unpacked and waiting for him in the lobby. He said, "Well, let's eat and see what the action is, once it gets dark."

Tired from their long ride, Dawn nodded wearily and got up from her chair seat to walk into the bar-room and occasional cafe. Maybe she'd be able to rest up a bit before they moved on again. She knew they'd be moving on. Since coming back to the gold fields, Ace had moved like spit on a hot stove, as if in search of something.

She liked it here in El Dorado. The hotel was spacious and cleaner than the one in San Francisco. The town was quiet for a gold rush camp, and there was a veranda in back where a girl could sit and read for a whole afternoon while she listened to the little laughing brook that ran behind the hotel. If only they could stay a full week, she might not mind another ride to the next will-o'-the-wisp Ace would be taking her to.

Her husband held out his arm and, automatically, Dawn took it. They started into the other room, but in the doorway Ace stiffened and stopped, turning his face to hers with a startled expression.

Dawn asked, "What's wrong,"

"You don't look right. Have you done something to your hair or . . . oh, sweet *Jesus!*"

"What's the matter with you? What have I done? You look like you've just seen a ghost!"

Ace's face was bleak as he nodded and said, "I think I have. You've grown another inch!"

Dawn laughed. "Is that all? I knew I was filling out a bit. You said you liked the way my breasts were starting to look."

"Damn it, kitten, I'm not talking about your tits! It's the top of your damned head that scares me! Why, you're almost as tall as me, now!"

"Well, I told you I was young when you married me. When does a girl stop growing, anyway?"

"I don't know. Sixteen, seventeen, maybe. How old do you think you really are?"

Dawn thought and said, "Let's see . . . thirteen, maybe fourteen?"

"Good God in the manger! What kind of a horse have I married? You must be at least five-foot-four right now and I'm only five-five! You'd better do something about it, damn it!"

"Oh, for goodness sake, let's eat, dearest. I can't do anything about my height. I can't even seem to make a baby with you."

Ace led her silently in to a table and studied her for a time in silence before he asked, ominously, "What was *that* supposed to mean?"

"What was what supposed to mean, dear?"

"That remark about our having children. Are you saying I'm not man enough?"

"Heavens, no. Why, we've made love enough to have a dozen kids by now. I 'spect it's something to do with my being so young, don't you?"

He stared at her for a time. "Funny how a person's bone structure's hidden by baby fat. You don't know who your real folks were, right?"

"Of course not. Why do you ask?"

A bargirl came over to take their order. Ace ordered venison and beans and waited until she'd left before he said, "You look like what we called a mountain white, back in Virginia. I sure as hell hope I'm wrong, but, yep, you've got those wide-set eyes and high cheekbones. That blonde hair and firm jaw says mountain white, sure as God made apples."

Interested, Dawn asked, "What's a mountain white?"

"Scotch-Irish, mostly. We have a mess of them, over in the western Virginia counties. They came in through Penn's state, back before the Revolution. Moved into the big central valley that runs down between the Blue Ridge and the Cumberlands, and mixed with Injuns. The breed was big and ornery and wildcat tough, so they spread from the Hudson all the way to the Alabama piney woods. If your folks was mountain whites . . ."

"You mean I might be a real Indian, partly?"

"Not much, with that blonde hair. Maybe some Cherokee or Shawnee. It's the Scotch-Irish blood I'm worried about. I've never met a Scotch-Irishman I didn't have to stand on a barrel to talk to!"

"But I'm only a girl."

Ace grunted. "Sure. Likely you'll never make it to six feet. Look at me, damn it! I'm five-foot-five!"

The bargirl brought their plates and Dawn had time to consider her words before answering. She ate a mouthful, saw Ace was still staring at her, his food untouched, and smiled. "Look at the bright side, dearest. If what you say is true, our babies will be nice and big. Won't that be nice?"

"Oh, sure. My pa was twice my size and I'll likely have sons who can whip me at twelve. You've made my day. Eat your damn beans!"

"Please, darling, don't be cross with me. I may be older than I thought. I may not grow much more at all."

"Two inches and you'll top me. How will that make you feel?"

"I don't see why it should make me feel anything. You're my husband and I love you. I didn't marry you for your size. I married you because you were—you know—my knight in shining armor."

"Some knight in shining armor! Sir Galahad is standing with his feet in a hole right now. You reckon if we saw a doctor he could maybe give you something to make you stop growing?"

"I don't know. It's worth a try. They say smoking stunts your growth. Would you teach me to smoke? Only the men smoked when I was with the Paiute and you told me it wasn't ladylike, but—"

"You can't smoke in public, but I'll teach you, later on, upstairs. Maybe you could start dipping snuff. Snuff is tobacco and a woman can get away with that, if she watches where she spits."

"What if I started drinking lots of coffee? I've been going easy on coffee, since I read it can stop a woman from having babies, but if it's so important—"

"Yeah, I'll order coffee right now," he cut in, holding up his hand to snap his fingers for the bargirl. He stopped and stared at his upraised hand, repeating the oddly silent movement of his fingers. "What the hell . . .?"

"What's the matter now, dearest?"

"Don't know. My hand is acting up again. I can't seem to snap my fingers!"

"It's the hand your father broke. You likely caught a chill in it, riding down from Angel's Camp."

"I hope so," said Ace, lowering the impotent hand and massaging it. "Our living like white folks depends on my hands. I'd better practice some before I get in a game hereabouts."

"They look all right to me. You can still move your fingers, can't you?"

"Hell, kitten, I don't win at cards by moving my fingers. I win by moving them right. I got this one trick with a double joint I can snap faster than the eyes can see and . . . Jesus, I can't do it! All of a sudden my hands are . . . just hands!"

"Do they hurt? Do you think you should see a doctor?"

Ace flexed his fingers thoughtfully and shook his head. "I know what a doctor would say. He'd say there was nothing wrong with either of 'em. Let's go up to our room."

"Aren't you going to finish supper?"

"Ain't hungry. Got to get out the cards and work these kinks out. I can't have clumsy hands in a card game. I've got to get back in shape."

"Why don't you just rest them a while, dearest?"

"A gambler can't afford to let his hands rest. My hands and Mister Colt are all that keep me from being just a useless little shrimp!"

It would be years before Dawn heard the word psychiatry, but she knew intuitively what was wrong with her husband. His hands were as healthy as they'd been the day she met him. It was his nerve that was failing as day by day his child bride continued to grow to the normal height her genes decreed. She would never be taller than five feet six inches, but Ace had started drinking heavily shortly after that first shock in El Dorado, and by the time she reached five-five, he was impotent in bed as well.

They traveled constantly now. From El Dorado to Sheep Ranch, from Angel's Camp to Poker Flat and back again, always on the move, as if running from some unseen terror.

Ace no longer trusted his clever hands, even sober,

and sobriety had become something of a rarity occasioned by poverty. He continued to gamble, resorting now to the tricks of the common card cheat. Once, when called on a false deal, Ace had stared for a long unblinking minute at the youth who accused him, his right hand tensed to move for his gun, then suddenly lowered his eyes and suggested drinks all around and another deal. His skill with Mister Colt's equalizer had left him too, or if it was still there, Ace's self-doubt warned him not to test it.

He almost went for his gun the first time a jovial miner called him Shorty, but that too was settled by a boyish smile and a round of drinks. Ace's charm increased as his helplessness grew, for like a baby he was relearning the fact that small creatures must be deadly or, if not deadly, cute.

By now Dawn's sympathy was turning to stolid distaste. She no longer missed his lovemaking. He seldom kissed her goodnight, and when he did, a kiss was the end of it.

They slept—when they slept together at all—back to back, Ace snoring in alcohol-dulled dreams and Dawn awake most of the night. A woman of the coming generations would have left him long before this. Dawn, having heard the word *divorce* only as a dirty word, never considered it, but she sometimes wished he'd drink himself to death and get it over with.

They were now back in Lost Chinaman. Dawn hadn't wanted to come, but Ace had heard about high stakes at Piggy O'Day's. When they arrived on the scene, Piggy greeted them as old friends. Apparently, as Brian Carlyle had suggested, the madam had cooled off. It would be some time before Dawn learned of the awesome warning the big Irishman had issued about anyone's harming a hair on her head the last time he'd packed in supplies.

The last place Dawn wanted to stay in was the whorehouse-hotel, so they camped not far from the old claim she and Nevada had worked, in what seemed a distant past.

As she sat on her heels by her Paiute fire, smoking a cigar the way Ace had taught her, Dawn neither knew nor cared when Ace would come back from the all-night brawl at Piggy's. It no longer seemed to matter whether she grew taller or not, but she'd learned to enjoy a good smoke when the firelight was too dim to read by.

She became aware she was not alone. Then, in Ho, a male voice asked, "Is it really you?"

Without turning, Dawn asked, "How goes the hunting this year, Spotted Elk?"

The Indian squatted at her side by the fire. "Not good. Crippled Deer is dead. The White Eyes shot him as he was picking through a trash pile."

"Have you hunger?"

"No. I am working for a White Eyes, tending his sheep up the hill. It is not a bad life. Just . . . not the same."

"I know. My life has changed for the worse, too. Do you know of my friend Coyote Singer?"

"He lives. His women make love to the White Eyes and bring him food. I do not speak to him when we meet on the trail."

"I'm sorry. His need must have been great."

"All our needs are great. Coyote Singer is no longer a Person. I don't want to talk about him. May I have some smoke?"

Dawn passed the cigar to him. "Keep it. It is not seemly for a man to smoke with a woman."

"I thank you for what is in your heart, little yellow-haired Ho, but we shall smoke together. We live in changing times, and I am not a man anymore either. I am more of a man than Coyote Singer, but . . ."

"I understand your words, but I deny them, Spotted Elk. You keep the smoke. You keep your memories, too. They are proud memories, and you shall ever be a man as long as you cling to them."

The Indian made a choking sound, then said, "I am going now. When I saw you sitting here, I wished to talk. Now I wish to be alone. It is permitted for a man to weep, when he is alone."

Dawn didn't look up as Spotted Elk got to his feet and faded into the night. She thought of getting out another cigar, decided against it, and decided to turn in.

She was in the tent, unrolling the sleeping bag, when Ace joined her, quite drunk, but obviously upset. He dropped to his knees at her side. "Dawn, you gotta help me. I just lost. I mean, this time I lost big!"

"What's new about that?" she asked. "We don't have anything left worth selling."

"Listen, I gave my marker to Trigger Evans. You know who he is, don't you?"

"Yes, another gunslinger from Texas. Half the men in Lost Chinaman seem to be gunslingers from Texas these days."

"Damn it girl, I gave him a marker for a thousand dollars!"

"So what? You haven't got a thousand dollars, have you? He'll just have to wait, like everyone else dumb enough to bet against one of your IOU's."

"He says he don't aim to wait, Dawn. He says I have 'til sunup."

"To raise a thousand dollars? That's insane."

"Well, they say he's a mite insane, too. Dawn, he's gonna kill me if I don't come up with the money."

A guilty thought leaped into her mind, but Dawn suppressed it. "You'll either have to fight him or run from him, then. I'd best start packing."

"Dawn, he used to ride with the Texas Rangers and Captain Love. I can't get away from a man like that. You have to help me."

"What am I supposed to do, strap on your guns and face him down? I'll allow I'm a mite bigger than you, these days, but I don't 'spect I'm that big, yet."

"Honey, there's this good old boy who struck a hardrock vein just up the wash. He doesn't gamble, but he says he'll give me a thousand dollars for, uh, a favor."

"Well, do him the favor, for heaven's sake! What does he want?"

Ace hesitated before he whispered, "'You. He's seen you around the camp, and well, he says it'd be worth a thousand dollars to him to spend just one night with you."

Dawn gaped at her husband, "He must be big as hell. A year ago you'd have shot him on the spot for even suggesting such a thing. I take it he'll still alive, darling?"

"Don't you use that mocking tone on me, girl. I know it's a hell of a thing to ask, but I don't see what else we can do. It'll only be this one night and . . ."

"You told him he could sleep with me *tonight?*"

"Well, sort of. He's waiting up the draw a piece. His name's Gus. Gus Swensen, and he's a decent enough cuss. I mean, what the hell, Dawn, it ain't like I was selling your cherry!"

"No," she said, coldly. "A knight in shining armor

saved me from that fate. I'm going to leave you, Ace. I know what promises we made in front of that judge in Sacramento, but a promise works two ways and you—you've turned into something filthy." She laughed harshly and added, "I had a visitor just a mite ago and we were talking about you. Funny, I didn't know it at the time."

"Dawn, that Texan's going to kill me if I don't have the money for him at sunup."

"That's too bad. I liked you, once upon a time."

Ace started to cry.

Dawn listened to him in disbelief as he sobbed hysterically and threw his head in her lap with his arms around her waist. She said, "Oh, for God's sake," and absently patted his head as one would comfort a hurt child. He wept and pleaded in meaningless phrases for a time as Dawn fought not to vomit.

She was heartsick and tired, ever so tired, and, please Jesus, if only he'd stop and let her sleep for a while . . .

But she'd get no sleep this night, she knew. They were going to have to run through the dark hills again, as if they'd repeated a bad dream, or even worse, grim-faced men would be riding out in the morning to tell her, once again, about a shootout in Piggy O'Day's. It was all too familiar, all so wearisome. How had she ever gotten herself into this treadmill of time? More important, how did she get out?

Dawn shook her sobbing husband to get his attention. "Listen to me, Ace. Are you listening to me?"

"Yes, Mamma, what do you want me to do?"

"I'm going to save your life. I'm going to get you the money and then I never want to see you again. Is that clear?"

"You'll do it? You'll pleasure my friend Gus for me?"

"I'll do it because it's the least messy way I'll ever be rid of you, I 'spect. When it's over, I'm going back to San Francisco and I never want you to come near me. I don't know much about Texas gunfights, but so help me, I'll slap you silly if ever I see your mealy-mouthed face again. Understand?"

Ace rose to his hands and knees, and crawled out of the tent. "I'll get Gus. I'm sure you'll like him."

Dawn gagged. Then she reached to unfasten her hair, muttering, "The devil himself would be an improvement, after you, Ace Purvis!"

Dawn lay in the tent, naked under one thin blanket, and tried to force her mind to be a blank void as she waited for what seemed an oddly long time, numb and dry-eyed in the darkness.

There was a rustle of tent cloth and a gruff male voice whispered, "You in there, honey?"

"I 'spect I am. Are you Gus?"

"Yep, Gus Swensen's the name and gold mining is my game. I own the Sweet Petunia shaft—lock, stock, and barrel. Uh, Ace told you about our deal, didn't he?"

"Yes. Couldn't you have made a better deal at Piggy's place?"

"Hell, Dawn honey, I'm a man who can afford the best and I pay for what I want when I want it. I've seen you around town and, do Jesus, you're about the prettiest little thing I ever laid eyes on, and that's a plain fact."

"Thank you. Shall we get it over with? I'm a mite tired."

"Hot damn, I like a gal who don"t mince words!"

Dawn lay there, stiff and cold, as she listened to the sound of a man disrobing. In all too short a time the unknown, unseen stranger lifted the blanket and slid onto the pallet beside her, running a rough palm over her cringing flesh as he gasped, "Jehoshaphat! You're naked as a jaybird, too. Do Jesus, you smell nice."

"It's French perfume. What's that you're wearing, naphtha soap?"

"Well, I washed up a mite afore I come down to visit," he said, putting an arm across her to grasp a shoulder and turn her unresisting body to his own. He explored the darkness with his lips and kissed her cheek. It registered as a numb surprise to Dawn that her visitor had a beard. And then he was kissing her on the lips, his tongue inside her disinterested mouth as he pawed her firm young breasts.

"Oh, you are something else!" he whispered, his lips against hers, as he rolled his body on top of her and forced her thighs apart with a hairy leg. *For God's sake*, she thought, *he's still wearing his socks.*

And then, as she offered no resistance, he mounted her properly and with a gasp of pleasure thrust home his penis.

Dawn gasped as he entered her. He was too heavy and his big thing hurt! But she'd made a pact and she meant to keep it if it killed her. She opened her thighs wider to admit his thrusts, telling herself that this, like all things, would pass.

"Can't you move it a little, honey?" he asked and Dawn, as Ace had taught her, flexed her buttocks to meet his thrusts in a passionless mockery of enjoyment. He sighed, "Oh, that's better!" and started to pound harder. It was such a silly thing, when one thought about it, Dawn decided. She'd gotten used to his larger size and it was no worse than it had been with Ace, after all. Perhaps, indeed, it was a bit nicer than her husband's juvenile rabbit motions. The stranger seemed to be taking longer, and his shaft filled her pleasantly. She wondered what he looked like. If he was at all handsome, this wouldn't be so bad.

Gus gasped, "Oh, I can't hold it back no longer. How about you? Are you fixing to come?"

"I think so," she lied. "Don't stop. Do it harder!"

And then, as she knew her ordeal was almost over for the moment, Dawn gave herself in mock passion, moaning soft lies as she met his savage thrusts with movements of her own.

Gus Swensen suddenly cried out and went limp atop her, sobbing, "Oh, my God, it was twice as good as I was expecting, and I was expecting a thousand dollars' worth!"

Dawn stroked his back with a cool palm and murmured, "That was lovely. Shall we rest a while?"

As the stranger rolled off her, he murmured, "I'm sorry. I reckon I'm a bit heavy for such a bitty gal at that. I didn't hurt you, did I?"

"No, you were very gentle."

"I tried not to hurt you, knowing how tiny you was. But I been doin' without for a spell, and near the end there, I sort of lost my head."

"It's all right. You didn't hurt me."

"Did I really make you come?"

"Of course. Couldn't you tell?"

"I thought I did. Some gals lie about it, though. You see, I don't really like it, 'lessen I pleasure the gal, too."

"That's very considerate of you."

"Well, I reckon as you could say I just plumb *like* women. I mean, as people, aside from what we just now done. You reckon that's unmanly of me, Miss Dawn?"

Dawn laughed and, remembering the size of his turgid member, said, "No, Gus, I'd say you were quite a man. What do you look like, anyway?"

Gus reached out to his pile of clothes on the earth nearby. "Not all that much, I reckon. I'm just a big dumb Swede."

Then he lit the match he'd taken from his pocket and for a moment Dawn gazed up at a once-blond giant old enough to be her father. The craggy features were well formed, and just before the match went out, their eyes met. Gus Swensen's eyes were glacial blue, but twinkled with obvious good humor at the world as he found it.

In the dark once again, Dawn said, "You're a nice-looking man, Gus. How come you have to buy this sort of thing?"

"Hell, I ain't got time for courting, Miss Dawn. The Sweet Petunia's a one-vein one-man shaft, and I've been working my head off from first light to first star. You likely noticed I ain't no kid, so I don't need me a woman all that much. You promise you won't laugh if I tell you something?"

"What is it? I won't laugh."

"You're the first gal I've had in over a year. I mean, I'll never see fifty again and I was startin' to think I'd outgrowed the need, but—well, I seen you around the camp, and hell, I reckon you noticed how you make me feel."

"That's very sweet of you, Gus. I'm glad you enjoyed it."

"You reckon we could do it some more?"

"If you like. You paid for a night, didn't you?"

There was a long silence. Then the man who'd bought her said, "That ain't nice, Miss Dawn. I know a man can't buy love, but damn it, I never paid for downright hostility!"

"I'm sorry, Gus. I'm not angry with you. It's . . . somebody else."

"Ace, huh? I was a mite surprised when he made the offer. I can see how it might fret a gal to have her husband pimping for her."

"Wait a minute. You say Ace made the offer to you? You're certain you didn't approach him first?"

"God, no! It never would have entered my mind, pretty as you be! I was surprised as thunder when he said you was a whore. I never in this world would have suspected it."

Dawn closed her eyes and muttered, "That dirty little good-for-nothing son of a bitch! Oh, that rotten, black-hearted little shrimp!"

"Did I say something wrong, Miss Dawn?"

With controlled malice, Dawn said, "No, you just set me free, and—shall I tell you something, Gus? I like you better than Ace, in every way. Did you know his thing is no bigger than your thumb? Did you know he licks me between the legs because he's not man enough to do it right?"

"Well, I've heard of Frenchmen doing sech. Never tried it, my ownself. I figure the tool God gave me was enough to use on most gals."

"Use it on me, Gus. I want you to put it in me and let yourself go crazy. I want to know what it's like, for once, to fuck a real man!"

"Great day in the morning, you sure talk wild, Miss Dawn. But I'll be only too happy to oblige a lady!"

They made love again and this time Dawn gave her-

self completely in mingled passion and revenge. He
was a nice-looking man and he *did* make love with
skill and virility. Then, with a sob of mingled desire
and rage, Dawn knew for the first time what a good
healthy orgasm could be. She screamed aloud as she
felt her vagina clamp down hard on the big man's
thrusting shaft. She dug her nails into Swensen's
sweating back and wrapped her legs around his
waist, sure she was going to die and go to heaven if
it lasted another minute. But it lasted longer than a
minute as the virile Swede, inspired by her ardor,
gave her one repeated orgasm after another until,
gasping for breath, he went limp. Rolling onto his
back, he lay looking up at the ceiling of the dark
tent. After a time he said, "I thank thee, Lord. If
you want to take me now, I'll come willing, for I've
seen the valley and I've seen the hill and after all
these years, I've had me a woman!"

"You want me to get on top?" Dawn asked.

"Not just yet, 'lessen you aim to kill me. Can't we
jest talk a mite? This business with your husband has
me plumb confused. I don't see how in thunder a man
could share a gal like you, even for a million in gold."

"It's a long story," she said. "Have you got a
smoke?"

Then, as they lay in each other's arms, sharing a
cheroot, Dawn filled him in on her life. Gus was a
good listener, but he cut in once or twice near the
end, asking things like "Hold on, now, you're saying this is the first time? That you ain't no whore at
all?"

Dawn explained about the gambling debt and Ace's
desperation. Gus was silent for a long time, then he
said, "Do Jesus, I'm so sorry, Miss Dawn. I mean,

I'd have never done what I just done . . . I thought you was . . . you know."

"A whore? I guess I am one, now. It's funny, though, it's not as bad as I thought it would be. I mean, damn it, I like you, Gus. I 'spect that makes the difference, don't you?"

He took her face in his hands. "If what we just done was for pleasure, then you ain't no whore at all. What do you aim to do about the worthless trash you married up with, Miss Dawn? I mean, he's done it once, he'll do it again, and the next paying customer may not be as much to your liking."

"I know. I told him it would only be this once— and I meant it. Once he gives the money to that Texan, we're done. I never want to see him again."

"You want to move up with me on my claim, seein' as how you and me seem to hit off so good?"

"No, Gus. I thank you for the offer, but it wouldn't work. It would cause talk and trouble for you, and I've decided it's best for a woman to stand on her own two feet. I've been looking for a man to protect me all my life, and all it's gotten for me is grief. Grief for the men, too. It's partly my fault that Ace is what he is today. I can see that now."

"Well, I'll tell you what, Miss Dawn. I'll pay off the little runt and run him out of town. Then I'll grubstake you to another thousand for your ownself."

"What do I have to do for it? We've about exhausted the possibilities."

"Shoot, you done all you has to, Miss Dawn. I ain't talking about the pleasure of your flesh, nice as they be. You see, I ain't as dumb an old Swede as I look. I knowed you was funning me, when I first crept in here with you. That last time, though, was real. I don't just mean the coming together. I mean the liking one another whilst we done it. That's about the friendliest thing two folks can do for each other, Miss Dawn. Next to liking somebody, a gift of gold ain't all that big a shux. 'Sides, I got me a whole mountain full of the trash."

Dawn and her elderly admirer were dressed and having breakfast by the morning campfire when Ace rode into the clearing. He was not alone. A tall lean youth with a tie-down holster rode at his side, a sardonic smile on his adenoidal face and a bad man's reputation to uphold. The two new arrivals dismounted and joined Dawn and her guest by the fire. Ace squatted, not looking at his wife as he went through the motions of warming his hands. Trigger Evans stood a few paces away, knowing a man drew faster standing tall.

Before Ace could ask, Gus Swensen threw him a large buckskin poke. "Here's your gold, sonny. I don't mind there's nothing else for you now, hereabouts. So pay your just debts and ride."

Ace said, "Dawn, pack our gear. We're moving to Middle Fork City."

Before Dawn could frame a denial, Swensen said, "She ain't goin' noplace, Ace. You sold her, so she don't belong to you no more."

Ace's eyes glittered dangerously. "What's this? Have you been putting bugs in my wife's ear, old timer?"

"She ain't your wife. A man don't sell his wife, pimp."

Ace got to his feet, red-faced. "You take that back or go for your gun, God damn your eyes!"

Dawn gasped, "Stop it, both of you!"

The older man chuckled and said, "I was hoping you'd say that, sonny."

They both reached for their holstered revolvers at the same moment.

Ace should have been faster. He knew he should be faster, but his hand seemed to move through gelid air as thick as glue as he stared into the eyes of the much older, much larger man. And then, just as the little gambler's fingers touched the ivory of his pistol grips, Gus Swensen's old cap-and-ball pepperbox roared and Ace Purvis died, a surprised look on his face and a little crimson hole between his eyebrows.

Another gun echoed in the clearing as Trigger, bewildered but acting out of instinct, drew and fired at the still-seated Swede. The big man jerked like a puppet on a string as the conical .44 round slammed into his chest. Then he fell on his side, moaning, "Dang it, Trigger, this wasn't no fight of your'n!"

The Texan raised his pistol to take dead aim on the man he'd wounded, neither listening to nor concerned with the meaning of Swensen's protest. But before he could fire, there was a whirring noise, cut short by a dull thunk, and the Texan froze in place, slack-jawed. Then, as slowly as a sawn-through tree, Trigger fell forward into the fire, still holding his gun, with a feathered arrow shaft between his shoulder blades.

It had all happened so fast Dawn had not had time to move. At sight of the arrow she remained frozen in time and space.

Then Spotted Elk stepped into the clearing, his face blank. "I was watching. Is your big friend dead?"

"I don't think so, Pull that arrow out and hide."

Spotted Elk said, "No. The point is broken off inside him. I can tell from where I stand. They will find it. I think we'd better make up a good story, don't you?"

Gus Swensen croaked something from where he lay on the ground near the tent and Dawn bent over him. "How bad is it, Gus?"

"Bad enough, I reckon. That Injun a friend? Or is ever'body buttin' in on fights, these days?"

"He's a friendly. Where were you hit?"

"Don't matter, Miss Dawn. Do you have paper and a writing stub in your possibles?"

"Yes—do you want me to write something for you?"

"Nope. Ain't legal 'lessen I writes it in my own hand. Get the paper, girl. I ain't got all that much time."

Dawn ducked inside the tent, rummaged for a pencil, and tore the blank flyleaf from a book, taking them back to Gus with the book itself to use as a writing surface. Meanwhile, Spotted Elk had come over to assist the dying man to a sitting position, asking, in his own limited English, what he could do to help.

Swensen ignored him and took the writing materials from Dawn, putting a couple of paragraphs of crude script down before he signed it. "This here's my last will and testament, Miss Dawn. Now listen and listen good. We're gonna have to tell us a few lies to make this work out right. You mind what you said about being losted? Well, we gotta tell 'em I'm your daddy, and that I just found you after all them years."

"You are my *father?*"

"Hell, no, but nobody hereabouts knows that. Just remember you're Dawn Swensen and that I'm leaving the Sweet Petunia and my other gear to you and

Ace, here. I put Ace in on account I didn't know, when I wrote this will a week ago, that this jasper from Texas was aiming to shoot him, see?"

"You're leaving a gold mine to *me?*"

"Ain't got nobody else I care to leave it to, but that ain't important. Remember, we was sittin' here, jawing polite, when Trigger rode in for a showdown with Ace and this here Injun saved you after Trigger shot the two of us men. You got that fixed in your head, pretty lady?"

"I think so. We'll worry about it after I fetch you a doctor."

"Hell, Miss Dawn, I don't aim to last that long. Take this paper and put it in your bodice for now. I'll leave it to you to coach your Injun, seein' as you know his lingo. Tell him to ease me back down, though. I reckon I'd feel better with my head a mite lower."

Dawn started to repeat his instructions, but Spotted Elk had understood, and he gently lowered the big man to a comfortable position on his side.

Dawn put the last will and testament away without reading it, putting a hand on Swensen's shoulder. "You just lie still and I'll ride into camp for Doc Forbes."

Swensen didn't answer.

"He breathes no more," Spotted Elk said. "Do you think they will believe our story?"

"Did you understand what he was saying?"

"Yes. It was a good story. The man was a mighty liar as well as a good person, I think."

Dawn's slight sad smile was quizzical as she kissed a finger and touched it to the half-open eyelids of the grizzled, once-handsome head near her knees. "Yes, he was good in every way. Those shots will have been heard. They will be coming soon. You'd better leave."

"You will need me to back your new version of what happened here."

"No. I know the kind of men the vigilantes are. They may believe you put an arrow in a White Eyes to save me, but they won't like it—and at the least, you will be beaten. Go quickly and I will thank you properly at a later time."

"I have been beaten before. I am not afraid. How else can you explain that arrow?"

"Leave your bow and quiver. I shall say I did it. They know I spent my youth with Real People and . . ."

"But hear me, this is a *man's* bow!"

"I know—but they won't. I shan't insult your bow by drawing it. I just need it to weave a good basket of lies. It is forbidden for one of your kind to kill one of mine, even with reason. A woman of my kind can get away with almost anything, once she makes up her mind."

Dawn's story was accepted by the Vigilance Committee. There was a proposal put before the meeting to hang the dead Texan anyway, but it was voted down as an unseemly waste of effort, and the more sensible majority decided to auction off his horse and belongings to pay for a proper funeral for all three victims.

The miner's committee accepted Gus Swensen's last will and testament with some surprise, but no real objection. Gus had been liked and respected as a hardworking man who paid his debts and gave no trouble to the small community. His handwriting was well known. The man himself had never commented all that much on his past, and when one member wondered aloud why Gus had never told anyone Dawn was his long-lost daughter, another said, "Hell, losing your family ain't a thing no man's likely to want to talk about. I mind when Miss Dawn first came over the Sierra with her brother. Old Gus wasn't hereabouts, then. Meetin' up with her after all this time, only to learn Nevada was dead, would be enough to put most men in a silent mood."

"Shoot, Nevada warn't her brother. He found her out on the flats with Injuns and—"

"Now, hold on, Luke, this meeting ain't to pass on what might or might not have gone on betwixt Nevada and the girl. Nevada was my friend and I'll hear no talk agin the dead. I votes we acecpt this here will as it was writ and not ask no more questions as could git a man kilt!"

There was a murmur of agreement and the would-be gossip was silenced.

Thus, possession of the Sweet Petunia mine passed to "the widow Purvis," as Dawn was now being called with some respect.

The gold-filled poke the big Swede had dropped at Ace's feet before killing him was hers, too, although unreported to either committee. So she hired an oxcart and had her meager possessions moved up to the mine and its nearby cabin.

The shaft, as Gus Swensen had said, was little more than a hole drilled into the hillside at a forty-five-degree angle for less than sixty feet, following the vein of gold-bearing quartz at a slight curve. A pile of salmon dust and a circle of flat stones set around an upright post driven into the earth puzzled Dawn until one of the Mexican carters explained it was a crude but serviceable Spanish gold mill. A gutter inside the circle of square-hewn stone blocks collected milled quartz as a mule or ox, hitched to the center post, dragged a large granite boulder over the ore-rough paving. Down the slope a hundred yards ran a small brook that furnished drinking water as well as a constant trickle through the long plank sluice box Gus had built. Dawn didn't have to be told what a sluice box was, or how the fine-ground mixture of gold and quartz was separated by gravity and the running water over its wooden riffles.

The cabin was a pleasant surprise. She'd known Gus had bathed before coming to visit her, but she'd assumed he lived as most miners did, in piglike bachelor sloth. But he had apparently had an orderly mind and fastidious habits. The logs of the cabin had been well set and chinked with adobe. The inside walls had been debarked to free the logs of insect hiding places. Gus had built rustic furniture consisting of shelves, a plank trestle table, two stools, and a bed shelf large enough for his burly frame. His clothes still hung on manzanitawood pegs driven into the walls. A few meager belongings were packed in an old leather-covered Saratoga trunk. His tools, harness, and other supplies had been neatly piled in a lean-to nailed to the back wall of the cabin, and he'd even gone to the trouble of digging a pit latrine on the downwind side of the clearing.

Dawn waited until the carters had been paid and were gone before she started unpacking her things and putting the cabin in order for her lonely but not unhappy first night on the mountain. She'd never had a home before, and rough-hewn as it was, it delighted her. She spread her own blankets on the corn-husk mattress of the dead man who'd made her his startled heiress. Smiling again, wistfully, she remembered the one and only night she'd had with a man she'd

never really know. It seemed almost as if Ace Purvis
had never happened, now. She missed Nevada—and
yes, she missed Gus Swensen. It was hard to think
of herself as the widow Purvis. And to think she'd
spent nearly two years with him!

As evening approached, Dawn built a fire in the
small adobe hearth at one end of the cabin and put
a pot on the coals to boil. She had to decide what to
eat. She knew it was time, but she wasn't hungry and
there was so much to choose from. She had the food
supplies she'd bought in town, not knowing in advance about the kegs of Boston beans and other
things in Swensen's well-stocked larder.

In the gathering dusk she went outside and moved
absently down to the little stream, smiling down at
emerald spears pointing to the sky near the water's
edge. Then she nodded and bent over to start picking.
Fresh arrowroot boiled with salt and a little jerked
venison, would do her nicely.

Near the top of the slope, watching from shadows
of a manzanita clump, two white men watched the
distant figure of the woman picking arrowroot in the
bottom of the ravine. One of them was absently rolling a smoke. His partner said, "Don't smoke, Windy.
The gal's half Injun and she might spot or smell it."

The other claim jumper shrugged and said, "Don't
make no never mind if she does, now. We're more'n
three miles from the next claim and she left her gun
and that damn bow an' arrow of hers in the cabin.
What are we waiting on?"

His older and wiser companion said, "For dark, you
idiot. Don't want no shots heard. Don't want nobody
to ever know jest what happened, see?"

"Do we have some fun with her, first? She's a
righty pretty little thing."

"Dang it, Windy, that's a *gold mine* we're after, not a piece of ass! She's gotta be kilt quiet and hid fast, so's we can put in the first claim after she's been missed a decent interval."

"Won't they 'spect somethin' happened to her, Jim?"

"Well sure, they'll 'spect. They'll 'spect the Injuns made off with her, or that she met a feller and traipsed off with him. Shit, it don't make no never mind what they 'spect, long as she's gone and we file on a deserted claim."

Dawn had finished filling the front of her skirt with arrowroot and was climbing the slope to the cabin. The one called Windy said, "Sweet Jesus, ain't she pretty! Look how the sunset shines on that yaller hair."

"It shines better on gold. Sun'll be down soon. We wait until star bright and move in. She don't even have a danged old watchdog!"

"Ain't got much sense, neither. You'd think a gal that pretty would know better than to try to live out in these hills by her ownself. How much do you reckon that mine is worth?"

"Don't know till we go to sell it. The Swede was taking out a hundred or two in dust a day, but he was workin' his ass off doin' it. I figure to sell to that Hearst jasper, once it's our'n. He's got hisself the labor to open up the mountain right."

"Yeah, it's only right the gold should be got out right. That bitty gal down there ain't got the strength to work fifty a day outten hard rock."

And so the two men waited as, down in the cabin, Dawn put her supper in the pot to boil and lit a whale oil lamp. The combined warm glows of lamp and hearth cast a cheery light on the peeled pine logs around her. As Dawn sat down, she breathed, "Oh, thank you, Gus!" with a smile on her lips and tears in her eyes.

Outside, the sky was a deep blue and the first stars were winking on as the claim jumpers slowly crept down the brush-covered slope.

Moving down behind them on silent feet came four watchful Indians who had trailed the men for hours. When the claim jumpers stopped behind a boulder, preparing for their final move, the quartet of Indians stopped in place, like tawny upright cats. One whispered, "You were right, Spotted Elk."

Spotted Elk nodded grimly and said, "Heya, friendly visitors do not approach a woman alone in such a manner. Use your clubbing sticks, my brothers. It is not my intention that their bodies be found, but if they are, there should be no arrow wounds."

Inside the cabin, Dawn heard nothing as she ate her supper and prepared for bed after her long wearisome day. She would never know about the short, savage, silent struggle on the hillside just above her cabin, for Spotted Elk and his comrades were not given to idle conversation with women. The little White-Eyed Ho was their friend and they would protect her. They had told her this many times. They saw no need to discuss it further.

The three Mexicans and the mule stopped milling ore as Dawn came out of the cabin with a pitcher in one hand and a cluster of tin cups in the other. The *gringa* who'd hired them had spoken pleasantly and was said to be *muy simpatico*, but one never knew where one stood with *los americanos* and she was headed their way. Pablo, the foreman she'd placed over the other day laborers, removed his straw sombrero and stood at respectful attention as the blonde *gringa* approached.

Dawn said, "My, isn't it hot, today? I've made us some *sangría*—or I hope I have. Would you taste it and see if I got it right, Señor Pablo?"

Pablo glanced at the sun and said, "You have made this for *us*, señora? It is not yet noon."

"Heavens, you've been working since first light and it's time you had a break. Here, I'll fill your cup."

Pablo watched, wooden-faced, as Dawn filled a cup with the mixture of wine and citrus juice and handed it to him, starting to fill another for a second workman. In Spanish, Pablo said, "Idiot, take the pitcher and see to yourself and Hernandez. She is our *patrona!*"

Shyly, the young man took the pitcher and cups from this strange young woman who'd hired them. They had thought, at first, she mocked when she addressed Pablo as señor, for he was a peon and everyone knew it. Most Americanos called them boy or Mex or greaser. La Señora Purvis called the foreman señor, or sir, and the others were addressed by their names. It was an odd habit, but not unpleasant.

Pablo saw that Dawn was holding out a cup of her own to be filled and asked shyly, "La señora wishes to drink, with us?"

"Oh, I hope it's all right. I don't know your customs all that well."

"We are honored, señora." The foreman smiled, holding up his glass in silent toast as he waited for Dawn to take the first sip. She insisted. "Please try it. I've been tasting it as I made it and I really don't know a thing about Mexican beverage."

"La señora drinks with Mexicans in a most becoming manner, and we would thank you if it was vinegar, but, by my God, this is fine *sangría.*"

"I didn't put too much sugar in it?"

"No, señora," he lied. "It is just right. May I ask where you learned to make it?"

"I had some in San Francisco, one time. I asked the bartender how he did it. When I saw the lemons and oranges they've just packed in to Lost Chinaman, I thought I'd try my hand at it. I've another pitcher for the men in the shaft, so if you'll excuse me . . ."

Pablo started to protest that he himself could serve the workmen in the shaft. Then he thought better of it and merely nodded. The men in the shaft had been grumbling. Even if the young woman's hospitality was calculated, it was still better treatment than they were used to.

Dawn walked away, leaving the filled pitcher with the mill hands. Pablo drained his cup and said, "All right, *muchachos,* back to work."

Hernandez said, "We haven't finished the *sangría.*"

The foreman glared at him and cursed. "When I say we drink *sangría,* we drink *sangría.* When I say we work, we work."

The scene was repeated at the mouth of the mine shaft. The foreman of that team, an older and more experienced miner, was used to being called señor, for even gringos respected a man with the skill to follow a vein. But in truth he'd seldom been served a cool drink by any boss, Anglo or Hispanic. After their short break, the miners went back to work with renewed energy and less suspicion of their odd young female employer.

Dawn returned to the cabin to work on her books. With a full crew, the mine was showing a modest daily profit. Her profit might have been greater if, as the men in town suggested, she worked with fewer greasers and paid them less, but Dawn had shoveled sand and gravel for Nevada's rocker box, and she knew what the work was like under a hot summer sun.

Native Californians of Mexican ancestry were allowed to file mining claims, as was anyone but an Indian. But holding a claim in a crude territorial court staffed by Americans was difficult even for one of Anglo-Saxon descent. So the few Mexicans of Calaveras County were content, or at least willing, to settle for a living wage. What it took a Mexican to live on was anybody's guess, and most mine owners paid as little as they could get away with. Dawn paid her workers the going rate for a white American, if a white American willing to work for wages could have been found.

And yet, despite dire warnings that the vein might run out any day, she was slowly but surely getting rich. Having learned of Piggy O'Day's hazy memory when it came to her strongbox at the saloon, Dawn kept her dust hidden, between mule trains, and sent it down to be assayed and deposited to her account in a Sacramento bank.

On a recent visit, her Indian friend Spotted Elk had brought her a young Indian camp dog as an unexplained gift. The small yellow-brown cur lay under the table now as she worked on her ledger. After resisting the impulse to name it Ace she'd settled on Shorty.

Shorty was whimpering now, as if he'd heard or sensed something. Dawn knew Indian dogs were trained never to make a sound, save in warning, so she put her pencil stub aside and went outside again.

A tall man was riding into the clearing on a fine Virginia walking horse, leading a pinto packpony. Dawn noticed that her foreman, Pablo, had thoughtfully positioned himself between her and the approaching rider, with a pick handle casually held in one hand. She called out, "It's all right, Señor Pablo!" as Brian Carlyle reined to a cautious halt.

Carlyle saw the Mexican step sullenly from his path, and moved his team to the cabin door where Dawn stood. Doffing his hat, he said, "God bless us both! Every time we meet, of late, it seems to be on a mountain."

Dawn laughed and waved a welcome. "My God, it's been a long time, hasn't it? Get down and I'll feed you. You heard about what happened to Ace, didn't you?"

"Ay, Piggy O'Day just told me. I suppose I should say I'm sorry, but I've never been a man to tell a joke with a straight face."

He dismounted and waved his hat at the pinto. "I brought your Indian baskets up for you, as soon as I heard where you was," he said. "Bejasus, them baskets and meself have been to Frisco and back, lookin' for yez."

Dawn smiled. "I'd forgotten about them. I'm sorry if I put you to so much bother."

"Small bother, lass. They're light, and I've had a look at 'em. It takes a Celt to know the fairy skill in clever weaving. Most of the pack is stuff you ordered at the general store. I thought as long as I was coming up here, I'd bring it. What would herself be doing with all them sacks of Mexican cornmeal? The stuff's the color of pasteboard and not much better to eat."

"I've a Mexican crew, and their women can't make tortillas with our American flour. Come inside and tell me what you've been doing with yourself these days, while I put the coffee on."

Carlyle said, "I'll unload the packpony, first." But Pablo, who'd been listening with quiet interest, moved forward to volunteer. "I will attend to it, señor. You will wish the packs in the lean-to, señora?"

Dawn explained that the food and pick heads went with the other supplies, while her basket collection was to brought directly in.

Then she ushered her Irish guest inside, shushed the growling watchdog, and waved him to a seat. She put the coffeepot on the coals to warm and joined Brian at the table. "I hear you've been doing well as a packer, Brian."

"Och, it's first names now, is it? Well then, Dawn, me lass, I've been doing well, but not well enough, for dreams cost more to feed than men or even horses."

"You're talking about your magic road?"

"Ay. They've punched one through as far as El Dorado and hired some dagos to carve another up through Murphy's and Angel's Camp. I have to pay a toll to use it, and it's not a well-made road at all, bejasus!"

"Can't you go around?"

"Of course I could go around, but that's what roads are for. To save man and beast useless steps. I save more than a day and the toll pays for itself by the time I'm done, but damn it, that could have been *my* road and *my* tolls!"

"There's talk of a stage line these days in Lost Chinaman. A man came up the other day to ask me to invest in one."

"Was he from Wells Fargo or Butterfield?"

"No, he wants to start his own."

"Jasus, I hope you turned him down?"

"I said I'd think about it. He seems to need an awful lot of money."

"Ay, money is the oil in the machinery of civilization and no small operator has enough to compete with Butterfield or the Wells Fargo Bank. I've been to Wells Fargo, offering them a deal on me road, but they said the grades were too steep, this far up the slope."

"What do you think, Brian?"

"Ah, Jasus, with a hundred men and the wherewithal to pay 'em, I'd have a road up here from Angel's in less than a year. But what's the good of talking? I couldn't even get one of those fat bankers to ride up here with me to see for himself."

"What kind of money are you talking about, Brian? How much would it take?"

He shrugged and said, "I could start it with ten thousand."

"That's a lot of money, even in California."

"Ay, it's the inflated prices here that makes doing anything worth doing so dear."

Pablo entered with the baskets and Dawn told him to pile them in one corner for now, as Carlyle, wrapped in his own thoughts, mused aloud, "You can't get a Mex or Chinee to work for less than a dollar a day and a white man wants ten to swamp out a saloon!"

Pablo's face was impassive as he carefully piled the baskets in the corner, but Dawn was embarrassed. She knew how even decent pioneers like Brian treated anyone not of northern European ancestry with good-natured but abrasive contempt. Didn't they think her other friends had feelings?

Dawn said, "Thank you, señor. We were about to have some coffee. Would you care to join us?"

The Mexican looked startled and shot a wary glance

at her big gringo guest, but Carlyle's face was un-
readable. Privately, Carlyle disapproved, not so much
because Pablo was Mexican as because he was hired
help. It was not his house, however, and under the
roof of host or hostess Brian Carlyle was prepared to
drink with the devil or an Englishman if his duties as
a guest required it.

He'd never had the Gaelic, and his brogue was less
thick now than when he'd come as a boy to Boston
after the potatoes failed. But while he worked to
Americanize his speech, his manners were those of a
Celt, and as the code of a guest under a friendly roof
demanded, Brian smiled agreeably at the Mexican.
"It's the coffee boiling I hear and that's a fact."

Gingerly, Pablo sat down, placing his sombrero on
the floor and putting his hands in his lap, eyes down-
cast. All gringos were obviously mad. If they weren't
spitting at you and calling you names, they seemed to
wish to adopt you. Were there no proper manners for
polite strangers among these barbarians?

Dawn got up and fetched the steaming pot and some
cups, placing on the table a bowl of what to Carlyle
looked like broken-up adobe bricks. He waited until
she'd poured three cups before he pointed at the bowl
and asked, "Are we supposed to eat that or chink the
cabin with it, lass?"

"They're a sort of Mexican hardtack." Dawn explained. "I swapped some salt with one of the men's
wives for a sack of them and they taste pretty good.
I forget what she said they were. What do you call
them, señor?"

"*Tostadas*, señora," murmured Pablo, not looking up.

Carlyle said, "Some sort of toast, eh?" and tried
one. "Not bad at all, bejasus, but they'd go better with
ale, if herself don't mind an honest opinion." For the

Mexican's edification he added, "Ale is what we call *cerveza*, señor."

Flustered, Pablo murmured, "*Sí*, yes, *tostadas* with *cerveza, muy bien.*"

It was a point in the big barbarian's favor. Everyone knew one ate sweets with coffee and salty corn crisps with dry wine or beer. Everyone, it seemed, except la señora. But since she was a saint as well as a mere woman, Pablo forgave her occasional oddities.

The Mexican drained his hot cup of what was truly awful coffee and got to his feet. "If la señora will allow me, I should be getting back to the *molino*. My worthless helpers must be watched."

As soon as they were alone again, Brian asked, "Aren't you after spoiling your help a wee bit, lass?"

Dawn said, "They could use a bit of spoiling, in this valley. Besides, they work like beavers for me, spoiled or not."

"Well, it's yourself is the boss. I've never gotten a Mex to work worth a damn for meself. Maybe if I ever build me road it's yourself I'll be after hiring for straw boss."

"I'd like that." She dimpled, adding, "Like some more coffee?"

"I'd love some more," he lied, "but I have to be getting back to the settlement. By the way, are you sure you're still on neighborly terms with those Digger Indians?"

"Of course, why do you ask?"

"Just some idle talk I heard in town. Some of the boys spotted an Indian on the skyline the other day. He ran off before they could ask him what he was about. They say other Diggers have been seen skulking around your camp. What do you suppose they're after?"

"Oh, it's just Spotted Elk's band. They know they have my permission to food-gather on my land, but my Mexicans make them shy."

"Ay, as I'd be after thinking Injuns might make your Mexicans feel. Some of the lads in Lost Chinaman seem to think they're dangerous. It's said a white man's not safe out here in these hills at night."

"Pooh, Spotted Elk's people are a poor ragged handful, gathered from the remnants of a dozen broken tribes. Spotted Elk comes to visit me, some nights. He gave me that pup under the table. Neither one would hurt a fly."

"I'll bow to yourself as the authority on Injuns in these parts, but it does seem odd that at least five men from Lost Chinaman have vanished in these hills in the last few weeks."

"I'm sure they vanished with no help from my Ho friends, Brian. I even have my Mexicans convinced they're harmless. Spotted Elk says it's an improvement over the way they used to get along. Before the Americans came, the Mexicans either converted them to Mother Church or shot them as vermin, depending on the weather or something. You're sure you won't stay for another cup? I wanted to ask you more about your road."

Brian got to his feet and sighed, "I can't be after staying, more's the pity, and I doubt I'll build me road, for the reasons I just told you. There's talk in the capital that if this Buchanan fellow wins the coming election, back in the Union, there may be federal funds for roads and all. If that should come to pass, a Waterford-born Paddy like meself will be far down the list when it comes to the government pork barrel. Och, well, as long as the roads get built, it's something, and now I'll be saying good day to ye, Dawn Purvis."

"Brian, I have well over ten thousand dollars in the bank in Sacramento."

"Do you, now? Well, a bank is a safer place to keep it than under your mattress, but I'd keep a bit of silver in the thatch, too, for banks are no safer than the men who run them. But I was after leaving, so . . ."

"Brian, I want to help you build your road."

He paused, smiling down at her. "I know your meaning, lass, but you don't know what you're after saying."

"Yes I do. You said you could start your road with ten thousand dollars, and I've got ten thousand dollars—"

"Whist! I'll not hear another word of it, Dawn Purvis. It's too great a risk. I've no security to offer, and if something were to be after going wrong . . ."

"Brian, damn it, I own a gold mine!"

"Ay, and gold's becoming a drug on the market with half the world digging it out of these hills. Do you know the price of bullion's dropped by a third since '49? I know the profit you're after making, for such things are common gossip in every camp. I know there's an end to every vein, too. You could peter out your shaft tomorrow, and then where would we be? No, lass, we'll be after leaving your money where it belongs. In the bank, collecting interest!"

"Oh—you!" she said in exasperation. "I'm a woman grown and a widow to boot, and you grownups still won't let me have my way!"

Carlyle laughed and opened the door. "It's a fine grown woman you are, too, these days, but you're right about not having your own way, if it means an Irish dreamer taking advantage of you!"

"What if *I* took advantage of *you,* then?"

He stopped and frowned. "How would you be after doing that?"

"I could drive a hard bargain. I could be as mean as those old bankers in Sacramento and hold you to a firm promise. That would make it fair, wouldn't it?"

"Och, what sort of a bargain could we be after making, lass? I have a few tools and some swaybacked horses. None of which would pay you back if you was to finance me for a month."

"How much would it take to start the road? Would ten thousand grubstake you?"

"Ten thousand dollars? Jasus, I'd mortgage me immortal soul for less! But where's your security, damn it? I couldn't raise a thousand on my tools and livestock if I threw in me head!"

"Brian, I don't want your horses, or even your head. I want you."

Carlyle blinked in surprise and then he smiled uncertainly. "What do you mean, you want me? If it's a frolic you want, what are we talking business for?"

"I'm speaking of business. I want you as security for my grubstake. I have no need of tools or horses, but I do need a husband. If I loan you the money, I expect you either to pay me back in six months or marry me. I think that's fair security on any loan, don't you?"

"You're daft, lass! That's the maddest deal I've ever heard of! And I've heard me share of mad deals since coming over the Sierra, too!"

"What's the matter with my offer? Am I that ugly, Brian?"

"Jasus, you're a queen among women, young as ye are, and ye know it. But I'm not the marrying kind, and if I was, you'd be after getting the short end of the stick."

"I don't see how. I need a husband, and you're the best man in Lost Chinaman. If you go broke, you'll need a rich wife, too, and I'm the richest widow woman in the county, so . . ."

Carlyle threw back his head and laughed. Then he saw the stricken look on her face and quickly became serious. "Jasus, a dozen men I know of would kill each other for such a chance, Dawn. It's not that I'm not taken with you, either. It's just that, well, the thought never crossed me mind."

"Don't you like me?"

"Of course I like you. I've always liked you. That's a hell of a reason to be after getting married, though. I mean, I haven't even begun to make me fortune and the thought of marrying anyone hadn't crossed me mind at all."

Dawn sighed and grinned. "Well, we'll just have to think of something else, then. I told you I don't want your durned old horses."

Carlyle looked down at his scribbled figures for a time, frowning. Then, cautiously, he asked, "What if I was after going along with such a mad mortgage, and built me road and paid you back in time?"

"You'd be off the hook, wouldn't you?"

He laughed again and said, "Bejasus, it's tempted I am and that's a fact. Leaving aside me virtue, what's the interest rate ye feel is fair on this fairy mortgage of yours?"

"Oh, ten percent seems fair enough. Eleven thousand or your hand in marriage in exactly six months. How does that set with you?"

"It sets with me as insane, but bejasus, I'll shake on it!"

Dawn got up and came over to him, gravely holding out her hand. He shook it just as gravely. Then, with a quizzical smile, he tried to draw her nearer to him, reaching out with his free hand to embrace her.

"None of that, now," she said, pulling back. "Not until we're married up proper."

He looked puzzled. "I thought it was yourself just said she wanted me, Dawn."

"Oh, I do, but as a husband, not a lover."

"Jasus, I was just going to kiss you."

"Maybe. But you'll get no free samples before our wedding night, Brian Carlyle. Meanwhile, if you'll let go my hand, I'll see about writing your check."

He watched, bemused, as Dawn got out her papers and prepared to finance his engineering project. She noted the puzzled smile on his face and asked, defensively, "What's so funny?"

"I was just wondering whether I'll curse meself the more if I fail to complete me road on time," he said. "Or if I'll win our bet and, winning it, forego me chance to pay the forfeit!"

The Indian was a stranger, but Dawn knew from his headband he was Miwok. He stood in the clearing, ignoring the Mexican workmen around him until Dawn came out of the cabin to ask what he wanted. Then he said, "Spotted Elk sent me. There is an old man camped up the slope. We think he is dying and he is not a bad person."

"Is he sick or hungry? Which band does he hunt with?"

"He is sick, or maybe just old. He hunts with no band of Real People. He is not one of us, but he shared tobacco with White Condor once, and another time he gave a child some funny sweet stuff. Spotted Elk thought you might be able to help him."

"I can try. I didn't know there were any White Eyes up on that part of the mountain."

"He is not a White Eyes. He is not a Real Person, either. We don't know what he is, but he has a good heart. Will you come?"

Dawn nodded and went inside to fetch the box of supplies she used to attend the cuts and bruises of her workmen and their dependents. The Indian youth led the way, walking slow for a Digger, without comment on Dawn's obvious inability to keep up with a Real Person in her boots and skirt. A trio of her Mexicans started to follow, but Dawn waved them back, knowing they made her Indian friends as nervous as they made the Mexicans.

The young Indian took her to a small lean-to hidden in a shallow draw two-thirds of the way to the ridge. The sick man, whoever he was, was on her land. That was odd, but not important if he was really ill.

Dawn had expected Spotted Elk and his followers to be waiting at the camp of the prospector they'd apparently befriended, but there was not a soul in sight as the guide pointed at the lean-to. "He is inside. Maybe he is still alive."

Dawn stepped over to the lean-to and lifted the canvas flap of the improvised doorway. An odd odor assailed her nostrils as she peered in at a shapeless form huddled under a blue blanket. There was the slight sound of breathing, but when Dawn called "How are you feeling?" a husky voice replied in a singsong language she couldn't understand.

She turned to ask the Indian a question and saw she was alone. The Ho, she knew, were nervous about dead bodies. The young guide had braved the sight of Changing Woman by coming this close to the camp of a dying man if in fact the stranger was dying.

Dawn stooped inside and knelt by the sick prospector's side, gingerly pulling the blanket away from his face.

She blinked in surprise at the frightened almond eyes regarding her. Though she'd seen Chinese in San Francisco, she'd hardly expected one as a neighbor in the mother lode country.

Again she asked how he felt, and this time the man managed to croak, "Wong belly bad. Wong belong die chop-chop, me savvy."

"Where are you hurting, Mister Wong? I have some medicine with me, though I'm no doctor."

The little old Chinese smiled fatalistically. "Better you go, now, missy. Wong belly sick. Missy no can fixum. Wong belong dead."

Seeing that she was in over her head, Dawn said, "I'll be right back, Mister Wong."

Then she started to retrace her steps down to the cabin. Partway down the slope, she saw her foreman, Pablo, moving cautiously uphill with a rifle. She called out to him, ordering him back to her camp to get help. Then she returned to the sick old Chinese, wondering, though it seemed impossible, if he could be the Lost Chinaman of the oddly named settlement.

Her second inspection found Wong asleep or unconscious. Dawn put a hand on his brow and he seemed to have no fever, so there was little point in trying to get any quinine down him.

Dawn was joined in a few minutes by Pablo and three other workmen. At Pablo's direction they cut a pair of saplings and improvised a litter. As they were moving the old man into position on it, Wong sobbed

something and reached feebly for a buckskin bag
Dawn hadn't noticed in the darkness and litter of the
squalid little shelter. Dawn placed it in his thin hand
and the old Chinese clutched it tightly to his chest,
crooning something in his own language without opening his eyes. Dawn said, "We'll bring all your possibles
down to my cabin, Mister Wong. You just lie still and
let us worry about it, hear?"

As they lifted the litter, Pablo asked, "Are you
thinking of having *el chino* in your cabin, señora?"

Dawn said, "I can't think of a better place to care
for him. Did you know he was up here, señor?"

"Of course not, señora. We would have run him off
your claim had we known. You said it was all right if
los indios gathered acorns on the property, but, *Madre
de Dios, this* one's a *chino!*"

"He's probably been skulking up here for years, like
a hermit. I wonder what he's been doing here."

"That I can tell you, señora. You gave him back the
poke of gold he has been stealing from your claim.
I know *los chinos.* They have been known to sneak
into mines at night, to help themselves to high grade
ore. They have no faith. Hence they have no honor."

"He hasn't been in the Sweet Petunia. Our night
watch would have caught him. I don't think there's
any gold up here, either. The quartz ends halfway up
the slope."

Pablo reached out and pulled the leather poke from
the unconscious man's clutching fingers. "Wherever he
stole it, señora, it is no longer his." Then, even as
Dawn told him to put it back, Pablo hefted the bag
with a frown. "It is too light for gold. What has the
pobrecito been stealing?"

Curious herself, Dawn allowed Pablo to open the
poke. He poured a couple of green pebbles out in his

free palm and frowned. "It is not gold. The idiot has a poke filled with common pebbles!"

Dawn said, "Well, put them back and let him keep them. He seemed very attached to them and they may be some sort of Chinese magic to him."

Pablo did as he was told and they carried the dying man to her cabin despite Pablo's insistence that it was wrong for her to have a heathen oriental under her roof.

For the next two days and nights, Dawn and her helpers nursed the mysterious and obviously very ill Chinese called Wong. They had no idea what was wrong with him, so there was little they could do but clean him up and try to get some liquid food into him. On the third night, either because Dawn's rough nursing had helped or simply because he felt a bit better near the end, Wong opened his eyes.

Dawn was unaware of it at first. She was seated at the fire, smoking, and reading a book by the flickering light when, somehow, she felt eyes on her and turned to smile at the pale yellow parchment face staring at her from the bunk across the room.

Wong licked his lips and tried to gather his thoughts, for the tongue of the Western barbarians grated on the mind and the words were so very hard in one's mouth. Then he said huskily, "I am Wong Lung How. I die chop-chop, I think. How I come along this place?"

"You're in my cabin at the Sweet Petunia, Mister Wong. My name is Dawn Purvis, and we don't want you to die, so you'll just have to get better."

"You missy belong along Sweet Petunia? Wong hear white lady own mine belly tough, my word. Wong hide long time. Lady no see."

He suddenly looked concerned, groped around on the mattress until he felt the poke Dawn had placed beside him under the blanket and relaxed, sighing, "Lady no take Wong's *yu?* Wong no savvy, but Wong belly glad."

"Are you talking about that poke of rocks, Mister Wong? Nobody's going to steal it from you. Your other possibles are in the shed, out back." Then she frowned and asked, "What was that you called it?"

"*Yu.* Amelicans call 'em jade. Wong find belly much *yu* in Califolly, my word. If Wong no die, Wong go home belly lich man. But now Wong die and allisame nebah go home so . . ."

"You just hush and we'll see about that, Mister Wong." Dawn leaned forward. "Do you know what you've got? It doesn't seem to be a fever and it doesn't seem to be a cough."

The old man sighed and said, "Wong no savvy why. Wong just savvy he die. You light fo' Wong, missy?"

"You want me to light the lamp?"

"No lighty lamp. Lighty paper, if you can."

"Oh, you mean you want me to write something for you?"

"Hai, that what Wong say, light on paper fo' Wong. Wong gottem blalah in San Francisco. Bye and bye, when Wong die, if missy bling paper along blalah, blalah send Wong's bones along Canton, you savvy?"

"You want me to tell your people in San Francisco you're sick, eh?"

"No, me want you tellum Wong dead. You takum *yu*, me mean jade. Blalah belong along San Francisco, pay you for tell him where Wong's bones hidee. You gottom jade. You gottom gold belong along Wong's tong, too. You do this, missy?"

"You just tell me how to find your folks and I'll see that they get word. I'll see that they get the rocks, too, seeing as you set such store by them."

Dawn got some writing paper and a pencil to take down the address of the dying man's brother in San Francisco's Chinatown. When she was done, Wong asked her, "You no savvy jade, missy?"

"Oh, I know what it is. They make rings and things out of it, don't they?"

"Yes, missy. Jade belly good. More bettah than gold, to Wong's people. You tell Wong something tlue, missy?"

"What's that, Mister Wong?"

"You know jade good joss, yet you no takum! You find Wong on plopety, yet you no get mad and hittem. You take Wong in you house and tly make bettah. You belly funny Amelican, missy."

"Oh, heavens, you weren't bothering anybody, and you were sick."

"Hai. You give Wong paper and lighting stickee. Wong light little bit fo' blalah, yes?"

Dawn went over to the bunk, and with her help Wong managed to scrawl a few Chinese characters under the address Dawn had written down. Then, exhausted by the effort, he closed his eyes and said, "Wong go sleep now, missy."

He was wrong. He didn't sleep that night. He died about ten minutes later.

Six months later, an angry, puzzled Brian Carlyle returned to Dawn's camp just as the sun was going down. Dawn met him at her door, and his defeated smile turned to a look of amazement as he stared at her swollen abdomen. "Jasus, is it herself's *expecting?*"

Dawn nodded. "I'm about seven or eight months along. Come inside, Brian. I've been waiting for you."

He followed her in. "You heard about the trouble we've been having down near El Dorado, then?"

"I heard something about Indians making off with your stock. I'm afraid I don't know the details."

"You don't, eh? Isn't it funny now, dear Dawn, how of all the men in this part of California, I alone seem to be having trouble with thieving Diggers?"

"Well, you know how hungry they are this time of the year."

"Do I, now? I know one thing for certain, Dawn Purvis. I know you're thick as thieves with half the Diggers in California, and I'm after learning you're a woman who's used to getting her own way!"

"Why, whatever do you mean, Brian?"

"Jasus, let's not be after beating about the bushes. It's too transparent, even for a poor Paddy like meself. You didn't want me to finish those last few miles of road, did you?"

"Are you suggesting I asked the Indians to steal your stock to slow you down?"

"Suggesting it, me eyebrow! I'm saying it! The deal is off, Dawn Purvis. You'll get your money, and with interest, for I've new stock and extra guards, but you'll have to wait, and sure, it's your own doing."

"You intend to break your word, then?"

"Mary, Mother of God! The woman sends her Indians to stop me and twits me about false words! I can see why you need a husband, lass, but you'll have to trap another man some other way. That's me last word on the matter, save to warn you to keep them damned Indians away from me camp if you value their red hides!"

"Oh, heavens, if I'd wanted to trap you, I'd have let you sleep with me six months ago and blamed this baby on you."

He tried to keep frowning. Then his grin betrayed him. "Ay, it might have worked, too. Why'd you sic them Indians on me with an arrow like that in your quiver, lass?"

"I trap my prey fair and square. You want some coffee?"

"Jasus, you admit your scheming ways, then?"

"Well, you seem to have them figured out. Is there any use in my denying anything?"

Relieved, he guffawed and slapped his thigh. "Well, in that case I'll have the coffee and a promise of no more tricks. We'll say no more of it."

Dawn nodded and put the coffee on to boil, taking a seat by the fire and smiling demurely in her apparent defeat. Mollified, Carlyle sat down at the table, facing her, and said, "We've got little more than a quarter mile to go. Me tollgate's built and I'll be after starting to repay you in a few weeks at the most. Do you want it sent up here to you or deposited to your account in Sacramento?"

"We'll have to work it out with the bank, Brian. I won't be here in two weeks. I just sold the mine."

"You *what?*"

"Sold the mine. I'm moving down to the capital."

"Ah, the baby and all, eh?"

"Oh, no. You see, the vein's about played out. Some men from an eastern syndicate were in Lost Chinaman investigating mine holdings, and I thought I'd better sell before word got around that the Sweet Petunia was played out. My workers are loyal, but it's hard to keep a thing like that to oneself, you see."

"That's for damned sure. What sort of a price did they offer?"

"Two hundred thousand. It should be enough to last me a while, even in the capital."

His jaw dropped and he gasped, "You got two hundred thousand for a hole in the ground? Jasus, were the tenderfoots blind as well as rich?"

"Oh, I'm afraid I played a little trick on them. You see, I never told them the mine was played out."

"Nobody ever does, but didn't they look at it?"

"Of course. They had a mining engineer from the East with them. I led them to the working face and they could see the vein was pinching. I explained the labor was eating up my profits as the amount of worthless rock we had to dig increased. I suppose they thought they were taking advantage of a poor young widow in a family way, don't you?"

Brian frowned, shook his head, and insisted, "Back up, there's something missing. How in the name of Jasus did you get them to buy out a pinched vein for all that money? You're holding something back, for I can see that fairy smile in your eyes, lass. How'd you work it?"

"Oh, that was easy. I took some dust, loaded both barrels of Gus Swensen's old double-barrel shotgun, and . . ."

"You little witch! You salted your shaft!"

"Well, sort of. I found a few veins of barren quartz my miners had passed up, fired a few ounces of gold dust into the rock and—" She broke out laughing and added, "You should have seen them, Brian! I led them right by the salted veins, as if I never suspected there was a speck of gold in those side lodes, and they almost broke their faces trying not to let on they'd spotted color in what I said was dross quartz. They nodded and hemmed and hawed about the pinched vein I showed them, and later, when I had ever so much trouble letting go my dear old daddy's mine, they kept upping the ante like a Chinaman playing three-card montel"

Carlyle roared and slapped his knee. Then he got his laughter under control and asked, "Won't they come after you, once they know there's no gold to speak of in the Sweet Petunia?"

"I don't see how they can, dear. I told them the truth, you see."

"Bejasus, I do see, and that's a fact. Och, are they ever going to feel the fools, though, once they learn they've been' sold an empty hole in the mountain! You're a cunning wee thing, Dawn Purvis of the big innocent eyes. Faith, I'm proud to be the match for you, though, for your other wee trick didn't work on meself, as near as you came before I figured it out."

"Well, some men are smarter than others. Coffee's ready, dear."

She poured them two cups and Brian sipped in re- stored good humor, going so far as to opine, "Your coffee's improving, too. If ever you do trap a father for that child you're after expecting, he'll be as well off as many a man, and that's the truth of it."

Dawn resumed her place by the fire and sipped her own cup, saying nothing. After a time, Carlyle said, "You really did sic them Indians on me, didn't you?"

"If you say so. What does it matter? You've told me you don't want me under any conditions."

"Well, I never said that, lass. I said I wouldn't be tricked into anything by a scheming woman—and admit it, you've grown to a woman with a fearsome will, and that's a fact."

"Drink your coffee and we'll say no more about it,

then. I'll just have to wait for my money and you . . .
No doubt you'll find a woman more to your liking, once
you've had time to start looking."

"Bejasus, I'll not be made to feel guilty about being
late with your money. Damn it, me delays and troubles
were your own doing, Dawn Purvis!"

"I'm not arguing, dear. Perhaps it's just as well you
saw through me. I'm not sure we could make a go of
it, anyhow. You're too strong a man, and as you say,
I'm too willful a woman. We both need someone
weaker and perhaps not quite so smart."

"Ah, Jasus, you think I don't see through that act
of yours either, don't you?"

Dawn laughed and said, "I give up. I've never been
able to pull the wool over your eyes, Irish!"

"Well, by the mother of God, you've tried. When's
that kid of yours expected, anyway?"

"I'm not sure. A month or two, why?"

"I'll adopt it, once it's born, but it'll have to be born
as Purvis, for I'll not have that sort of gossip about us,
once we're wed."

"Are we getting married, then? I thought you said
you'd seen through me and that the deal was off."

Brian put down his cup and fixed her with a mock
scowl. "I did and it is, for I'll not be tricked and I'll
not be badgered. A dacent woman waits for himself to
ask her before she sics a pack of naked Diggers on
him, and I'll have no more tricks."

"I don't understand you, Brian. First you say we
are and now you say . . ."

"Jasus, if you'd shut up and let me finish, I'd get to
the heart of me delicate proposing. You're a woman to
match me mountains, Dawn. I'll marry you and be
proud of it, but I do what I want, when I want, on me
own terms. Is that understood?"

"You're the boss, dear."

"That's what I was just after telling you. Now, do you want to marry up here in Lost Chinaman or do we settle accounts in Sacramento?"

"Whatever you say, Brian. Do you want some more coffee?"

"No. I have to get back to work. I'll be back in three days. Will that give you time to pack and be ready to follow me to Sacramento?"

Dawn smiled into the fire and said, "It will have to be, won't it?"

They were married in Sacramento, Brain insisting on a rectory service in the frame Catholic church near the waterfront, where he glared through the brief ceremony at an elderly priest who'd made no comment on Dawn's obvious condition.

After the mother lode country, Sacramento seemed a city worthy to rival San Francisco in Dawn's eyes, though both were mushroom towns of raw lumber, muddy streets, and unplanned sprawl.

The house he'd rented with an option to buy was the first real house she could remember visiting, let alone being mistress of it all. Dawn wanted to furnish it with her own money, but Brian insisted she bank her profits from the sale of the Sweet Petunia with her other funds. He gave her an account with the merchants of the river port, which enabled her to furnish all fourteen rooms to her heart's content. Brian's only contribution to the interior decor was an insistence on lace curtains for every window. Back in his native Boston, Celtic society had been divided into those who had lace curtains visible from the street and those who did not. On this one point he was adamant. She could have had a stuffed moose in every room.

It was a dark-brown time for interior decoration, no matter how much or how little was being spent. This was partly because the fashion-setting Queen Victoria's taste ran to somber colors, and partly because a world heated by coal and wood dictated draperies and furnishings that didn't show soot. The walls had been papered in black-striped maroon before they moved in. Dawn's uneducated but not naturally vulgar taste ran to simplicity, for the era. The heavy mahogany furniture, upholstered in maroon plush or dark red morocco leather, blended well with the maroon interior draperies and sepia prints in dull gilt frames she chose for the front parlor. A small sewing room off the main hall was well illuminated by a north light, and it was on these walls, above the new Singer machine Brian had bought her, that she hung her Indian baskets of warm earth colors. The ground floor, from front entrance to kitchen door, was as sedate as anyone could wish, although for California a bit conservative.

Upstairs, Dawn allowed her fancy more play. Brian, on first seeing the master bedroom, smiled and said, "Jasus, it looks like an expensive San Francisco whorehouse. Where'd you ever find gilt brocade and blood-red velvet in Sacramento, lass?"

"Don't you like it, dearest? I thought we'd have more color up here."

"Och, I like it fine, lass. But all that gilt will be turning green as soon as the soot settles into things up here."

"Our window faces west, into the prevailing breeze and across the river, dear. Let me show you the nursery. I wanted to be sure the baby has light and cross ventilation."

Brian followed her into the next room, keeping his thoughts to himself. He'd agreed the coming child would bear his last name, and Dawn had suggested, if it was a boy, they name him August after her late father, the long-lost Gus Swensen. Secretly, Brian was hoping for a girl. The late Ace Purvis had been a puny wee thing, and if the child took after its father, he'd be the shortest Carlyle in recorded Waterford history.

Brian pronounced the nursery a success and said something about getting back to work. Dawn asked if he wasn't having his midday dinner at home, but he said, "I'm riding out this afternoon to survey the new waterline from Placerville, lass. The way this town's been growing, the wells are giving out."

"I've noticed the water from my kitchen pump is brackish. Do you think it's safe to drink?"

"It is for now, but it won't be this time next year. The salt from the bay is working up through the water table, between all the new wells in town and the irrigation pumps around the city. I'm building the dam at Placerville on shares, but I've told the city council it's pay as they go on the aqueduct. The tolls we're collecting on our mountain road won't keep us and me work crew going." He kissed her absently on the forehead. "And now I'm off."

He left, and Dawn went down to the kitchen to tell the Mexican cook, Felicidad, they'd be eating alone for the next few days. Brian hadn't said so, but she knew he'd be away the better part of the week. This habit of her new husband's was a thing she'd have to learn to live with, she supposed. She'd known when she set her cap for him that Brian was an engineer. She hadn't considered the amount of time his hammering California into shape was going to steal from her.

Perhaps when the baby came things would be a little less lonely. She knew the child would keep her busy, and she knew how little, really, she had to offer

Brian under his own roof, for though they were married, her condition precluded lovemaking.

Leaving the Mexican girl to make dinner, Dawn went into her sewing room to run up another set of diapers for the coming event. She sat at her Singer, pleased with the wonders of modern civilization as she worked the foot treadle and guided the yard goods through the magically dancing stitcher. Isaac Singer's invention freed a woman's mind as well as her fingers, and she found herself daydreaming of what it would be like, once she had her figure back. Brian was a man to fit her frustrated dreams about having made love to Nevada, the lost love of her girlhood. Save for that one exciting memory of the night in Gus Swensen's arms, Dawn knew she'd missed years of real lovemaking while married to little Ace Purvis. She'd never seen Nevada or even Brian in the nude, but she assumed that since both were bigger than the late Gus Swensen, she had much to look forward to.

The cook came in to say "Señora, there is a man at the door. He say he has business with yourself."

Dawn said, "Well, show him in, Felicidad. I'll receive him in the parlor."

"*Por favor*, señora. The man is a *chino!*"

"A Chinese? Oh, I 'spect it's about poor Mister Wong. You go back to the kitchen, dear. I'll tend to it."

Felicidad did as she was told, muttering to herself, as Dawn went to the door and admitted a grave middle-aged man in a deep-green coat with a choke collar and wide sleeves. Like others of his generation, the Chinese wore the front of his head shaved, and his remaining steel-gray hair hung down behind him in a long braided queue. As Dawn greeted him, he bowed stiffly and said, "I am Wong Fu, Mrs. Carlyle. I have taken the liberty of coming here on my late brother's request. You are the lady who sent us his belongings and news of his death, are you not?"

"Oh, you must be the brother he talked about. Let's sit in here, shall we? My word, you do speak tolerable English, Mister Wong. I'm afraid I had a time understanding your poor brother."

"He was not given to conversing with your kind, madam. I am a business man in San Francisco, and let us face it, Wong Lung How was eccentric."

Dawn waved him to a seat and asked, "Would you like some coffee, sir?" But the Chinese remained on his feet and said, "No, thank you. My, um, business with you can be settled with few words and while you seem to be the sort of person my late brother indicated in his last message to us, others may not approve of your hospitality."

"Heavens, it's my house, Mr. Wong."

"Just so, and I am—shall we say?—a chink." He permitted himself a dry smile before adding, softly, "A white lady must be cautious with the sons of Han, madam. Has not your husband warned you of this?"

"My husband is a gentleman, Mister Wong, as was your poor brother when I found him dying up in the hills. Did you come here to trade insults, or is there something I can do for you?"

"Forgive me, madam. My uneasiness has made me rude. Your treatment of my dying brother was not unheard of. I am not unaware that some of your people are kind. But tell me, did you really know what was in that bag you sent to us with your message?"

"You mean the jade? Of course I know what jade is. My husband says you people value it more highly than gold."

"We do, madam. The jade my brother collected will more than pay for shipping his remains back to Canton. There is the matter to be settled about his having found some of it on your mining claim."

"I don't care where he found it. It was his. I know there's jade up in the mother lode and that some people have been selling a little of it from time to time. But . . ."

"I must tell you, as an honest merchant, madam, that the bag of jade you sent us was worth triple its weight in gold. By rights, you have a claim to a share in my brother's find."

"Well, I don't want it. I'd have never known he had it, or that he was even there, if he hadn't gotten sick. So I'd say we were even, wouldn't you?"

Wong sighed and said, "My brother was right. You are what he said you were, a simple, decent human being. You leave me no choice in the matter. I must pay you for your kindness to him."

"Damn it, Mister Wong, you don't owe me anything for the little I was able to do for your brother. I'm sorry he was too far gone when I found him to do more than make him comfortable and send word to you. What I did was simple Christian charity."

"I am familiar with Christian charity, Mrs. Carlyle," the elderly merchant cut in, taking a small red silk purse from his sleeve. "My brother wanted you to have this. My people have customs of their own, though, frankly, I thought he assumed too much when he wrote his last message to me. Now that we have spoken, I feel he may have been right."

Dawn opened the little purse and took out a heavy gold ring with Chinese characters engraved in its face. It was obviously a seal of some sort. She slipped it on her finger and said, "It's lovely, Mr. Wong. I'll be honored to wear it in memory of your poor brother."

"Please, madam, hide the seal of Ong Leong away

and tell no one you have it until the time comes, if it ever does, that you have need for it."

"Need for it? What is it, Mr. Wong, a wishing ring?"

"No. It is the secret seal of Ong Leong. My late brother and I were initiated as young men into a certain, shall we say, society. He wanted to ensure your future as best as he was able and directed that you be given the Power."

"Power? Power to do what, Mr. Wong?"

"To call upon Ong Leong Tong, if and when you ever have need of our services. If you press that seal into wax and send it to me at my San Francisco address, men will come to do your bidding."

"Heavens, you mean I can use this to call up a bunch of Chinese? What would I ever do with them, Mr. Wong?"

"Anything you wished, Mrs. Carlyle. If you need money, they will bring you money. If you need protection, they will protect you. If you desire revenge, they will avenge you. Your claim on us is limited only by our powers to satisfy your request."

Dawn laughed and said, "Good Lord, you remind me of one of my husband's stories about the wee people! How many magic wishes do I get with this ring of fairy gold, sir?"

"Within reason, as many as you need. My late brother, in his youth, was a hatchet man. His claims on Ong Leong were very strong, and you were given every one of them with his dying breath."

Dawn removed the ring and replaced it in the purse, not knowing what to say and not sure she felt comfortable with the odd bequest. Wong reached in his voluminous sleeve again and took out a small ivory figure, handing it to her. "This is my own small token of my esteem, madam. If you find it barbarous to your taste, I will understand."

"Oh, it's so lovely!" Dawn protested, holding the serene little carving up to the light. "It looks like a little Chinese princess, and my, isn't she a friendly little thing? Do I have to hide her away too, Mr. Wong?"

Wong said, "No, she is proudly displayed in certain Chinese homes."

"Well, then I'll just put her up here on my mantel, where everyone can see her. Does she have a name, or is she just a beautiful Chinese lady, Mr. Wong?"

Wong's face softened as he lowered his eyes and murmured, "Her name is Kuan Yin. Even before meeting you, I knew she belonged in the house of a sister."

Dawn forced her lips around the unfamiliar name and mused, "You call her Kuan Yin? Well, she's awfully pretty and I thank you for her. Was she a famous Chinese beauty or something?"

"She was, once," explained Wong, adding, "It is written that a lovely girl named Kuan Yin gave up her place in paradise for a frightened sinner. Lord Buddha, taking pity on her, and in honor of her good deed, transformed her into his guardian angel of mercy."

"Oh, what a nice story. That explains her sweet friendly expression, doesn't it?"

The first of Dawn's sons was born that fall at home in Sacramento. To Brian's puzzled relief, he seemed a strong lusty boy. Brian would always assume he took after his mother's side, for Swensen was a Norse name, after all, and while his wife was not a woman of great size, he'd heard her father, the old miner who'd lost her as a baby and only found her again just before he died, had been a big raw-boned Swede. The late Ace Purvis had once mentioned being the runt of his own litter, too, so Brian assumed that the boy, christened August Xavier Carlyle, wouldn't take after his real father after all.

The birth had been an easy one, and Dawn recovered from her uncomplicated lying-in within days. Her figure, if anything, was improved by having borne a child, for to Brian's way of thinking she'd been a whalebone and whipcord little thing. Nursing the baby seemed to soften her a bit, and her almost Indian tan was fading to a becoming shade of old ivory, due to the softer light of the Sacramento delta country and her new habit of wearing hats.

Their first real wedding night, celebrated in the privacy of their red-draped four-poster, was more than Brian dreamed it would be, but less than Dawn expected. Brian was a lusty bull of a man who ate steak and potatoes with every meal, and his lovemaking, while vigorous, was as simple and direct as his other appetites.

He was virile, his stamina awesome, and he'd been endowed by nature with a big muscular body and an almost frightening penis. But after her first orgasm, Dawn couldn't help wondering what it would have been like to make love to a man endowed with Brian's virility and little Ace's imagination.

She couldn't suggest it, she knew. Brian had twitted her more than once about poor Ace, and she'd lulled his sexual jealousy by assuring him he was twice the man, in every way, her first husband had been. Brian's penetration was twice, or mayhaps thrice, as thrilling, and each time, she'd sigh softly, "Oh, my, *yes*, this is so *nice!*"

But then, as her husky lover pumped on and on, almost like one of the steam pile drivers he was using to build that new dock down by the river, she'd find herself wishing they could change positions, for God's sake! With some difficulty she'd gotten him to make love without that damned flannel night shirt he'd shyly worn to bed the first night, though he insisted she wear at least the black lace peignoir he'd bought her, explaining, when she protested, that it wasn't "dacent" for a woman to sleep in the nude.

Lace excited Brian, probably more than her naked form might have, and since it opened down the front, the black lace lent a certain bordello excitement to their otherwise plebian frontal sex. She toyed with the idea of black stockings and presenting her derriere to him as a surprise, but while the idea intrigued her, she didn't have the nerve.

Cunnilingus, she knew, would strike him as a terrible perversion. In a moment of post-coital candor he'd mentioned that Frenchmen—a race he placed on a par with the English and lower than Mexicans—made war with their feet and love with their mouth.

Some of Ace's other love games had never appealed to Dawn while she'd lived with him. Yet sometimes as she lay in Brian's arms she'd catch herself fantasizing about them, combining the two men, or even Gus or Nevada, into impossible orgies. Her passion at such times was accepted by Brian as the natural response to his own virility, a prowess he accepted as his due for hard work and clean living.

Dawn found herself pregnant again within months and accepted this with neither bitterness nor regret. A little brother or sister would be good for baby Gus and a welcome break in what was becoming, for Dawn, routine.

Brian's comings and goings, like his lovemaking, were neither unpleasant nor surprising. As an engineer he was in his element, for the new raw state was in need of men who knew the arts he'd studied in the East. He was away as often as he was home, riding out on surveys or supervising the construction of roads, bridges, dams, and irrigation projects. The second child was a daughter, Rose Maureen, and Brian gained a bit in Dawn's estimation by showing no more favor to the child he knew to be his than he lavished on little Gus.

Dawn was mildly annoyed by her husband's attitude toward her mind, however, for he tended to treat his young wife much as he did the children. Brian brought home gifts for the three of them, and Dawn knew he'd have faced wildcats bare-fisted for any of them. But he refused to discuss "men's business" with her. Dawn's own money from the sale of the Sweet Petunia was hers, he said, to do with as she liked. Yet when she tried to discuss investments or the bewildering political situation in the East, he dismissed her as not having the ability to fathom what he considered manly mysteries. Hence she was forced to follow the Lincoln-Douglas debates in the newspapers, keeping her opinions to herself, for her husband was a registered Whig and didn't think either the Southern Democrats or the new Republican party would amount to much in California politics.

Dawn had been taught by Nevada to ride a horse with a gentle hand on the reins, and so she didn't argue, even when she saw, as time went by, that Brian was more of an engineer than a businessman, and hopeless as a political forecaster.

It took Brian some time to discover this, and had he been a less secure man, the shocking fact that his wife had been thinking and acting on her own might have led to a fearsome row. As it was, it led only to a friendly argument.

It happened one night at supper when Brian admitted, sheepishly, that he'd taken a terrible beating on the Pony Express.

"I'll never understand how the Pony Express went bankrupt," he said, over the steak and mashed potatoes he never seemed to tire of.

Dawn smiled fondly at him acrosss the candlelit table and said, "They paid too much for horses and equipment, dear. The telegraph line had been planned even before they started the overland mail, so everyone should have known it was just a stopgap until the wire reached the coast. With it almost here, everyone's stopped sending mail, so . . ."

"Och, how were they to know Western Union would string them wires in less than eighteen months, lass? Jasus, if we'd have stuck with the ponies another three years or so, the original investment would have paid us back. There's no way to send a letter or package over that newfangled wire, even now. Do you suppose, when the novelty wears off . . .?"

"The Pony Express was too expensive for any but urgent messages, dearest. Those riders did a fine job while it lasted, but it's over. Nobody's going to pay ten dollars an ounce for mail when they can get it the same day over the wire."

"I know. It's to be slow mail by overland coach and important news by the damned Western Union's wire, and I've devil a cent to show for it."

"Look at the bright side, dear. California will have the news from East the same day, now."

"Och, the telegraph's a wonder and the world has shrunk since Morse came up with such a grand idea. I just didn't think our world would be after shrinking on us so suddenly. I'm afraid I've lost us a bundle on the ponies, darling."

Dawn hesitated. Then she said, "I put a few dollars into Western Union a year ago, dear. I didn't think you'd mind."

Brian looked up from his plate and gasped, "You did *what*, lass?"

"I bought five hundred shares of Western Union. It was from my own account, and you said I was to use it as I wished."

"I meant for the house, damn it! You had no right to play the stock market without telling me about it, Dawn!"

"Would you have approved?"

"Five hundred shares of a mad electrician's dream? Of course I wouldn't have approved! You could have lost the whole thing, betting on the wire!"

"I know, dearest, but I seem to have doubled my original investment. I read in the papers last week that Western Union shares are up one hundred. So I don't suppose any harm was done, do you?"

Brian stared at her for a time and tried to look fierce. Then, despite himself, he grinned. "If you'll forgive me losing on the Pony Express, I'll overlook your madness, just this once. What else have you been after buying behind me back? And don't say you haven't, for I know that fairy gleam in your eye, Mrs. Carlyle."

Dawn smiled shyly and said, "Well, I haven't been investing so much as moving things about. You remember that stock I held in the Butterfield Stage Line?"

"Ay, a good investment it was, too, even if it was meself advised you to buy it before we were wed."

"Well, I traded my Butterfield stock at par for Wells Fargo, after reading about the fight in Washington about the overland mail routes."

"Jasus, I've been reading longer than yourself and

I'll be damned if I can see any difference between the two stage lines, north or south."

"There'll be a tremendous change in the traffic if Texas follows through on its threats, dear. The Butterfield line runs through Apache Pass, and if war breaks out between the Southern states and the Union . . ."

"*War!*" he cut in, "who in thunder said there was to be a war? Them eastern politicians have been arguing abolition for a generation and—"

"And Lincoln's election has brought it to a head," she insisted. "The Whigs have waffled over the issue with the Democrats for years, but Lincoln's new Republican party means to put it to the acid test. I've known a few Texans, and I don't think they'll back down, so for the time being the Butterfield Stage will be out of the running. Wells Fargo, on the other hand, runs over South Pass and across the Nevada desert from the northern midwest states. Aside from having a safer route, they're in banking as well as transportation, so the stock is on sounder footing than Butterfield's, even without trouble with Apache and Texas guerrillas. All in all, I think I was lucky to trade at par, don't you?"

He clucked indulgently, at his child-wife's untoward babblings on a subject far beyond a woman's grasp. "Playing the stock market and forecasting war, bejasus! You've grown a cocky wee head since you left them Indians and learned to read, Dawn Carlyle. You know you're wrong, don't you? I have it from me friends in the party that us Whigs have enough power in Congress to force another compromise, once Lincoln and them Southern Democrats wear themselves down with all their wild talk of state's rights and the Union forever. Ay, and in the next election we'll pick up the pieces, too!"

Dawn was smiling calmly. "I don't think so, dearest. Since John Brown's raid, the country's not in the mood for compromise. I'm afraid the Whigs are finished as a party. They've avoided taking a stand so long that the ground's been cut from under their shilly-shally position. Your Whig friends will have to switch to either Democrat or Republican if they hope to be elected dogcatcher in any town, north or south."

"Och, let's get off politics! It's a dirty business for a man to be thinking about, let alone a woman. I'll grant your ideas on the stage lines make sense, so what do you think of me buying them shares in the new mines near Murphy's Camp?"

Dawn shrugged and said, "We know the gold is there, but I'd get out of gold if I were you. The easy placers and veins have been skimmed, and there's more money to be made these days in land and lumber."

Carlyle quickly disagreed. "Och, there's land and lumber to be had for little more than the asking, lass. The Great Valley's only a third settled, and as for lumber, there's naught but trees between Frisco and the Oregon line."

"I know, dear. That's why I've been buying it. While it's still cheap. The lands that are easy to irrigate have mostly been claimed and they're cutting the last redwoods south of San Francisco right now. I have an option on some timberlands near Red Bluff—"

"Timber near Red Bluff, woman? Have you gone daft? Of course there's timber near Red Bluff. The whole damned country's a solid forest!"

"It won't be for long, dear. Once again, the cream's been skimmed. I was lucky to get the timber rights to land right above the river. When the price is right, *my* logs will be easy to float to market. The man who sold me the municipal bonds says they're going to be building a new subdivision, east of town."

"You bought what, goddamm it? You let them sell you on Sacramento's worthless municipal bonds? Jasus, what's the matter with you? Why didn't you ask me about them bonds?"

"Oh, you were out on a survey, and I guess it slipped my mind by the time you got back."

He looked at Dawn sharply. "Ay, I know what a dull mind you have. You outfoxed yourself on Sacramento bonds, though. I have it on good authority that the capital will soon be moving to Frisco, once and for all."

"I don't think so, dearest. I know they've been arguing about it for years, but the people in Pueblo de Los Angeles will never stand for a capital in San Francisco, and San Francisco will go to war before it sees the capital moved to Los Angeles, and anyway, Sacramento will have to grow, capital or not. It's the natural outlet for the produce of the Great Valley as well as the transshipping point for the gold fields. Besides, I only put a little money into municipal bonds, and the interest rate's over six percent, so—"

"Back up and tell me what you're after calling only a little money, lass. I've a right to know it if me wife's a self-made pauper."

Dawn murmured, "Oh, I invested less than ten thousand in them. Finish your plate. I had Felicidad make that deep-dish pie you like so much."

Brian shook his head and might have made a cutting remark had not the front doorbell started ringing insistently. Brian got to his feet. "I'll tend to it, lass. I left word with the party to send a message about the situation back east."

Dawn waited for him as Felicidad cleared the table for coffee and dessert. Brian returned with a puzzled frown and resumed his place, muttering, "Jasus, they've gone mad at the statehouse and that's a fact."

"What's happened? You look worried."

"Do I? Well, mayhaps it's because I am. You know I'm beholden to me party for the public works contracts I've been getting, don't you?"

"Of course. Public works and politics go hand in hand."

"Ay, and the hands are after trembling. Your darling telegraph hasn't put the Pony Express out of business just yet, for a rider just arrived with the latest news from the East, and all of it's bad!"

"What is it, Brian? What's happening in Washington."

"Och, it's happening all over. The Southern states are pulling out of the Union and Lincoln's called out the militia! It looks like you were right about Texas, and them fools at the California Statehouse want *my* advice! The Democrats are voting to side with the South and the Black Republicans are for the Union— and no Whig born of mortal woman has ever been able to make up his mind on any subject!"

"I hope you told them you're for the Union?"

"I told them I was after making roads and bridges, not civil wars. I don't care which way California goes, as long as it goes some damned way, bejasus!"

"Darling, you're going to have to take a public stand for the Union if you aim to stay in business!"

"Oh, I am, am I? What makes you so sure this state will stay with the Union, Fey Woman of the Western World?"

"It's simple. The Union's going to win and the men who've come out here are a winning breed. You can call it fey, or you can call it common sense, but if you value your hide, you'll do as I say for a change!"

He started to grumble. Then he shrugged and said, "Well, you were right about the war coming. I may as well go along with you on which side will be after winning."

The Civil War years were boom times in California, whose gold largely financed the desperate Union, and Washington was grateful. A large section in the southern part of the new state was openly for the Confederacy, and volunteer contingents trekked east to join both sides in the horrendous struggle beyond the mountain walls that kept California's face to the Pacific.

Though suspected as a Copperhead, or Southern sympathizer, by some of the more radical Republicans who now controlled the purse strings, Brian Carlyle was known and respected as a skilled engineer who kept his word, got the work done on time, and paid his bills.

Brian would never guess how much of this was his young wife's doing, for when red-faced men with overdue bills appeared in her husband's absence, Dawn insisted that her cash payments be accepted with no further discussion. Her husband, as she explained, was a busy man who shouldn't be bothered by the mere details of day-to-day transactions.

The merchants and contractors were no fools. They didn't quite grasp the full details of Carlyle's erratic transactions, but word got around that it was easier to deal with herself, who paid within thirty days and insisted on a ten percent discount for doing so.

Brian contracted to build fortified gun emplacements for the army on both sides of the Golden Gate, for Confederate raiders were out in force and the news of their depredations made disturbing news as it came over the wires of Western Union.

The news reached Brian before other contractors could bid on the job, because Dawn, as a stockholder in Western Union, had made certain arrangements at the telegraph office. Other early news could be turned to profit, and Dawn, on her own, bought wheat futures a day before the Sacramento papers carried word of the shortage of farm labor in the East occasioned by the full mobilization of the Union Army. Later, when the Confederate raider *Alabama* caught the north Pacific whaling fleet at anchor off Alaska and decimated it, Dawn would foresee the shortage of lamp oil and invest an experimental sum in the wild schemes of a young man in Humboldt County who was drilling, he said, for oil.

When he read of the madness in the papers, Brian dismissed it as a crackpot venture, for while Drake's well in Pennsylvania seemed to be producing barrels of the ugly black goo, it was well established that rock oil, or petroleum, was worthless evil-smelling stuff that wouldn't burn worth a damn in any lamp. His dismissal of another young man in the East was just as adamant, for while Johnny Rockefeller's distillation process seemed to work well enough, it violated engineering logic. Why go to so much trouble to obtain liquid fuel when the Good Lord had provided mankind with a sea full of whales?

When Dawn discovered she was expecting another child, she insisted on following her husband to San Francisco. For once, Brian didn't argue. He was involved in more than the military installations now, and the riverboat trip on weekends was a bother. His harbor defense contracts for the army had attracted the notice of San Francisco's politicians, and his honesty and Irish charm had opened doors for him at the new city hall. Dawn's advice that he register as a Republican as the old Whigs faded from the scene hadn't hurt him, etiher, though he didn't like to admit it.

The original Deluxe Hotel on Market Street had burned down and been rebuilt; hence there were no ghosts from her first marriage to haunt Dawn as she moved in with Felicidad and the children. The city, since last she'd seen it, had grown more substantial, and the nameless hill where she'd met Brian that day was neither nameless nor covered with poppies now. Commanding a magnificent view of the city and bay, the steep hill had been covered with a network of impossibly graded streets and surveyed into building lots. Dragging building materials to the top was exhausting for dray horses and cost the earth, but the men who'd elected to build on the hill had money to burn, and they were finding the once-fashionable Rincon Hill, south of Market Street, crowded and cramped for new lots. Hence the next decade would see the rapid climb of housing on Nob Hill, named for the "nabobs," or "nobs"—rich people envied by Californians and, indeed, the whole country.

For they were rich, the nabobs of Nob Hill. Rich in a boisterous childlike way that would vanish only with the next century's wars and income taxes. Some came from wealthy backgrounds. As younger sons and poor relations coming to California to find their fortunes, they stumbled into fortunes never dreamed of by their snobbish relatives in Boston, London, or Paris. Others, from humble farms or a hundred teeming slums, had become as rich or richer overnight. As the gold rush was replaced by civil war, with its insatiable demands for the products of her hills and sunny farms and ranches,

California was the cornucopia of the Union. The men who controlled her produce were hard pressed to spend the money they were making in the boom.

Fine marble fireplaces and statuary shared house-room with vulgar floors of gold coins set in cement. Imported oriental rugs lay beneath the glass-eyed stares of mooseheads mounted on oak-paneled walls. Bound sets of Shakespeare lined the libraries of rough-hewn men who could barely read. Cut-crystal chandeliers illuminated vast rooms, blue with the rancid smoke of corncob pipe or imported Havana Perfecto. The new-rich smoked what they wanted, ate what they wanted, and slept with partners of their choice. Decent former farm girls, wellborn European society women, and the notorious Lola Montez, who was said to charge a thousand dollars a night, could be seen at the same table in many a Nob Hill dining room. For Nob Hill society was based on simple wealth; nothing else mattered to those who divided their world into those who had it and those who didn't.

Brian Carlyle never thought of building their new home anywhere else, though even with his booming business, he was hard pressed to raise cash for their lot on the western slope. Left to Brian, the mansion would have been as ornate and gingerbready as he could afford. But as Brian was busy with his roads along the tricky terrain of the Pacific shoreline, Dawn was able to supervise much of the building. Riding up once a day from the hotel, she gently talked the builders out of a Jacobin chimney here and a feudal turret there. Her own taste hardly ran to Cape Cod, since she was, after all, a Victorian whose education had been limited at best. Yet she had a feel for balance and a love of the warm earth colors favored by her Indian background. The painters, after some hesitation

—himself had ordered canary yellow with kelly green trim—agreed that the warm dove-gray siding with cream trim and umber shutters pinned the house to the sandy hillside well and would doubtless stand up to the soot from the city below.

The interior décor would not have won a prize in Queen Victoria's London, though many a Back Bay Bostonian would have felt at home with the ferns and goldfish of the bay windows in her parlor. Dawn had lived comfortably with the black and maroon of her Sacramento wallpaper, so she saw no reason to change colors, although she chose a floral pattern from the selection at Gump's, the new department store at the foot of the hill.

Much of the furniture had been brought by steamboat from her old home in Sacramento. Giving in to Brian, she filled out the larger rooms with gilt Louis XVI furniture, insisting only on dark-brown upholstery rather than the red plush Brian preferred.

She was adamant about the flooring; although allowing Brian to have the foyer paved with Mexican double eagles, she insisted on parquet in the rest of the rambling hillside house.

Brian's grumbling came to an end shortly after they moved in. He'd invited a new client to dinner— an Irishman, the younger son of the earl of Dunraven, who'd come to California, he said, to invest in a distillery. The young man's wife was French, with aristocratic features and a limited command of English. After dinner, as the men discussed their business over brandy, Dawn took the French girl on a tour of the house and gardens. Celeste pronounced her hostess's new home *formidable*.

When they'd gone, Brian exclaimed, "They liked us, lass. I mean, they liked us as people, and himself said we had a grand house! I told you who he was, didn't I?"

"Yes, dear, you said he was the Earl of something. Is he going to let you build his distillery for him?"

"Aw, Jasus, I didn't have the heart to take advantage of him. I told him about the barley lands up near Weed. That's the only place he should be after building. You need mountain water and good hard barley for the brewing of The Creature. Wasn't that wife of himself the looker, though? Himself was after saying she was a countess, left over from poor old King Louis's time. Jasus, to think of Carlyle with a French countess and the son of a belted earl under his roof at the same time!"

"They seemed like nice people."

"Nice, they was *grand gentry!* And himself it was who lit me smoke when we shared Havanas in the drawing room. Jasus, herself was taken with you, too! Whatever did yez talk about?"

"Oh, we just looked in at the children and she taught me the French words for some of the flowers out back."

"Do you know what himself said you was, Dawn Carlyle? Himself said you was a lady. You know what else he said? He said we had a civilized house. That's the very word himself used, civilized. I wonder what he meant by that?"

"I'm not sure, dearest. Celeste said it was *formidable.* I got the idea she liked it."

"Jasus, so did I, and to think of the houses them two has been in! I was wondering, though, about them coins we had set in the foyer. I mean, it seemed to me the two of them seemed surprised when they came to the door and glanced down at the floor. I saw the look that passed between them, and well, I didn't care all that much for it and that's a fact. It was all right, once they was inside and meeting you in the drawing room, but them coins, now, do you think a bearskin rug would be after toning it down a bit?"

"You want my advice, Brian?"

"Well, you do have a flair for making a house look dacent and I'd be a fool to deny it. At the risk of turnin' your pretty head, I'll tell you I've been complimented on the Carlyle house in the street out front. You know how we argued about the gray siding a few months ago? Well, the Dobsons down the block are having theirs repainted the same color! What do you think of that, Dawn, me girl?"

"I think it's a good idea, dear. I hated that shade of mustard they started out with."

He laughed and said, "It's settled, then. I'll take no rear pew when it comes to the building of a house, for the timbers in this one would stand up to a broadside from the Royal Navy and it's every one I chose meself. But if you'll admit I'm the master builder of the family, I'll be man enough to admit you've an eye for color and decoration I skipped in me schooling. If I was to put that foyer on your hands, me darling, what would you be after doing to make it look like the entrance to a gintleman's house?"

"Well," she said, "since you asked me, I'd start by ripping out those Mexican coins and putting them in the bank where they belong."

"I guessed that much. What then—marble? How about black and white marble, set in squares or maybe the Carlyle monogram?"

"Terrazzo," said Dawn, firmly. "You know what terrazzo is, don't you, dear?"

"Och, a cheap substitute for marble it is. Made by the Eye-talians of stone chips and mortar, polished and waxed to be aping after the real marble they can't afford."

"It doesn't have to look like that! What's that flint-like stone we have so much of here in the bay area? Don't you call it *chert?*"

"Ay, there's cliffs of it, out by the Golden Gate. I think it's a form of flint, red with the iron in it. You'd not use such dross in our foyer, would you?"

"Yes, and that dull-green serpentine from the hills to the south. I'd separate the moss green and dull rose with bands of tan gold-quartz from the mother lode. The design I have in mind is from a Was-Ho basket. Would you like to see it?"

"Jasus, you'd use a Digger Indian design in our front foyer? It sounds terrible. But you were right about the outside trim, so I'll say no more."

"You'll let me do it? The circle of Acorn Woman has a dot in its very center. Would you like it if I put one of your coins there?"

"Wouldn't it look a bit, well, jumped-up Irish?"

"It might, but it's your foyer, too."

"Och, I just told you to do it your own way, lass. I can't even picture what you have in mind, but I told you the inside of this house was yours to do as you please, and Carlyle is a man of his word."

Later that night, Brian was surprised and pleased with his wife's responses to his lovemaking. As he finished and prepared to fall asleep, he heard Dawn's chuckle and asked, "What is it, darling? What fairy scheme are you after hatching now?"

"I was just thinking," Dawn replied, "that you really are becoming terribly civilized, dearest."

"Jasus, what's that supposed to mean? I didn't understand it when himself said it about me house, this evening."

"I wasn't sure, either, until just now. Have I told you lately that I love you, Brian Carlyle?"

"Hell, of course you love me. Haven't we always been dacent to each other, lass?"

"I suppose we have. Tonight you seemed to outdo yourself in decency though. And damn it, you really are a very nice person, you know?"

"Oh, women! If I live to be a hundred I'll never understand the half of what they say, and that's the fact of the matter. Can I be off to sleep now, or do you want to talk about how nice I am?"

"Good night, darling. You need your rest, and I know who and what you are." He didn't hear as she added, under her breath, "I suppose I could have done a lot worse, at that."

In the East, the Civil War dragged on for five years and would seem an eternity to the people it scarred, North and South. In California, the time passed quickly in an all-too-brief golden age of overnight fortunes and what seemed a neverending building boom. Houses sprang like mushrooms from the steep slopes of Nob Hill, and Dawn was in her element as the belle of San Francisco society. The round of parties and intimate political dinners was punctuated, once, by the birth of Dawn's second son, Brian Junior. In the even climate and comfortable security of her new life, the news of Lee's surrender at Appomattox ended the war, and the boom, with unseemly haste.

In the five years that had passed, Dawn had not been idle with her stock portfolio. Foreseeing the drop in bullion prices as the agony in the East whimpered to a close, she unloaded her gold shares at the same time Brian was buying into the new Comstock silver lode on the far side of the Sierra.

Dawn couldn't understand it. Couldn't anyone else add and subtract? Didn't any of them read history? Every wartime government lowered the prices of silver and gold as soon as they saw peace ahead. It was simple arithmetic. Washington would pay off its war debts with inflated paper currency. On the other hand, the new Homestead Act was going to mean another land rush in the semiarid southern counties. Converting her bullion shares to water rights seemed simple common sense. Hadn't *any* of the men thought to wonder where the new homesteaders were going to get irrigation water?

Despite his profession, Brian hadn't planned on any irrigation schemes. Caught flatfooted by the end of the war, he found himself with cancelled contracts and unpaid bills. Having learned in her girlhood that men, red or white, would tell a woman what was bothering them in their own good time, Dawn said nothing until the night Brian brought it up at the dinner table.

"I hate to do it, lass," he said, "but it's a mortgage on this house I'll have to be thinking of taking out. I've got to have ready cash, and the damned politicians are too busy trying to impeach President Johnson to be paying their damned bills!"

Dawn let him go on at some length about the overhead of his business before she put down her wineglass and murmured, "We could probably unload my Central Pacific shares at a tidy profit, now that the grants for the transcontinental railroad have been printed in the papers."

Brian blinked. "What Central Pacific shares? You didn't buy into *that* mad scheme, did you?"

"I got a very good buy on them, dear. The promoters were desperate for money, and well, I did have a little inside information, thanks to my holdings in Western Union."

"Desperate for money, were they? Jasus, of course they were desperate for money! Save for Leland Stanford, who managed to get himself elected to the state-house before the voters wised up, the whole lot are a pack of paupers! Jasus, you know what C. P. Huntington was before he started passing himself off as a railroad baron? He was a two-bit storekeeper known for giving short measure! Without Stanford's political pull, they'd have been laughed out of Washington for suggesting they knew how to put a railroad over the Sierra!"

"That's probably true, dear, but you see, they *did* have Governor Stanford's pull, and they have gotten Congress to finance the shares with land grants. So when they offered shares on the market at shoestring prices . . ."

"Jasus, none of them rascals have shoes to offer! Let alone a shoestring between them! It's a get-rich-quick pipedream at this stage!"

"Come now, you know the railroad has to be built. You've said yourself that the overland stage takes too long."

"Och, I know what I said and I know there's to be a railroad, someday, but not this soon! Jasus, I crossed them mountains and the desert beyond back in '50 and I know what's involved! Stanford and Huntington are a crooked lawyer and a penny-pinching merchant. Between the two of 'em, there's not enough engineering know-how to build a chicken coop, let alone a transcontinental railroad!"

"Well, whether they build it or not, the stock has more than doubled in price since I bought it. We should be able to sell it for—oh, fifty thousand. Would that help us?"

"Fifty thousand dollars? Jasus, it'd be manna from heaven, if anyone was fool enough to buy it at that price."

"Oh, I'm sure I could unload a good block of it on Mr. Huntington. They say, now that the government's backing the venture, he's been trying to buy up a controlling interest in the company."

"C. P. Huntington's buying back his own watered stock? Back up a bit and let's think it through, lass. Old Huntington's not the sort of lad to buy a pig in a poke. He must know something we don't about them shares of yours!"

"I don't see what the mystery is. Mr. Huntington may not be much of an engineer, but they do say he knows his way through a business ledger. He and his business cronies needed Governor Stanford to get the contract. Now that they have it, they're fighting for control of the company."

Brian nodded and said, "Ay, I think we'll be after holding on to them shares of yours after all, lass."

Dawn smiled fondly across the table at him and sipped her wine. He was such a dear, once you got the hang of making him see things your way.

Then Brian said, "Ay, I'll mortgage this house and we'll just wait out this railroad madness until we see what them rascals are up to."

"I don't like the idea of mortgaging our home, dear. How much do you need to keep your construction company afloat for now?"

"Och, fifty would do it, but I'll not be after taking a penny of me own wife's money. I can raise enough on this house to last us until I get paid on some of them damned defense contracts."

"But darling, we don't *have* to sign a mortgage. I've enough in my savings alone!"

"Whist! You know how I feel about your savings, woman. What kind of a man do you think Carlyle is?"

She started to say a proud stubborn fool, but she contented herself with a resigned nod as she tried to decide which of her several options she should follow in the next few days.

One of the nicer things people called Collis P. Huntington was The Octopus. To Dawn he rather resembled a canny coyote sniffing a suspicious bait as he tried to spy the jaws of a trap.

They'd met in the back room of the San Francisco Yacht Club, an establishment not as grand as its name implied; the earthy financiers of San Francisco felt comfortable near the waterfront and in the company of other men who paid to see Lola Montez perform her notorious Spider Dance atop a grand piano of an evening.

Over his plate of raw bay oysters the wily storekeeper *cum* railroad magnate muttered, "Let me see if I get this straight, Miz Carlyle. You're offering me a block of C.P. shares at little more than par for . . . for . . . damn it, what are you *really* up to, gal?"

"I told you. I want you to pay my husband for a survey."

"But, damn it, we don't aim to follow that pass you and your brother come over that time. It's too far south for one thing, and even if it wasn't, it's too high. You couldn't get over it with a locomotive in a hundred years."

"I'm sure my husband will agree, once he's surveyed it, Mr. Huntington. But he has to survey *something,* if you mean to pay him all that money for his time."

"I don't get it, gal. You want me to pay him a hundred thousand of your own money, just to go off on a wild-goose chase?"

"Yes, fifty thousand down and fifty more when he comes back to tell you the pass is unfeasible. I don't see what's so complicated about it."

"It's complicated enough. Why can't you just give him the damn money and save us all a lot of bother?"

He popped an oyster in his mouth, swallowed, and studied Dawn for a time. "You got a reason. Everybody has a reason. You never come here to offer me that stock in exchange for such a fool deal without you had a damn good reason. What is it—another man?"

"Sir! Is that any question to ask a lady?"

"Hell, girl, it ain't no never mind of mine why you want your husband out of town for a spell. Let's see if I understand this, though. You give me back my stock at par and I'm to hire your husband to make a worthless survey, paying him with your own money, right?"

"That's it. Do we have a deal?"

"Don't see why not. When do I get my hands on that stock?"

"Right now, sir. I brought it with me in this carpetbag. Needless to say, I have the money, too."

Huntington looked surprised. "You trust me enough to pay in advance?"

"Why not, Mr. Huntington? Can't you be trusted?"

He laughed and said, "Maybe I can and maybe I can't. Maybe this Lucrezia Borgia act of yours appeals to the devil in us all. You knew all along I'd do anything to get my hands on them shares, didn't you?"

"I was hoping so, sir. You have a reputation as a

shrewd business man and, as you can see, there's no risk involved in it from your end."

"I can see that. I can see your husband shooting you and that other jasper if he should come back down offen the mountain ahead of time, too! I'd best make sure he does a good survey up there, right?"

"Well, I can see there's no sense in trying to fool a man of the world, but you will be discreet about it, won't you, Mr. Huntington?"

"Call me Seep." He grinned, adding, "All my friends call me Seep, and some of my enemies, too. You're a dangerous gal, but damn it, I like you. If I was a man who liked to live dangerously, I'd maybe give that other hombre a run for his money, even if you do think he's worth a hundred thousand to be alone with. You have any other railroad shares, gal?"

"I have a block of Union Pacific on margin. Do you want them, too?"

"Not as a gift. Get rid of 'em before the news comes over the wire."

"Why, Seep, is there something wrong with U.P. shares? I thought your Central Pacific was to meet the U.P. midway and . . ."

"Hell, gal, there's nothing wrong with the Union Pacific railroad. It's the watered stock they've sold on it that's gonna make a stink in God's own heaven! A skunk named Durant and a crooked congressman named Ames have watered U.P. shares past simple greed and into sheer stupidity. The scandal figures to break any day. Vice President Colfax has been trying to whitewash it, but you won't be able to give away U.P. stock once the news gets out. That damned Durant has sold a hundred percent of the company nearly a hundred times over, and there just ain't that much whitewash, even on Capitol Hill!"

"Heavens! Thank you for telling me, Seep. But isn't it unusual for you to pass on such a tip?"

"It is, and I'm trying to figure out why I just done it. I reckon I just hate to see another fox get skinned, and hell, I told you you could call me Seep."

Dawn smiled, slightly bewildered, and C. P. Huntington chose to read his own cunning into it as he swallowed another oyster. "Yep, you had me figured from the start. You know I'd skin a man for a dollar, but that I wouldn't hurt a fly for no good reason. Not many folks know I'm a man of my word, but you did, and you been square with me. Most gals would have come to me with some fool story about their husband's pride or some such fairy tale, but you come right out and admitted you wanted to be alone with your lover. I like anybody, male or female, who has enough hair on their chest to know what they want and just up and git it! We'd make a hell of a pair, Dawn Carlyle, but you're too dangerous a woman for the likes of me."

Dawn laughed aloud this time. "I can see it's no use trying to pull the wool over *your* eyes, Seep."

Then she handed over the carpetbag, noting that he, in turn, didn't bother to check its contents. After a few more words of small talk she left the arachnoid Huntington to his dreams and oysters.

She'd intended to go straight home but instead went to her broker's office on Market Street.

Getting right to the point, she said, "I want to dump my Union Pacific shares at par, but keep a record of whom you sell them to."

Her broker nodded sagely. "I've heard the Crédit Mobilier manipulations are getting out of hand, too, Mrs. Carlyle. But tell me, what does it matter whom we sell them to, as long as we sell the worthless shares?"

"That's simple. I have to know who bought them if I ever intend to buy them back, don't I?"

The broker gasped, "You intend to buy U.P. shares *back*, ma'am? I thought we just agreed they're worthless!"

"Heavens, can't you add and subtract, Mr. Canfield? Right now Union Pacific is selling at an inflated value, so naturally we should sell them before the scandal breaks and they drop in price!"

"I understand that, ma'am. In a day or so they should be worthless, but—"

"Not worthless," Dawn cut in. "Cheap, but hardly worthless. The Union Pacific shareholders are going to take a terrible drubbing and the shares we sell for dollars this week should be selling for pennies by this time next month. That's when I want you to buy them back. I'm sure the holders will be delighted to sell at any offer."

"On that, there's hardly an argument, Mrs. Carlyle. But why do you want shares in a defunct railroad line?"

"Not defunct, Mr. Canfield. Just in receivership and undoubtedly under new management. The transcontinental railroad is going to be built! The vice president and other party hacks who've backed the Union Pacific will have to see that it's built if they ever expect to be elected dogcatcher again. Congress has already given away miles and miles of federal land to finance the railroad. They'll give away more, refinance the line, and . . . Heavens, you're supposed to be a stock broker!"

Canfield stared at Dawn in utter fascination. "My God, I thought I was until just now! Do you have any idea of the killing we'll make if U.P. weathers the Crédit Mobilier scandal?"

Dawn nodded. "Of course. It seemed obvious as soon as I heard the news."

The other children were a bit small to tag along, but Dawn decided to take young Gus with them as she accompanied Brian on the survey that summer. The boy was immature for his nearly ten years, and roughing it up the mountain would be good for him. Brian agreed with good grace, for he enjoyed his wife's company, the boy was no bother, and the pace would be slow. Each survey point had to be recorded and mapped with care if the CPRR was to have its money's worth. As nursemaid Dawn brought Felicidad, who really was a terrible cook and couldn't be trusted to supervise the newer servants back on Nob Hill.

They were camped by a glacier-fed stream near timberline the night her young son discovered the Milky Way. Dawn and her husband were bedded in their own tent, upslope from those of the camp wranglers and the one Gus shared with Felicidad. Fortunately, they were not making love when the child burst in on them, crying, "Mommy! Daddy! Come out and look! The sky is on fire!"

Indulgently, Brian swung his legs off the cot and led the boy outside, both in their nightshirts, as Dawn followed. She smiled in the darkness at the way Brian spoiled the boy she'd had by Gus Swensen. For she'd wondered, when Brian Junior had been born, if her husband's treatment of his stepson might not harden. To his credit, Brian treated all three children with equal and unfailing good humor. She heard him now, saying, "You can't see it down near sea level, son, but up here the air's much clearer. That long white stripe of stardust is called the Milky Way."

"But, Daddy, I'm not talking about all those little new stars. I mean that streak of shiny stuff across the sky."

"Ay, that's the Milky Way. It looks like a cloud of fairy dust, but it's made of stars like the others. They're too far off to make out each one, but together they form that arc of lighter sky against the dark of night. Can you find the Big Dipper for me, lad?"

"Oh, that's easy, Daddy. It looks so bright up here in the mountains. Is that the North Star over there?"

"Ay, you can see the dimmer stars of the Little Dipper, too, now that we're above the ocean mists. Och, look there! Did you see that shooting star, just now?"

"I saw it! I saw it! Do stars fall down, Daddy?"

"Well, not often. You'll see a lot of shooting stars up here, lad, if you keep your eyes open for them. 'Tis said the wee people grant a wish on every one you see, too. What sort of wishing would you be after, this night, Gus me lad?"

The boy thought and said, "Oh, I wish we could live up here all the time, Daddy. It's all so clean and pretty, and I saw a frog over there in the creek this afternoon."

"Ay, it was probably a prince in disguise. You wouldn't like it here in the winter, Gus. It's terrible cold this far up the slope in the winter."

"Can we come up here every summer, Daddy?"

"Well, mayhaps not every summer, but, when you're older, you can come along with me on me surveying. Would you like that, Gus?"

"Oh, yes, Daddy. I want to be an engineer, just like you, when I grow up."

"Ay. Well, if you intend to grow up healthy, you'd

best be off to bed. We rise and shine with the sun, you ken, and we'll be breaking camp in the morn. So off with ye, and pleasant dreaming."

The boy nodded. Then, seeing his mother standing by in the starlight, he said, "Goodnight, Mommy. I'm sorry if I woke you up."

Dawn waited until he'd gone back to join the snoring Felicidad in her nearby tent before she put a hand on Brian's shoulder, stood on tiptoe, and kissed him gently.

He returned her kiss but whispered warningly, "We'd best save that for our own tent, lass."

"Brian," she said, "I want to make love."

"Och, there's no reluctance on my part, woman. Let's duck inside and be after starting the same!"

"I don't want to make love in the tent, dearest. Will you walk with me to a place I found this afternoon?"

"Jasus, you want to do it out here in the open? What's got into you?"

"Starlight, dear. Come on, I promise no one will see us."

He took her hand, muttering to himself about female notions as he allowed himself to be led barefoot through the cool night grass to the place about a quarter mile up the slope where Dawn had found the hollow lined with scented fern between three granite boulders. She stripped her nightgown off, sinking naked to the ferny ground as she murmured, "Nevada and I camped in this hollow, coming over the pass so long ago. I found it and remembered, this afternoon when I was strolling with Gus."

Brian removed his own nightshirt and draped it over a boulder before he dropped to the ferns beside her. "Ay, you told me how you used to hide from Shoshoni in the rocks. You know what I don't understand about this pass of yours, lass? I don't understand whatever possessed the C.P. people to consider it as a railroad right-of-way."

"Don't you want to make love to me?"

"Och, don't I always? It's not that you're not the most lovely fey creature any man could be after holding in his arms. It's just that, well, I feel so naked, out in the open like this!"

"Silly, you are naked, and so am I! Doesn't the night air feel delicious on your skin?"

"It feels more like goosebumps," he began. Then, as his rough palm caressed her naked flesh, he murmured, "Och, Jasus, you are a fey thing spun from dreams and stardust, Dawn Carlyle!"

She lay back in the sweet-smelling fern as he mounted her, thrusting his cool flesh into hers with a moan of passion, and the firmness of the earth beneath her buttocks added force to his efforts as their pubic bones ground together. Dawn locked her thighs around his bobbing hips and stared up at the star-spangled heavens beyond the dark outline of his head. It was easy to imagine it was Nevada making love to her in this place they'd shared so long ago. Yet, though she'd planned it that way in the beginning, it was Brian and only Brian she felt inside her as she sobbed, "Oh, God, I'm coming! Tonight I can feel the earth turning and turning under me as we spin through the universe on our little muddy star!"

"Jasus, Jasus! Och, Jasus!" he moaned, as his own shuddering orgasm swept up from his feet buried in the fern-covered sand.

He collapsed for a moment, catching his breath before he nibbled her ear and suggested, "Let's try for another, darling. You were right, this is a magic place you found. Tell me something, naughty lass. Was it this you thought of when you found the place this afternoon?"

She started to say she'd thought of it years ago, but aloud she merely purred and said, "Not this afternoon. It came to me when you and my son were sharing the stars tonight. It came to me that I wanted to share them, too, and—oh, look, another shooting star!"

He moved his semen-lubricated shaft deeper and sighed, "You have a fairy wish coming, lass. What would you have this night from the wee people?"

"I have my wish for the night, dearest. Just keep doing what you're doing and . . . Brian, I really do love you. Did you know that?"

He thrust deep and kissed her neck, growling, "Of course I know it. Was there ever any doubt?"

She didn't answer. She knew he didn't expect her to. It must be nice, she thought, to be a simple steak and potatoes man.

Dawn enjoyed the pointless survey more than her husband. With each twist of the path to the spine of the Sierra, Brian grew more confused with C. P. Huntington's choice of routes, but Dawn was impressed as never before with his skill and engineering know-how. Their life together had settled into a comfortable groove of mutual disinterest as Dawn had taken over the running of the mansion on Nob Hill and Brian had gone about his mysterious business with maps and instruments in what had been, up to now, a man's work far from wife and family.

Dawn had been truly surprised at the detail involved in her husband's profession as she watched Brian and his crew at work. At home, Brian seemed a simple, somewhat rough-cut Waterford lad, pushing forty, bemused by his wife's newfound polish as a hostess, and inclined to eat too much steak and drink a bit more porter than was good for his waistline. Out in the field he was in his element. His brogue sounded right as he bossed his hardworking surveyors and camp roustabouts. Brian, working harder than any of his twelve-man team, tanned and hardened a bit in the clear mountain sun.

The trip had done wonders for young Gus. The private school he attended over on Russian Hill was said to be the finest in San Francisco, but her son and the friends he brought home from school on occasion seemed a softer, paler breed than one would have expected from the descendants of men and women who'd crossed the Great American Desert in Conestoga wagons.

Dawn knew that she herself had been paled by the Frisco fogs and softened by the luxuries of Nob Hill, but, she thought, a boy of ten who called his mother "Mommy" was a bit much.

But the boy seemed to thrive on camp life, and as his skin tanned and his hair bleached in the Sierra sunlight he looked at least two years older to his delighted mother. Dawn had told the camp hands not to spoil the boy, and they'd taken her at her word, calling Gus "Little Britches" and making him help with the chores. Once, when Gus fell from his pony as he galloped it across a grassy slope, the laconic camp cook who reached him first and saw he'd suffered no injury to anything save his dignity, shifted his cud of tobacco and asked mildly, "Well, kid, do you aim to lay there taking a sunbath, or do you aim to climb back on that bronc and ride the son of a bitch?"

Gus rubbed a dirty hand across his face, grinned

sheepishly, and yelled back, "There was never a pony that couldn't be rode, and never a rider that couldn't be throwed."

It was a far cry from the somewhat prissy speech of a private-school lad, and Dawn was pleased at the change.

One morning, as Brian and his stake men were farther up the slope at work, Dawn listened in silent wonder as young Gus, washing his tin plate in the sand of a running mountain stream, sang to himself in a clear and hauntingly beautiful key:

> Och, will ye come away with me
> To yon pure foaming fountains?
> And we'll pick the wild thyme
> That grows high among yon mountains.

She waited until he'd finished his chore as well as the song and returned to her at the campfire before she murmured, "That was lovely, Gus. Where did you ever learn such a pretty song?"

"Athair taught it to me, Mommy."

"Athair?"

"Oh, that means Father, in the Gaelic. Athair says I'm not to call him Daddy anymore, for it's going on ten I am and I mustn't talk like a sissy."

Dawn felt a mild pang of . . . jealousy. "I've never heard him sing. You're quite attached to him, aren't you, son?"

"Of course. He's my father. Athair says when I'm a wee bit older I can come along on other trips and that when I grow up I can be an engineer, too."

"What about your music lessons, Gus? I thought, when you grew up, you were going to write an opera."

"Oh, I'm going to do that, too, Mommy. Athair says

it's all right for a gentleman to dabble in the arts, as long as he has a trade."

"I suppose so. Uh, you do know about your real father, don't you, dear?"

"You mean the man you married before Athair, Mommy? Himself told me my real Daddy was a nice man, too."

"Does it bother you—that himself is not your real father?"

"It used to, before we talked about it. Athair says it's not to, though. He told me he loves me as much as Sister and Baby Brother when I asked him about it. I 'spect he meant it, don't you, Mommy?"

"Yes, dear. I 'spect he did, and by the way, do you have to call me Mommy?"

"It's your name, isn't it? What should I call you if I can't call you Mommy? I don't know the Gaelic for mother."

"How about just plain Mom? I don't know any Gaelic, and I'm not sure I want to. Will you just call me Mom?"

"All right, if you'll stop celling me August when you introduce me to folks."

Dawn laughed and said, "We have a deal, Gus. Oh-oh, himself and the others are coming back early, and himself is wearing a terrible scowl this morning, isn't he?"

Brian joined them at the fire, seated himself on a log, and muttered, "Madness, the whole thing is insane!"

"What's the matter, dearest?" asked Dawn, as if she hadn't guessed.

"There's just no way to lay track at a nine percent grade up this damnfool pass. I told Huntington that when he hired me. I know you and Nevada came over it that time, but neither of yez was after driving a locomotive. The Sierra's even steeper on the far side, and a tunnel is out of the question. Them Chinamen Stanford has been importing would have to drive through more than five miles of solid granite and . . . Och, what's the use of talking? They'll have to use another pass."

"But you'll still be paid for the survey, won't you, dear?"

"Ay, that's in the contract, but that's not the point. I just don't like to be *beaten* this way! It's no use, though. We'll be after striking camp and reporting back this day. Next to giving up, there's nothing worse than wasting time and trouble on the impossible."

Gus piped up, "But we're almost to the top, Athair! I wanted to see the other side of the Sierra where Mommy—I mean, Mom—was raised by the Injuns!"

Brian started to shake his head. Then he smiled wryly. "Ay, we'll ride up and take a peek before we leave, then. Will you be after coming, too, Dawn Carlyle?"

"To pick wild mountain thyme?"

Brian laughed. "Why not? We'll never find a place up there to lay a railroad track. I see the lad's been teaching you me Irish songs, eh?"

"Yes. How come you've never sung it to *me*, Brian?"

"Och, it's but a wee ditty I sang one day without thinking. I have the voice of a bullfrog drunk on porter and that's the truth of it."

Dawn waited until her husband had rested over a cup of coffee and the three of them were saddled up before she asked him to sing for her. Brian grumbled and protested for about a mile, but then, as they neared the top of the pass, he cleared his throat sheepishly and began to croon "Wild Mountain Thyme" in a surprisingly beautiful Irish tenor. Gus joined in, harmonizing with his stepfather, and by the time they reached the grassy saddle between the snow-covered peaks on either side of the pass Dawn had picked up the words of the simple tune and joined in.

The haunting refrain echoed from the rocky slopes as they reined in their mounts to gaze eastward across the shimmering dusty flats of the Great Basin, which lay at their feet like a tawny carpet stretched to the shimmering far horizon.

Young Gus stared in silent wonder as the song died in his throat. Dawn and Brian sat their mounts on either side, wrapped in their own silent thoughts. Gus asked, "Is that where the Indians found you, Mom?"

"Yes, dear. Somewhere out there in the middle of it."

"Gee, I knew what a desert was, but it's so . . . so big! Do you 'spose your Indian friends are still out there somewhere?"

"Not the ones who found me, Gus. I'm afraid I don't have many Indian friends any more. The Diggers have been pushed into reservations, and the last time I asked about Spotted Elk and his band, nobody could tell me whatever became of them. It's funny, I owe them so much, and there's nothing I've ever been able to do for any of them."

Brian said, "Och, you've given many a barrel of flour to your Diggers, darling." But Dawn shivered as if a cold draft had suddenly come up the pass behind her as she murmured, "They never really needed my charity. The only thing they really needed was to be left alone, and that was the one gift I couldn't exchange for a gathering basket. I'd like to ride back now. I'm suddenly feeling very cold up here."

As Dawn wheeled her horse, Gus fell in beside her

and piped up, "I never really understood how lucky you were to be found in the desert, Mom. It's awful down there. Don't you think it's lucky that you're still alive?"

Dawn smiled gently down at her son and across him to the silent Brian as she nodded and answered, "Yes, son, things could have turned out a lot worse for me than they have at that."

The "wedding of the rails" took place at Promontory Point, Utah, in 1869. Ex-Governor Stanford, in token of Brian Carlyle's efforts on behalf of the great adventure, sent him a golden railroad spike. Actually, it was a common steel spike electroplated with fourteen-karat gold, for Leland Stanford was a pragmatic man in his most generous moods and he was politician enough to give out many "golden" spikes.

C. P. Huntington, having paid good money for a worthless survey, felt he'd done enough for the Carlyle family and, as they met socially from time to time, watched Dawn with a wary eye. His spies had told him the woman had gone along with her husband on the fool venture, and Seep Huntington worried about people he couldn't figure out. He'd already started yet another company of his own that would become in time, the mighty Southern Pacific railroad empire of the Southwest. And one day Huntington would skin the notorious Jay Gould in a fight for control of railroad traffic west of the Mississippi. He'd skin a lot of people and do a lot of good as well as harm to the economy of the growing young state. But he'd never really understand Dawn Carlyle, and as a cautious man, he'd keep a friendly distance and try to avoid crossing swords with her in any business deal. His same spies had told him how shrewd the innocent-eyed young belle of Nob Hill society could be in a proxy fight. But what the hell, he liked her.

By this time Dawn was in her early thirties and the prime of her beauty. A miscarriage in her late twenties had resulted, according to her doctors, in a tipped womb, leaving little chance for a fourth child. The news had not upset her as much as it might have. The three she had were enough for any mother to cope with.

Neither little Brian Junior nor his older sister, Rose, were old enough to wander far from the grounds of the mansion, but as Gus reached early adolescence, he simply refused to stay put. Hardened by the weekend and summer vacation work at his stepfather's construction firm, Gus had not grown into the prissy youth his mother had feared he might. At eleven, he lost a fight with an older boy who laughed at his velvet knickers. Brian took him down to the waterfront, bought him a pair of long jeans, and spent a week teaching him something called counterpunching. By the time his first black eye cleared up, Gus had stalked and beaten the older boy in a schoolboy fight such as legends are made of. Some of Brian's laborers contributed boxing lessons of their own, and despite his piano lessons, Gus Carlyle never lost another fight. What worried Dawn was that as he grew bigger and stronger he relished such adventures.

The vigilantes had cleared up the worst street gangs of San Francisco, but it was still a notoriously tough town. When Dawn voiced her fears to her husband, Brian took a good-natured view of his stepson's wanderings and said he'd warned the lad to stay "north of the slot." The only place white men fought with knives, Brian said, was in the mission district south of Market Street.

When Dawn pointed out that Gus had returned from an exploration of North Beach with a torn shirt and broken knuckles, Brian shrugged it off as wild oats, which he said he'd felt at the same age in the north end of Boston. Dawn didn't know what to do. She suspected, with good reason, that Brian rather gloried in the exploits of "young Carlyle."

Rose Maureen, as if to make up for her older brother's wild nature, was growing into a well-behaved young miss who seldom ventured farther than the front garden. She was a daddy's girl who gave her mother little trouble, but Dawn sometimes wondered if she had any brains at all.

Brian Junior was a placid little boy who liked to draw and play with his toys in the backyard. He seemed healthy enough but inclined to be sluggish, and Dawn could only hope he'd outgrow his baby fat in time. He looked very much like a fat version of his Irish father, and indeed, Brian himself was putting on more weight than a man of forty-odd should be carrying. When she mentioned his thickening waist and suggested he cut down on second helpings, Brian merely snorted that he was no fatter than any other middle-aged businessman he knew. But it wasn't age; it was the softer living, now that Brian was spending most of his time at his firm on Van Ness Avenue.

The hard fieldwork was left to Brian's younger associates as Carlyle and Sons grew in prestige. Brian's connection with the transcontinental railroad had been inflated with the retelling, and though he didn't suspect it, Dawn's shrewd financial dealings had been credited to him, too. Since nothing succeeds like success, Carlyle and Sons was swamped with building contracts.

Few of his clients would ever guess how he'd argued

with his wife the time she bought into the new sugar
refinery at Alverado, or how he'd scoffed at her suggestion that investing in the new steamship line to
"them cannibal-infested Sandwich Islands" might be
a good buy.

It didn't matter that their "smart Irishman" lacked
a certain sense of business foresight. The men who
hired Brian got good value for their money. His in-
creasingly conservative nature assured conscientious
civil engineering and construction that erred, if at all,
on the side of safety.

Brian prided himself on solid workmanship, and
these days he could afford to turn down unsound
engineering schemes.

One night, having dinner alone with Dawn on the
patio, he explained with some annoyance about a
building subdivision he'd refused to have anything to
do with. "There ought to be a law about building on
faults, and that's a fact."

"Building on what, dear?" asked Dawn, listlessly.
She really knew very little about engineering—and
damn it, he was having a third helping of mashed
potatoes!

Brian said, "A fault is a great crack in the bedrock.
You know we have a few wee earthquakes here in
California from time to time and it's known them
things take place along fault lines. But would they
listen to me? They would not. They've set their minds
to putting up them new houses right across a fault
line you can see with your naked eyes. Mark me
words, there's going to be a terrible disaster down
there one day."

Brian reached for the gravy boat, noted the look in
his wife's eye, and then, as if to change the subject,
said, "Leland Stanford was asking about that Chinese

idol you have on the knickknack shelf in the front parlor the other day."

"Kuan Yin? I've had her there for years. A lot of our guests have commented on the lovely workmanship."

"Ay, it's well-carved ivory, but it's still chink, if you get me meaning."

"I don't understand, dearest. What difference does it make who carved it, as long as it's pretty?"

"It makes a lot of difference these days. I was after telling Stanford we don't know any chinks, personal. I think you'd better be after moving Miss Heathen to an upstairs room, if you're all that set on keeping the damned thing at all."

"I don't know what you mean. What's the problem?"

"The chinks are the problem. The damned railroad never should have brought them in in the first place. Have you been down in Chinatown of late? Och, never mind, I know you haven't, for the smell of that warren is enough to knock a team of horses down. Jasus, the slope below Grant Street is teeming with the yellow pigtailed boogers and they seem to breed like rabbits. One of the lads at the club was telling me the other day that at the rate we're going the state will be a Chinese province by the turn of the century."

"Heavens, Chinatown is hardly a square mile at the most, and I've never had a bit of trouble from any of them."

"Och, it's not as individuals that they're so bad. Hell, I've had chinks work for me in the past and I'll be the first to say they work like beavers. It's the numbers that are after causing the problem. It was thought, once they built the railroad, they'd all go home, but the boogers keep coming. A lot of shortsighted rascals are still importing chinks, and everybody knows, now, that chinks *stay* after they work off their passage contracts."

"I'm missing something, dear. If Chinamen are hard workers and not bothering anyone, why are your friends so afraid of them?"

"Och, who's afraid of a chink? There'd be little enough trouble if only there was jobs for the rascals after they worked off their passage contract. But nobody wants to hire a free chink, and since they won't go home . . ."

"Wait a minute. If they're importing Chinese labor because they work so hard, why isn't there any work for them? It's all very confusing."

"Och, that's because you've no head for business, lass. You see, the chinks who've been here a while ask for a white man's wages, which would be fair enough if they lived like white men, but they don't. They live on fish heads and rice and save their money, and before you know it, they have more in the bank than the saints ever intended for a working lad. I mean, a coolie is one thing, a business competitor is another."

"I thought thrift was a virtue, dear."

"Well and it is, within reason, but you see, them chinks don't contribute to the economy. You take a white lad who makes an honest dollar, now, and what does he do with it? He spends it, like a dacent Christian. The chinks just take from the state of California, they don't put nothing back in the pot."

"Wouldn't you say the transcontinental railroad was a fair contribution to the economy, Brian? I've been using a very good Chinese laundry down the slope, too. I have no idea what sort of food they eat at night, but I must say our sheets and pillowcases are coming back ever so much whiter than when I sent them down to North Beach."

"Jasus! You've been letting chinks do our laundry? No wonder people have been asking about your Chinee idol! Don't you know them Irish washerwomen along North Beach depend on our trade, lass?"

"If you feel sorry for the drunken slut who used to do my sheets, I can send her some money, or better yet, a barrel of beer. Maenwhile, I like to sleep on clean linens. What does Governor Stanford intend to do about his Yellow Peril, in the meanwhile?"

"Och, Stanford's for a peaceful settlement. He'd like to pass a law just keeping the rascals on the other side where they belong. It's keeping a lid on the Chinese problem until the politicians can solve it that's at the root of it all. You see, for every party man who sides with Stanford, there's another who wants to keep the cheap labor of contract coolies flowing. Meanwhile, with Denis Kearney and his harbor toughs stirring up a hornet's nest about yon chinks, we'd best be after putting away our Chinese gods and sending our linen out to a dacent Irish laundress."

Dawn grimaced and asked, "Who, or what, is Denis Kearney?"

"You don't know about the American Workman's party? Jasus, I thought you read every page of the papers! That rascal Kearney has been offering free drinks for a Chinaman's pigtail, delivered in any bar on the Barbary Coast!"

"Good Lord, that's terrible! I did read something about an organized labor movement in the papers, but how are the working men to orgnaize if they start by fighting among each other? I mean, the Chinese, however this Kearney may dislike them, are, after all, workingmen. Right?"

"Wrong. A coolie is not a working man, he's a chink. Denis Kearney stands for white labor, bimetalism, free land to them as wants it, and some of that Owenite stuff that Jew, Karl Marx, has been after spouting out about in London."

"You mean he's a socialist?"

"Jasus, I don't know what he is, and I don't think he knows, either. He was a Fenian back in Ireland. Now he's just a troublemaker with a new tale for every troubled mind to follow. I don't think Kearney will ever get his new party past rioting in the streets, but meanwhile, us dacent folk should sit back and let Kearney's toughs and the hatchet men fight it out, so . . ."

Dawn, remembering a chance remark from years ago, cut in with, "Did you say hatchet men? Just what is a hatchet man, dear? That old man who died up at the Sweet Petunia was supposed to be a hatchet man, whatever that means."

Brian looked surprised and frowned. "Was he, now? You told me he was just a crazy old Chinee, picking pebbles from among the rocks. A hatchet man, you see, is a professional murderer, working for one of them tongs down in Chinatown."

"Oh, you can't be serious, dearest! Old Wong wouldn't have hurt a fly. He used to give sweets to the Digger children."

"Ay. Well, maybe his tong wasn't at war with your Diggers, then. If Wong was a hatchet man, he was a killer. You see, when the tongs are after a man, they send him a wee jade hatchet as a warning. Then, if he don't leave town or mend his ways, they send a man with a real hatchet to bury in his skull."

He put a forkful of potatoes in his mouth and chewed a moment. "They do say some of the younger tong men have taken to using six-guns, though. Sam Colt's wondrous inventions are having a grand effect on the old traditions of this world, and that's a fact."

Dawn said, "Dear me, it's coming back to me now. Wong's brother did say something about a tong, that time. I should have written it down. I think he said they were Orange Gongs, or Hong Kongs, or something."

"Jasus, it wasn't the Ong Leong Tong, was it?"

"You know, I think that was what he called it! But what do you know about Chinese tongs, dear?"

"Och, well, as a member of the vigilance committee it's me duty to keep informed."

"You're still a vigilante? I thought you all disbanded years ago, once the Barbary Coast gangs were cleared off the waterfront."

"Well, we haven't had to hang a Sidney Duck in years, but we sort of get together to talk over old times and to keep an eye on the municipals. If this business between Kearney's toughs and the tongs gets out of hand, the uniformed police will be after needing more than a little help. We've been watching both sides, you see, and it's a toss-up between Kearney and Ong Leong. Old Wong's bunch is a bad one. 'Tis said Ong Leong controls half the vice and gambling in the city, and that's not counting Chinatown."

"In other words, the white toughs are mad at the oriental toughs for competing with them as criminals?"

"Ay, you can't beat a chink for competing, be it a laundry or a lottery or the letting of a little blood for hire. What's for dessert?"

"You're still *hungry?*"

"Of course I'm hungry. It's a hard-working man I am, and I saved room for me dessert. The cook tells me it's apple pie this night, so do we ring for it or would you be after another helping of steak and potatoes, lass?"

Dawn sighed and said, "I'll ring for dessert, but I don't want any. Somehow, I seem to have lost my appetite."

Some sage once observed that a man who was not a liberal at twenty had no heart, while a man who was not a conservative at forty had no brain. As the original forty-niners felt their way into middle age in the uneasy '70s, many a hell-for-leather pioneer sported an Ingersoll watchchain across a growing, ultra-respectable paunch. Good-old-boys who'd bellied up to the bar with jovial laughter at the news of each new strike began to eye the neighbors on their San Francisco block with an eye to the sort of gents who might be coming to court their daughters. Hickory shirt and buckskins were replaced by starched linen and broadcloth as the moosehead in the drawing room was replaced with an often fictitious family crest, complete with family tree and the unstated hint that while one may have dabbled in mining shares or a railroad, the money had been in the family for generations.

Some few "old timers" went the other way and gloried in a Wild West that had never existed save in the romantic penny dreadfuls of Ned Buntline and other inventive hack writers. But, as former market-hunters and frontier vagabonds like Buffalo Bill and Wild Bill Hickok sported shoulder-length hair and elaborate fringed costumes, most of the men who'd built the western two-thirds of the nation affected dress and manners suited to a rather stuffy banker or their own version of a proper English gent.

The British Empire of Good Queen Victoria set the fashions of the century, and while America was now peopled by immigrants of three-fourths non-British stock, it thought of itself, rather truculently, as an

Anglo-Saxon nation. Charles Darwin's outrageous notions had been partially accepted and vastly perverted by the educated community by now, and while the notion that man had descended from lower animals seemed preposterous, the idea of survival of the fittest had been eagerly embraced—to account for the fact that English-speaking people had a perfect right to take over most of the globe.

With this fancied right went a firm conviction that lesser breeds were acting against natural law in resisting or competing with the self-appointed carriers of "the white man's burden."

In San Francisco, the pragmatic definition of an Anglo-Saxon included almost anyone of European ancestry, for the Irish and Italian communities joined vociferously in upholding the natural superiority of Anglo-Saxon Americans against non-Caucasians. Many a San Franciscan who could barely speak English would one day sign the petition by "Concerned Citizens" that read, in part:

Be it resolved that:

Not one virtuous Chinaman has been brought to America, and here the Chinese have no proper ties of lawfully-wed wives or legitimate children.

That the Chinese have no legal title to Real Estate and pay no taxes.

That the Chinese subsists on rice, fish, and cheap vegetable fare and afford no trade to American food merchants or farmers.

That the Chinese are of no benefit to the country.

That the Six Companies, or Tongs, have secretly established judicial tribunals, jails, and prisons, and secretly exercise life and death judicial authority over the Chinese.

That all Chinese laboring men are slaves who take away the just employment opportunities deserved by white men.

That Chinese merchants, dedicated to cheating and hoarding, bring no benefits to American bankers or importers etc.

The list of accusations went on for some pages. Signed by hundreds of San Franciscans, it was forwarded to President Grant, who, bemused, did nothing about it.

But Californians were used to being ignored by Washington and, like most westerners, used to taking matters into their own hands. In the fifties they'd settled the problem of the Barbary Coast gangs by simply forming ad hoc vigilance committees and wiping them out with pistol and rope. The seventies would be troubled times as the gold and railroad booms wound down in a series of sudden bankruptcies and mass unemployment. Despite their button shoes and derby hats, the men of San Francisco were still as inclined to easy solutions and hasty judgments as any buckskin hero of Ned Buntline's *Wild West*, if perhaps less dedicated to the code of the West that never, in fact, existed.

The Chinese riots started in 1871, when Gus Carlyle was in his early teens. To Denis Kearney's credit, the lynchings began in Los Angeles, where yet another band of disgruntled white men suddenly started murdering Chinese for reasons never too clear, save that the whites were drunk and unemployed and it was a hot night. The small Chinese community in southern California was decimated, and many of the panic-stricken refugees fled to the larger ghetto in San Francisco, where, to Denis Kearney's *dis*credit, the semi-socialist Workman's Party, inflamed by Kearney's disorganized rantings, joined the loafers and toughs of San Francisco in a similar venture.

The San Francisco Chinese, however, were many in number and not without some skill as street fighters. For the first few days and nights, white terrorists had their way with hapless orientals they caught on the streets surrounding Chinatown. Growing bolder with drink and the ease with which it seemed one could hang a screaming coolie from a lamp post by his pigtail, a band of loafers from Telegraph Hill made the mistake of a frontal assault on Chinatown itself. When the smoke cleared away, a dozen white men lay dead or dying along Grant Avenue. Brian Carlyle had been right about the erstwhile hatchet men having guns. Ong Leong and the other tongs struck back with savagery and hate to match their tormentors', and the streets ran red between Nob Hill and the Embarcadero.

The Carlyle mansion faced the other way, on the far side of Nob Hill. So the full horror of the situation reached Dawn and her family only through vague rumors and the occasional firecracker rattle of small-arms fire in the night.

Brian, before reporting to his vigilance committee, told Dawn to bar the doors and windows and to keep the servants as well as the children off the streets. For once, Dawn found herself in complete agreement with her husband.

It was the third night of the Chinese riots when Dawn noticed her eldest son's absence at the dinner table. A hurried search of the house revealed that he'd gone out, against his parents' orders. It took Dawn only

a few minutes to get the details from Brian Junior,
who, after trying not to betray his big brother's secret,
burst into tears and admitted Gus had gone out "to see
the fun."

Dawn was white-lipped, but her jaw was set as she
went upstairs and started to change her clothes. The
maid Felicidad came is as Dawn was pulling on an old
pair of hiking boots and, glancing at the pistol on the
bed beside her mistress, gasped, "No, señora! We must
wait until the man of the house returns!"

Dawn stood up, smoothed the front of her dark linen
riding habit, and picked up the revolver. "I want you
to bar the door after me, Felicidad. You're to open it
to no one until I come back with my son."

"Señora, this is madness! You don't know where to
begin looking! Why don't you send the butler and footman to look for Master August?"

"And have four men from this household missing?
I'm going myself. I'd know my son's figure at any
distance and I'm tougher than old Jarvis and the new
footman put together!"

"Then I, Felicidad, shall go with you, señora."

"No you won't! I need someone here to guard the
house and you're the second toughest adult on the
premises right now. If himself returns while I'm out,
tell him I just stepped over to the Huntington house
and that he's to wait for me here."

"You wish I should lie to the master?"

"Wish, hell, I'm telling you, girl! Now, go back down
and make sure the children don't see me slipping out.
For God's sake, Felicidad, move!"

Not waiting to see if her orders were really being
obeyed, Dawn slid the revolver inside her bodice and
went down the backstairs. She moved through the

darkened garden with a grim stride any Indian would have recognized as that of a mother cougar looking for a lost cub.

The street lamps were out as Dawn strode up the slope, crossed Powell Street, and moved toward the steep steps leading down the east slope of the hill to the blackened-out battle-area between her anxious gaze and the moonlit expanse of the bay. The night was punctuated by odd little flurries of disjointed sound and flashing light, but the riot area, if that was what it was, was surprisingly silent for an early San Francisco evening. Dawn wondered what was missing as she moved down toward Chinatown to the northeast, and then, as a dog barked somewhere in the night, it came to her that what was missing was the sound of normal traffic. The clopping of hooves and the rattle of steel-rimmed wagon wheels over the cobbled streets had become an unheard but ever-present sound of the waterfront area. Like the sudden silence of crickets in the country, the absence of the sounds had attracted her attention to them. The streets were moonlit and the cool, damp night air carried sounds normally masked by the rumble of traffic and voices on the busy streets. It seemed to Dawn, as she passed each dark and shuttered house, that she had somehow been transported to a ghost city inhabited by shadows who occasionally screamed or fired a shot at some unreal distance. There was nobody on this particular block. The houses were empty shells. It was all a shoddy make-believe stage setting someone had erected overnight on the hills of a deserted Indian-haunted bay beyond the Great American Desert. San Francisco wasn't real.

But as she reached Grant Street, a burly drunken white man staggered around a corner, blocking her path with a bottle in one hand and a length of two-by-four in the other. "I see you, China Doll. Whatcha doin' out here away from your joss sticks 'n' opium pipes, huh?"

Dawn didn't hesitate as she moved toward him. "Get out of my way, you son of a bitch. I'm not going to say it again."

"Hey, you a white gal? What the fuck's a white gal doin' here in Chinatown?"

Dawn didn't answer. She drew the revolver from under her bodice, aimed it in the general direction of the white man's groin, and fired. The drunk howled in terror and disbelief as the roar of the shot echoed from the shuttered buildings on either side. Then he was running as fast as his legs could carry him and Dawn knew she'd missed him. At this point she was beyond caring. Now that she'd reached Chinatown, her desperate search was bogging down in a multitude of choices. Which way had that damned kid of hers gone, once he reached Grant? Chinatown was an amorphous area more than a mile square and laced with streets and twisting alleyways. Gus could be anywhere! Which way should she look first?

To the north, a gun roared in the night and Dawn headed for the sound, her own weapon muzzle-down in her right hand as she swept the dark shadows with her eyes for any sign of movement. Dawn stiffened as something small and black darted across the moonlit cobbles in front of her, but even as she swung her pistol up to aim, she saw it was only a wharf rat. Nothing else was moving as far as she could see.

She turned a corner and stiffened as she realized that the gently swaying shadow under the broken street lamp was the corpse of a hanging man. Dawn forced herself to approach and felt a wave of weak-kneed relief as she saw that the lynch victim was an elderly Chinese. Then, since it was a man, even if it wasn't anyone she knew, Dawn dragged a trash barrel from a nearby doorway, mounted it beside the hanged man, and tucked her gun away. She took a clasp knife from a side pocket and sawed through the rope, gagging as the corpse fell to the damp pavement with a dull thud. Holding the lamppost for support, Dawn lowered herself back to the pavement and stared down at the sprawled dead form near the trash barrel. Now that she'd cut him down, what was she supposed to do with him?

Dawn was suddenly aware she was no longer alone on the seemingly deserted street. A voice said, quietly, "Why missy do that? Missy no belong along white fellah?"

She looked around her at the circle of Chinese who'd suddenly materialized from the night mists. Seeing it was useless to go for her weapon, she licked her lips and said, "I am looking for my son. He's a tall blond boy in a dark high-necked sweater and jeans. Have any of you gentlemen seen him?"

The Chinese who'd first addressed her said, "You son white fellah and he come Chinatown, he dead, my word. Why you cut Chinee fellah down flom lampee? You maybe clazy lady, missy?"

"I'll give you a reward if you help me find my son. He's only a baby and he's never hurt anybody, Chinese or white. Won't you help me?"

The English-speaking oriental translated her request in singsong Cantonese, to be met with a burst of incredulous mocking laughter by the others. The Chinese gang had moved in closer around her, not unlike wolves around a crippled deer, and she quickly fumbled in her side pocket before holding up a golden ring. "Wait," she stammered. "I want you to look at this, please."

The leader of the gang took the summoning ring from her roughly. It was his, whatever it was, by right of conquest. The white woman was not bad-looking, either. Since she'd shown such odd consideration for a victim of her kinsmen, mayhaps he'd let her live, once they'd had some sport with her.

Then, as he held the ring up to the dim light to examine it, his jaw dropped. "Where missy get this? You cuttem off dead Chinee fellah?"

"It was given to me many years ago by a man named Wong. Do you know what it means?"

The gang leader held a hurried consultation with his fellows before he said, grudgingly, "Better missy come along Fong Low. Better we go chop-chop, savvy?"

Dawn allowed the Chinese and his followers to lead her into a nearby dark alley, asking, "Where are you taking me?" But the man refused to answer, merely taking her by the sleeve to lead her none too gently through nearly total darkness. Around her, others seemed to be singing or screaming at one another in their strange tongue.

Later, Dawn would have no idea of how far or in what direction she'd been half-led, half-dragged, through the back alleyways of Chinatown. In time, a door opened in the inky blackness and she was shoved inside, blinking in the incense-scented lamplight of a small room decorated in red and gilt. Dawn stood alone for a time as her guides left her. Then the beaded curtains at one end of the room parted and a small dark young Chinese in black western clothes entered. He bowed to Dawn with a stiff smile. "It's so good of you to honor us with your visit, Mrs. Carlyle."

"You know me?" Dawn blinked. "Who are you, sir, and where are we?"

The Chinese said, "I have known you for years, madam. My illustrious uncle, whose name need not concern us, pointed you out on the street to me one day. As to who I am and where we are, it may be better if you never know. You have used the bidding ring you were given by my kinsman. May I ask what your desires may be on this most unfortunate night?"

"I'm looking for my son. He's a good boy, but I'm afraid he's out on the streets—"

"You speak of your son, August Carlyle? This is not a good time for a white boy to be on the streets of Chinatown, madam."

"I know. He told his younger brother he wanted to see what was going on. He's not one of the hoodlums you people have been having trouble with, sir. I'll admit Gus may seem a little wild, but . . ."

"Please, madam, you are wasting time telling me things I know already. Did you think we would be watching you all these years without knowing what sort of children you have?"

"You know Gus, too?"

"Of course. He is, as you say, inclined to wander. He is also a decent enough young man, for his kind. You see, Mrs. Carlyle, we know who calls us Ching-Ching-Chinaman and pelts our laundry lines with horse manure. We know when one of your people merely walks among us in idle interest at our customs and ways, and which of them stare at us with ill-concealed dislike."

"My son Gus likes everyone. He'd never throw horse manure at anyone, sir."

"Again we speak of what is already known, madam. One time, not long ago, your son was with some friends at a nearby noodle shop. I don't know whether he liked our lo mein or not, but I know he paid, and when one of his white friends made a rude remark to the waitress, your son chided him. It was perhaps a small enough expression of common decency, but these days my people are grateful for small favors. Now, as to what brings you out on such a terrible night, you have done more than enough. May I suggest you allow me to have some of my friends escort you to the safety of your own part of town?"

"I have to find my child, sir."

"Of course. As he must find his mother safe and well when he returns to his home. You were most fortunate in meeting the men you did, Mrs. Carlyle. The next band you encounter on your aimless wandering may be from a rival tong, or even worse, white ruffians from the waterfront. I suggest you go home and wait. If your son is in Chinatown, and alive, we shall see that he gets home safely."

"I'll go mad waiting up on Nob Hill without a word about Gus. How long do you think it will take your friends to find him?"

The hatchet man shrugged and said, "That is written on the wind, I fear. Suffice it to say, we shall do our best. Will you allow me to have you seen safely to your district? Forgive me if I seem rude, but seeing you safely to your very door may not be prudent on either side."

"Can't I wait here?"

"Madam, you can do anything you like. I can only make suggestions to the holder of a summoning ring. I suggest you follow my advice, but your every wish is my command."

"All right, my wish is to stay right here until my son is safe in my arms again!"

"In that case, may I offer you some tea and more comfortable quarters while you wait? If you will step this way, I shall see to your son's whereabouts after seeing to your comfort."

Dawn started to say she didn't give a hang about anything but where Gus might be, but she contented herself with a nod and followed the young man into a larger, more sumptuously furnished room. The hatchet man clapped his hands, and a young woman in a red silk gown appeared with a tea tray. The hatchet man indicated a pile of satin pillows on a teak divan. "If you will excuse me, then, I shall order a search of such territory as I control in these troubled times."

The man said something to the girl in Cantonese and left Dawn alone with her. The girl smiled shyly and began to pour green tea into a tiny eggshell-thin blue cup. When Dawn tried to thank her, the girl giggled uncertainly and Dawn knew she spoke no English. Dawn had read somewhere that the Indian tribes had emigrated from Asia to America, so she tried a few words of Ho. The Chinese girl looked, if anything, more confused.

Apparently the American Indian had been on this continent some time. Dawn had noticed a similar tonality in Cantonese and Ho, but the vocabulary was completely changed by time, if, indeed, there had ever been any similarity.

Dawn sipped the unsweetened tea and returned the cup to the tray the girl had placed on the ebony table by the dais. She didn't want refreshments. She wanted her son back. She knew she was going to box his ears the moment she saw him, but dear God, let him be found safe and well!

It seemed a million years but was little more than

an hour before the hatchet man came back with an uncertain smile. He bowed and said, "Your son is alive. If you will come with me, I shall take you to him, madam."

"Where is he?" she gasped. "Why didn't you bring him with you?"

"Calm yourself, madam. The boy has been injured, but he is in no real danger. It would seem Ong Leong is deeper than ever in debt to the house of Carlyle, but I digress. Come. We have not far to go."

Dawn sprang to her feet and followed him, hardly noting the fact that the path he led her through seemed to be a dimly illuminated series of passageways between the cheek-by-jowl buildings of Chinatown. They went up and down flights of steps through oddly furnished living quarters, basements, and, once, a steaming kitchen. And then, at last, they were in a black-and-gold-paneled chamber smelling of sandalwood and some oddly pungent sweetness. Dawn saw her son stretched naked to the waist on a pile of satin pillows. His head lay in the lap of a beautiful Chinese girl of perhaps sixteen. At the white youth's side knelt an elderly man in a dark-blue smock and a small black silk skullcap. The Chinese who'd led her to Gus murmured, "As you see, he was in a fight."

Dawn gasped as she sank to her knees by her son's side. The boy's chest and upper arms were covered with bruises. His face was swollen, his upper lip was split, and the girl who held his head lifted a damp towel to reveal an ugly gash on the boy's forehead. As Dawn took one of Gus's hands in both of hers, he opened his eyes, looked up at her with a crooked little smile, and said, "Hi, Mom. I 'spect you're sore at me, huh?"

"What happened to you? You look like a train ran over you! Didn't your father tell you not to go out tonight?"

"Aw, Mom, I just wanted to help. I didn't mean to get in trouble."

The hatchet man explained, "Your son came to the noodle shop where this young woman works. He told her and her family to come away with him where they would be safe. I gather he meant your home. The people he offered his protection to speak little English and in any case would not have left Chinatown on such a night, but as I said, your house has indebted my house yet again."

"Oh, that's ridiculous. The fool kid didn't help anyone and now look at him! When I get you home, Gus Carlyle, I'm going to give you a good tanning!"

Gus said, "Yeah, 'spect I deserve one, Mom."

But the hatchet man went on. "Your son was not as unworthy as you may think, Mrs. Carlyle. It seems he was not the only white man who'd noticed the charms of my female cousin, here. Shortly after he arrived, the shop was invaded by a band of six other white men. I shall not offend your ears by telling you what they intended. The girl, and Ong Leong, owe the preservation of her honor to the house of Carlyle."

"Gus, my little Gus, took on a half dozen other boys?"

"They were not boys. They were men, and he took them on indeed. The shop is now a shambles, but such damage is easily repaired. When our tong men responded to the alarm raised by the girl's father, there was little left for them to do. Your son, it would seem, is an awesome fighter. Two of the hoodlums lay unconscious on the floor. The rest had fled."

The girl holding Gus's head smiled shyly at Dawn and said in quite good English, "He was a dragon! I laughed at him when he came in to say he was going to protect me, but then those others came, and Gus was no longer a silly boy. His eyes blazed like burning joss and his fists became flashing hammers of steel. When they hit him, he just laughed, and his laughter was the laughter of a dragon, too!"

The hatchet man said something in Cantonese and the girl fell silent with lowered eyes. The tong leader said to Dawn, "His cuts and bruises are not as serious as they look. The doctor, here, tells me he should be able to walk in an hour or so. Suffice it to say, he shall be carried to your door, but we must wait until the night calms itself. Judging by our past experiences in such matters, the mobs will be safely sleeping off their drunken rage by midnight."

"We can't wait that long. I have to get word to my husband. If he comes home to find us both missing . . ."

"You anticipate me yet again, Mrs. Carlyle. By now your husband will have received the message I sent. He is at the police station with the other vigilantes. The police, with commendable wisdom, have assigned interior guard duty to their civilian volunteers."

"Then my husband's safe, too? I was so afraid he'd be in the thick of things."

"One would imagine that's what the police thought, too. The San Francisco police have rather surprised us in the past few nights. In Los Angeles, the police stood by as our people were being robbed and murdered. It would seem, despite their occasional rude remarks to the sons of Han, the San Francisco police are true professionals. This, too, shall be remembered. No jade hatchet shall ever be sent to any officer who served this night, no matter how he may insult us in the future."

Gus suddenly tried to raise his head as he muttered, "I'm feeling better now. Where's my shirt?"

The elderly Chinese snapped something in his own language and the hatchet man said, "Lie still, young friend. You received a nasty blow from that club and you must rest until the good doctor is more pleased with the pupils of your eyes. Your shirt was torn. You will be given a new one before you leave. Would you like a drink?"

Gus shot his mother a wary look and asked, "You mean a real drink? I don't know as Mom, here, thinks I'm old enough."

The hatchet man chuckled and said, "You are old enough. With madam's permission?"

Dawn nodded. "I could use a good stiff belt myself, about now!"

The hatchet man motioned to the girl, who slid her thighs out from under the boy's head as she lowered him gently to the pillows. Then she went to a nearby cabinet to return with a small earthenware bottle and three cups on a brass tray. She poured three tiny drinks and held the tray in turn to Gus, the hatchet man, and Dawn, as the boy propped himself up on one elbow. The hatchet man held his cup toward the boy and his mother in a silent toast. Then, as Dawn followed his example and sipped the mysterious fiery liquid, Gus coughed and gasped, "Jasus! What is this stuff?" Then, catching himself, he stammered, "Sorry, Mom, I never meant to cuss."

"That's all right," said Dawn, with a resigned little smile, adding, "I 'spect if you're old enough to drink with your Mom, you're old enough to cuss like your Dad."

* * *

Both Denis Kearney and the Chinese would survive the riots of '71. Within two short years the racial pressure would be partially removed from the Chinese community as the farcical Modoc Indian War flared up in the northern part of the state. The so-called Indian uprising was little more than a rampage on the part of a small band of frustrated Ho-speaking youths, but their raiding and occasional ambushing of a lone white occasioned a reaction all out of proportion to the danger.

Gus found his mother in the back garden, where she and little Rose were planting bulbs. As Brian's work and growing corpulence slowly changed him into a lackluster lover, Dawn found herself more inclined to busy herself with improvements in the house and garden, if only to burn up energy.

Gus squatted down beside them and picked up a bulb as if to help, but he merely toyed with it as he said, "Mom, I've been thinking about joining up."

"Joining up with what, dear?" asked Dawn, absently.

"The volunteers, Mom. They're recruiting out at the Presidio, and well, Sam Gump and I were thinking of signing on for the duration."

Dawn stopped what she was doing to stare at her son, open-mouthed. "You want to join the army? Whatever for? There's no war, and for God's sake, your father gives you a bigger allowance than the thirteen dollars a month of an army private!"

"Aw, it's not the money, Mom. We just thought we'd give the volunteers a hand up north. That Captain Jack and his Modoc have been killing folks all summer and nobody seems to be able to catch 'em. Sam and I were saying what they need up there are some real westerners who know the country and . . ."

"Oh, nonsense!" Dawn cut in. "What do you know about Modoc Country? Have you ever been up there in the lava flats?"

"Well, no, but . . ."

"That's what I mean. I don't know the country up there, either, but I know my Ho, and I've been following your silly so-called war in the papers. The whole thing's pathetic, and it would be funny if only those few whites and Indians didn't have to keep getting their fool selves killed."

"I know you like Diggers, Mom, but Captain Jack's a renegade and . . ."

"Now, how in blue blazes can an Indian be a renegade, Gus? Didn't you learn any English at those fine schools we've been sending you to all these years? A renegade is a traitor to his own people. How many Indians do you 'spect Captain Jack and his band have killed? The poor little fool is just lashing out, and frankly I can't say I blame him. The Modoc have been pushed off their old lands into broken lava fields a lizard would have poor hunting on. You know why they've been raiding farms and ranches near their so-called reservation? Simply to get something to eat!"

"The government was feeding 'em, Mom. The fighting started when they refused government rations and attacked the Indian agent."

"I know what sort of garbage Washington calls Indian rations, but let's not argue the right or wrong of it. You're not going. I won't have you led into an ambush by those foolish officers we seem to have in charge of that crazy campaign up north. Why, one good mountain man and a squad of men who knew what they were doing would have rounded up those poor Modoc in a week, but . . ."

"That's my point, Mom. Everybody knows the army's

making a fool of itself in the Modoc War. If Sam and I showed them how to do it, they'd likely make us officers and . . ."

Rose Maureen suddenly piped up, "Oh, you just want to get yourself killed over that fool Chinese gal, Gus. You don't know any more about the army than you do about girls!"

Dawn started to shush her daughter. Then, noting the flush on her eldest son's face, she suddenly got to her feet. "Let's go over to the gazebo for a minute, Gus. Rose, you stay here, and mind you don't plant any more of those tulips upside down!"

She led the protesting Gus to the wrought iron gazebo set against the retaining wall at the back of the lot and sat him down beside her. "All right, Gus, what did Rose mean about a Chinese girl? Have you been pestering that Ching Li at the noodle shop again?"

"Aw, gee, Mom, I don't see why everybody's so down on the Chinese."

"I'm not down on anyone, Gus. Have you been courting Ching Li, or haven't you?"

"Well, sort of. I know you and Athair would have a fit if I really up and married a Chinese, but damn it all, I just can't seem to get her out of my mind and . . . Hell, I don't see why two people who like each other have to fret so much about the slant of their durned old eyes!"

"All right, you're in love with a Chinese girl. Does that mean you have to run around killing Indians? Honestly, Gus, if I live to be a hundred, I'll never understand you men!"

Gus looked startled and gasped, "You wouldn't mind if I married up with a Chinese gal, Mom?"

"Not if she was a nice Chinese girl. I judge people

by their hearts, and from the few times I've spoken to her, your Ching Li seems like a sweet little thing, but it's not that simple, Gus."

"I know, Athair would have a fit if he knew."

"Your father would have a fit if you married a Protestant, but he's not the problem. You know he loves you and that he's a good-natured man. If there were some way you could marry Ching Li, he'd keep his thoughts to himself and treat her as kindly as he does everyone else, for all his bluster."

"You mean, we could have your blessing, Mom?"

"Of course, but your father and I are not the world you and Ching Li live in, son. For one thing, it's against the law for a white person to marry a Chinese or Indian in the state of California. Have you thought about that?"

"Ching Li has. She says I'm silly. I told her we could maybe go back east or something, but she says that's silly, too, and . . . and Mom, she says she's going to have to marry up with a damned old Chinaman!"

Dawn tried not to smile as she soothed him. "That doesn't sound like such a bad idea, son. Her father and mother are Chinese. I imagine a Chinese husband would be what they've had in mind for her."

"She don't love him, Mom. She told me herself she doesn't even know the old man. They're going to make her marry him, anyway."

"Against her will?"

"Well, not exactly. She says it's her duty to please her folks, but how could she love an old chink?"

"You know what you just did, Gus? You just explained why you can't marry the girl!"

"I did? How'd I do that, Mom? I just said she was spurning me for . . ."

"An old chink. A man you know nothing about except that he's Chinese. How do you feel about your Ching Li in the arms of a naked Chinaman, Gus? Does it make you a little sick to your stomach?"

"Oh God, yes, Mom! She's so little and pretty, and I know she's never even been kissed and—"

"Gus, listen to me. The way you feel about your Ching Li in the arms of some strange Chinese is just the way a lot of the white people you know would feel about you in the arms of a Chinese girl! You say she's never been kissed, so I can only hope that includes you. You haven't gotten the girl in trouble, have you, son?"

"Mom! She's not that kind of a girl!"

"All right, I know what we're dealing with, then. You've paid court to a pretty girl and she's turned you down. I know you're upset and I know there's little I can do or say to help, but you're not going to make things any better by running off to fight Indians. I'd sooner see you drunk!"

"Mom, you don't understand at all. I've read about love and I've heard about love, but this awful empty feeling is driving me crazy, and if I could maybe invite Ching Li and her folks to dinner or something . . ."

"What would that do for you, son?"

"Well, Ching Li says she knows how folks would feel, but if I could bring her up here to Nob Hill and let her see you ain't like the folks she's worried about—"

"In other words, you think she'd be honored to have dinner with white people. My God, no wonder you say ain't. Do you know what you are, Gus? You're becoming an unmitigated young snob. You can cuss and say ain't all day, and it still won't help. You really do think you're better than people of other colors and creeds, don't you?"

"Mom! I offered to *marry* Ching Li!"

"Oh my, and to think she turned down the honor! Did it cross your mind for one minute that a mere Chinese might not want to share steak and mashed potatoes with your ever-so-nice family?"

"Mom, she's as civilized as we are."

"Of course. Maybe she and her family think she's *more* civilized. We don't have a monopoly on snobbery, you know. Has she ever given you any reason to think you're more than a customer for her father's noodles?"

"Mom, she *knows* I *love* her!"

"I see. She's supposed to drop everything and roll over and butter herself for the first white boy who says he loves her, eh? Oh, my poor baby. You have so much to learn—and they wasted so much time trying to teach you French!"

"I don't see what my being white has to do with it," he said sullenly.

"Really? What else have you to offer the girl except the honor of your stooping to her supposed level? A lot of men chase fat girls for much the same reason. They're so surprised when they discover that a woman may not always fall in love with a man just because he thinks he's shooting fish in a barrel. Now, listen to me, Gus. I know just what's happened. You've been hanging around Chinatown for two reasons. One is because it's novel and sort of exciting to be around people and things so unusual. The other is that it makes you feel superior. Wait, I know you've been very friendly to your Chinese toys, but that's what they've really been to you, simply pretty exotic toys. You've found it easy to make friends down there because you're a big white boy who'll fight for them and you like to be fawned on a bit, as who doesn't?"

"Mom, Ching Li's not a toy. I love her!"

"Perhaps you do. But you've failed to grasp that under her tawny skin and exotic almond eyes, Ching Li is a *person!* You've been mooning about the noodle shop, talking and joking with her, and you've built a daydream romance out of it. You thought just being white would give you an edge over the Chinese boys who probably think she's rather pretty, too. Now that you know it hasn't, you're all upset and confused, but it's really very simple. She doesn't love you, she has never loved you, and she's engaged to another man. You're simply going to have to put it out of your mind."

Gus stared stubbornly at the plank flooring and sighed, "It's not that simple at all, Mom. You *got* the man *you* loved. You just don't know what it's like."

Dawn looked away and murmured, "I'm afraid I do, Gus. You see, before there was your father, there was another man. A boy called Nevada. I loved him very much, and I never got him, as you put it. So I'm not as much a stranger to your feelings as you might think."

Gus looked up in surprise. "Uncle Nevada? You never said he was in love with you. I remember your telling us about how he found you out in the desert and all, but I always thought you were sort of a kid sister to him or something."

"I guess I was. He never knew how much I loved him. Loved him and wanted him, the way you want your Ching Li. I've often thought, had he lived a little longer . . . Well, the thing is, I got over it."

"That's when you married up with my father, right?"

"Yes," Dawn lied, "and your father made me very happy before I lost him, too."

"Yes, you told me how he was killed defending you and granddad. But Athair's made up for it, hasn't he,

Mom? I mean, you are happy together, aren't you?"

"Of course, dear. Whatever made you ask a thing like that?"

"I don't know. I remember how we went up to the mountains that time and how happy the two of you seemed."

"Aren't we still the same, Gus?"

"I guess so. I guess, as folks get older, they don't josh around and spend as much time together, huh?"

"Well, we've both been very busy, the last few years. I didn't know we seemed any cooler to one another. He's been very good to us all, you know."

"Oh, sure, Mom, I didn't mean you two were peeved with each other or anything. It's just that, I dunno, it ain't the same as when we kids were little."

"Oh, we're still very happy. Just getting old and set in our ways, I suppose," mused Dawn, even as she considered how long it had been since she and Brian had made love. Good heavens, had it really been last month? Yes, it had, and she'd feigned her orgasm, if only to get his bloated belly away from hers. Dear God, was it really that obvious to the children?

Dawn suddenly brightened. "Himself will be having a birthday in less than two weeks. What do you say to a surprise party?"

"Mom, I don't know if I'll be here in two weeks, if I'm to join the volunteers and all."

"We'll talk about it after your father's birthday party, Gus. I don't want to hear another word about Captain Jack's ragged Modoc gang until he's blown out the cake. Heavens, I'd better make it a big cake. Between the two of us, we've certainly accumulated a lot of candles!"

"Mom, I promised Sam. I don't want him to think I'm chicken!"

"We'll invite him to the party, too, along with his sister Nancy. She's a very pretty little thing, and I'm going to need you there to play the piano and sing for us. You know himself enjoys singing, but he won't sing for me unless you join in the harmony."

Gus would argue and sulk for days, she knew, but the matter was settled as far as she was concerned. She'd intended a quiet gathering of Brian's friends and business associates for the coming birthday get-together, but it was time they had some young people at the house and there were a dozen or more pretty young things whose mothers Dawn knew well enough to invite.

While she was about it, she thought, she'd better see that there were some boys to catch Rose Maureen's attention. She certainly didn't want to go through a thing like this again. All in all, it might be better if she started paying a bit more attention to her children's infatuations. She couldn't stop the fool kids from trying to make her a grandmother before she was forty, but with a little motherly guidance the three of them might be steered into sensible choices.

The birthday party for himself was less than a surprise, thanks to Felicidad's big mouth, but Brian was a good sport about pretending total astonishment when he came home that night to find the backyard decorated with Chinese lanterns and filled with people, young and old.

The children and teenagers of Nob Hill made a curious contrast to their elders as Dawn watched them during her supervision of the fete. Despite a certain tendency to run to flab, and despite their fine clothes, the millionaires and near-millionaires of Nob Hill, together with their wives, betrayed their oddly assorted ethnic and social backgrounds. You could put a bearded mountain man in a starched shirt and a frock coat, but you couldn't make him look used to them. You could take a farm girl off the farm, but you couldn't take the farm off her with a gallon of perfume and a bucket of expensive cosmetics. Those of educated background tended toward stuffy respectability or self-indulgent theatrical poses as country squires or latterday Davy Crocketts. Though few went as far as the self-proclaimed "Emperor Norton" who roamed the bars in an admiral's uniform, handing out his own homemade money and occasionally pausing to "knight" a bemused policeman.

Their children, however, were San Franciscans, an odd breed future Californians would be able to tell at a glance.

It was environmental rather than inborn, Dawn knew. In an era where a woman's limbs were never mentioned in public, the legs of the San Francisco girls was a topic of sniggering legend. Growing up on the steep hillsides by the bay had endowed the second generation with trim muscular figures that made both boys and girls seem somehow related to the same mountain tribe, whatever their background. The climate had left its stamp on them, too. San Francisco's Presidio was the only army post where neither summer uniforms nor winter overcoats were issued, and while it was almost always cool, it was seldom either really hot or cold. The San Francisco boys were a bit pasty-faced from the constant fogs and overcast; the girls, with thinner skins, had the pale peaches-and-cream complexions of wellborn English girls. Neither freckles nor sun-bleached blond hair was in evidence, and growing up in a climate that encouraged Western European dress, both sexes of the new San Franciscans tended to be neatly buttoned into their everlasting fall wardrobes. The girls for the most part wore stylish Paris gowns from puberty on. The boys tended to wear the same dark wool suits and neatly fastened starched collars.

Aside from those few, like Gus, who tended to rebel against convention, there was a certain smug uniformity to the younger generation that belied their years. They were patrician in their manners and proud of their city, looking pained when one of the older people called it Frisco. Dawn was rather pleased with the way the town was turning out, but she wondered if she'd ever be quite comfortable with the self-conscious pride it was developing so soon after rising from its flea-infested sand dunes by the bay.

Her daughter, Rose Maureen, had dressed for the occasion in a dark maroon dress far too sedate for her years, but the girl was not going unnoticed by the boys she'd invited to her father's party. Rose was becoming a vapidly pretty young thing as she matured. She had a lot of her father's peasant bone structure, but the soft light and steep hills had slimmed and paled her to a fair imitation of a well-bred Irish gentlewoman. If she kept her figure past the first baby, Dawn supposed she'd escape looking like a North Beach washerwoman.

Brian Junior had inherited his father's looks. He seemed, in fact, to be more like Brian had been when she'd met him than his older and stockier father, these days. Like the others, Brian Junior had been toned up and conditioned by the hills and active life of his peers, once he'd gotten old enough to stop moping petulantly around the house. He had his own gelding stabled out by the marina and was growing quite athletic as he discovered why boys and girls were different. Dawn watched him serving punch to some sweet young thing and felt a pang of motherly pride, mixed with regret, as her eyes swept past to the figure of her husband, standing with some other men near the upright piano the servants had brought out from the house.

It seemed as if by some grotesque reversal of time Brian Senior and Junior were trading bodies as they got older. Her son was now becoming a tall muscular young man as his father deteriorated into a large pudgy child with a cigar in his mouth. Her husband's hair was becoming thin rather than gray, and Dawn knew he was going to be one of those big, pink, baby-faced men in old age. It wasn't fair. Brian was only ten or twelve years older than she, if he'd told the truth. How could a man not yet fifty look so . . . so banal?

One of the guests had apparently requested a song, and Brian called over to Gus, who joined the older group near the piano. Gus was about as neatly dressed this evening as he ever was, but he still looked like a farmhand who'd somehow wandered into Nob Hill society as he ran his fingers through his unruly straw-colored hair and seated himself at the piano. Dawn knew her eldest boy was popular, despite his sore-thumb contrast to the sleeker-looking young men now gathering around him. Gus played well, yet never with the skill one would have hoped from all those music lessons, and Dawn brightened as her son ran his big rawboned hands over the keyboard in a warm-up arpeggio.

The conversation stopped as the assembled guests turned to the piano, and as she'd hoped, Gus began to play "Wild Mountain Thyme."

Brian took the cigar from his mouth and began to

sing as Gus joined in, following his stepfather's tenor
with a deeper harmony of his own. Brian had lost his
shyness about singing in public and his voice was perhaps the one thing he'd improved with practice in the
last few years. Dawn listened, her head filled with a
bittersweet memory of the first time she'd heard the
plaintive old Irish song as the two of them sang:

> If you ever leave me, Dear
> Faith, I'll just have to find another
> To help me pick wild thyme
> Where it's growing on yon mountain . . .

Dawn frowned as the full meaning of that verse
sank in. How odd, she thought, that she'd never really
heard the song that way before. Brian hadn't turned
away, exactly, but . . . where *was* the strong young
man she'd married? It wasn't fair. It hadn't been that
many years ago, and damn it, she was still a young
woman. A woman much too young for an aging fat
man, at any rate. They hadn't made love in days.
Months, if one counted enjoying it. Dawn tried to tell
herself it wasn't Brian's fault, but it *was*. It wasn't age
that was coming between them. It was Brian's calm
acceptance of his growing girth and seeming lack of
interest. She knew he wasn't impotent. On the increas-
ingly rare occasions they made love, his virile member
functioned well enough. What was the matter with
him? Brian said it was because he was growing older
and was worn out from his long hours at the office,
but he wasn't old and he'd been a rutting bull of a
man when he'd been working beside his work gangs
for sixteen hours at a stretch. He didn't have a drinking problem, Dawn knew. Brian was a two-fisted
eater, but he drank and smoked as he ate, without

much imagination and a seemingly bottomless capacity. She'd never really seen him drunk, as a matter of fact. Once, when she'd commented on the huge quantity of needled steam-beer she'd seen him put away at Governor Stanford's dinner party, Brian had simply shrugged it off, saying there wasn't enough steam-beer in San Francisco to make a man his size drunk. It had taken all Dawn's willpower not to blurt out that there were few men his size in San Francisco. They'd reached an armed truce on the subject of his appetite in the past few years. Dawn no longer commented on his overeating and Brian neither sulked nor called the salad greens she served her children "rabbit food."

One of the other older men had joined Brian, and the two of them were now singing "Sweet Betsy from Pike" as some of the younger guests tried not to look pained. The younger San Franciscans seemed to turn from the roughneck tales of the Great Crossing in inverse ratio to how wild and woolly their parents remembered the Gold Rush. Dawn wondered if *their* children and grandchildren would remember it at all, assuming San Francisco had sprung full-blown from dragon's teeth, like Rome. Or would they, perhaps, join in the already glorified legends of the recent past as they, in turn, rejected the pretenses of the first native sons and daughters of the Golden West?

She'd found some copies of Ned Buntline's magazine in Brian Junior's room and scanned through them before making up her mind whether to forbid him his penny dreadfuls. It was astonishing how the eastern writers were portraying the young states west of the Big Muddy. Ned Buntline, whoever he might be, seemed to think life in the West consisted of endless Indian fights and stagecoach robberies, engaged in by strange-looking men with Louis Napoleon beards and woolly chaps. Dawn was amused to discover that on the cover of one magazine sturdy Colonel Billy was wearing the fringed buckskins of a Shoshoni *squaw*.

A familiar voice broke into Dawn's thought train and she turned to see Canfield, her stockbroker, sidling up to her with two glasses of punch. Canfield said, "You look tired, ma'am. I thought you could use a drink."

The fussy little man tried not to talk business, but it was all he ever thought of. Anxious to get her own mind away from its wandering, Dawn smiled at him as she accepted the punch. "I was hoping we could have a moment to discuss your last memo, Mr. Canfield. I'm keeping an open mind on Southern Pacific, but frankly I think my portfolio's overloaded with heavy industry."

"We're living in an industrial age, ma'am."

"You mean we've been living in one, sir. I've been following the figures on Carnegie, Krupp and Bessemer. Steel and rails are peaking out. There's a limit to how many blast furnaces and coal mines the world needs."

"Oh, come now, Mrs. Carlyle. Andrew Carnegie's become one of the richest men in the world with his Pittsburgh empire. And as for Krupp—"

"Oh, no doubt they'll go on to greater glory. My point is that the main advances in heavy industry have been made. The future will see bigger steel ships and more powerful locomotives, but from here on to at least the end of this century there won't be any basic changes in steel, rails, mining, and so forth. We don't make money investing in fat-cat stocks that pay six percent, Mr. Canfield. The few killings I've made have been in buying into growth."

Canfield nodded sagely and sighed, "I can't argue

with that, ma'am. Those Western Union shares you bought when there was a single copper wire stretched from the Mississippi to this coast have made a modest fortune for you in their own right. But about this opportunity to buy into the Southern Pacific's new extension across the Imperial Valley . . ."

"I don't want any more S.P. stock. Have you been following Denis Kearney's latest outbursts against the Octopus?"

"Come, now, Kearney's just a troublemaker. Nobody listens to his socialist ravings, ma'am."

"You mean nobody who lives on Nob Hill, don't you? I agree he's a troublemaker, but a lot of small businessmen, farmers, and underpaid workers are listening and repeating his demands for government regulations on freight tariffs. You'll have to admit that the Southern Pacific has been a bit roughshod in its methods."

"Oh, C.P. Huntington's been a bit greedy, next to Central Pacific and U.P., but he's got the gang in Sacramento in his hip pocket and Kearney hasn't been able to elect any of his people to anything important."

"The Working Man's party doesn't have to win election to the statehouse. They merely have to convince the regular party men we do elect that somebody ought to put a muzzle on C. P. Huntington."

"I doubt if anyone in California could do that, Mrs. Carlyle."

"Oh, Seep will survive. The railroad and ranching barons have too much accumulated power to be put out of business in our lifetimes, but I don't see much profit in it for me, fighting on their side. As I said, I'd rather have my money in growth, not in a holding action."

"You may be right, but some of these new companies you're interested in seem a bit harebrained to me, ma'am. For instance, those Standard of Ohio shares are terribly overpriced for a high-risk venture like rock oil. Young Rockefeller is expanding too fast and taking terrible risks with that oil business he started. I have it on good authority he knows absolutely nothing about geology. The man was a mere bookkeeper when he begged, borrowed, and stole enough to build his first refinery."

Dawn cut in, with an impish grin, "And C. P. Huntington was running a general store when he decided it might be nice to have a transcontinental railroad. John D. Rockefeller is worth one million dollars at the age of thirty-seven. He's selling shares to buy out his brother's interest in Standard Oil, and in less than five years we won't be able to afford Standard of Ohio at any price. That's why we're buying in now."

"But you're buying too many shares, ma'am! What if Standard Oil should fail? Where's he going to sell all that oil?"

"He'll sell it. That's what I mean about growth stocks. The world is changing, Mr. Canfield. Changing faster than it's changed in at least two thousand years. Did you know a man named Karl Otto is working on an internal combustion engine in Germany, right now?"

Canfield looked blank. "What on earth is an internal combustion engine, Mrs. Carlyle?"

"I'm not sure I understand, either, but the magazine article I read said it burns naphtha, and John D. Rockefeller is producing naphtha as a by-product to his lamp oil in Ohio. Another new invention I'm interested in is that writing machine of Charles Thurber's. Does he have any shares on the market?"

"The so-called typewriter is impractical, ma'am. Everyone who's tried to manufacture one has gone broke."

"As did Goodyear with his sulfurized rubber and Howe with his sewing machine, but they'll perfect the typewriter. They have to. There's just too much paperwork today, and not enough clerks who can write a fast, legible hand. But leaving that aside, what about Nobel of Sweden? Did you order me that block I suggested?"

"I couldn't get it at your bid, ma'am. Nobel seems to be developing into a blue-chip stock a bit sooner than one would have expected."

"You didn't expect *dynamite* to sell? Heavens, they've been using it over in the Comstock for nearly five years!"

"I know, ma'am, and Nobel of Sweden has been getting rich off their patent. The stock is selling dear and only paying five percent, so . . ."

"Oh, you were right to withdraw my bid, then. I really do have to learn to get in on these things sooner. How about Edison of New Jersey?"

"I picked up a block of a hundred on margin. The firm's been losing money on research and we got it cheap. Frankly, I don't see what you wanted with it. They say Edison is a bit mad. Since he made a few dollars with his stock ticker, he's been wasting time on pure research instead of mass-producing his stock tickers like any sensible young man would be expected to. The company's profits have been marginal, at best, up to now."

"Give them time. Petroleum, electricity, new chemicals, and new ideas are the wave of the future."

"Forgive me, but you lost money on that scheme to grow figs in the Central Valley, and we've yet to see a profit from those vineyards in the Napa valley."

"*Touché*—but there has to be risk or there'd be no need for investment money. I don't know why figs

won't set fruit in California, but some day we'll have
the answer and we will grow figs here instead of importing them all the way from Greece. As for the
poor showing of my vineyards, that's another mystery
we'll have the answer to, with time. My hands tell me
dusting the vines with sulfur seems to help and I've
sent for some French books by a Professor Pasteur,
who seems to know a lot about winemaking. Meanwhile, the vinegar we've been getting in place of wine
seems to be paying the upkeep on the vineyards."

Canfield was starting to look glazed, so Dawn released him with a question he could answer about her
Western Union shares. He reassured her about their
being gilt-edged, as she knew already, and made his
way over to another group near the buffet, leaving
Dawn once more with her lonely musings about her
growing boredom.

Her husband was singing some song about an Irishman's goat and Dawn was not amused. She put the
half-empty glass of warm punch on a nearby table and
went inside to supervise the kitchen help. The kitchen
help didn't need supervision. The party, like everything else she planned, was running smooth as silk.
But dear God, she thought, was that all there was to
life? She wasn't forty, and her life had settled into a
banal rut. It was a comfortable rut, she was willing
to allow. Her husband was probably as good a husband as any woman could expect, and her children
seemed to be pleasant enough young strangers, but
what was the point of it all?

Dawn's gloomy train of thought was relieved by the
appearance of three new arrivals across the crowded
room. Seeing that her husband was oblivious to their
guests, she made her way over to do the honors. She
recognized their neighbor from up Nob Hill, the

courtly Mark Hopkins, who was said to be one of the
least offensive robber barons. With him were a tall
dark man and a shorter one who blinked at the lantern
light uncomfortably, like an owl forced from shelter
in daylight.

Holding out her gloved hand to Hopkins, she said,
"Mark, how nice of you to come."

Mark Hopkins looked uncertain and replied, "I had
no idea you were having a party, ma'am. I, uh, came
with these other gents on buisness."

Dawn smiled at the two men with Hopkins as she
waited to be introduced. Then her heart skipped a
beat. The man with the funny eyes was a total stranger
to her. The tall dark man with the silver streaks in his
curly black hair was Joaquín Murrieta!

Somewhere in the distance Mark Hopkins was saying, "You probably know Boss Buckley, here. May I
present State Senator Lopez?"

Hopkins chuckled as he added, "They're both durned
Democrats, but business is business."

By this time Brian had spotted his guests and torn
himself away from the songfest by the piano, so Dawn
was given time to compose her thoughts as her husband joined them near the entrance. The man she
knew as the notorious bandit was calm-faced, and she
couldn't tell what he was thinking. Had he recognized
her, too? It had been a long time since that anxious
night in the faraway canyon, and she'd been a mere
child.

Boss Buckley was saying something about a sewer
contract in an anxious tone, and Brian suggested they
talk about it in his den. Dawn stammered something
about seeing to the other guests and turned away. She
knew who Boss Buckley was, now. They called him
the Blind Boss, and he was said to be the man one saw

if one wanted to do business with the city of San Francisco. Like Hopkins, he was one of the more amiable robber barons of California, in that he seemed content with the lion's share of anything he was party to. He was generous to his followers, and during the Chinese riots he'd worked for peace. His notorious political thugs, "Buckley's Lambs," had left the Chinese alone. Their orders were simply to break the heads of any longshoreman or city worker who voted the wrong way. Buckley ran the local Democrats while Hopkins was reputed to be high in Republican circles. This didn't puzzle Dawn half as much as the part the bandit Murrietta might be playing in her husband's business these days!

Dawn saw that the punchbowl was low and had just instructed one of the help to refill it from the kitchen when she became aware of the tall figure looming at her side. She smiled up uncertainly and asked, "Would you like some punch, Senator Lopez?"

The sardonic Mexican replied, "La señora has always been famous for her sangria. It is said she used to drink with Mexicans before it became fashionable."

Dawn looked around for Brian and the others. Murrietta said, "They are off discussing their own brand of highway robbery. I came over with Hopkins as his houseguest, not as a coconspirator. What do you think of that monstrous house of his up the hill? Did you know he plans an even bigger one, with fairytale towers and stained glass windows?"

Dawn saw they were not within earshot of anyone and sighed, "You're not making this very easy for us . . . Senator."

"I know. The intelligent move would be to join the others in your husband's den and assume you hadn't recognized me. You have grown even more beautiful

since last we met and I have always been more curious
than common sense would call for."

Dawn filled a Waterford cup and handed it to him,
meeting his eyes as she smiled and said, "I'm afraid I
have no idea what you're talking about . . . Senator."

He held the cup, untasted, and said, "Please don't
take this for the flirtatious gallantry it may seem. I
only came over to reassure you."

"Reassure me, sir? I didn't know I had anything to
worry about."

"Ah, yes, I forgot you were a witch. From time to
time I run across people who might have known me
in my youth and some of them seem quite disturbed
to learn my head is not floating in that glass jar after
all."

"I see. I heard Captain Love was shot in some
vaguely reported brawl a while back. My husband
knows nothing about anyone I might have met in my
youth, *Senator*."

Murrietta/Lopez smiled thinly. "If I thought you
would believe me I would assure you I had nothing
to do with the demise of Captain Love. The man was
a drunkard and a wife-beater. His killing was long
overdue, but he died at the hands of another Anglo.
I know little more than you about the details."

Despite herself, Dawn couldn't resist asking, "Have
you *any* idea who that poor man in the jar might have
been, Senator?"

He shrugged. "No. They say Love caught the notorious bandit down near Tule Lake. An artist has
painted a portrait from the somewhat grotesque trophy, and some of my people keep prints of it as a
reminder of their hero and Robin Hood. So you see,
even if I should be accused . . ."

Then he smiled warmly and added, "But I am

speaking foolishly. I know who my friends are, and by the way, they call me Roberto. I am most uncomfortable with Senator. It makes me feel so old and stuffy."

Dawn smiled and said, "In that case let's make it Roberto and Dawn. I've forgotten what those other people we might remember were called."

"I agree. Let us remember them only as a frightened man and a very pretty young witch who touched something in him with her magic at a moment in time he could have gone either way. But before we lay the past to rest forever, could you bring me up to date on a few things? What happened to that fortunate little man with the nervous hands?"

"You mean Ace? He was killed in a gunfight."

"Ah? This does not surprise me. Your current husband is good to you?"

Dawn hesitated, then nodded. "Yes, we have three children, and Brian has been very sweet, in his own way."

"How fortunate for him. But I see he and the others have finished their dark plots agains the taxpayers, and I fear I must rejoin Mark and my old mentor, Buckley."

As Murrietta put his cup down, untasted, Dawn held out her hand to him. "Is Blind Boss Buckley as bad as Three Fingers Jack?"

Murrietta laughed and said, "Worse. Poor Jack had no imagination when it came to robbery, and by the way, Boss Buckley isn't really blind. He has cataracts, but he sees well enough, and misses nothing. If we're not discreet, he'll think I'm trying to steal you from your husband."

He kissed her gloved hand and released it. But before he turned away, he asked, "Well?"

"Well what, Roberto?"

The erstwhile bandit smiled crookedly and sighed, "Never mind. Alas, there are things one can steal and things one cannot."

As he turned and was threading his way through the crowd, one of the boys bumped his elbow. The once-deadly Murrietta accepted the youth's stammer of apology with a pleasant smile before moving on.

How odd it was, Dawn thought, that nothing in San Francisco was ever quite what it seemed. Like the fog from the sea, names and reputations shifted mysteriously, and just as you thought you knew the answers, they changed the questions.

Dawn moved over by the piano, where her husband joined her after seeing his callers out. He muttered, "Sorry about that, lass. Damned business emergency. I'm afraid that sewer deal's fallen through."

Dawn grimaced. "Do we have to talk about sewers, dear? We're having a party!"

"Ay, and a grand party it's been. So to hell with auld Buckley and his worries about the public till. What did you think of Senator Lopez?"

"I thought he was rather charming. Why do you ask?"

"He's all right, I guess. Buckley says he's honest enough, but a bit of a womanizer. I told him the Don Juan game was a wasted effort as far as my auld woman was concerned."

Then he noticed the look in Dawn's eye and added, "What's the matter? Did I say something wrong?"

"No, dear. Your auld woman isn't about to run off with a dashing Mexican." Then, despite herself, she asked, "By the way, did they say whether the senator's married or not?"

Brian thought for a moment before he replied. "I

don't think he is. But it wouldn't matter if he was. Them good-looking spiks all serenade the gals whether they're married or not. There's no substance to the breed. All flash and empty words. Give me a meat-and-potatoes American every time."

Dawn looked away and murmured, "We'd better mingle with our guests, dear. Why don't you sing some more?"

"Well, I haven't sung the one about Finnegan's Wake yet. Do you think it's too bawdy for Nob Hill?"

"No, dear. I think the children might enjoy it."

A Chinese sage once cursed an enemy by saying, "May you live in interesting times!" Dawn had never heard the expression, but she would have understood it after the bank crash of 1875, for her boring but comfortable round of dinner parties and meaningless errands ended with a literal bang shortly after the Bank of California failed that year, touching off a financial panic and a rash of suicides and street riots.

The rioters were workmen and small businessmen whose savings had been wiped out when the badly overextended banks fell like a line of dominoes after a sudden shift in bullion prices touched off a run on cash savings and a sudden calling-in of extended loans. The suicides were a mixed lot of bankers facing prison and middle-aged businessmen facing bankruptcy in a new economy they didn't understand. The get-rich-quick Gold Rush days had drawn to a close, and it was no longer possible for any man, young or old, to make it overnight with a prospector's pan or a deck of cards. One of the many men who shot himself was Dawn's stockbroker, Canfield. She heard the report of his .44 just as she entered the reception room of his office and, together with his male secretary, burst into his oak-paneled inner sanctum to find him behind his desk with half his head blown off.

"Oh, my God!" sobbed the secretary, as Dawn, taking in the scene with pale lips and a firm set to her jaw, snapped, 'The damn fool's dead. Do you have the combination to the safe?"

The fuzzy little man at her side nodded, then caught himself and stammered, "We can't touch anything until the police get here, Mrs. Carlyle." But Dawn snapped, 'The police are fighting for their lives on Market Street. Get that safe open. Some of those securities in there are mine!"

"It's illegal for us to touch his papers before the bank examiners have had a look at them, ma'am. We were issued a summons just before you arrived. I think that was why poor Mr. Canfield was so upset. Oh, my word, you don't think I'm in trouble, do you?"

Dawn stepped around behind the desk, lifting the hem of her skirt to avoid the blood on the carpet, and bent over to pick up Canfield's still warm revolver. "Here's what we're going to do. We're going to take every scrap of paper out of the safe, take a private room in the saloon across the street, and find out if we're in trouble or not. Come on, we're wasting time."

"Oh, ma'am, I can't open the safe without authorization!"

Dawn hefted the revolver, pointed it at the secretary's belt buckle, and said, "I'm authorizing you, as a stockholder in this company and a lady who's got the drop on you with a .44. Open the safe. Now!"

A few minutes later they were safely in the rear of the saloon across the street as Dawn faced the pallid secretary over a pile of handwritten papers and printed stock certificates piled between them on the bare wood table. The gun had been left with the broker's body for the police to find when they responded to the sound of the shot, if, indeed, they ever would. Dawn knew she could handle the mousey little man with her bare hands if she had to.

The secretary sipped at his stein of beer without tasting it and asked, in a hushed tone, "Have you found anything, Mrs. Carlyle?"

Dawn's voice registered disgust as she replied, "He should have killed himself years ago. Fortunately, I have a little more than half my older stock certificates under lock and key at home. The son of a bitch was buying for me on margin and pocketing the cash, wasn't he?"

"I'm not sure I understand just how Mr. Canfield conducted his affairs, ma'am."

"Of course not. He just had you working on his books to keep you from falling in the bay, right? You know perfectly well he was taking my orders and my checks and bidding on the stocks I ordered with marginal down payments. There isn't a thing here I can cash before I pay off the rest of what's due on them, and in case you didn't read the papers this morning, nobody in San Francisco has a bank account right now!"

"Oh, I'm sure the banks will have to make good, Mrs. Carlyle. The Bank of California just announced it was shipping in its gold reserves to cover the sudden local run and—"

"Oh, shut up and let me think. Let's see, the dividends I have coming on the sound stocks I still have will keep us eating, and our bills are paid up for the month. It'll be three months before anyone sues for past-due bills, so that gives us ninety days' leeway. Damn! I hate to think of letting go these shares in

Standard Oil and Edison, though. The Edison margin can wait at least a month, but unless I make a margin on Standard Oil . . . Here, you'll want this. I'd burn it, if I were you."

"What . . . what is it?" asked the secretary, taking the printed form from Dawn's hand as she said, "It's your signature on a stock order, you idiot. Canfield signed most of these himself, but you should be in jail for ordering this block of A&P on credit."

The man stared at the incriminating order blank as if it were a snake about to bite him and gasped, "This is your A&P bid, Mrs. Carlyle."

"I know. I have the canceled check to prove I paid cash for it, too. Oh, stop looking so innocent and get rid of it. By the way, just what is your name?"

"My . . . name?"

"You do have a name, don't you? If you're going to be working for me, I have to call you something besides Rover or Spot."

"My name is Murdstone, Justin Murdstone, ma'am. But I don't understand. What do you mean, I'm going to be working for you? I work for Canfield Associates and . . . Oh, dear . . ."

"That's right, Canfield Associates just blew its fool head off and you're either going to be working for me or in jail—until I get this mess cleaned up."

She waited until he'd had time to digest the part about jail before she asked, in a pleasanter tone, "How about it, Justin? You're going to have to wait to be paid, but I'll see that you and your family eat, at least."

"What . . . what am I supposed to be doing for you, ma'am?"

"The same thing you've always done for Canfield. You're going to lie a lot. Right now, the streets are filled with broken glass and gunsmoke, but sooner or later the accountants will get around to the late Canfield Associates. They'll find the safe empty, but fortunately you'll have the ledgers and papers in a safe place. Knowing of the trouble in the streets, you took them home with you after calling the police and locking up the office like the faithful employee you were."

"You want me to give these papers from Mr. Canfield's safe to the bank examiners, after all?"

"Of course. They'll want them. We're going to have to make a few changes in the books—and isn't it lucky I came by to pick up my own stock certificates just before the poor man killed himself?"

Understanding crept across Murdstone's weak-chinned face as he nodded and said slyly, "The ledgers should prove I had nothing to do with his cheating anyone, shouldn't they?"

"Of course. I'll leave that part to you. In return, I want you to insert a few things. You'd better run back across the street and get some order blanks, checkbooks, and—oh, a pen and ink. Send a message to the police as you leave, but don't tell anyone where you can be found for a few hours. We're going to be too busy to talk to the police just now. Oh, here's a twenty-dollar goldpiece. On your way out, slip it to the manager with as lewd a wink as you can manage and tell him we don't want to be disturbed."

"Oh, Mrs. Carlyle!"

"I know. That's what I want him to think we're doing back here. Get a move on, will you?"

Dawn had sent her carriage home from Canfield's office before crossing to the saloon with the secretary. She hadn't told her coachman of the suicide or when she intended to return. She intended to flag down a hackney to get home, but the broad expanse of Market Street was filled with late afternoon crowds of angry screaming men and women, so after making her way through the chaos as best she could, Dawn climbed the slope of Nob Hill on foot.

It was harder going now than it had been that day she met Brian atop its then barren crest. It wasn't just that Dawn was older and exhausted after her exciting day downtown. The city planners, with no regard for the lay of the land, had run the street grid of San Francisco up and over the hills in a Philadelphia gridiron as if draping a checkered tablecloth over a curvaceous sleeping beauty, with Nob Hill her ample hip. The paved sidewalk ran up at an impossible angle and there was no way to tack back and forth. Dawn had read about plans for a cable car line up Powell Street to relieve the strain on human and animal muscle, but work hadn't started on it. Meanwhile, the climb gave her time to sort her thoughts a bit on the weary way home.

The checks she'd inserted in Canfield's records, drawn on her nonexistent account in the defunct Bank of California, wouldn't pay the margin on her stocks but should afford a smokescreen for the examiners to wade through. As long as she had the opportunity, Dawn paid by worthless checks for gilt-edged stocks she'd never have a better opportunity to buy at any price. Justin Murdstone had said that Canfield's books were so balled up now, it would take a team of examiners six months to figure them out. That had been the general idea. For a man who made his living bilking widows and orphans, Canfield had a very poor ability to cover his financial tracks. It was odd, Dawn thought, how her instilled Indian skill at backtracking and laying false trails could be used in ways no Indian ever dreamed of.

She was a bit confused herself as she ran her hours of careful forgery through her memory on the way home. She wasn't sure, just now, if she'd recouped some of her losses or made a profit. On paper she now owned more, and owed more, than when she'd started out that morning of the bank crash. With luck, by the time the lawyers got through fighting over just what had been done to what, and by whom, she'd break even. Meanwhile she'd bought time to raise the ready cash everyone was going to need once things got back to normal.

Dawn realized they'd been watching for her from the house when her daughter Rose dashed out to meet her as she approached the gate. Rose called out, "Where on earth have you been, Mother? The boys have been looking all over for you!"

"I've been attending a few errands, dear. Is your father home for supper yet?"

"That's why Gus and Brian have been trying to find you, Mother. I don't understand what's happened to the banks, but it's terrible. Dad came home about two hours ago, crying, and then Gus sent for the doctor."

"Your father needs a doctor because he's crying about the news?"

"Oh, no, Mother. The doctor says it's a heart attack. He says Athair never should have run all the way home like that at his age."

Dawn pushed past the girl and mounted the porch steps two at a time. Behind her, Rose added, "The doctor says he's going to be all right, if only we can keep him calm."

Dawn sighed, "We'll have to do just that, then, won't we?"

Upstairs she found her husband stretched out across the four-poster in his underclothes, with the doctor seated in a chair near the head of the bed. The doctor nodded to Dawn and said, "He seems to be out of danger for the moment, ma'am. I'm not sure whether it was his heart or simply exhaustion, but we can't afford to take chances. I've given him some opium tincture to calm him and I want him in bed for at least the next few days."

Dawn nodded and moved to the far side of the bed to place a hand on Brian's sweaty pink forehead. She murmured, "Is he running a fever?"

"It's just plain sweat. I've told him he's overweight and I don't know what possessed him to run all the way up this hill from Van Ness in a wool suit! Your son tells me he was ranting and raving and smashing things when he suddenly collapsed."

Both Dawn and the doctor had assumed Brian was unconscious or asleep, but he suddenly sat up and sobbed, "Ruined! It's ruined I am by them damned thieving Sassanachs!"

The doctor put a hand on Brian's shoulder, as Dawn said, "Oh, for heaven's sake, stop carrying on like a baby, dear! The State Guard's been called out to patrol the streets, and the governor has promised an investigation. It's going to be all right."

But Brian insisted. "We're bankrupt! Carlyle and Sons can't even meet its payroll next week, and Jasus, what am I to tell me men?"

"You'll tell them the truth. They can read the papers. I doubt if half the workmen in San Francisco will receive their next pay checks. Meanwhile, they still have their jobs and I think we can manage enough between us to see that nobody actually goes hungry.

You just rest, now. Later we'll work out some way to see your men through this crisis."

"Jasus, woman, what are you going to do? Send sacks of groceries around to their homes?"

"If we have to. Our own bills are paid up, and I can buy enough food on credit for a regiment if it comes to that. I doubt it will, though. I have enough cash on hand to dole out partial wages next week, and a few weeks after. You just lie back and let Gus and me worry about your men."

"There's nothing anyone can do! Do you think anyone will be after paying us for the work we've done after what's happened to the banks?"

"You'll be paid in time, dear. Everyone will be paid in time. In the meanwhile, the city will just have to get by on credit and good will. I mean, it's not as if we're dealing with strangers, is it?"

"Christ, you'll be after paying the doctor, here, with a side of ham from the pantry! Carlyle has always been a man who paid his bills on time, and in cash!"

The doctor smiled. "I shan't be billing you for this visit for at least thirty days, Brian. Your wife is right. The sun is going down, and at the worst, nothing is going to happen to anyone tonight. So lean back and enjoy it. Would you like some more medicine?"

"I don't need medicine! Jasus! I need the wherewithal to meet me obligations—and me payroll's in the damned Bank of California!"

But before they could argue the point further, Brian suddenly slumped back, closed his eyes, and began to snore softly. The doctor glanced at Dawn. "It took a while for the opium to take effect. Your husband is a big man," he said.

Dawn resisted observing it was mostly fat, and contented herself with a nod of agreement.

She said something about seeing to the children's supper and left her husband's care for the moment to the doctor.

Going down the stairs, she met Gus. Her son's face was flushed and he was winded. "Is Athair still alive, Mom? They told me you'd come home and . . ."

"He's going to be all right, dear. Go change your shirt. You're soaked through. Where on earth have you been running?"

"You name it and I've been there, Mom. When Athair got all glassy-eyed and fell down like that I ran first down to Gump's. Rose said you'd mentioned something about going there this afternoon, but when I got there—"

"Never mind, we're all home safe and sound, and that's really all that matters. Is Junior here?"

"He's in the parlor with Rose and the others."

"Others?"

"The men from the office. It's something about the bank run and what's to be done at work."

"You go and change. I'll see to it, Gus."

Dawn found the parlor filled with worried-looking men. Rose had served them tiny demitasse cups of coffee. Dawn recognized Brian's bookkeeper and the head draftsman, Donovan, but most of the others were just vaguely familiar faces to her. Dawn noticed Donovan toying with an unlit cigar and said with a smile, "For heaven's sake light up, Mr. Donovan. Rose, would you be a dear and see if we have some porter and ale on ice in the pantry?"

She saw the relieved look that passed among her male visitors. Turning to her younger son, she said, "Brian, would you go into your father's den and break out a box of cigars for these gentlemen? I fear we may have a long night's work cut out for us."

Donovan, who'd apparently been appointed spokes-man, smiled. "We just come over to see how himself was getting on, Mrs. Carlyle."

"My husband has had a mild heart attack, but the doctor says he'll be his old self in a day or so. Mean-while, I know you'll want to know how and where you all stand with Carlyle and Sons. I can start by telling you there's no problem we can't handle if only we'll all pull together."

Donovan nodded and said, "That's the way I was putting it to the boys just now, ma'am." But one of the less well-dressed workmen blurted, "Is it true our payroll's locked in that terrible bank, Mum?"

Dawn said, flatly, "You'll all be paid, in cash or kind. I'll have to go over the books before I can answer truthfully whether we'll have to pay part cash and part script. You all know we have over a million in outstanding due bills for work that's already been done by the firm. I have no idea how long it's going to take to collect any part of our accounts receivable, but if anyone in San Francisco ever intends to pay their bills again, Carlyle and Sons is in good shape."

The bookkeeper refused to meet Dawn's eyes as she turned to him. "Would you be able to have the books ready for me in the morning, Mr. Boyde? The sooner we go over them together the sooner I'll be able to tell these other gentlemen just where they stand."

Boyde stammered, "I'm not sure himself would want that, mum. Meaning no offense, but—"

"I know the weekend's coming up," Dawn cut in, "but I intend to work through the Sabbath if I must, sir. I'm sure the Lord and himself will understand it's an emergency."

"It's your husband I'm working for, mum," insisted Boyde.

Donovan frowned at him. "What's the matter with you, Tom? Don't you want these lads to get paid?"

Boyde's face was stubborn. "I'm working for himself and I take no orders from anyone else, see?"

Dawn's smile was pleasant but her voice had an edge to it as she said, "You're fired, Mr. Boyde. I assume you have a key to the office, Mr. Donovan?"

Boyde blinked and gasped, "Now wait a minute. You can't fire me!"

"I just did. My husband is unwell and someone has to run the firm until he's back on his feet."

"But, damn it, you're a woman!"

There was a muttering agreement from some of the other men in the room and Dawn steeled herself for a showdown.

Before she had to reply, Brian Junior came in from the den with a cigar box, just as Gus entered from the hall. Dawn's smile was glacial as she turned to Gus. "Would you tell these gentlemen how old you are, dear?"

Gus looked blank but answered, "I'm twenty-one going on twenty-two."

"There seems to be some discussion about the management of Carlyle and Sons. As long as I have my two sons here, we may as well get a few things straight. Would you be a good boy and tell Mr. Boyde he's fired, dear?"

Gus blinked. "You want *me* to fire him, Mom?"

"Yes, dear. Your father isn't up to it and Mr. Boyde doesn't seem to think I'm in charge until himself is better."

Gus nodded in sudden understanding, and facing the older men in the room, said, "Until I say otherwise, if my mother tells you a team of horseflies can haul a Mormon plough, I don't want any argument. You men just hitch the little buggers to the plough and say giddyup!"

There was a startled reaction but no open rebellion this time. Gus, while young, was taller than any other man in the room. Boyde smiled sheepishly and said, "Well, as long as it's yourself in charge, young sir . . ."

But Dawn insisted. "Gus, I want him fired."

Gus, with a shrug, said, "You're fired, Boyde. Your pay will be in the mail and your hat's in the hall."

Boyde's face was ugly as he stammered, "Why, you young pup! I've half a mind to invite you outside!" and a smaller man in dark blue work clothes said, "I'm with you, Boyde! It ain't dacent for them to treat us so!"

Gus smiled crookedly at the two of them and asked, "All right, is there anyone else here who wants a piece of the action?"

Brian Junior's face was pale as he stepped up beside his elder brother and added, "I'll stand with you against the whole bunch, Gus!"

Then Donovan roared, "Now that'll be enough out of all of yez! Neither of these lads will have to fight anyone while Donovan draws breath! Get out of here, Boyde, and take wee Sean with you before I spits in his eye and drowns him!"

The bookkeeper, suddenly deflated, turned to Dawn and pleaded, "I'm married, mum. I have three kids."

Dawn nodded and said, "So do I, so we're starting even. I think you'd best leave, Mr. Boyde. Oh, and take Sean Murphy with you."

"Jasus, mum, have you no mercy for a poor dumb mick whose only crime was talking out of turn?"

"You didn't talk out of turn, sir. You threatened my

sons. I could forgive your arrogance to me, but . . ."

"Mom," Gus cut in. "Let them stay. I think we've got it settled."

Dawn hesitated, then looked thoughtfully at the two who'd defied her. "Is it settled, gentlemen?"

Boyde looked ready to burst into tears as he blurted, "Oh, yes, mum!" and Sean Murphy added, "Yourself is the boss, and that's a fact. I'll break the back of any man here who says different, Miz Carlyle!"

Dawn shrugged and said, "All right, if my son wants to keep you on, I shan't stand in the way."

There was a mass sigh of relief in the crowded room. Then, as Brian Junior started handing out the cigars, Dawn sat down with a stern smile. "All right. Now that we've got that straight, here's how we're going to work together to save Carlyle and Sons . . ."

It was just as well Dawn was alone in her husband's office when she learned why the bookkeeper had been so reluctant to let her see the company ledgers. She'd thought Boyde was hiding something and had agreed to keep him on partly to have him handy when it was time to have him arrested for whatever dishonesty he was trying to cover up. But as she carefully sorted through her husband's disordered desk, she learned with growing dismay that the bookkeeper was a loyal employee.

Loyal, that was, to Brian. The first few checks made out to one Helen Bordon didn't seem important. Dawn knew that one of Brian's workmen, a blaster who'd been killed in an accident down the coast, had been named Bordon. So at first she assumed her husband had been helping the man's widow. Five hundred here and a thousand there seemed a bit generous when the checks were dated within one month, but Brian had always been an open-handed man. Then she found the canceled check for five thousand made out to the same woman and began to reconsider.

Dawn rummaged through the older payroll vouchers until she found the entry where Jim Bordon's death was noted, along with a thousand-dollar compensation to his widow. There were no children listed as the late James Bordon's dependents and—yes, here it was— Brian had picked up the mortgage on the Bordon's house on Chestnut Street. Dawn wrote the address on a separate slip of foolscap and set it aside.

Later, when she found the delivery order for an expensive bedroom suite she certainly didn't remember receiving, the address matched.

Dawn sat quietly in the deserted office for a time as she thought about that. She could think, if she tried, of a dozen rational explanations, but none was as convincing as Brian's all too familiar sexual jealousy. She remembered how he'd made her throw away all the nightclothes she'd had while she'd been married to Ace Purvis. Yes, it would be like Brian to insist on a new bed for his recently widowed . . . mistress!

So there it was, like a gobbet of phlegm on her own pillow, and what was she going to do about it?

Her first impulse was to rush home and confront her husband with the evidence, but Dawn knew that would be a waste of time, and time was of the essence. She was working through the first weekend after the bank crash, to forge ahead of the firm's creditors and competitors while the courts as well as the banks were closed. No matter how she felt about her husband at the moment, it was her duty to save Carlyle and Sons, for the sons were hers!

One of the junior draftsmen, working with Dawn over the usually quiet Sabbath, came in to announce she had a visitor. He handed Dawn the man's card, and she grimaced. "Show him in. He's late."

When the client she'd sent for entered the office, Dawn repeated her remark about his being late, and the man frowned. "See here, young woman, I happen to be a very busy man and . . . where's Carlyle?"

"You're talking to Carlyle. I'm Dawn Carlyle. My husband is indisposed, Mr. Sullivan. I'm running the firm until he's back on his feet, and as I was saying, you were expected over an hour ago. Here, take these vouchers and read them over."

"Vouchers? What are you talking about? Carlyle and Sons is subcontracting to Sullivan Construction, and we usually pay ninety days after accepting."

"These are not usual times, Mr. Sullivan. As you see, I'm going to have to pay the workmen I have on your foundations for the bridge you've bid on for the state, up in Marin County. Our payroll funds were in the Bank of California. Yours were not. I took the liberty of checking on that before I sent for you."

"All right, Sullivan Construction is still solvent, for which I give thanks to the Lord and my own healthy suspicions of the darling B.O.C. If you think I'm about to pull Carlyle and Sons' chestnuts out of the fire with my own money, girl, you're mad as well as impertinent!"

"If I can't pay my help, I can't build your bridge foundations, Mr. Sullivan."

"That's your concern, not mine. Your husband signed the contract. He has to build them as he agreed to do, or forfeit his bid and our agreed-on penalty clause!"

"That's true. You have us over a barrel, and the state of California has you over the same one. Unless that bridge is finished on time, nobody gets paid!

We're going to have to pull together in these trying times, Mr. Sullivan."

Sullivan leafed through the payroll vouchers and snapped, "You expect me to lay out this kind of money for foundations and abutments when I haven't even started my own steelwork? Goddammit, woman, I won't see a penny from the state for a good eighteen months!"

"You won't see it then unless you finish your bridge on time. You did post a bond with Sacramento when you bid on the project, didn't you?"

"That's none of your business. I won't lose my bond. I'll just get another contractor and . . ."

"Brian's bid was a thousand dollars lower than his nearest competitor, and knowing you're in a bind for time, no other firm is going to make you a better offer. Leaving aside the money, you've approved our blueprints and the work has been started. Calling in another subcontractor is going to set you back at least six weeks, and in the end you won't save a dime. In fact, there's just no way for you not to lose money if you refuse to advance us enough to stay afloat."

"I'll be damned if I'll be badgered into parting with money before it's due! It's not my fault your husband was improvident, and damn it, this is naked blackmail!"

"I didn't know a man named Sullivan would be so enamored of the Protestant ethic, but getting to your more insulting remark, I hardly think you could get any court of law to agree I was blackmailing you. I've only told you the simple facts. Carlyle and Sons is insolvent. I'll show you the books if you doubt me."

"Look here, I don't doubt you folks got wiped out in the crash. Half the businessmen in San Francisco did. But damn it, it's not my fault!"

"I never said it was. I merely said you were going to have to bail us out or sink alongside us. As you see, our men draw less than five dollars a day, and with less than six weeks' work on your foundations, it only comes to a little over a thousand . . ."

"It's not fair! Nobody ever pays a subcontractor in advance!"

"I know. The bond you posted with Sacramento comes to a little over a hundred thousand, doesn't it?"

"Damn it, I can add a column of figures, young woman. You might at least be a little more polite when you shove a gun in a man's ribs!"

Dawn smiled. "I didn't think I had to, Mr. Sullivan. My husband has always spoken highly of your common sense. If I've been a bit blunt, it was simply to save time. We could have shilly-shallied away a good hour or so before you agreed, and as you see, it's nearly three. Some of our workmen have threatened to quit unless I can assure them they'll be getting paid next week."

Grudgingly, Sullivan said, "It's understood that the payroll is the only expense of yours I'll have to pick up? What about the cement and aggregate?"

"We have the concrete for your foundations on hand, Mr. Sullivan. I can promse you on-time delivery and no further requests for an advance before Sacramento pays you for the job."

Sullivan agreed to pay Dawn's workmen and grumped out of the office. One small straw had been removed from the camel's back.

Dawn went back to work on the books with renewed interest, ear-marking several other due bills that could wait. The junior draftsman returned about three forty-five to announce another visitor.

The man was named Turino and he hadn't sent a

card. Turino was a small excited man who appeared on the verge of screaming, but his voice was ominously calm as he got right to the point. "The cement your husband ordered last month has not been paid for, ma'am."

Dawn smiled at him and replied, "I know. I just tried to get the contractor to advance us some money on it, but he refused. You know, of course, we haven't a penny."

"But, ma'am, I am not in business for my health. I too have lost money in the crash. My creditors are hounding me. I don't wish to be unkind, but unless I am paid, I shall have to have my cement back. It is not one sack of cement we are speaking of, you understand. *Dio Carne!* Your husband owes me for a thousand tons of fine-screen hydraulic."

"We're going to need more," Dawn cut in. "I was just talking to our site engineer and he tells me they're going to have to use a high-grade hydraulic mix because of the high water-table across the bay."

She handed Turino an order blank and said, "You'll note we want this delivered on site this time. The middle of next week will be fine."

The supplier stared down at the paper in his hands as if it had just bit him. "You want *more* cement? I just told you I'm going to have to ask for the return of the cement I sent you if I don't see some money!"

"Pooh, where are you going to sell it, sir? You know construction will be at a standstill in the bay area until they unravel this silly business with the banks. I've just given you a very good order and you'll note we're meeting your asking price without a quibble."

"Forgive me, I mean no disrespect, but you are insane, Mrs. Carlyle! How long do you think I could remain in business by giving away my cement?"

"Heavens, nobody's asking you to give anything away, Mr. Turino. Your profit on this deal will come to several thousand dollars, once we pay you."

"Ahah! But when, may I ask, will such an unlikely event take place?"

"I have no idea. Frankly, if I didn't respect your common sense, I'd lie and promise you the moon. You know you'd deliver if I promised you payment in full within thirty days, don't you?"

"Of course, but . . ."

"But I'd be betraying the trust of a friend and one of our best suppliers, wouldn't I? Wouldn't you rather I told you the truth? All right, the truth is that we're scraping the bottom of the barrel. The truth is that if we don't fulfill our contracts we won't ever be able to pay you. You do understand, don't you?"

Turino frowned and sighed, "All right, I can wait for the money on the cement I've delivered. Another load is out of the question."

"But Mr. Turino, we're going to need more cement. Where are we going to get it if you won't advance us more credit?"

Turino shook his head stubbornly and said, "I just can't do it. I too have a payroll to meet. My mill is shut down and I have no money to pay for the hauling, either."

"Well, you must have a few tons in your bins, and if I got some of our hands to drive a wagon out . . ."

"No, no, and again no, Mrs. Carlyle. I will wait for payment on past due accounts, but that is the most I can offer. I am not trying to be a hard man. My hands are simply tied."

Dawn considered sobbing, decided the little man was too bright for that old ploy, and simply sighed in resignation.

After Turino left, the draftsman came back with a worried look and asked, "Is he going to sue us like he says, ma'am?"

"No. You're sure we have enough cement for those underwater abutments over in Marin County on hand?"

"Yes, ma'am. More than enough—if we can keep Turino from carting it away as he threatened."

"He isn't going to cart anything away. He can't afford the freight. But I do want a twenty-four-hour guard on the site. You know how the squatters always carry away unguarded lumber, and with the State Guard rounding up unemployed rioters, we're going to have more than the usual number of hoboes skulking around across the bay."

"We've hired some Pinkertons, Mrs. Carlyle, The agency says it can wait ninety days before they have to be paid."

"That was good thinking. We'll be finished over there well before Pinkerton's bill comes in. Is there anyone else out front?"

"No, ma'am, but if you don't mind my asking, how are we going to pay them jaspers from the gravel pits? They're threatening to sue us."

"They probably will. I've spoken to my lawyers about it, though. The court calendar is filled up for the next two years, thanks to this bank crash. If I'm not here when the summons comes in, just leave it here on my desk."

"You don't want us to duck the process servers, ma'am? I mean, with himself sick and Boyde away, I could say I only work here and ask the lad with the summons to come back in a few weeks."

"That's what everyone in San Francisco will be doing. I think our best bet is to accept all court actions politely and avoid upsetting anyone. As I said, we shan't be on the court dockets for months, if not years, and meanwhile our creditors will be having their more desperate thoughts about the people who *are* ducking them."

"I see what you mean, ma'am. But how long do you think we'll have to bob and weave like this?"

Dawn shrugged and said, "I have no idea. As long as we have to, I suppose."

Justin Murdstone's face was filled with open admiration as he met Dawn in the back room of their rendezvous saloon a few weeks later. He said, "I don't know how you did it, Mrs. Carlyle, but you were right. While the big boys have been fighting over the carcass, a lot of scraps have been overlooked. Do you know what I paid for this block of Southern Pacific?"

"I hope under par," Dawn sighed with an ill-concealed grimace of distaste. She'd roamed the Great Basin with Indians long enough to know the value of carrion in a hungry moon, but did Murdstone have to remind her so much of a grinning coyote as he licked his chops at others' misfortune?

Murdstone said, "People have gone mad for ready cash. I sold the municipal bonds as you suggested, then bid on this Southern Pacific and got it for a tenth of its true value. Jesus, if only I had some real cash to deal with, I could buy half the state in this confusion!"

"How much hard cash do we have left, at the moment?"

"Well, counting silver certificates, we've made about fifty thousand in the past week. I hope you know what you're doing, accepting paper money, though. In this panic, gold specie's buying paper at six-bits to the dollar."

"The Bank of California failed. I doubt if Washington's about to go bankrupt, Mr. Murdstone. That's a good price for paper money. I think we'd best forget about stocks and bonds for now, and corner as much paper money as we can with the little gold we can scrape together."

"You want to convert *all* your gold to paper, ma'am?"

"At a twenty-five percent profit? You bet your life I do!"

"But, ma'am, a lot of people don't trust paper money, especially with the way the banks have been closing. Everybody wants silver or gold!"

"I know. I've never understood what's so confounded special about either. You can't even make a decent knife out of either metal. Do you know what money is, Mr. Murdstone? Money is just the white man's wampum. You can't do anything with a dollar, be it silver, gold, or paper. Money is only a token. A token you can buy things with. It's the *things* that we need the money for. Things like land and houses and food and clothing."

"And stocks and bonds?"

"They're just tokens, too. People don't ride on Southern Pacific stocks. They ride in cars, on steel rails and redwood ties. When you own a share in a railroad, you own steam and iron. The paper certificate just lets people know it. The poor idiots who've been dumping their shares have forgotten that. The *Bank* of California failed. *Calfiornia* is still out there, growing by the minute!"

Murdstone shrugged and said, "Well, you're the owner of more of it now than you were a week ago, ma'am. I used to think poor old Canfield was the bee's knees when it came to buying cheap and selling dear, but you've shown me the elephant. I thought you had a fifty-fifty chance of getting some of your money back after the crash. I never figured you'd be showing a profit before they cleaned the glass off Market Street!"

Dawn shrugged again and said, "I merely followed the example of J. P. Morgan and the Rothschilds."

"My God, do you know the Morgans and the Rothschilds, ma'am?"

"Of course not. But their business methods are no secret. I think it was J. P. Morgan who said he always watched the way the crowd was running and simply ran the other way. I read it in *Leslie's Illustrated Weekly* once, and it seemed to make sense."

"You sure have made a killing taking his advice, then. What did Baron Rothschild say?"

"I have no idea whether he ever said anything. I've merely been watching the House of Rothschild in the financial section. They always sell when people are buying and buy when people are selling. I imagine right now they're buying U. S. Treasury notes for seventy-five cents on the dollar, don't you?"

"But they can afford to take such chances. They have millions to lose, Mrs. Carlyle!"

"Nobody has millions to lose. Keep that in mind the next time you use expense money to buy extra shares for yourself. I don't mind a little skimming of the cream, Mr. Murdstone, but if you get greedy, we're not going to be working together much longer."

Murdstone looked shocked. "Surely you don't think I'd cheat you, ma'am?"

"I don't think it, I know it. You see, I have an advantage over you in counting my money, sir. You cheat on paper. I keep the figures in my head. Right now, I still need you. Pad that expense account again and I may find your services too dear."

Before Murdstone could protest further, Dawn got to her feet with a smile. "And now, if you'll excuse me, I have to attend to more important business. I'll send word to you when I've time to have another accounting with you. And do try to be a bit more careful with those fingers of yours. You'd really make quite a good broker if you'd pay more attention to my instructions and less to temptation."

She left him speechless and went out to her carriage. The young coachman at the reins knew his mistress was thoughtful of her team and started to take the usual long way home up the gentler slope of Nob Hill from the west. But Dawn was in a hurry and told him to drive directly up Hyde from Market. Like most carriage horses in San Francisco, the team was stocky and chosen for power rather than speed. Newcomers tended to laugh at the curried plough horses pulling the carriages of San Francisco society, until they tried to attempt one of the city's hills with a high-stepping team of Kentucky trotters.

Arriving at the Carlyle mansion, Dawn found her daughter waiting anxiously for her in the entrance. Rose said something about a young man coming to dine with them that evening, and Dawn brushed by with a hasty approval. Ordinarily, she'd have taken more interest in her daughter's budding social life, but at the moment she had more important things on her mind. She gave Rose permission to supervise the dinner, party, or whatever, and went up to Brian's room.

Her jaw was set perhaps a trifle firmly, but she smiled pleasantly as she entered the bedroom. Brian was propped up in bed with the afternoon papers in his lap, a cigar between his teeth, and a stein of porter on the table at his side.

"I see you're feeling better, dear," she said. "The doctor tells me you'll be up and around in a day or so."

Brian growled, "Jasus, I've been ready to go back to work for a couple of days now, and it's cramped I am from laying here like a lump. Gus just left. He says things are going well at the office, but I have to get down there. I'm going to work in the morning and that'll be the end of it!"

"If you say so, dear. I have some more papers for you to sign, if you feel up to it."

"Of course I feel up to it! Where's me pen and what am I signing this time?"

"We got the contract from Dalton and Grimm for the new brewery wing on Front Street. Himself has to put his John Henry on it, of course. Then, there's some other vouchers, loan extensions, and so forth. We seem to be coming out of the woods, but we're still desperately short of working capital."

Brian shoved the papers to one side and groped for the inkstand beyond his beer. "Ay, I've been reading about the recovery in the papers. The whole town's broke, but the worst of the panic's past and people are starting to make sense again."

Dawn watched him with some concern as he took the papers from her, propped them on his knee, and began to sign the first one. She'd counted on his being as foggy from medication this afternoon as he'd been the last few times, but he was obviously alert.

Well, what of it? They were going to have to have a confrontation sooner or later and there was no sense in putting it off. Brian signed twice more before he suddenly frowned. "What's this?"

"Oh, that's the deed to this house, dear. I had to raise some more bond money for the brewery contract, so I decided to mortgage the house. Naturally, I have to have it in my name before I can do that."

"Damn it, lass, you had no right to even think of such a deed without consulting meself!"

"But I am consulting you, dear. It's hardly as if we've never considered it, you know. I've had to talk you out of mortgaging the house more than once in the past. This time, however, it's a real emergency."

"I don't understand. Gus tells me you've pulled a rabbit out of the hat and that Carlyle and Sons is back in the black. Has the lad been drawing the long bow to cheer me up?"

"Gus never lies. He's been a big help down at the office and things are getting back to normal, but as you can read for yourself in the papers, everyone in town is strapped for cash and we're no exception. Heavens, why don't you just sign the deed over and let me worry about the small details?"

"How much are we getting for the mortgage, then?"

"Fifty thousand. That's enough to put Carlyle and Sons back on its feet for the foreseeable future."

Brian smiled. "Jasus, that's for damned sure! Where on earth did you find a bank who'll loan that kind of money in this depression?"

Dawn looked away and said, "It's a private party. I'm working through poor Mr. Canfield's secretary, Murdstone. He's been very helpful in ferreting out unsuspected sources."

Brian started to sign. Then he said, "I'd best have a talk with Murdstone, first. I might be able to talk this party of his into a bigger loan."

Dawn shook her head and said, "You won't be able to. Fifty is the most you can hope for and we don't have time to dicker, even if you were really up to it. I told Mr. Murdstone I'd have your signature on the deed in the morning. Do sign like a sensble dear and let me get you the money in time for your first day back on the job."

Brian shrugged and said, "Well, I hate to risk me own family home this way, but you've been right as rain about everything else and it'll be a relief not to be after ducking creditors on me first day back on the job."

He signed and handed the deed to his wife. Dawn kept her face desperately calm as she put the deed casually aside and changed the subject with a comment about another, less important paper she wanted him to sign.

The house was hers. Nobody would ever be able to take it away from her now. And even wide awake, Brian hadn't forced her into the showdown she dreaded. She had just enough cash on hand to cover the dummy mortgage Murdstone had drawn up to a fictitious lender, and knowing the books of her husband's firm better than he did, Dawn knew he'd be apt neither to pay off the loan nor to ask foolish questions for at least a year. A year was not a long time, but at least it would give her the breathing spell she needed to consider her next move.

Mrs. DeWitt was a rather imposing woman in shantung silk and her late forties. She wasn't quite as grand as she thought she was. Nobody could have been. But Dawn could see her guest was a woman very used to having her own way, as they faced each other over tea in the front parlor.

Mrs. DeWitt helped herself to another gingersnap as Dawn poured her a second cup of tea. Then, having restrained herself about as long as her petulant expression indicated she was capable of, the woman said, "I know your daughter Rose is a lovely girl, Mrs. Carlyle, but you'll simply have to make her see she's being a bit, well . . ."

"Presumptuous?" asked Dawn, with a steely glint in her smile.

Mrs. DeWitt shifted uneasily in her chair. "It's not as if my husband and I don't *like* the girl. But my son Roger *is* an *officer*, and well, we *are* Episcopalian, you know."

"I see. I was going to raise my children as Paiutes, but my husband insisted they be baptized Catholics. Silly of him, wasn't it?"

"My dear, I have nothing against the Catholic Church, as a religion. But there are social distinctions to consider."

"That's true. A Protestant cavalryman with a shanty-Irish wife could be in a terrible fix if Red Cloud's Sioux found out about it, couldn't he? Rose tells me your son has been posted to the Dakota Territory as of six weeks from yesterday. No doubt his leaving the Presidio has brought them to this—what would you call it?—foolish decision."

"Roger had no right to propose marriage without consulting his father and me. But you know how foolish a young man can be on the eve of a military campaign."

"That's true. He's only twenty-three, too. I hope you gave him a good scolding and sent him to bed without any supper?"

Mrs. DeWitt looked pained and said, "Please don't be impertinent. I know the name DeWitt means nothing to people such as your daughter and yourself, but . . ."

"Oh, I know who you are, Mrs. DeWitt. When your son started paying court to my only daughter I took the liberty of having you investigated."

"You did *what?*"

"Investigated. Looked into. Your son is almost as great a snob as you are, so when he started spouting off about his family tree to us one night, I thought I'd better have a look into his background. Have you read what that new young writer, Mark Twain, has to say about people who boast about their ancestors?"

"I'd hardly read anything written by that rustic reporter from Virginia City, Mrs. Carlyle."

"You should. He's very amusing. He said people who brag about their ancestors are admitting the best people in their family are dead and buried. Anyway, I asked around about you and your husband. As you've been busting a gut not to say, the wife of a shanty-Irish contractor has a lot of contacts in unseemly circles. It's surprising what you can find out by talking to servants, Chinese laundrymen, and so forth."

"All right, I assume you've been listening to gossip about the people from our neighborhood, as I have about your own background. Tell me, is it true your first husband was a gunman and gambler?"

"He sure was. His name was Ace Purvis. You may have met him when your husband found you in the whorehouse in Poker Flat. Ace never had much use for the cribs upstairs, but there was usually a game going in the piano room."

The other woman rose grandly to her feet and stammered, "I don't know what you're talking about, but I refuse to stay here another moment and listen to your wild insulting accusations!"

Dawn shrugged and said, "The miners came in '49, the whores in '51, and then they got together and produced the Native Son. You can flounce out of here and be damned to you, sister. I don't want my daughter married to that mealy-mouthed young simp of yours, either!"

Mrs. DeWitt gasped, started to say something, and then, as Dawn laughed in her face, stormed out without another word, her face livid.

Dawn was gentler with her daughter when the girl came in from the garden after watching her sweetheart's mother drive off in a huff.

Rose was pallid with worry as she joined her mother. "Well, how did it go, Mother?"

Dawn sighed and said, "I don't think the DeWitts approve of us all that much, dear. You may have to sneak up to Roger's window with a ladder and elope, if you really can't wait."

"But why, Mother?" Rose sobbed. "I know the De-Witts are very rich, but Athair is rich, too! Is it because I'm Irish?"

"You're only half Irish, but that's neither here nor there. Poor Cedric DeWitt has managed to make some money in the last few years selling barrels or something, and its made him remember some remote relations who stole New York from the Indians. Surely you don't want that dragon you just left for a mother-in-law, do you?"

"I told Roger I'd convert from Catholic to Protestant. That would make me better, wouldn't it?"

"Oh, dear! Protestant wouldn't be enough. You'd have to be High Church Episcopalian, and no, it wouldn't make you better. It would just make you foolish. Would you ask Roger to become a Catholic?"

"I couldn't. It would ruin his career. Most of the officers in the regular army are Protestants, and he worked so hard to get through West Point, Mother!"

"Yes, I imagine it would be hard sledding for a boy

with Roger's brains. Oh, well, he'll be off to butcher Indians in a few weeks, anyway."

"Mother, I know you don't like Roger, but we're in *love!*"

"I know, dear. That's why I think you need a change of scene. Your father needs Gus down at the office, but I've been planning a nice surprise for you and Junior. Have you been reading about the big exposition in Philadelphia this summer? It's the first centennial, and heavens, everyone will be there. I've bought tickets for the three of us on the Transcontinental Express, and we're leaving next week. You'll want to shop for some new clothes, of course. Why don't we go to the Emporium in the morning and . . ."

"But, Mother, what about Roger?"

"Oh, I'm sure he'll be safe enough this summer. The army's issued new Gatling guns in case the Indians make a fuss about those Black Hills of theirs."

"Mother, please don't be sarcastic. Roger and I are really serious about getting married before he leaves for the front."

"Darling, if it were up to me, I'd grit my teeth and give you my blessing, but the boy's not going to marry you against his parents' wishes and there's nothing I can do about it."

"Well, I'm not going off to Philadelphia on any durned old train!"

"Yes you are, dear. Roger's old enough to defy his mother, if he had the backbone, but you're still under age, and even if you weren't, I'm bigger than you are."

"Mother, that's not fair! Can't we discuss this like grown women?"

"Not until you've grown up a mite. The Carlyle family is not a parliamentary democracy, Rose. It's a dictatorship. Like Brazil. They say the Emperor, Dom

Pedro, will be at the Centennial, too. Won't that be fun?"

Dawn had never really known how huge the United States was, despite her wanderings over the Great Basin, until she awoke the second morning on the Union Pacific Pullman car to stare out the window in wonder at the passing landscape. They were still west of the South Pass, according to her time table, and heavens, even going fifty miles an hour, they didn't seem to be making a dent in the empty wilderness! Had she really once crossed that tawny expanse in a covered wagon? No wonder it had taken the old timers three months to reach the coast from the Big Muddy. The Missouri was no longer a mythical legend from her childhood, now. She knew she'd actually see it, and cross it, in only a few more days. Yet, in truth, her first morning on the train was a bit of a letdown after the novelty of boarding the marvelous Palace Car and sleeping fitfully at fifty miles an hour.

The children were bored and restive, too, as they had breakfast in the dining car, and Dawn was struck once more by how soon the human mind accustomed itself to new surroundings.

Brian Junior roused himself from toying with his bacon and eggs as he glimpsed something through the window. "Mustangs!" he gasped. "I just saw a herd of mustangs, Mom!"

But when Dawn looked out, there was nothing to be seen but more of the same monotonous dry plains that seemed to roll on forever. "They're gone, now," he said. "How soon do we get to Salt Lake City?"

Dawn said it would be that evening and asked Rose if she'd like some more jelly with her toast, but the girl was pouting again and her mother didn't press it.

The next few days were much the same, as the linens grew grimy with smoke, the drinking water more tepid, and the scenery a bit more interesting. By the time they detrained in Philadelphia and got to their hotel near Grace Church, Dawn was stiff and convinced there had to be a better way to travel three thousand miles than in a stuffy Pullman with a pair of complaining brats. She knew they'd eventually have to go back the same way and decided to put it out of her mind. All she really wanted was a long hot soak and a good night's sleep between clean sheets. The next time one of her children fell in love she wasn't going to say a word even if it was with a three-toed sloth!

Dawn slept well, despite the bustle of the traffic in the great city all around, but as she lay abed the next morning, vaguely wondering where she was and how she'd gotten there, Rose burst in on her, fully dressed. "Oh, Mother! It's awful! The Sioux are on the warpath!"

"Sioux? Warpath?" Dawn muttered, as she propped herself up in bed.

Rose said, "I just got the morning papers! The Indians are killing settlers in the Black Hills and General Terry is marching against them in full force!"

Understanding sank in as Dawn reached for the water pitcher by the bed to do something about the dry taste in her mouth. "Oh, your Roger was supposed to be posted to Terry's command, wasn't he?"

"Yes, Mother, the Seventh Cavalry. Colonel Custer's Gerry Owens. He'll have left the Presidio by now."

"Oh, stop it, Rose! We left well before Roger could have, and the campaign should be over by the time Roger catches up with them in the Dakota Territory." She grimaced as she swallowed. "Those poor Sioux won't last a week against regulars with Gatling guns. Your Roger will barely get there in time to escort the survivors back to the reservation. Where is Junior?"

"He's downstairs, watching the parade."

"Is that what that noise is? What time is it?"

"It's nearly nine, Mother. Listen, you know all about Indians. This paper says Red Cloud has ten thousand warriors . . ."

"Don't be silly. There aren't ten thousand fighting Indians left in the whole country. Do you know the size of an average hunting band? It's less than thirty braves and their dependents. You know how many so-called warriors Custer fought a few years back at his so-called battle of the Washita? There were about a dozen. Most of the victims were women and children. Then Custer shot their ponies. The whole thing is pretty disgusting."

"But, Mother, Red Cloud massacred all those settlers . . ."

"What settlers are you talking about? There aren't supposed to *be* white settlers in the Black Hills. It's Indian Treaty land. Do you know how many white people have been killed in all the Indian Wars from the time the Pilgrims landed on Plymouth Rock?"

"I have no idea, Mother. It must have been millions, if you count all the massacres!"

"I'm counting all the massacres. They're a matter of record, and as you know, I'm interested in Indians. You see, when they raid a farm and kill off one family, that's a massacre. When we attack a village and shoot a whole band, it's a battle. Anyway, starting with the French and Indian Wars, roughly fifteen hundred white people have been killed by Indians in all the years we've been killing them. More white people will

die of typhoid this summer than in all the Indian wars
we've ever had. So let me get dressed and we'll see
about driving out to the fairgrounds."

To honor the hundredth birthday of the United
States, the wonders of the civilized and not-so-civilized
world had been assembled on the outskirts of Philadelphia. Oriental pagodas and papier maché Turkish
minarets nestled between prefabricated Victorian pa-
vilions housing new inventions of the Age of Steam
and Iron. Near the center of the fairgrounds sprawled
the vast Machinery Hall, copied from the London
Crystal Palace in wrought-iron spider-webbing and
translucent greenhouse glass, and dominated by the
massive Corliss Engine, the largest steam engine ever
constructed.

Dawn and her children stood in the crowd gaping up
at the Corliss Engine as it squatted on mighty castiron
haunches, waving its walking beam slowly from
church-steeple height as its huge twin pistons powered
acres of lesser machines all around via a maze of
leather belts, tumbling rods, and chain-link transmis-
sion lines. Brian Junior was entranced, and Dawn was
relieved to note that even Rose seemed to have forgotten her heroic cavalryman for the moment. Yet
Dawn herself felt strangely detached as she stood
alone in the crowd.

Dawn was impressed by the talking telegraph unveiled by a young Scots-Canadian named Bell, and
after hearing her son's voice as he spoke to her from
a distant booth on the device, she made a note to invest in the new Bell Telephone Company. She had
more money to invest, these days, after weathering the
bank crash of the year before with a tidy profit to show
for a few months of shrewd bargaining. Yet she won-

dered, even as she wrote down the address of the inventor's brokerage house, what she really wanted with more stock in anything.

She and her family were financially secure, she knew. Even if the boys never inherited their father's somewhat speculative business, their futures were assured. Gus had a standing offer to serve on the board of the steamship company she owned stock in, and if Brian Junior grew up with a lick of sense he'd find any number of positions open to him. The home on Nob Hill was in her name, now. Nothing Brian Senior or anyone else could do would ever endanger it again. If the children were orphaned tomorrow, they were set for life. Yet, as long as she'd come all this way to listen to the fool contraption, a hundred shares of Bell Telephone might be a wise investment.

And so Dawn accumulated business brochures and stock prospectuses as her children sampled Turkish candy and purchased Centennial souvenirs. Brian Junior bought a huge lithograph of the painting unveiled in honor of the occasion. It was called "The Spirit of Seventy-six" and Dawn wondered vaguely where they were going to hang it once they returned to San Francisco. Rose spent much of her generous allowance on imported French perfumes and soaps as well as a dozen yards of white damask churned out with frightening speed by a new card-operated power loom as they watched. Rose said she wanted the shimmering damask for her wedding gown, and Dawn withheld comment. With any luck the Sioux would scalp the simpering DeWitt boy before she had to face the grim prospect of her daughter in that tacky material.

The closest Dawn came to purchasing anything other than food and beverage at the exposition was when she spied what looked like a well-dressed, well-fed Indian squaw selling basketry, jewelry, and "genuine Navajo blankets" at a stand near the Siamese pavilion. One of the baskets caught her eye and she picked it up, recognizing the traditional Paiute motif woven in sepia and cornhusk buff. But what was a waterbasket design doing on an obvious winnowing platter? And where was the imperfection? Didn't anyone remember Spider Woman's curse on weavers who tried to emulate the Spirits?

Dawn asked the woman selling the Indianware about this in Ho and, when the middle-aged squaw looked blank, repeated her question in the Na-Déné jargon. The woman licked her lips and said, "Princess Silver Buffalo no savvy white lady."

Dawn laughed wryly and put the synthetic Indian basket back in its stack beside the synthetic Navajo. She was too kind to point out that Na-Déné didn't name their girls after hunted animals, and that if they had, the plains buffalo were not familiar to the southwest desert tribes. The basket was a fake, as were the machine-woven blankets with their too-bright German dyes. How strange it was that even as Phil Terry's troopers were marching into the Black Hills against one of the last tribes of true Indians, this made-up travesty was hawking mass-produced "Indian" wares.

The world was out of joint that year, Dawn felt, as she walked in the wake of her children through the sprawling mixture of confused cultures. So much had changed in the few short years since she'd followed Runs Down Antelope through the Great Basin, and even now America seemed a surreal mixture of fact and fancy. Could it really be true that men were talking over telegraph wires and lighting rooms with electricity here in Philadelphia, while only a few miles north of the railroad they'd just ridden on in Pullman

Palace cars a shaman with the unlikely name of Sitting Bull was gathering his clansmen to defy the United States Army?

The few Real People left were living in a dream, Dawn knew, yet all around her, as she walked through the crowds of the exhibition, the White Eyes, too, dealt in so curious a mixture of fact and fiction as to make the head swim. She remembered reading in the papers about a man in Deadwood just a few weeks ago and how surprised she'd been when she'd thought, *Wild Bill Hickok? But he's not real! He's one of those characters in Ned Buntline's Western Magazine!*

And now the papers were saying that Buffalo Bill, for God's sake, was rushing off to fight the Sioux after a successful tour of the East with his Wild West Show. Her White-Eyed associates were as mad, it would seem, as poor Sitting Bull and the few Real People left. Was there anyone, anywhere in the world, who saw things as she did?

Perhaps not. Perhaps she was, after all, the same lostling between worlds she'd been when Nevada had found her alone in the Great Basin.

Calling a halt to their visit, Dawn took her children back to the hotel and purchased tickets for New York. Philadelphia was a smaller, less interesting city than she'd imagined and Dawn felt anxious to move on. She didn't know what she'd find in New York, but she knew she needed to find something, anything, to occupy her mind. New York was a larger, dirtier version of Philadelphia. Like its sister cities all across the nation, New York was celebrating the centennial with parades and fireworks, but the crowds and humid heat depressed Dawn. Like most San Franciscans, she'd come to think of the East as a more refined, more civilized place than her windswept city by the bay. Yet while there were fewer self-conscious "western characters" in New York, the drably dressed men and women she found all about her seemed no different from the people on Market Street. The women, if anything, were less fashionable and the men seemed more wilted in the heat of summer.

Dawn checked them into the Astor Hotel, noting that the best hotel in New York was no grander than San Francisco's Palace, after all, and that the food at Delmonico's, while good enough, was little different from what she'd grown accustomed to in any decent San Francisco establishment. Dawn had heard that travel broadened one. To the extent that she'd learned that Philadelphia and New York had nothing more to offer than the younger San Francisco, she supposed travel had indeed broadened her insights. Perhaps, when she got home, she'd be more content with her lot, but dear God, was this all there was to living?

Her children were grown and no longer needed her. Her husband, as good a husband, she supposed, as any woman had a right to expect, was becoming a strange fat man she saw only on weekends, and didn't really want to see too much of then. Yet she wasn't old enough for life to wind down on her like this.

A product of the Victorian Age, Dawn had never heard the term sexual frustration, though more sophisticated in such matters than most women of her generation. Sex was still a topic expressed, if at all, in sniggering whispers or, at best, in occasional blushing suggestions between lovers in a darkened room. Yet, though the writings of Sigmund Freud lay in the future, Dawn's common sense told her much about her growing dissappointment with her life. It didn't tell her, however, what to do about it.

Dawn had never had a recorded birthday. An educated guess at her own age, now, would have been almost forty, give or take a few years. In an era when middle age began at thirty, Dawn could hardly think of herself as a young woman. Yet the cruel shark of time had been kind to her features, and if there was any gray in her ash-blonde hair, it failed to show in her mirror. She felt as energetic as ever, and if childbirth had rounded her once boyish figure a bit, it was still a figure many a younger woman envied, and Dawn was not unaware of the glances men cast her way as she walked through a lobby or into a dining room.

How had this happened? How had she suddenly become a Nob Hill dowager whose alarmingly aging children kept threatening her with grandmotherhood?

"Damn you, Changing Woman!" she often sighed, in half-mocking memory of her early religious training. "I know you decreed long ago that what was Sea should become Land and what was Up should come Down, but honestly, did you have to work so hard, and quickly, on me?"

As she knew, Changing Woman had done more to the world all around her than to the girl who'd learned of her at the knees of a digger squaw. Dawn felt little different from the girl she'd been when Nevada found her alone in the Great Basin. Yet Nevada himself was dust. Ace Purvis and half the people she'd known at Lost Chinaman Camp had followed Nevada into the Long Sleep. And poor Yvette, the last she'd heard, was a raving lunatic in the Sacramento asylum. Madam Piggy was said to be living in Folsom, retired and modestly wealthy, but crippled by veneral disease and surrounded by the plaster saints who seemed to be her only company.

And Brian . . .? Brian was someone else these days. The tall husky young man she'd chosen to be the father of her children no longer existed. Changing Woman had been cruel to Dawn, there, even as she'd worked her magic on the three children so that they'd grown cornstalk tall. It was almost as if her once-handsome husband had been taken from her as a sacrifice in exchange, for all three of them made their mother proud these days. Gus had polished off some of his rough edges as he grew into young manhood and was becoming a respected member of the adult business world. Brian Junior was a husky clean-cut youth with no trace of the sluggishness she'd worried about. And Rose, as her own baby fat melted with maturity, was becoming a breathtaking young beauty. If only—Dawn prayed to both Changing Woman and the newer God she'd learned of later—the damned fool girl would develop some common sense to go with her looks!

Dawn thought Rose would go insane that summer after they read the headlines: TRAGEDY ON THE LITTLE BIG HORN. CUSTER AND ENTIRE COMMAND MASSACRED BY SAVAGE SIOUX!

But after a night of raging tears, Rose had lapsed into a stoic calm as they waited for the full casualty lists to be published by the War Department. The calm worried Dawn almost as much as the hysteria, for the scar left by Nevada's untimely death had never really healed, and poor dim-witted Roger DeWitt seemed such an unlovely candidate for a martyred first love.

And then one evening as they were about to go out to dine, Dawn found her daughter doubled over with laughter in her own room, holding a Western Union telegram in her hand. Dawn thought at first it might be more hysteria, but as she sat on the bed and put a gentle hand on her daughter's arm, Rose gasped, "It's from Roger. He never left the Presidio. He's in the hospital with the *mumps!*"

Despite herself, Dawn laughed. Then she squeezed the girl's arm and murmured, "I'm sure he'll be all right, dear. At least you know he's safe."

"Oh, that's what this night letter is all about, Mother. He sent a night letter because he says it's cheaper and gives him more words to reassure me. He seems to think I was terribly worried."

"Well, weren't you?"

Rose thought a moment, then she smiled and sighed, "Yes, I was, but honestly, Mother, Roger really is a bit pompous for a boy who's never seen a day in the field. He says his only regret is that he missed the chance to stand by his brother officers in the final fray. That's what he called it, the final fray. Don't you think that's a little silly of him, Mother?"

Dawn murmured something in Ho, and Rose asked, "What was that, an Indian curse?"

Dawn smiled and said softly, "It was more a prayer. I just thanked Changing Woman for something."

"What was it, Mother? Roger's safety?"

"That's close enough, dear. Let's go eat."

Not long after Dawn and the children returned to San Francisco the coming of the cable car wrought subtle changes on Nob Hill. The cheery clanging of the crossing bells was heard less often than the somewhat ghostly whisper of the underground steel cables that pulled the little vehicles up and over the impossible slopes. The cables ran twenty-four hours a day in their steel slots between the rails at an unvarying six miles an hour. The cars stopped and started by gripping the moving steam-powered cables with an in-

genious brake-handle device Dawn would never understand. Visitors to the neighborhood, walking a
seemingly deserted street at night, were puzzled by
the echoing hiss between the empty tracks. Small boys
soon learned one of San Francisco's more enduring
sports when they found that a paper bag, tied to a
length of twine dropped in the cable car slot, would
run along the street like a rabbit for miles before the
string broke or a passing horse stepped on the mysteriously motivated scrap of trash.

Brian Junior would just miss this display of urchin
ingenuity, for he'd grown into his first real interest in
girls by now and no longer played with marbles, either.

Gus had met a girl while Dawn had been in the
East. Brian Senior's only comment was that at least
she wasn't Chinese, but Dawn liked Miss Matson.
That she was Presbyterian seemed unimportant to a
mother who'd once prayed to the Elder Gods of Ho
than it did to either Brian or the girl's somewhat uneasy parents. Her future in-laws, when they came to
call, proved easier to manage than had the self-important Mrs. DeWitt. Perhaps, Dawn thought, this was
because they were more secure in both their faith and
social position than the puffed-up parents of poor
puffed-up Roger.

Ruth Matson's mother broached the subject of religion after dinner, as she and Dawn retired to the
sitting room to leave the fathers to cigars, brandy, and
the new land boom in Los Angeles. When Ruth's
mother asked what Dawn thought about her son's
promise to raise any future children as Protestants,
Dawn smiled and asked, "What's the problem, then?"

"You have no objections to your grandchildren being
raised in my daughter's faith, Mrs. Carlyle?"

"Call me Dawn. You probably know I'm a convert to my husband's faith, ah, Mrs. Matson?"

"Please, Dawn, my friends call me Prue. Gus did mention your childhood to us once, at dinner. I must say it makes a thrilling story. Is it true you had no religion at all when they found you as a child in the desert?"

"Well, I wouldn't say I had no religion, but I'll allow I had a lot to learn. I was a married woman before I got it straight that the Lord Jesus wasn't the son of Changing Woman and the Great Spirit."

She saw she'd shocked her guest and quickly added, "Please don't be offended, Prue. You see, I'm trying to explain how I feel about religion as I've come to understand it. Becoming a Christian as a young adult may have given me a perspective many white people don't understand."

"You mean . . . you still believe in heathen Indian gods?"

"No, of course not. Not if you mean in the rain-dance and gourd-shaking way, at any rate. It may seem odd or even sacrilegious, but to the extent that I understand the Lord, the Great Spirit, or whatever we call Him, it's the *spirit* of His law and not the *letter* that counts."

"I'm afraid I don't understand you."

"Very few people do. That's why we fight among ourselves over who loves the Prince of Peace the most. What I'm trying to say, however badly, is that I don't think it matters all that much *how* my grandchildren pray as it does that they pray to *someone*, and that He answers their prayers with a father and mother who love them. Maybe, if it's not asking too much, He'll see that their father and mother love one another, too."

Prudence Matson nodded in sudden understanding. "We're not as far apart in religious matters as I might have feared, Dawn. I may have a little trouble with my husband about it, but don't worry, I think I can make him see his way to give them his blessing."

"Heavens, Prue, I knew we had our husbands whipped as soon as they discovered they both hated the Southern Pacific and smoked the same cigars!"

Yet even as the houses of Carlyle and Matson were making uneasy peace on Nob Hill, the democratic cable car was making its own small changes in the world they'd known, for the Powell Street line neither started nor ended atop Nob Hill. It ran up and over the wealthy neighborhood from Market Street to Fisherman's Wharf and the squalid shanties of the North Beach Cannery Row. The fare was cheap, and many a workman who'd never thought of climbing the steep slopes of the hill to see the homes of the nabobs for himself now passed them on his way to and from work. Denis Kearney now took his underpaid or unemployed followers on six-mile-an-hour tours of Millionaire's Row to shout from his vantage point on the open platform, "Look at 'em, will yez! Livin' up here like Olympian gods whilst the likes of us fight Chinamen for scraps amid the soot and the smoke and the mudflats below!"

Kearney won 51 out of a 155 seats at the convention for the new California constitution in Sacramento. The delegates from the Workmen's party contributed more noise and confusion than constructive legislation but shook more moderate delegates into drafting a far cry from the state constitution sought by Senator Stanford and the Establishment. For amid the bluster and conflicting demands of the exploited masses of California lay a few gems of truth. A handful of men and women who'd gotten first to the trough were running the state, and ran it for their own comfort and profit. In the end, Kearney would fail to nationalize the railroads or distribute free lands to the workers as he promised. But more rational men would take up his simplistic cries for justice. If they couldn't make California a socialist Utopia, they'd put serious crimps in the sprawling empires of the robber barons by the bay.

The first inkling of what lay ahead reached Carlyle and Sons shortly after Gus and Ruth Matson married. Dawn didn't learn of it from her husband, for Brian spent fewer nights at home since learning that his wife no longer felt up to his occasional sexual advances. Gus dropped by alone one evening, as Dawn sat on the veranda to give discreet privacy to Rose and her latest beau. Dawn was flattered that he'd come alone because he wanted to talk to her. Ruth was a dear daughter-in-law, but somehow Gus never spoke as freely in the company of his young wife, and this evening he seemed troubled.

After a bit of small talk, Gus got to the heart of what was bothering him. "It's this blacklist that Sullivan and the other big contractors are passing around, Mom. They want me to fire Garson and O'Bannion as trouble-makers."

"Are they troublemakers, dear?"

"Well, no, not to Carlyle and Sons. But Garson's brother-in-law is an official of the Grange, and O'Bannion's a member of the Workmen's Party. Sullivan says unless we all stick together we'll be having our men joining unions and Lord knows what else."

"I see. What does himself have to say about these dangerous subversives, Gus?"

Gus looked uncomfortable. "Athair hasn't been spending much time at the office since his heart attack,

Mom. He, ah, sort of lets me run things down there these days."

Dawn suppressed a grimace of distaste and the chance to say she knew damned well where himself was spending his time. "All right, what do you want to do about the blacklist, Gus?"

"I just don't know, Mom. We'd be ruined by a union, but if it was up to me, I'd wait and see how serious O'Bannion was about organizing one before I fired him."

"That seems reasonable. Tell me, what's so terrible about your men organizing a union, Gus? Do you feel you've been paying them too little?"

"Of course not, Mom! Carlyle and Sons pays top dollar for honest work. Why, some of our straw bosses take home as much as twelve dollars a week—and that's more than a brakeman on the cable makes!"

"Hmmm, that seems fair enough. By the way, have you met the Davis boy Rose has been keeping company with?"

Gus looked annoyed. "I met them at the social the other night, Mom. He seems like a nice enough chap. What's this got to do with O'Bannion and that damned blacklist?"

"I was just thinking. Howard Davis is inside, right now, with Rose. He is a nice young man, and tonight he brought me a lovely box of chocolates. He brought flowers, too—for Rose, of course."

"That seems only proper, Mom. What are you getting at?"

"I was just wondering how often Mr. O'Bannion brings home chocolates, or if he used to give his poor wife flowers every time he came to call. I suppose he must have managed flowers, but a five-pound box of chocolates would be a problem for a man taking home less than twelve dollars a week, don't you think?"

Gus looked confused and said, "But, Mom, it's not the same. Howie Davis is a gentleman."

"You mean he has an allowance greater than the wages of any three men you have working for you? I'm not sure just what a gentleman is, Gus, but I do buy the food for this house and I do know what groceries cost in this town, no matter who has to buy them."

"Come on, Mom. Carlyle and Sons pays a living wage."

"I suppose it does. If by living you mean meat two or three times a week, a few schooners of beer of an evening, and a two-room shack on North Beach. What sort of wages is this union of O'Bannion's talking about, Gus?"

"Oh, there's no limit to the demands of men like Denis Kearney. Do you know he says that someday men will get as much as five dollars a day for common labor?"

"Well, we know Denis Kearney's a dreamer, dear, but let's be realistic. If you leave Mr. O'Bannion alone, it's quite likely he'll never organize anything. And if he does, how much more can we afford to pay before we have to fight?"

"Oh, I suppose we could pay the men a few extra dollars, passing it on to labor costs in our bids, but that's not the point, Mom. It's the principle of unions we're against."

"I'm not sure I like the idea, either, dear. But sooner or later I fear we'll just have to accept them, as we accepted the Chinese. Do you remember how every-one expected the Chinese to murder us all in our beds just a few short years ago, Gus? Somehow, we still seem to be here, and I suspect Carlyle and Sons will survive this current labor unrest, too."

Gus smiled, allowing his mind to dwell a moment on an almond-eyed girl he'd almost forgotten. "You may be right, Mom. I think I'll just sit tight and wait it out. I don't suppose O'Bannion's plotting any anarchy tonight, anyway."

"I don't either. Are you going to tell him, dear?"

"Tell? Tell whom what, Mom?"

"Mr. O'Bannion. That his job is safe, of course. Don't you imagine he's worried about being on that silly blacklist?"

"Gee, Mom, I don't see how he could even know about it."

"Oh, he knows, Gus. A man fighting to feed his family makes it a point to know such things. If I were you, I'd call him in and have a talk with him."

"What would I say, Mom? The man's an ignorant mick. We don't talk the same language."

"Heavens, you have been spending a lot of time at the Chamber of Commerce, haven't you? For God's sake, Gus, just call the poor man in and tell him you'll not be after giving him the auld boot!"

It was at the wedding of Brian Junior that Dawn suddenly awoke, with a start, to the fact that another great bite of time's cruel shark had been spent in limbo.

It hadn't been an uncomfortable limbo. She had a box at the opera now and had even picked up enough French and Italian to understand much of what went on down on the stage—although it seemed, from her bored vantage point in the gilded box, that many of

the tenor's agonized rantings could have been avoided
with a bit of common sense. Much of her time these
days was spent at fashion shows, for the women of
San Francisco who *counted* were becoming famous for
their trim figures and Parisian manner of dress. The
rather plain young thing that Junior married had been
flattered and a bit overwhelmed to have her trousseau
chosen by her future mother-in-law. Rose, like Gus,
had married into families who had charge accounts at
Gump's, but poor little Mary Simmons, while from a
good family, had been almost literally snatched from
the convent by her Nob Hill suitor.

This time, at least, there was no religious problem,
and the bride's family had the wherewithal for a
decent church wedding in a less fashionable parish
on Columbus Avenue. It was as the young couple
drove away from the steps in a shower of rice and
good wishes that Dawn suddenly thought, numbly,
"That's it. They're all grown up. I don't have any
babies anymore!"

She suddenly covered her face with a white-gloved
hand. At her side, her husband took her by the elbow,
jovially mumbling, "There, there, Mother. You're not
losing a son. You're gaining a daughter."

He'd said the same sort of thing at the last two
weddings and Dawn had merely nodded. This time
she said, "Oh, for God's sake, Brian, put a sock in it!"

"Did I say something wrong, auld girl?"

Dawn saw the bride's mother approaching and
pasted a smile across her own face as she told her
husband, "I'm just tired, dear. Why don't you run
along to your club? I'm sure you'll be more comfortable out of that boiled shirt."

Brian looked away as he stammered, "Well, and I

am expected for an early supper and some cards with the boys, but if you'll be needing me up at the house this evening . . ."

"You run along and . . . play, dear. Oh, here's Molly Simmons. Wasn't it a lovely wedding, Molly dear?"

Her new in-law, a brown little sparrow in borrowed finery, flashed an alarming set of dentures at Dawn. "Oh, it was so beautiful I wanted to cry," she gushed. "Himself and me was married in a civil ceremony, you know, but I always promised meself, when it was time for me Mary to be wed, we'd do the best for her. Not that it's been easy."

Who was this horrid little woman, Dawn wondered, as Molly Simmons droned on about the sacrifices she and her shopkeeper husband had made to bring their only daughter up a dacent Catholic girl and all and all.

Dawn found herself wanting to ask Mrs. Simmons how old she was, for even allowing for a change-of-life baby, her son's new mother-in-law was *old!* Her hair was not gray, but that was probably due to a rinse. The poor woman looked like she'd been soaked in brine and dried out like a raisin in the sun.

Brian excused himself with another awkward remark about his "club," and Dawn forced herself to listen to Molly Simmons, if only to take her mind off the probable pending scene on Chestnut Street. Discreet inquiries had informed Dawn of her husband's problems with the other woman. Helen Bordon was said to be a bit of a shrew who often badgered Brian in public about getting a divorce from his "old Indian squaw," and while she knew divorce was unthinkable to Brian or anyone else on Nob Hill, his obligatory attendance at his son's wedding would no doubt make for a stormy evening for the poor dear.

Molly Simmons was saying, "To think I could be a grandmother before I'm forty-five!" Dawn was startled into forgetting her husband's mistress as she asked, cautiously, "Oh, are you that old, dear? I would have taken you for perhaps thirty-eight or so."

Pleased, Molly Simmons flushed and confided, "No, I try to take good care of myself, but between us girls, I'm going on forty-four, and if we give them nine months . . ."

"My, that does make you a very young grandmother, doesn't it?" It was insane! This poor little prune of a woman was not much older than *she* was!

As if she'd read Dawn's thoughts, or just wanted to be annoying, Molly Simmons said, "Well, I imagine I won't be the only young grandmother in the family, Dawn me dear. For you've got a good ten years on me to the younger side, I'd be thinking."

Dawn shook her head, thoughtfully, and said, "No, I think we must be about the same age." She smiled wryly and added, "I'm afraid I've beaten you to grand-motherhood, too. My oldest boy, Gus, just had a son last month. Otherwise, he'd have been here with Rose and the rest of the family."

"Oh, me eyebrow, how pleased you must be, Dawn darling!"

"Pleased? Oh, you mean about my grandson? Yes, I guess I am. I've only seen him twice. His mother hasn't been feeling well and they live so far down the Peninsula these days."

"That's your Brian's older brother, the one who married the Protestant, isn't it?" asked Molly Simmons in an understanding tone.

But she didn't understand, Dawn thought. None of

them understood how . . . how weird it made her feel
to hold a small pink bundle in her arms and think,
"My God, I'm a grandmother! How did this happen?
Doesn't a woman get to *live* a few years before they
tell her she's a grandmother?"

Everyone was very nice about it, though. Friends
still complimented her on her youthful appearance
and her sons made gallant little jokes about feeling so
foolish calling a real looker Mom.

But nobody understood. Dawn herself didn't understand how she could feel so split in two by time. She
knew, objectively, that she'd lived through the now
legendary days of the Gold Rush and that many a
young man, now grown, thought of the Civil War as
something that had happened shortly after the siege of
Troy. Yet another part of her waited, as she'd waited
so longingly when she'd loved Nevada, for the lost
little girl the Indians had found to *grow up*.

"Well, I must say you've been very lucky with your
teeth," Molly Simmons was saying with a touch of
envy. Dawn murmured something meaningless about
having a good dentist even as she searched her memory for some milestone, any milestone, that read, "Here.
This was the year, this was the point in time when
you stopped being a child and became an adult."

Perhaps, she thought, it was because she'd never
had a birthday, or in truth, a childhood. As an Indian,
she'd been expected to do a woman's work with digging stick and gathering basket from the moment they
found her. As a white, she'd been plunged into an
adult world from the beginning, even though Nevada,
alone among the men she'd ever known, had refused
to see her as anything but a skinny kid. Well, she
wasn't a skinny kid anymore, but she didn't feel like
a grandmother either. She didn't feel a day older than

when she'd been running barefoot from the Bannocks with the other Indian girls. She just felt . . . cheated.

She wasn't sure what time had taken from her. She still had her looks and health, and a more comfortable life and income, than this poor little sparrow with the awful teeth could ever dream of. But something was still missing, and despite her wealth and position she couldn't buy it. She didn't know, in fact, just what it was. She only knew she wanted it, before it was too late.

The death of Brian Carlyle took place, no doubt amid considerable drama, at the house of his kept woman, Helen Bordon. The news of his fatal heart attack reached Dawn as she was making up her guest list for the christening and reception for her granddaughter, Mavis Carlyle. The butler brought the hand-delivered note as Dawn was thinking how fortunate that Molly Simmons's real name was Mavis and that she'd talked them out of naming the child Dawn, after her. She dismissed the butler with a nod and opened the small white envelope with the Malay kriss she used as a letter knife.

For a time she stared numbly at the words, written in spidery copperplate by an obviously fussy as well as embarrassed Mr. Boyde. Helen Bordon had apparently sent for her lover's bookkeeper shortly after the doctor covered Brian's face with a sheet. Doubtless Helen Bordon had wanted to discuss the books of Carlyle and Sons a bit before informing her lover's family of his death. Well, she'd get that out of Boyde when he called in person. She'd pretty well established in the bookkeeper's mind, by now, that she was one woman he'd take orders from!

Dawn folded the note neatly and put it back in the

envelope, wondering, even as she did so, why she took so much time and care with the meaningless task. So Brian was dead, was he? Small wonder, the way he'd been making such a pig of himself all these years. Was she supposed to *do* something about it? Oddly, she didn't feel like doing anything. She didn't feel anything at all. Shouldn't she at least feel *relieved?*

Dawn tucked the note neatly in a pigeonhole of her library desk and stared at her guest list for a time before she murmured, "Oh, bother! The least the poor thing could have done was die at a less inconvenient time!"

The christening would have to be postponed until after the funeral, she supposed, and she'd have to tell the children of their father's passing.

"Damn you, Brian Carlyle!" she muttered aloud, "I have to write notes to just everybody and I don't know what you'd want me to say!"

She picked up her pen and scrawled across a scrap of foolscap, "Dear Rose, Your father just dropped dead in that love nest on Chestnut Street. Flowers are optional."

Then, having gotten that out of her system, Dawn took another sheet and began to compose a more rational note to each of the children as well as the family lawyer and others. She wrote tersely correct messages without pause, and by the time she'd finished, her mind was back in control of her emotions. It was important, she knew, to keep a cool head at a time like this. The smell of carrion always drew scavengers, and the scent of a dead Nob Hiller would carry far. Dawn still remembered how those dreadful little men had peddled tintypes of Civil War graves to grieving families after the War, and the claims on the Harrison estate pressed by fraudulent relatives.

Yes, she was a widow woman once again, and Brian had led such an untidy life these past few years.

Dawn reached in a drawer for a small silk bag and took out the ring old Wong had bequeathed to her so long ago. She held a match to a stick of red sealing wax, dropped a small puddle of it on a blank sheet, and pressed the seal into it as it cooled. Then she addressed an envelope to a certain jade shop on Grant Avenue and placed her wordless message inside.

Getting to her feet, Dawn pulled the bell rope and, when the butler came, handed him the packet of envelopes with instructions to see that each was delivered. "I'm afraid we're going to be having quite a few guests in the next few days, Jarvis. I think we'd best keep a cold buffet ready for odd servings and—oh, yes, we'd better order plenty of cigars and porter."

The butler nodded gravely. "Will the master be coming home to supper then, tonight, mum?"

"No, the master died this afternoon. I don't intend a wake here at the house, but we'd best have plenty of porter on hand, anyway."

The butler's face blanched but he betrayed no other reaction. He said, "I understand, mum," and withdrew without another word.

So the servants knew, did they? Well, that simplified things in a way. At least she wouldn't be expected to display crocodile tears in the privacy of her own home. The black veil she intended to order for the funeral would relieve her of any need to hide her feelings in public for the next few days.

How odd, she thought, that she'd never before considered why widows wore those veils. Some funeral customs of the White Eyes were quite civilized, when one thought about them objectively.

* * *

It rained the day of Brian's funeral. Dawn didn't remember, until she got home, how it had rained the day they buried Ace. She wondered if she was supposed to feel some significance about that, but decided it was too much bother. Snow might have been more appropriate to the feelings she'd had as she'd noted the curtained carriage standing against the skyline of the hill behind Brian's grave. Dawn neither knew nor cared whether Helen Bordon had watched from there out of discretion, sincere grief, or a sense of showmanship. Dawn was sure others had noticed, but no one had said anything, and perhaps at least a few of the mourners hadn't known about the house on Chestnut Street after all.

Gus and his wife, Ruth, drove Dawn home and offered to stay with her, but Dawn protested. They had a long drive down to San Mateo and she wanted to be alone. They said they understood and left her to toss aside her stuffy veil with a sigh of relief and an oddly gamin sense of mischief. The servants were solicitous and the butler was absolutely unctuous until Dawn sent him off to his quarters with orders not to disturb her.

She went to the kitchen and, finding it empty, made herself some coffee to have with jam and bread. Then, feeling as though she were playing hooky like the schoolgirl she'd never been, Dawn curled up in the bay window of the parlor and had a secret picnic, watching the rain run down the panes in the gathering twilight.

The old Chinese lamplighter had just turned on the street lamp out front when an oilcloth-covered sulky pulled up at the hitching post by Dawn's gate. A tall man in an Inverness cape got down from the single seat of the sulky and swiftly tied his reins to the horse-head post as Dawn, wondering who on earth he was, put down her tray and went to open the door, smoothing bread crumbs from the front of her dress as she moved through the dimly lit hallway.

The man she admitted looked familiar, yet Dawn had trouble placing him as he swept the wet deerstalker cap from his iron-gray curls and said, with a formal bow, "I came as soon as I heard, Mrs. Carlyle. Actually, I was just checking in at the Palace when one of your late husband's business associates told me the dreadful news."

The slightly British accent, mellowed by a hint of an older, softer tongue, jogged Dawn's memory and she gasped, "Oh, you're the earl of Dunraven! I didn't recognize you at first. Please come in—uh, do I call you Earl?"

Her visitor smiled and said, "No, my friends call me Fitz. It's actually George FitzRoy, but I don't like George and at least a dozen people would have to die before I'd be in line for the title." Then he remembered his errand and gasped, "Oh, I say, that was dreadfully unfeeling of me, wasn't it?"

Dawn waved him into the parlor, smiling back as she asked, "Because you mentioned death? It's a word we live with every day, Fitz. Frankly, I'm a little weary of trying to pretend I can't think of it without a maidenly shudder. Would you like some coffee? I've some porter on ice, if you'd prefer that."

"Coffee will suit me, mum," he said, as Dawn took his wet cloak from him and draped it on a rack just outside the parlor door. As he sat beside her on the horsehair sofa near the window seat, he added with a slight sigh, "I've been here long enough, I suppose, but I'll never understand why you Americans drink cold beer."

Dawn laughed as she poured him a cup. Then, noting the expression on his face, said, "I know, we're supposed to be ever so solemn at a time like this, but as I told you, I've spent the whole afternoon listening to condolences and . . ."

"I know the feeling," he cut in, with a sardonic little smile of his own. "When my wife passed on, six months ago, I had this dreadful urge to grin like an idiot at her funeral. I mean, I really was quite fond of the old girl, but all those long faces, and all that dreary music, well . . ."

"Oh, dear, Celeste is dead, too? I'm so sorry, Fitz. I never really got to know her, but she seemed so sweet."

"Please, I came to offer my sympathies to you, mum!" And then, quite suddenly, both of them laughed out loud. FitzRoy managed to pull himself together almost at once, but Dawn howled, doubled over with insanely unexpected mirth. Then she recovered enough to sit up, giggle, and look away, saying, "Aren't we awful?"

"Quite uncivilized," said FitzRoy, soberly.

Then they both laughed like children again.

Dawn let herself go, somehow sure that he understood, even as she tried to understand herself. Then she wiped her face, gasped, and said, "My God, that felt good! You must think I'm mad."

"No," he replied, gently, "I think you feel safe with a friend who understands."

Reconsidering what he'd just said, he quickly added, "I've always considered you and poor Brian my friends, you know. I was green as grass when I arrived in California with a bit of silver in the thatch and a head full of dreams about becoming the whiskey baron of the western world. I owe such success as I've had to the generous advice of you and your late husband."

"Oh? Didn't you ever build your distillery up near Weed, after all?"

He shook his head. "No. I learned soon enough I'd have my hands full just growing the barley and malting it. Brian was right about the north end of the valley being best for barley, but the climate's so different here that our old British methods just won't take. I kept at it, though, and by the time I got the hang of things, I'd found myself with a near monopoly. You're looking at the man who grows the barley and makes the malt for half the stills and breweries in California."

He named some brands and Dawn said, "Oh, we have some of that steam-beer on ice! I never dreamed you made it!"

"I don't," Fitz insisted. "We're living in a new age of specialization. Instead of one man making lock, stock, and barrel, each makes the thing he's best at. My malt, another firm's bottle, yet another firm's stoppers, labels, and so forth."

"Oh, I see. It's like subcontracting. I never thought of that with my poor vineyards up in the Napa. My tenants up there have been trying to do the whole thing, and all we've been getting is raisins and vinegar."

Dawn suddenly realized she was talking shop at what might seem a grotesque time and changed the subject by asking Fitz about his own recent loss. Her visitor shrugged and said, "It was merciful when it ended, I fear. Poor Celeste never completely recovered from a bad miscarriage, and near the end she was in considerable pain."

"Oh, I'm so sorry. Did the two of you have any other children?"

"No, it bothered Celeste more than me, but it would

have been nice. Sometimes I think it was her inability to bear that brought on her female complaints."

He shuddered as if a cold draft had swept over him. "It's not one of my favorite topics of conversation, these days. As I said, it was quite unpleasant for both of us, near the end."

Before Dawn could think of a suitable reply, Fitz-Roy glanced past her out the window and said, "Hello, you seem to have visitors at the gate."

Dawn turned to see a knot of dark, wet figures standing undecided in the rain near FitzRoy's sulky. She got to her feet. "Oh dear, it's some of the workmen from Brian's firm. Excuse me a moment, will you?"

She went to the door and swung it open, calling out, "For Heaven's sake come up here out of that rain, boys."

The band of seven, led by Gavin O'Bannion, came awkwardly up the walk. O'Bannion stopped at the foot of the steps and removed his dripping cap as the others followed suit. O'Bannion stammered, "It's our respects we'd be after paying, Miz Carlyle. We don't expect to come in, but . . ."

"You'll come in and get dry and we'll share some ale and porter to the memory of himself!" Dawn insisted firmly, as she held out a hand to the bashful O'Bannion. The straw boss came up the steps, bowing his head to kiss the back of Dawn's hand with an oddly courtly gesture. Then, as Dawn led the way inside, each man crossed himself in the doorway and muttered, "God's blessings on this house!" before passing on into the front parlor.

FitzRoy was on his feet, and as Dawn introduced the flustered workmen to him, Fitz shook hands with each in turn and asked about their counties. Dawn had no idea what their murmured Wexford, Mayo, Sligo, Clare, and so forth really meant, but it seemed very important to Irishmen for some reason. When O'Bannion learned FitzRoy was from Belfast he seemed overjoyed, for the tall stranger in the gentleman's frock coat had obviously made him uneasy at first.

Dawn noticed, as she seated her guests and rang for the butler, that Fitz had dropped his Oxford accent and assumed one much like that of her late husband and his men. She couldn't help wondering if the lilting brogue by which Irishmen identified one another didn't thicken as they got farther from the River Shannon's shore. Brian had once told her the purest English spoken could be heard in Dublin, yet they all seemed to outbrogue one another with each passing year away from the Auld Sod.

She knew for a fact there were more Fenians in San Francisco alone than in all the Irish counties put together.

The servants brought refreshments and cigars, and as the room filled with the smell of good tobacco and cheap wet wool, each man in turn expressed his grief and attempted to canonize the late Brian Carlyle. To hear the way they spoke of himself might have suggested, to one who hadn't lived with the man, that he'd been Staint Patrick and Cuchulain rolled into one.

Dawn listened with polite respect and nods of agreement as her guests outdid one another in eulogy. Much of the bitterness of the last few years had faded with each hour since his death, and Dawn supposed, in his fashion, poor Brian had done his best. She found herself agreeing, to her own surprise, about some of his virtues, and managed to keep a straight face when they ventured into hyperbole. He'd been, she thought, exactly what she should have expected when first she

chose him from among the even rougher men around
Lost Chinaman. He'd been a good father and a generous provider, and if, in the end, she'd outgrown his
uncouth ways, it had been, she supposed, as much her
fault as his.

After what seemed a million years the delegation
ran out of nice things to say, and O'Bannion, taking
out his Ingersoll pocket watch with a self-important
air, ushered himself and the men firmly out to catch
the cable car back to their warren. Dawn saw them to
the door and returned to her guest with a wan smile,
murmuring, "I'm sorry I had to put you through that,
Fitz, but I'm glad they came. The old customs do have
a way of comforting one, don't they?"

"That's why they're old customs." He nodded gravely, adding, "The purpose of the Irish wake is to leave
everyone so tired they'll get a good night's sleep."

Dawn laughed and said, "My God, they did go on
about himself, didn't they? Do you think it means
they really liked him, or would they have done the
same for anyone?"

"It was genuine. I've been to enough wakes to
know."

"Did your neighbors carry on like that when Celeste
passed away?"

"Hardly. People like us are supposed to keep a stiff
upper lip."

"People like us? I'm hardly related to any earls,
Fitz."

"Perhaps not, but your people must have been
gentlefolk, Dawn. That's neither praise nor cause for
rejoicing. It's a simple fact of life. I think, sometimes,
the born commoner has the more pragmatic approach
to our mayfly existence in a brutish world."

"You mean steak and potatoes were all God meant us to have?"

"Nine-tenths of the human race will never enjoy that much. Nine out of ten of us will never really ask for more. Sometimes I wish . . . but what's the use? It's the people like us who drag the rest of the world, kicking and screaming, out of the caves and into what we hope is progress. We'd still be in those caves, you know, if some long-forgotten fool hadn't wondered if there wasn't more to life than a mastodon steak and that lass with the well-turned ankle in the next cave over."

Dawn nodded and said, almost to herself, "Brian was more than a contented peasant, yet somehow he never quite became what I thought he would. He used to talk so much of his dreams for the future, but this *is* the future he dreamed of creating. Somewhere along the way, he faltered."

"Perhaps you just took different paths, Dawn. You have to remember he was older than you, and a man's dreams change as he sees how often time hammers them into unplanned shapes. I've heard good things about Carlyle and Sons over the years. May I ask just what he did that upset you so?"

Dawn started to tell him, knowing he was one of the few old friends who might understand. Then she caught herself. "My husband's dead. The past is dead. So be it. Let's talk about you. What brings you down here to the bay? You've yet to tell me what you're doing in San Francisco, Fitz."

He shrugged and said, "I'm expanding my business a bit, now that the malt kilns are practically running themselves up in Weed. Since Celeste died, I've found myself with a lot of time on my hands, and like you,

I can't just lean back and enjoy my ill-gotten gains."

"Is my restlessness that obvious?"

"Quite. You haven't stopped tapping that one foot since I came in this evening. What *are* you going to do, now that the funeral and all that muck are out of the way?"

"I don't really know. I thought, once I got things in order, I'd give this house to my oldest boy, Gus, and maybe travel a bit."

"The Grand Tour? Forgive me, my dear, but you're not old enough for that old widow's dodge. One has to be very young or very old to enjoy mucking about in museums and cathedrals. I took my Grand Tour when I was twenty. It was a dreadful bore, and the hotels on the Continent are rather grim."

"Oh, I don't know. I've always wanted to see Paris and the Grand Canal in Venice."

"Paris was meant for male enjoyment," he insisted. "As for the Grand Canal, it's filled with sewage, and besides, a gondola ride alone in the moonlight is the most depressing thing one can imagine."

"Perhaps I'll have to get someone to take me," she said, half joking.

He sighed and said, "That shouldn't present such a problem for you. You're not planning to run off to Venice with anyone in the next few weeks, are you?"

"Heavens, no. Why do you ask?"

"I have to run down to Riverside next week. I'm thinking of buying an orange grove. If these new navel oranges prove half as exciting as they're supposed to, I should be able to settle the deal and be back in San Francisco before the end of the month."

"Oh? Why is it so important I be here when you get back?"

He took his own watch out, said, "Good Lord!" and

got to his feet. "We'd better put off talking about it until I get back. It's after midnight and I fear I've already said too much, considering."

Helen Bordon looked less the tart Dawn had imagined and much less the lady her expression and haughty tone were intended to achieve. She obviously thought she'd scored an advantage in having Dawn call on her at the Chestnut Street address rather than the other way around, but Dawn came willingly. Curious about her late husband's love nest, she saw little advantage in Machiavellian maneuvers when, to her, the game they played was so simple.

Like the well-rounded blue-eyed brunette Helen, the mustard-yellow frame house between Van Ness and the Presidio was furnished to Brian's somewhat expansive taste. Ivory Belfast lace curtains in the bow windows echoed the whiter Chantilly over the blue watered-silk of the kept woman's well-filled bodice. Agains walls papered in wine and ebony paisley, the heavy mahogany furniture was Steamboat Victorian, upholstered in crimson plush. Dawn noticed there were no plants, and that despite the incense smouldering in the brass burner in the hall, the house was filled with ghosts of boiled cabbage and potatoes past.

After a meaningless exchange of cautious pleasantries, Dawn got to the point of her visit. "I don't want you bothering my son Gus again. My lawyers tell me you have no claim whatever on the house of Carlyle, but in view of, ah, services rendered, I've made certain arrangements Brian might have wanted."

Dawn opened the carpetbag on her lap and took out a sheaf of envelopes, handing them over to the woman sitting stiffly across the coffee table. "This house is yours, free and clear. Here's a bank book with a checking and savings account in your name. I assume you had sense enough to get something out of Brian over the years, but that's neither here nor there. I've deposited ten thousand to your account and signed over a hundred shares of Southern Pacific to you. So you see there's really no reason why you should ever approach my son or his bookkeeper, Mr. Boyde, again."

Helen Bordon held the envelopes in both hands without looking at them. She sniffed and said, "It's not near enough. I'm a woman alone, and I was his wife in all but name for all these years!"

"California doesn't recognize common law marriage between a married man and . . . whatever, Mrs. Bordon. I'm afraid it's going to have to *be* enough. I don't really owe you a cent, you know. I'm jut trying to be civilized about this awkward situation we find ourselves in."

"Brian loved me. He told me that once the children were grown and settled down he was going to divorce you and marry me!"

"I'm sure he did, my dear, but you see, he *didn't* marry you. He *died*. You really should have tried to get him to eat more salads and drink less porter. Anyway, you seem to be missing my point. I have one other paper I want you to sign. It's a quit claim, disavowing any and all connections you may have ever had with my late husband. We both know you have no claims against his estate, but I would so like to clean up all these little loose ends and let the poor dear rest in peace."

"I'll sign nothing! You can't buy my love for Brian!" Helen Bordon exclaimed, even as she clung to the booty Dawn had just given her. She added, "I have a lawyer, too. He tells me I have a very good case as

Brian's common law widow, after all these years I've given him!"

"Your lawyer's a fool, then." Dawn reached in her bag for a small flat box of satinwood. "I'm trying to be nice about this, not so much for you or Brian as for his memory. We had our difficulties, but what's past is past and he was my husband and the father of my children. It's my children and grandchildren I'm thinking of right now. Would you take this and open it, dear?"

Wordlessly, Helen Bordon took the small Chinese box and pried open the lid with her thumbnail. She stared for a moment at the small jade hatchet in its nest of pink satin, then licked her lips and gasped, "Don't be ridiculous! Do I look like a Chinaman?"

"I'll pass on what you look like, sister. You do know what I've just handed you, don't you?"

"Of course. Everyone in town knows about those crazy Chinese hatchet men, but damn it, we're white!" She let her lips curl a bit as she added, "That is, I'm white. Brian told me once that you were some sort of Paiute breed."

"Hmm, let's say that I am, for the sake of getting this business over with. Let's say that I'm a squaw, or better yet, a savage. Let's say that I'm just about fed up with you, too. Are you going to sign my quit claim, or would you rather keep my tong warning until someone comes some night to redeem it?"

"You must be joking! This is a white neighborhood!"

"True. Close to the Golden Gate fog banks and the mudflats just to the north, too. I suppose your visitors would have to exercise a certain bit of caution coming and going, don't you?"

"Do you know what I'm going to do the moment

you leave? I'm going directly to the police with this silly thing and I'm going to tell them you threatened me, a white woman, with a Chinese tong murder!"

"Did I say murder? I didn't ask my friends on Grant Street to murder anyone. I merely said a certain slut was annoying me and they said not to worry about it anymore. Frankly, I have no idea whether they intend to cut your head off or shanghai you off to some Cantonese whorehouse. I suppose that will depend on what they think of you when they come. You're really quite attractive, in a blowsy sort of way."

"Get out of my house! I'm going to the law about this!"

"My dear, do you really think they'll believe you? What would you think if you were a paddy copper and some distraught young thing with no visible means of support came to you with a tale of being threatened in such a bizarre way by a grandmother from Nob Hill?"

"They'll believe me! I'll make them believe me!"

Dawn got to her feet with a shrug. "Have it your way, then. I doubt we'll ever be seeing each other again, so I guess this is good-bye."

She made it almost to the front door before Helen Bordon came after her. "Wait! Suppose I sign? Suppose I sign and later I find I need more money?"

"You could always take in washing, if you're not up to servicing the next rich man you find whose wife doesn't understand him."

"It's not fair. I'm entitled to much more than you've offered after all I did for Brian."

"We live in an unjust world. I'll want the hatchet back, if you intend to be a good little girl and do as you're told."

Helen Bordon hesitated, then sighed. "Heavens, I

don't see why we have to carry on like this. Come back in the parlor and I'll sign your damned old paper."

Dawn foollowed her, smiling softly as she purred, "Now you're being sensible. But then, somehow I knew you would be."

"I still don't understand," Dawn was saying as she and George FitzRoy walked between the large oak casks in the gloom of her barnlike Napa Valley winery. "We never got anything but vinegar before you suggested those few simple changes."

Fitz held a tin cup under a spigot and drew about an ounce of wine as he replied. "It was simple enough on the surface, I suppose, but your inexperienced hands were letting too much air get in. I'm not sure I understand that French chemist in detail, but there's more to making liquor than stuffing a barrel full of smashed grapes and letting it rot. According to Pasteur, the timing is what's important. The little boogers that break down the sugar into alcohol give way to other boogers who turn alcohol into acid at the next stage of fermentation. Fortunately, the vinegar bugs need air and . . . here, taste this."

Dawn sipped at the wine he'd drawn for her and smiled. "Oh, my, it's just like Burgundy, isn't it?"

"Oh, let's not get sickening, old girl. It's an acceptable dry red table wine and it ought to fetch a handsome price in San Francisco. But Burgundy? Not quite."

She laughed and took another sip, insisting, "I like it, and maybe this place will be able to do more than simply pay its taxes, now that you've shown us how. Somehow, I've never been very lucky in my land investments. Manufacturing stocks have all done amaz-

ingly well for me—Edison of Jersey has even gone up,
since they came out with that new electric lamp of
theirs—but my farmlands? Nothing!"

"That's because you Americans are better manu-
facturers than farmers," he said, gently. He took the
cup from her, sipped thoughtfully, and replaced it on
the nearby workbench. "There's an art to making
things grow, just as there is to building a steam engine
or a highway. You chaps are the Romans of this age,
I fear. The poor Romans were never able to feed themselves, either, you know. They were great soldiers and
grand engineers, but they had to get their grain from
Cleopatra. America needs more peasants, like myself."

"Heaven's, Fitz, I'd hardly call you a peasant!"

"Really? Perhaps that's because you Anglo-Saxons,
like the French, use the word with its class-conscious
meaning. The true peasant is a man who lives off
the land. A man, if you will, who likes and understands
it. Did you know the Celts in Brittany grow more on
those stony hills of theirs, acre for acre, than your
American farmers are getting from the rich prairie
soils of your Midwest right now? I was appalled the
last time I rode the train east to see what your Homestead Act has done to the land back there, and I'm
afraid you Californians have a lot to learn, too. You
Americans don't *farm* land. You *mine* it."

"Well, I'd be the first to admit I'm not a farm girl,
Fitz. All I do know is that those barley lands of yours
up north are the richest in the big valley. You must
be doing something right."

"It's called fertilizer and crop rotation, old girl.
Can't make malt sans barley, and the Americans I
hired up in Weed had a lot to learn, considering they
all claimed to be farm lads when I signed them on.

By the way, have you sent for those goat figs, as I suggested?"

Dawn led the way to the doorway and out into the sunlight. She nodded and said, "My tenants down near Fresno had never heard of goat figs, but I did manage to find a Greek importer in the city·who knew what you were talking about. He's sent to Smyrna for some seedlings, and he seemed surprised we were trying to grow Greek figs without a few wild goat-fig trees here and there in the grove. How did you know the cultivated figs won't set fruit without their scruffy little cousins for neighbors, Fitz?"

"I told you I took the Grand Tour when I was twenty."

"Yes, but good Lord, did you learn about cross-fertilizing in Paris or Rome?"

"No, I mucked about in the farmlands between them a bit. You see, I'd seen a few cathedrals and museums in Britain already, but the land on the Continent was new to me. I fear I've always had a rather uncouth habit of chatting with gardeners and gamekeepers more than my mother approved of. She used to warn me we were gentry, but my misspent youth has paid off since coming to your country. I do hope you'll keep this a secret, old girl, but I really do enjoy being up to my elbows in good rich garden soil. Must be from my father's side, what?"

Dawn smiled as she sat down on a redwood bench circling the bole of an old Spanish walnut tree and asked, dreamily, "Have you ever tasted camas, gathered in early spring from a south-facing slope?"

He sat beside her and said, "Of course. I'd heard the Indians dug them for food and resolved to give camas a try. They're not bad, with a bit of salt pork in the pot."

"You're one of the few white men I've ever met who's tasted camas. Have you ever eaten manzanita?"

"Nibbled the fruits a bit. Can't say I really thought much of them. They reminded me of our Irish hedge-row medlars, with a soapy aftertaste. How do you feel about acorn mush?"

"My God, have you eaten digger bread, too?"

"Tried it. Can't say it was my cup of tea, but then, we have more of a choice than the poor diggers. I suppose if one had nothing better, acorn mush would serve."

"I haven't tasted it in years," she sighed. "I was raised on Indian food, you know."

"Quite. You told me the story. I have some diggers working for me up in Weed. If you'd like, I could send for some acorn flour."

She started to nod, then she shook her head. "I'm afraid I'd find it tasteless now. I used to try to make Indian food for Brian and the children, but they never really liked it, and to tell the truth, I've developed my own palate a bit since Hungry Moon found me in the desert. Do you know, lately I've been having a hard time believing it all really happened? I remember staring out the window of the train as it crossed the Great Basin and thinking it must have been a dream. I mean, I *know* it's possible to live out there in those sage flats and jagged rimrocks, but after all these years on the lush side of the Sierra . . ."

"I know," he said. "I went back to Ireland a few years ago. After California, the fields and woods I remembered from my boyhood seemed small and mean. Our grand family mansion had no indoor plumbing and the walls were clammy and smelled of mildew. Isn't it odd how you can't go back to the way it was? I mean, you can go back to the places, but you can't return to the way you remember them. Like it or not, I fear we're both Californians now."

"I suppose we are, but I still mean to see Venice before I die."

"Hmm. When were you planning on leaving?"

"I don't know. There's really nothing keeping me here now. I can't seem to get Gus and his wife to move back to Nob Hill, but the servants keep it like a jewel box whether anyone's there or not. My sons and son-in-law between them are managing the family business quite well, and I've grown bored with playing the stock market. I find I have more money in my account than I'll ever be able to spend in such years as I may have left."

Fitz gazed fondly at her in the dappled light of the old walnut and murmured, "My, yes, you're quite decrepit these days. Before you wander off to the elephant's boneyard, however, have you read the *Bluebird of Happiness?*"

"Of course. But there's no bluebird waiting for me back on Nob Hill. Just an old empty house too big for a woman whose family has grown up and drifted away."

He stared down at the bare earth between his boot tips and asked, quietly, "Have you considered starting over again? You're not really as long in the tooth as you make out, you know."

"Oh, for God's sake, I'm an old woman, Fitz. Even if I found a man who was interested in a barren grandmother, what on earth would I do with him?"

"Well, since I've at least six or seven years on you, I'm not one to offer suggestions, but I do seem to remember the chap got on top, or was it the other way around?"

"Why, Fitz, I do believe you're becoming a dirty old man!"

"Quite. Dirty old man with honorable intentions, however. If you'd let me, I'd take you for that gondola ride down the Grand Canal, Dawn. I'm quite good at mending things about the house, too."

"Good Lord, you can't be serious! I know you don't want my money, so what could you want with a worn-out shoe my age?"

"Well, if you must know, I'm a cannibal. I was going to keep it from you until I fattened you up a bit, but if you'll marry me, I promise not to eat you before we get back from Venice."

Dawn laughed but said, "Be serious, Fitz. You know I'm very fond of you, but we're too old to fall in love like a couple of children."

"I was rather hoping we could do it as a grown man and woman. Frankly, I don't know whether what I feel for you is love or propinquity, but I do know it makes a lot of sense. We share the same interests. We want the same things. Who knows, we may be on to something better than the pounding heartthrobs and all that rot."

Dawn laughed and said, "That was the most unromantic proposal I've had since I was a budding young thing in the gold fields. But at least you're not waving a club at me."

"Would it be accepted if I were to fall to one knee and sob lies about moonlight and roses, Dawn?"

She put a hand on his sleeve and murmured, "No. I've had my fill of romantic lies, Fitz. I've had terrible luck with the men I've chosen. The first man I loved died, leaving me a virgin. The second was an emoitonal cripple who lied as much to himself as to me. You knew Brian."

"Dawn, I can't say a word against Brian."

"I know, and it's to your credit he liked you, too. He was a good man and he tried to be a good husband. We simply outgrew each other, and I suppose it was as much my fault as his."

"Quite. Perhaps we'd better drop the subject and get back to the new pinot vines we've just heeled in."

"Dear Fitz, I don't want to talk about grapes. I want to talk about us. I'm trying to explain how I feel about . . . what's happening."

"You're gun-shy." He smiled boyishly. "I can't say I can blame you. Do you want me to withdraw my bid entirely or dare I assume you need time to think?"

Dawn smiled up at him. "If I ever do marry again it will have to be you or someone as understanding, Fitz."

Fitz returned her smile with more gallantry than hope. "I shan't ask for a blindfold and a last cigarette, dearest. What you're saying is that you simply don't love me, isn't it?"

Dawn shook her head. "What I'm saying is that I simply don't know, Fitz. If I were advising any other woman I'd say she was a fool to turn you down, with or without the moonlight and roses. But you're right. I'm gun-shy. I've been hurt too many times."

"I can wait, if there's any hope at all, Dawn."

"Fitz, that's not fair to ask of any man. Neither of us is getting any younger and you know you're quite a catch for any woman."

He touched her cheek. "I don't want any woman. I want you. Meanwhile, shall we have a look at those new vines? They say we'll have to wait at least seven years before they bear fruit, but I'm a patient man."

* * *

In the end Dawn probably would have married Fitz, for like his wine he improved with age, and as she got to know him better she found him one of the finest men she would ever know.

But fate had other plans for them both.

One afternoon by merest chance Dawn dropped by Gump's to select a present for the wedding of a friend's daughter. The store was crowded that afternoon and a woman bumped Dawn's elbow, causing her to drop her purse. As she knelt to pick it up a tall man bent down to help her.

"Allow me, ma'am."

As they both stood up, he handed her the purse with a polite touch to the brim of his Stetson. Dawn smiled her thanks and then her jaw dropped as if she'd seen a ghost, for she had.

The man's eyes widened, too. Then he blurted, "Dawn! Is it really you?"

She couldn't answer. She felt as if she'd been punched in the heart with a big soft hammer as the ghost of Nevada Jones, an older but still handsome Nevada Jones, grinned crookedly and said, "Yeah, it's me. The bad penny in the flesh."

"Nevada! You . . . you've been dead for years!"

He took her elbow with a warning look around. "The man you mentioned is dead. Let's get out of here and I'll tell you more about it."

In a daze, Dawn allowed herself to be led from Gump's and across the street to a tearoom, where Nevada got her to a back booth and sat across from her, still holding her hand. He took off his sombrero, and she saw that his hairline had receded a bit and that his hair was flecked with silver. She bit her lip and struggled for words. "They told me you'd been shot in the back, Nevada! You were killed in Angel's

Camp when Wabash Brown betrayed you to the law!"

His eyes seemed to drink in her hair, her eyes, her voice. "Yeah, that was a mean trick old Wabash pulled on that poor jasper. He was a card shark Wabash didn't like and I suppose he figured it was a favor to me. I sure was a foolish kid in those days."

"Oh, my God! All these years I thought you were dead—and now you tell me it was all a mistake?"

His eyes met hers. "It was no mistake. Wabash did it to get the law off my trail. I staggered into Angel's with two bullets in me and Wabash nursed me back to health. Old Wabash figured he owed me for past favors on the way west. He was living with a Mexican gal up the slope, and between them they got me back on my feet in about six months. Time I was able to come looking for you, they said you'd married Ace Purvis, so . . ."

The silence between them finally became more than Dawn could bear.

"You mean, all this time . . . Dear God, if only I'd known!"

The waitress came over and Nevada ordered tea for them. Dawn watched, frozen, as the man Nevada handled it with such casual ease. There was something odd here. It was Nevada, yet it wasn't. The boy she'd loved in her girlhood had been a raw tough cowboy. This man, whoever he was, seemed a total stranger.

As the waitress left, Nevada turned back to Dawn. "I heard about Ace getting killed along with your father. I was down in the Mojave, hauling borax. Time I could make it back to the mother lode you'd married Brian Carlyle. You sure married a lot of folks, Dawn. How is old Brian these days? You got any kids?"

"Brian is dead, Nevada. And I'm a grandmother."

The old Nevada might not have noticed the bitterness in her eyes. This new stranger nodded and said, "Yeah, I was in love with you, too. I suppose God sort of had it in for us, at that."

She looked down at her gloved hands and murmured, "You know you could have had me a dozen times and a dozen ways, don't you?"

His voice was oddly gentle. "Yeah, like I said, I was young and foolish in those days. But you know what? I'm not sorry. Not sorry I didn't take advantage of you, I mean. I suppose, over the years, I kept your memory in some sort of phantom locket. Like the poets say, it's better to have loved and lost."

Dawn was recovering her breath by now, and some of her old resentment. She said, "Goddammit, Nevada! You might have told me you were still alive!"

"After you'd married another man?"

"You big goof! You must have known I'd have come to you!"

He stared at her soberly, then said, "Yeah, I knew. I'd had time to do some thinking while my other wounds were healing."

"Then why didn't you . . ."

"Do what? Steal another man's wife? I thought about it, Dawn. I knew I could take Ace Purvis in a gunfight —and when they told me you'd married Brian I considered the odds, seriously. But I didn't want you that way, kid."

"Kid? I just told you I'm a grandmother!"

"Yeah. I noticed the French perfume, too, kid. You'll always be a kid to me, and I wanted you happy, not riding the owlhoot trail with a no-good saddle bum like me."

"Nevada, that's a hundred dollar suit—and I notice you've lost your good-old-boy accent. You haven't spent all these years gunfighting or even punching cows."

"Well, I've had time on my hands and done some reading, I suppose. We've both apparently done some growing since we last saw each other."

Over their tea, Nevada brought her up to date on his new life. After being pronounced dead as far as the law cared, he'd changed his name back to Campbell and headed south along the Sierra. In the great desert to the south he'd prospected and struck, of all things, borax. It seemed half the soap in California owed its existence these days to the Campbell Mineral Combine. He'd never married in the years he'd spent growing wealthy in southern California, and just a few months ago he'd retired and bought a new home in San Francisco. Had not they bumped into each other that afternoon, they might never have known they were almost neighbors.

It took them all too short a time to finish their tea and there was still much catching up to do. Dawn said, "You're coming home with me for supper. But, uh, the children remember Uncle Nevada as my older brother and . . ."

"Uncle Nevada was killed a while back, wasn't he? These days they call me Bill. Wild Bill Campbell, the king of Death Valley."

"Oh, no! That's worse than Nevada Jones!"

"Well, let's just call me Bill. You're still Dawn, aren't you?"

She suddenly covered her eyes and sobbed, "Yes, darling, I'm still Dawn. But you can call me Kid."

After all these years, it wasn't quite as simple as it had seemed the moment she discovered Nevada was still alive.

Her family accepted "Mom's new beau" without demur, for Nevada, or Uncle Bill, was an easy man to like and the children wanted to see their mother happy.

But the long-lost love of Dawn's girlhood was a stranger after all these years. Alone, they spoke of old times and the adventures they'd had together. But it was as if they spoke of children they'd once known. Neither she nor Nevada was young now. They were middle-aged people who'd led separate lives for a generation, and each had been changed, for better or worse, by time.

Bill, as Dawn now called him, was given to occasional lapses into frontier talk and seemed comfortable in a wide-brimmed hat and Justin boots, but he'd educated and refined himself almost as much as she had, having started with the three R's and the English language. He charmed the children with his occasional tales of the West they'd never know, but she noticed he never included himself in any of the tales and tended to report the way things had actually been, with none of the pulp western heroics so many old timers seemed to remember.

She knew the Nevada who had returned was even nicer than the Nevada she'd lost. Yet there were many things about him she no longer understood. And there was Fitz.

Fitz would never be the dream prince of her youth. But he was the sort of man an older, wiser Dawn knew she'd be a fool not to marry. It wasn't just his refinement and breeding. Bill Campbell knew his wine lists and had been to Paris, too. The thing she respected most about Fitz was that he respected her and every other living creature on earth. Fitz was right about being born to grow things. He had a way with animals as well as a green thumb with plants. She knew she'd never have another child, but she knew her grandchildren would be surrounded by flowers as long as Fitz drew breath. His casual comments to her gardener had transformed her back garden as if it had been sprinkled with fairy dust. Fitz could drive out with her to a new property and tell, from the road, whether the crops were being overwatered, under-fertilized, or simply not loved enough. Her fig trees were producing bountiful crops. Her vineyards were the envy of northern California and her wines were sought by the best restaurants in San Francisco.

Almost like icing on her cake, Fitz shared her interests as well. He seemed to be one of the few white men she could talk with about Indian handicrafts. And she, in turn, could understand him when he spoke of the new French painters. She'd laughed in mock horror when he took her to see the new paintings at the art gallery near the Civic Center. And then, as he'd explained how the thick daubs of raw color were meant to blend into sunlight and shadow from across the room, she suddenly found herself saying, "Oh, I do see what Mister Manet is trying to do! It *is* the way sunlight strikes old stone on a warm afternoon!"

But there was Bill, or as she'd always think of him, Nevada. The two suitors were aware of each other, of course. Dawn made it a point to introduce them at a party she gave for new neighbors.

Fitz kept to himself any jealousy he may have felt as she'd expected he would. To her relief, Bill Campbell was as correct and polite about it as she'd hoped he'd be. If anything, the two men seemed to *like* each other.

She found them chatting about cattle, of course, when she rejoined them after seeing to another guest. Bill was saying, "I'd put my money into white-faced cows if I was starting up again, Fitz. The folks back east are getting tired of chewing that stringy longhorn beef we've been shipping all these years." And Fitz said, "I quite agree the range breeds have had their day. But what do you think of milking shorthorns for the smaller ranches?"

Bill said, "Small ranches? Sure. But white-faces can take care of themselves on winter ranges and . . ." Then they both saw Dawn and he paused as Fitz, in obvious agreement, nodded. "Hardly interesting for our hostess, eh?"

"Oh, but I am interested in cattle," Dawn said. "You both know I just bought some land on the Salinas and it seems irrigating it would cost more than I anticipated."

Fitz said, "Cattle are the cash crop for dry range, of course. I'd suggest sheep for the coast ranges, but I know how you westerners feel about sheep."

But Bill Campbell shook his head and said, "That's *Wild West Magazine* nonsense, Fitz. They mix sheep and cattle in Australia, and it works just fine."

Fitz said, "I know. The sheep crop the leafy herbs and the cattle eat the grass. But I thought you cattlemen were against the idea."

"Shucks, those range wars over in Montana aren't between cattlemen and sheep men, Fitz. It's a fight between hogs."

"Hogs, on the Montana range?"

"Two-legged hogs, Fitz. There's enough grazing for all the sheep and cows the good Lord ever meant to put on a section of land up there. The cowboys and sheepherders are shooting each other because they want it all."

The men went on with their conversation as Dawn spied new arrivals and excused herself to make them welcome. Had that been Nevada speaking of gun-slingers in such a disgusted tone? Apparently he had grown a bit. How was a woman to choose between two such obviously fine men?

Did she have to choose? Was she really in love with either of them?

Dawn thought about that as she made the usual meaningless remarks to her new arrivals. She thought she still loved Nevada. The Nevada she'd lost. Or was she still, perhaps, in love with a dream?

As she ushered some shy young people to the buffet Dawn stared thoughtfully across the room to where Fritz and Bill were enjoying a friendly discussion about cows. They were both so handsome and both so nice, but what did she really feel for either of them?

Nothing was settled that evening. Or for the next few weeks. Both men escorted her to various functions about San Francisco and she couldn't choose between them. It seemed better, or at any rate *safer*, to simply leave things the way they were.

She knew that not every woman her age could hope to have two fine beaus escorting her on alternate eve-nings, and she suspected her neighbors of having a field day with her reputation. But she couldn't get *hurt* this way. Had it been left to Dawn, the stalemate might have continued.

But nothing lasts forever. In the end it was Fitz who brought things to a head. They'd been to the opera, had a late snack, and the evening had been lovely. Dawn said so as they rode up to her veranda to say good-night. As he helped her down from the carriage, Fitz said, very matter-of-factly, "He's going to get away if you're not careful, my dear."

"Get away? Who are we talking about, Fitz?"

"Bill Campbell. He's very much in love with you, you know."

"Oh? When did he tell you that?"

"Gentlemen don't discuss such things behind a lady's back, my dear. Let's say a little bird told me he's in love with you and that you're in love with him."

Dawn looked away as she murmured, "I'm not sure how I feel about either of you, Fitz. What was that you said about him getting away?"

By this time they were on the veranda. But Fitz held back as she opened the door as if to invite him in. "He didn't say he was giving up the chase, but I know the signs. He did ask me some rather leading questions. Not about you. About me. The sort of questions only a chap who has a woman's best interests at heart would ever ask another man."

"Oh, Lord, he didn't ask if your intentions were honorable, did he?"

"No. He knows my intentions are as honorable as his own. I got the impression he was trying to determine if I was good enough for you. I mean, make you happy and all that rot."

Dawn laughed uncertainly. "You poor dear! Whatever did you tell him about yourself?"

"That we got along quite well, but that I didn't think you loved me."

"Fitz! That's not fair! You have no right to say how I might or might not feel about you!"

Fitz smiled, quite boyish in the soft light from the hall lamp, as he replied, gently, "I had every right. I saw you first. I think I know you, too, Dawn. I know you well enough to read your eyes when you look at Bill Campbell. Do you want to lose him with this silly game you've been playing, or shall we talk about it, as friends?"

And then Dawn broke down and leaned against Fitz, sobbing, as she gave vent to her fears and uncertainties. He held her, as a kind father holds a frightened child, and she was grateful once more for his gentle strength as she poured out more than Nevada would have wanted her to.

Fitz shushed her as she got to the staged gunfight in Angel's camp. "Steady on, old girl," he warned. "You're giving away family secrets."

"I'd trust you with my life, Fitz, and, dammit, I don't want to lose you, either!"

He didn't answer for a moment, and when he did his voice was husky. He said, "You'll never lose me, Dawn. If I can't have you as my wife, I'll always cherish you as a friend."

Dawn looked up at him, eyes moist in the lamplight. "I love both of you, Fitz. It's just that Nevada . . ."

"I understand, and we'd better remember never to call him that again, my dear. Now, what are we to do about this sticky wicket?"

Dawn managed a weak laugh and asked, "What can I do? Propose to the dear old fool?"

Fitz smiled down at her, wryly. "Why not? Obviously one of us has to, and it would sound terribly silly coming from me!"

And so Dawn lived happily ever after, or at any rate until the early 1890s.

As far as they were ever able to put it together, Dawn must have been in her late forties or early fifties when she married Bill Campbell, alias Nevada Jones, but she was as nervous as any bride as they left for their long delayed honeymoon. Nevada had suggested a pack-trip up to the High Sierra and some old campsites he remembered fondly. But Dawn insisted on a trip to Los Angeles, aware at last why poor Brian had never wanted her in any bed she might have shared with another.

The marriage was consummated in the lower berth of the night Pullman, somewhere south of Salinas, and though Nevada was nearly sixty and she would have preferred more privacy, Dawn's first orgasm in his arms came quickly. Nevada had been willing to wait until they reached the hotel in Los Angeles, but Dawn was as impatient as her bridegroom—and terribly worried. She was wise enough by now to know how one's sexual fantasies can doom one to disappointment—and she'd had many years to dream of sex with Nevada. But, perhaps because of her hard-earned common sense, his long delayed lovemaking exceeded her wildest expectations and it was all she could do to keep from screaming with passion and joy as she found herself really doing it instead of only dreaming of it.

Nevada had the firm hard body of an athlete twenty years younger, with the lovemaking skills only time and many women could teach a man.

That part annoyed Dawn a bit, at first. His first efforts were the simple natural thrusts of any healthy male animal, and she responded in kind. Then, as they climaxed and she knew he was prolonging the pleasure with practiced skill, she felt a wave of jealousy rising in her heaving breasts, though she knew how silly it would sound to twit a man his age with past affairs.

Then Nevada kissed her moist shoulder and murmured, "You know, darling, I'm trying to be big about this, but I'm jealous as all hell."

Her arms around him, her lips against his ear, she murmured, "*You're* jealous?"

"Yeah. I keep telling myself I'm being a damned

old fool, but I can't help kicking myself for not being, well, the first."

She laughed and said, "Darling, I'm a grandmother, for God's sake!"

"I know, and it ain't like I've been a saint all these years, either. But damn it, you move it so nice and . . . Yeah, I'm a fool and that's all there is to it."

She laughed and held him closer. "Would you like it better if I just lay still, pretending to be twelve years old?"

He nibbled her ear and sighed, "God, no! It's just that one part of me's in heaven and another fool part . . ."

"Nevada, I was just thinking the same thing! Even while I was coming, I was sort of mad at you for being so *good* at it!"

"You were? Hell, Dawn, you knew I was sort of a randy cuss, even before I met up with you. I thought gals liked a man who knew how to do it right."

"We do and we don't, dearest. I guess all of us, man or woman, want a lover who's a—well, a skilled virgin."

He raised his head to smile down at her in the moonlight streaming through the window. He laughed and said, "You know what we both are?"

"A couple of silly kids?"

"That's about the size of it. You know what we'd be if both of us were still newcomers to this sort of thing at our ages?"

"A pair of frustrated old farts?"

And then they were both laughing. Laughing loud enough to be heard in the other berths and not really caring, and Dawn knew it was going to be all right. She knew she wasn't ever going to ask Nevada where he'd learned that trick with his fingers, and that he'd never ask which of her previous husbands had taught her how good it was with an ankle on either side of his neck. She simply raised her wide-spread thighs until he automatically hooked an elbow inside each of her knees and gasped, "Oh, *yes*, sweet baby!" and threw aside all inhibitions. And this time, when she climaxed, Dawn moaned aloud and didn't care if they heard her in the locomotive. A bride had certain rights on her honeymoon and she'd become a grandmother while waiting for this one!

Los Angeles was growing but was still a dusty little city sprawled on the semidesert flats of a treacherous seasonal stream. But to a honeymoon couple in love it was Paris and the Vale of Kashmir rolled into one.

They didn't do anything important in Los Angeles, or as Dawn would always remember it, they didn't do anything important in broad daylight. They drove out to the village of Santa Monica, pronounced the Pacific a success, and took in the tar pits at Hancock's ranch, which they pronounced evil-smelling.

The nights were spent in lovemaking with the sweet scent of night-blooming cactus wafting across their damp flesh through the french doors leading out to a private patio. Dawn wanted it to last forever, but they were expected back in two weeks. And so their trip to Los Angeles ended, but to Dawn's delight, the honeymoon didn't.

Dawn would always remember the next ten years as a short sweet dream and a fulfilling lifetime. Nevada fitted into the family as if it had been his from the beginning, and sometimes Dawn forgot poor Ace or Brian had ever existed. The children and grandchildren welcomed and grew fond of Nevada, though they never knew him by that name. He in turn accepted them as his own, and they seemed a replacement for the lost family of his boyhood.

There were times when Dawn drew back, as if for a better look, to search for some flaw, any flaw, in her newfound love. But though common sense denied its being possible, Nevada remained everything she'd dreamed he could be while thinking she'd lost him forever.

Dawn was objective enough to see that this was partly because any decent husband would have been a vast improvement after the luck she'd had with the first two. But it was more than that. Nevada was simply a very fine man who loved and understood his wife.

He was not without flaws, but in Dawn's eyes even occasional lapses into rough frontier humor or a stubborn insistence that salad was "rabbit food" and that cigar ashes were "good for the rug" could be endearing. He was a true gentleman and an understanding husband when it really counted.

When Fitz died quietly in his sleep six years after she married Nevada, Dawn hesitated only for a moment before asking Nevada to escort her to the funeral, and when she broke down in church despite all efforts to control her grief, her husband took her hand and murmured, "Don't try and hold it in, darling. I liked him, too."

The children came to Nevada for advice, and Dawn was surprised to hear some of it. Nevada said her business holdings were none of his concern. Yet, when asked, he showed a keen grasp of finance, and once saved Gus from a risky investment that even Dawn thought good on paper.

One night he found her crying as she sat alone in the bay window just at sunset. Wordlessly, he sat on the sill nearby and lit a smoke as he waited for her to tell him what was troubling her.

She said, "I just found some more gray hairs on my brush. Would you think it cheap of me if I had my hair rinsed darker?"

He said, "It's your hair, kid. I like it fine the way it is, but if it pleases you, you can have it green or purple."

"I don't want it green or purple. I want it young again. I'm so afraid of growing old."

He nodded but observed, "Nobody likes it much. But we'd have been in a hell of a fix if you'd stayed twelve forever. You've got some old to go, kid. Every time I look at you, you get prettier."

"But I can't *stay* this way, darling. The grand-children are growing like weeds and . . ."

"Hell, Dawn, be fair to the poor little tykes! You want them to stay little forever? As I remember, being a kid wasn't all that much. Adults have more fun with adulthood than infants have with infancy. Besides, nothing we can do will stop Changing Woman."

"Oh, you do remember the old Indian stories I used to tell you?"

"Sure. Had some wasted years to think about them. Old Changing Woman has been busy as hell since I found you out on the desert and that's a fact. But she's been sort of nice to us, lately, and like I said, you're still pretty as a picture to me."

Dawn dabbed at her eyes and nodded. "I have no complaints about the last few summers, either, darling. It's just that I wish Changing Woman would leave us alone for a while. Wouldn't it be grand if everything could stay just the way it is for, oh, a hundred years or so?"

"Might get tedious. I'm sort of looking forward to

the twentieth century. For one thing, there's been times I never thought I'd make it. For another, it sounds like things will get even more interesting. Did you know some German feller has a horseless carriage running up and down the roads over there, scaring livestock? And there's this gent at the Smithsonian who says he thinks he's figured out how birds fly. Wouldn't that be something for us and the kids to see?"

"I suppose so, if only . . . Nevada, aren't you even a little bit afraid of . . . Changing Woman?"

He stared out into the gloaming light, his profile still youthful in the kinder rays of sundown. Then he said, "Sure I'm afraid. I've thought I was about to die more than once, and every time, it scared me skinny. Sometimes it scares me to think of how high Up might be, or how long Forever has to be. I guess everybody is, kid."

"What do you do about it, Nevada?"

"The same as everybody else has to do about it. I thank the Lord for letting me get this far, and I try not to wonder about what's coming."

Dawn murmured something in the singsong dialect of the Ho and he asked her what she'd said. She replied, "I just asked Changing Woman to take me first. I don't know what I'd do if I lost you again, darling."

He grimaced. "That hardly seems fair to me, kid. What in thunder am I supposed to do alone down here if you go running off with Changing Woman ahead of me?"

She giggled at the look on his face. "You're a man. Men are supposed to be tough. Besides, if I know you, you'll be poking that old thing of yours in someone before I'm cold in my grave!"

And then he took one of her shoulders in each big hand and was shaking her like a naughty child, his eyes filled with tears, as he cried out, "Don't you talk that way, Dawn! Don't you ever talk that way to me again!"

Then he saw he'd frightened her and let go as if her flesh was red hot. "Damn it, kid. You're getting me all worked up over a damn fool female notion! You had no call to get us both all blubbered up about dying! You're not an old lady and I'm not an old man, and if you doubt my word I'll carry you upstairs to our bed and prove it!"

Dawn laughed mischievously and asked, "At this hour? The street lamps aren't even lit yet!"

He suddenly swept her off her feet and carried her toward the stairs. "Hell, kid, who needs a street lamp? I got all any man needs, right here in my arms!"

And so, protesting mildly, Dawn was carried up to her bedroom and one of the happiest nights she'd ever had. Neither of them could know, as they made love in the red rays of sunset, it would be the last night she'd ever spend in Nevada's arms.

For years the fleas of San Francisco, like the ankles they bit from time to time, had remained a subject nice people didn't talk about. The wild sandhill fleas had been there long before the town was built. When they found their gopher and seagull victims replaced by people and wall-to-wall housing, the fleas simply moved inside and kept on about their business of biting as usual. Visitors often commented on the itching little welts they received in the best hotels and theaters, but San Franciscans merely looked surprised and said, "Really? Odd, I've never seen a flea in *my* house!"

This was only partly true. Housewives of San Francisco waged a constant war against sand fleas with naphtha sprays and sulfur dust in every crack they could possibly find. But try as they might, there were always a few hidden here and there. Many people, like Dawn, seemed either resistant or immune to flea-bites or had learned to ignore the slight but constant itching of their ankles. Unlike other species, the San Francisco flea never lived on its victim but leaped up from a crack or thick carpeting to snatch a quick meal and drop away. Hence, nobody was ever bitten above the knee.

But any bite was enough, once some unfortunate rat left a never-identified ship tied up at the Embarcadero. Later, the health department would assume the ship had come from the Orient, and nothing more would ever really be known. The unseen rat would die of the plague it carried in its dirty fur, but not before infecting other rats and their fleas in the filthy maze of dockyards and warehouses near the waterfront. The first human who died, almost inevitably, was a Chinese stevedore. The authorities, who were consulted by worried attending physicians, understandably but fool-ishly tried to keep it quiet.

It didn't work. The first news of the black plague was easy enough to keep out of the newspapers, but the infected rats and their fleas didn't read the *San Francisco Examiner*. Rats died by the score all over town and their infected fleas, hungry for blood, left the cooling corpses to seek nourishment elsewhere.

Just how many people died in the almost secret epidemic will never be known. Their numbers were certainly modest, considering the gravity of the dis-ease: it had once wiped out nearly a third of the white race.

The doctors of 1890 were a far cry from the helpless physicians of the Middle Ages, and the San Francisco Sanitation Department acted upon more modern knowledge of the plague. Rats were killed in wholesale numbers, and sewers and back alleys were dusted with arsenic and sulfur compounds. In the end, after young William Randolph Hearst's *Examiner* released the story and demanded an accounting, the authorities would place the maximum number of victims at a dozen. In truth, there were more, and Nevada was one of them.

He never complained of the flea bite that killed him, but there must have been one. The first Dawn knew of her husband's illness was when he turned to her at dinner and said, "I seem to be off my feed a bit, darling. The food is delicious, but I think I'd like to lie down."

She summoned the doctor at once, of course. A beloved husband past sixty is not to be dismissed with a mere "something he ate."

The doctor's first visit was wasted effort. Neither he nor many other American physicians had ever seen a case of black plague, and the low-grade fever Nevada was running caused no alarm. The doctor poked and prodded, found no signs of heart trouble or high blood pressure, and left, prescribing quinine for the fever.

By midnight Nevada was in terrible pain. His cries of agony awoke the whole house, and Dawn sent the footman to fetch the doctor again before going in to him and turning up the bed lamp. She gasped as she saw the discolored lumps at the base of his jaw and under one armpit. She had no idea what had caused them, of course, but Nevada, unfortunately for his peace of mind, was a self-educated man. When she remarked on his swollen bruises and held up the mirror he demanded, Nevada gasped and said, "Get out of here and take the servants with you! I know what this is, kid! I saw a case in Mexico one time!"

"Don't be silly!" she replied. "We'll not leave you, no matter what it is. By the way, is it a secret, or can I know what all this fuss is about, too?"

"It's not funny. It's bubonic plague. The Black Death. Your only chance is the wise F's: Flee Fast, Flee Far, and Flee Forever!"

"Nobody's going to flee anywhere, and the doctor's on his way."

"Damn it, Dawn, no doctor can help me now. I've a one-in-a-million chance of pulling through no matter what they do. Get yourself and the servants out of here before everyone in this house catches it from me!"

Dawn shook her head firmly. "If it's catching, I've doubtless caught it. I'll send the servants away, if it'll relieve your mind, but we'll see this through together, whatever it is."

He suddenly rolled his eyes and screamed mindlessly for a full minute as Dawn gripped his sweating hand in both of hers. Then, as the spasm passed, he groaned and said, "Sorry. I didn't mean to be such a sissy, but Jesus, it hurts! Get out of here, darling. I can't bear the thought of your feeling one tenth of this damned thing."

"Let me give you some more quinine, and we'll see what the doctor can do for you when he gets here. I have some opium, if you think that might help."

"Nothing will help. They say if the buboes break within three days, there's a chance. I'll just have to sit tight and enjoy it."

"Would it help if I lanced them? I could sterilize a needle—"

"Good God, no! They say that's the worse thing you can do! I'll be all right, one way or the other, if you leave, darling. Won't you get yourself to safety, for my sake? I can't stand the thought of your coming down with it, too."

"If I come down with it, I come down with it. I'm not afraid, Nevada. I used to be afraid, but I've no complaints if it ends tomorrow. But you'll see, we'll both be chipper and tearing each other's clothes off in a day or two."

He smiled wanly and said, "It has been a good ten years, hasn't it, darling? Jesus, it seems like yesterday— and do you know what? I still feel like a newlywed everytime I hold you in my arms."

"Silly, we *are* newlyweds. What's a few years to a couple who've just discovered what all the poetic fuss was about?"

Another spasm hit him and he suppressed a scream with gritted teeth, waiting until it passed. "By God, it has been grand, hasn't it?"

"Just close your eyes and try to rest until the doctor gets here, dearest." Dawn soothed him, releasing his hand to go for some damp cloths.

By the time she'd stripped and sponged him, the doctor had returned. He took one look at Nevada, gasped, "My God!" and ran out of the room.

Dawn started to rise to follow, but the shift of her weight on the mattress seemed to distress Nevada and she quickly soothed him with a wipe of moist cotton to his scarlet brow. She heard the front door slam and muttered, "Damned fool!" Desperately, she wondered what she was going to do for her husband without a doctor or any clue as to the treatment for the plague.

Dawn waited for a time until he'd lapsed into an exhausted calm. Then, careful not to disturb him, she slipped to the bell pull and summoned the butler.

She waited, but there was no answer to her signal.

Dawn tiptoed from the room and went out into the hall, calling down the stairwell to Jarvis. There was no answer, so Dawn went downstairs. The lower floors were dark, and an uneasy thrill made the hairs on the back of Dawn's neck tingle as she realized, even before she reached the servant's wing, that the house was empty except for herself and her desperately ill husband.

Lighting a candle, Dawn searched the quarters anyway, hoping she was wrong. Another candle burned in the room of old Felicidad, who'd become useless as a servant in recent years and, from the untidy evidence of hurried packing, was no more loyal than the others who'd fled on hearing the dread whisper of the Black Death.

Dawn went back upstairs, resisting an impulse to check the silver en route. If the servants had taken time to rob her as they fled, so be it. She could replace household treasures. It had taken her half a lifetime to find a husband worth keeping.

Nevada was calling out again by the time she reached his side. She saw his naked body glistening with sweat and quickly wiped him down with cool moist cotton. He rolled his eyes and said something incoherent in a ghastly gargle. He tried to clear his throat, and Dawn gasped in dismay as he coughed a fine spray of frothy blood over her and the soiled bed linens. But the coughing seemed to ease his breathing for the moment and he lay quietly for a time.

It was perhaps an hour before Dawn heard a soft frightened tapping and, turning, saw Felicidad in the doorway. The old Mexican woman held a garish plaster Madonna in one arm and a bottle of cut crystal in the other. She whispered, "Please, señora. I have brought the holy water from the church. The priest, he would not come."

Dawn was touched, but her voice was firm as she said, "Put the Virgin and the holy water over there on the dresser and fetch me some hot coffee, dear. I was afraid you'd run away with the others."

"*Si*, I did run away, señora," the elderly servant confessed. "I came back because I was ashamed."

"I understand, dear. Bring a cup back for yourself while you're about it. I fear we have a long night ahead of us."

"Is *el patrón* going to die, señora?"

"I don't know."

"Before I go for the coffee, may I light a candle to the Mother of God?"

Dawn nodded, and Felicidad took a candle stub from the pocket of her apron, lighting it from the bedside lamp and dropping to her knees in front of her improvised shrine atop the dresser after placing the small votive light in front of the chipped plaster saint. She prayed silently for a moment, then got to her feet and tiptoed out on her errand. Dawn licked her dry lips as she glanced at the badly sculpted, almost pagan Virgin and murmured, "Heya, Changing Woman, leave us in peace for just a little longer. Give me another few summers with this man and I'll go gladly with you before I'm sixty!"

Almost as if in answer to her spoken words, a male voice called out. Dawn cried, "In here! Please help us, whoever you are!" A young Chinese in a white uniform came in, followed by a white youth wearing a gauze mask below his nervous eyes. The Oriental said, "I am Doctor Chang, San Francisco Health Department. Your family physician reported another case of plague and . . ." Chang stepped over to the bed with a frown, took Nevada's wrist in his hand, and sighed, "That's what it is, Charlie. You'd better get the boys in here with the fumigants."

His white assistant ducked out hurriedly as Chang explained. "Our orders are to isolate and cordon off these outbreaks, ma'am. I'm afraid we're going to have to quarantine this house. We'll see that food's brought in, and after we fumigate . . ."

"The hell with the house!" Dawn cut in. "What are you going to do about my husband?"

The young doctor sighed. "From the looks of things, there's little we can do but try and make him comfortable. I see you've been sponging him, and I've some painkillers that may relieve him a bit. Tell me, have you been examined yourself, by your doctor?"

"The fool ran like a rabbit the moment he saw my husband, but I'm all right. I feel just fine."

"Would you mind removing your clothes, ma'am?"

"You can't be serious, young man!"

"I'm very serious, and I know I'm a dreadful Chinaman, but the niceties are less important, right now, than seeing if you have any flea bites!"

"I've never been bothered by the Frisco fleas. Is that what's wrong with my husband? He wase bitten by a flea?"

"We're pretty sure that's how it's spread, ma'am. There's a pneumonic form, but thank God, all the victims we've isolated in this current outbreak seem to have been bitten by fleas. We still don't know whether the local sand fleas or oriental rat fleas are carrying it."

"My husband says it's the Black Death. I do so hope you'll tell me he's wrong?"

"I'm afraid not, ma'am. It's the real thing, and now, if you'll just let me examine you . . ."

"Can you do anything for me if I *do* have the plague?"

She could see the answer in his eyes, so with a bitter little laugh, Dawn said, "Let's worry about my husband, then. I'm not shy about undressing for you, but why waste time? If I have it, I have it. What I really want to know is whether he'll live or not?"

Doctor Chang looked away and said, "I just don't know. Despite my family name, I've never seen bubonic plague before. According to the little that's been written by modern physicians with the nerve to really investigate it, the mortality rate runs well above seventy-five percent. Tell me, how old a man is your husband?"

"He's just a little over sixty, Doctor, and you can see he's in very good condition for a man his age." She put a hand on Nevada's flushed brow as she added, half to herself, "He's so in love with *life*, Doctor."

"I want you to go and bathe and change your clothes, ma'am," the doctor said gently, adding, "I'll do my best for him, and, of course you'll be nearby if he should need you."

"You've got to save him. I know you're a brave young man and I know you know more about all this than I do. You'll save him, won't you?"

"I'll try," said Cyrus Chang, with more confidence in his tone than he felt in his heart. Chang was a brave man, and as good a physician as the training of his day provided, but he knew the unconscious man on the bed was in the hands of God. With the best of luck, the plague would run its course within seventy-two hours, leaving Chang with a miraculous "cure" or another body to dispose of by quiet cremation. He'd worry about getting an obviously Catholic widow to agree to the cremation when and if the time came.

All he could do, for now, was post the quarantine sign and spread the poison bait and insecticide.

Young Doctor Chang's calculation was off by nearly twenty-four hours. Nevada was a strong muscular man, and it took him almost four days to die. Those four nightmare days and nights, and the quarantine period that followed, were the closest thing to hell Dawn had ever been through.

She agreed, numbly, to the cremation. Two weeks after the lifting of the quarantine, she also agreed to the seemingly pointless memorial services at her church on Larkin Street.

All her children and their families were there, for Nevada had been a friend to his stepchildren and grandchildren. Others who crowded into the small dark church were friends from all over the bay area. Yet it seemed to Dawn, as she sat veiled in her pew between Gus and Junior, that she was alone. A hundred words of sympathy were pressed on her from every side, yet she'd never felt so alone in her life. Even as a lost naked child in the Great Basin, Dawn had felt that someone, somehow, would come to her. Now she just felt old and drained. What was to become of her? Where would she go? Where did she belong in this vast empty world around her?

She found herself being led from the church on the arm of her oldest son, with his gentle wife Ruth saying something about her coming to live with them in San Mateo. Dawn shook her veiled head and said, "I'd better go home, dear. The garden needs tending to. Did you know we put in some tea roses that came all the way from Bulgaria?"

Ruth said, "Mother, we'll see that your roses are watered. The children love you so. Just come home with us for a few months until we decide your future for you."

Dawn laughed harshly. "Oh, I have my future all cut out for me." It seemed as if she'd brushed away some mental cobwebs as she added in an oddly fighting tone, "Judging from the last time this sort of thing happened, I'll be beating off the buzzards with my broom. Did you know some son of a bitch has already made me an offer for the borax shares? I'm supposed to be a dotty old widow, you see, and it's best to strike while the iron's still hot."

Gus patted her gloved hand soothingly. "Don't worry yourself about business matters, Mom. Junior and I will take care of you. I've already told Lawyer Sloane he's to refer all such things to me."

Dawn frowned. "Why? I just lost another husband, not my brains! Heavens, Gus, you know you haven't the slightest notion of my agricultural holdings, and as for my stocks and bonds . . ."

"We'll be going over the books in a few days, Mom. You just come on home with us and rest yourself a bit."

"I'll do no such thing, and you children leave my damned books the hell alone! Heavens, I've been cooped up for weeks in that stuffy old house, and it's time I got back to tending my holdings. I'm going to have to see that some of his old partners receive their share of his estate—and let's see, there was that irrigation scheme he was interested in down near Bakersfield . . ."

Ruth started to say something, but Gus shook his head. "Mom's going to be all right, honey. Next to her cooking, there's nothing she enjoys more than a good scrap!"

And a good scrap she had, for as she'd foreseen, the

vultures did move in from all sides in the wake of her recent bereavement. Dawn hired a whole new staff of servants for the house on Nob Hill, not bothering to answer the written apologies from the servants who'd deserted her in panic when the plague had struck down her husband. She hired a male secretary and a young woman who played the new typewriter well and, despite the loneliness of her empty upstairs rooms, found new strength and meaning as she salvaged business schemes gone agley by the untimely death of "Bill Campbell."

Female suffrage lay a full generation in the future, so the position of a woman of property was a more precarious thing in the nineties than it would be in the coming century. Dawn had grown up and still lived in a man's world, and few businessmen of the era avoided the chance to take advantage of widows and orphans. She was still dressed in mourning when a vicious proxy fight broke out between Dawn and the male stockholders in one of the firms in which Dawn had been left a controlling interest.

She enjoyed every minute of it. A "mere woman" and "fussy old widow" she might well be, she told her attackers at a stormy board meeting, as she unleashed her own legal staff on them. But she still had her wits about her, and a keen business head that put their collective scheming minds to shame.

She won the proxy fight. She laughed when Leland Stanford tried to buy her block of Southern Pacific stock in exchange for a scholarship to his new university for her oldest grandson and honeyed words about seeing she had enough to live on for the rest of her life. Her grandson was a bit young to be thinking of college, she reminded Brian's old "friend," and as for enough money for the rest of her life, she had the money and more besides. In an age when a million dollars was a legendary fortune, Dawn was one of the wealthiest women on Nob Hill, and she intended to die richer, thank you very much.

And so Dawn profited, as she'd known she would, from the great freight rate wars between competing railroads in the southern part of the state, betting, as always, on the powerful Southern Pacific to beat its rivals to their knees with its vast side interests and a near-monopoly on the cunningly chosen routes through the lush valley farmlands.

Knowing the value of keeping eggs in more than one basket, Dawn had invested in the alien Santa Fe Railroad when its tracks reached Los Angeles. As she'd told Nevada just before he died, the barren scrublands in the Los Angeles basin he'd thought worthless doubled in price each year. Her worried brokers begged her to sell some hillside range she'd picked up for a song near Hollywood Ranch before the boom ended, but Dawn held firm. The city of Los Angeles was spreading like wildfire now, and she knew someday its suburbs would reach as far west as the cheatgrass range and irrigated bean fields of the Hollywood area.

She'd hold on to her lands. She'd hold her interests in a hundred growing companies. The water rights poor Brian had bought all those years ago were still hers. She'd hold them, too, despite the offers pouring in on her.

Perhaps it was this habit of holding on, as she accumulated more, that worried Brian Junior. Perhaps, in fact, he was simply the ingrate Dawn accused him of being when, in 1895, he attempted to wrest control of her Riverside orange groves from her. It was a shock she'd never recover from.

By now the agribusiness patterns of California had set in their more modern form. In a land blessed with eternal sunshine and rich soil, but lacking in water, the small one-family farm had never prospered. Since the Civil War and the passage of the Homestead Act, small farmers had eagerly staked out claims of a quarter section or the full square mile allowed on desert land by revised and updated legislation. But it took money to farm the California way. Irrigation was expensive, and the pattern of huge monoculture fields set in early as small-holders failed repeatedly on tiny farms that were eagerly snapped up for back taxes by larger, more prosperous neighbors.

The big property owners were often absentee land-lords who lived as far away as London or, in one case, Russia. No part of the world would ever surpass California in proving the old bromide about the rich get-ting richer as the poor got poorer, for along with their wealth, the land barons had political power and the collusion of the canning and freight monopolies. It was to combat their powerful rivals that some few surviving small-holders attempted to form co-ops.

When Dawn, the holder of a large citrus ranch near Riverside, joined and gave her blessings to the Orange Growers Protective Union of Southern California, or Sunkist, Brian Junior struck.

Dawn's puzzled young secretary admitted a rather officious little man to her study, and Dawn's expression was one of confusion rather than dismay as she studied the summons he handed her. She read it over twice before she stared up at the process server and frowned. "Sanity hearing? I don't understand. Nobody around here is crazy, damn it."

The man shrugged and said, "I wouldn't know,

mum," leaving Dawn to puzzle the matter out with her lawyers.

The lawyers took a grimmer view of the matter than Dawn as they explained how Brian Junior's reasoning went. The silly boy apparently thought there was something wrong with Sunkist. She'd straighten it out next time she visited with him and the children.

But Brian Junior avoided her until the day of the hearing, and even in the stuffy courtroom in City Hall, he refused to meet her eyes. The judge, a man about Dawn's age with a balding head and a disinterested expression, seemed more pained than puzzled by the complaint. Brian Junior's lawyers had amassed a vast brief, outlining the eccentric doings of this rather attractive woman whose relatives wanted her declared an incompetent. His Honor could make little sense of the complicated tangle of business dealings. How much did these damned Carlyles and/or Campbells *own* between them, for Pete's sake? And who or what was Sunkist?

Brian Junior's attorney attempted to explain, as Dawn studied her youngest son's averted profile in the half-empty courtroom. Junior had been putting on weight, she saw. He wasn't as old as Brian Senior had been when she'd first met him, yet his father's tendency to fat was beginning to appear. If anything, he was going to be even more porcine in middle age. And poor Brian himself, to give him his due, had never worn such a petulant self-important expression at his worst.

The judge was saying, "Let me see if I get this straight, Counselor. You're arguing that the defendant in joining this Sunkist thing has been acting against her own best interest and should be protected from her . . . What's a generous impulse? It has no point in law."

The opposing lawyer said, "Mrs. Campbell is a generous warm-hearted woman, Your Honor. She obviously has been influenced into giving away her own business advantages by agreeing to cooperate with these johnny-come-lately small-holders who mean to rob her. The poor woman is a lonely widow near sixty and—"

"Objection!" cried Dawn's young lawyer, leaping to his feet.

The judge nodded and said, "The defendant's age is not the question before this court, Counselor, and for the record, the Court happens to be sixty-three. How does this farmer's co-op intend to rob the defendant, exactly?"

"They've agreed to all sorts of socialist schemes, Your Honor. Why, they've assessed their own membership for funds to build their own orange crates and freight wagons. Mrs. Campbell, by agreeing to a set price for her oranges, has forfeited any right to act in her own best interests, should the opportunity present itself."

The argument went on as Dawn listened—puzzled and dreading the questioning she knew was coming soon. What was she going to tell the judge? What must he think of a woman whose own family thought her a silly old lunatic? Damn it, why *had* she signed with Sunkist? She could hardly remember the arguments of those young farmers who'd called on her that day, but she'd liked their looks and their words must have made sense at the time.

Dawn felt a movement beside her and turned as Gus sat down beside her, whispering, "Hi, Mom. We came as soon as we heard about this insanity!"

"I'm *not* insane!" she blurted, her eyes blurring with tears as she saw Rose Maureen and her husband coming down the aisle toward her.

Gus took her hand and squeezed it. "You're sharp as a tack, Mom. It's Junior who's gone out of his head."

By this time Rose was sliding in beside her, too. Dawn's son-in-law, Howard Davis, remained on his feet to stare hard at Brian Junior; failing to catch his eye, he shouted, "You stupid bastard!"

The judge looked up with a frown to call for order as Howard took a seat behind Dawn, muttering, "I never did like the mealy-mouthed little prig, even when we were kids."

The judge sighed and asked the room at large, "Would someone tell the Court what's going on? Who are these people? What's all this cussing about?"

Gus got to his feet and said, "I'm Dawn Carlyle Campbell's son August, Your Honor. This lady here is my sister, Rose, and the gent with her is my brother-in-law, Howard Davis."

"Are you appearing as witness for the defense or the plaintiff, young man?"

"We're here to tell you that my half-brother, Brian is a selfish turncoat swine, sir. If my mother's ever done a crazy thing in her life it was giving birth to that snake-in-the-grass over there!"

The judge smiled coldly, and said, "These family disputes are distressing to everyone, young man, but these are serious charges and a dreadful amount of money seems to be involved. Tell me, as a friend of the court, is it your contention that your mother is competent to handle her own money?"

"I don't see why not, sir. She *made* the money, didn't she?"

"Hmm, your point's well taken, but many of these

holdings do seem to be in the names of her two late husbands. I'm afraid we're going to have to try the case. The Court calls as first witness the plaintiff, Brian Carlyle, Junior."

But Junior didn't take the stand. Instead he suddenly fled the court room, eyes averted and face beet-red as, behind him, his own lawyer shouted, "Come back here, you fool!"

Dawn sighed and thought, "Oh, God, now he's going to call me to the stand!" But the judge's voice was bemused and gentle as he shrugged and said, "Dismissed. What's next on the calendar, bailiff?"

Dawn turned to the grinning faces around her as the portly bailiff started reading off strange words about total strangers. She asked her laughing lawyer, "What does he mean? When do I have to defend myself?"

"You don't, we've won," explained the lawyer. Gus said, "Come on, Mother. We're all going to dinner to celebrate. Ruthie and the kids are expecting me to bring you home for the weekend, and I'll not take no for an answer."

As Dawn got up, Rose added, "And after you get back from San Mateo you're spending a few days with us, Mother. Little Howie has been working on a hand-colored valentine for you and he'll be terribly disappointed if you don't spend a few days with us."

"But I don't understand. It's not anywhere near Valentine's Day, and I have so many things to attend to on Nob Hill . . ."

Howard said, "Every day is Valentine's Day for you at our house, Ginga. Come on, I've made reservations at the Palace for us."

"Ginga?" Dawn frowned, "Who's Ginga?"

"Didn't you know?" Rose smiled, trying not to cry.

"Ginga is what all the children call you. When we can get you to visit. I forget which one started it. Wasn't it your boy Freddy, Gus?"

Gus nodded and said, "Yes, we were afraid he'd never outgrow his baby talk, but he's in school now and sounds almost human, even if he still calls Ginga, Ginga."

"Oh, dear, I forgot," said Dawn. "Brian Junior's daughter, Mavis, is having a birthday in a few days. If I'm to drive to San Mateo with you, we'll have to stop off at Gump's for her present."

Gus started to object. Then he smiled down at his mother and said gently, "Of course we will, Mom. I should have known you'd want to."

After Junior's rebellion, Dawn took a firmer hand on her affairs and resumed the name Carlyle, which seemed to carry more weight in the business world and in any case caused her less pain when she signed a check or purchase order.

The Gay Nineties were gayer in memory than they were in fact to those who had to live through them. By now, San Francisco was bursting its seams and becoming a dreadfully odorous city. If mechanical and engineering wonders had made the state a faster, noisier place, the abuse of California's virgin lands had aged her terribly. California rather resembled a tired worn-out former belle, decked out in garish finery as she faced the looming turn of the century.

In 1898, her business affairs in tidy order and still full of life, Dawn finally took the Grand Tour she'd been promising herself for years. This time the view from her Pullman window was more cluttered as she crossed the vast expanse to the east. The buffalo no longer roamed beside the U.P. tracks, and the Indians had been fenced in, out of sight.

New York was bigger and brighter than she'd remembered it. Four-story buildings extended as far north as the Bloomingdale and Central Park, and the streets were illuminated by electricity. A few horse cars still toiled to haul people up and down the island, but the new electric traction cars clanged under her her window at the Broadway Astor half the night, and Dawn didn't get a good night's sleep until her Cunard liner steamed majestically off for Southampton.

She put off visiting Ireland on the way, knowing there was Fenian trouble in Dublin again and somehow sure Fitz had been right about her being disappointed after hearing all the glorious exile songs of the Auld Sod. She intended to visit London on the return leg, for she had so much time and there was so much to see.

She saw Paris, was delighted to see that it lived up to its reputation as the most beautiful city in the world, and got as far as Venice, where, ironically, the news that was to cut short her tour caught up with her.

Fitz had been right about a lonely gondola ride being lonely indeed. The young man poling her along sang off key, and the Grand Canal was filled with floating odorous filth. Dawn cut her pilgrimage short and returned to her hotel. She bought an American newspaper in the lobby and took it to her room after a quiet lonely meal.

She read the news about the latest Cuban troubles with little interest until, with the gift of foresight her friends and enemies found so uncanny, she suddenly pursed her lips and muttered, "Damn that Hearst boy. He's going to get us into a war with Spain!"

Well, she thought, what of it? Everyone knew poor,

mismanaged Spain was no danger to anyone. Even
should war break out, what effect could it possibly
have on California? Yet even as she tried to ignore the
nagging of her intuition, she knew her trip was over.
She had to get home. She didn't know why she had to
or what she'd find there, but she knew it was terribly
important.

Despite the tremendous changes in her lifetime,
Around the World in Eighty Days was still a dream.
By the time Dawn reached Paris on the Orient Express,
Le Monde's headlines screamed that America had gone
to war with the tottering Spanish empire. She wasted
nearly a week booking passage across the Atlantic from
Le Havre, for there was a maddening delay as the
French shipping company hesitated over new insur-
ance rates and worried about the suddenly truculent
young U.S. Navy's arrogant proclamations of block-
ades and possible aid to its fearsome Spanish foe. By
the time the transatlantic cables had reassured Europe
that America was only at war with Spain and that
the fighting would not extend to the Bay of Biscay, the
small American army had been mobilized and sent to
Florida. It was still there when Dawn arrived in New
York, but as she was riding the train back across the
country to San Francisco, the Indian-fighting U.S.
Army, with no Indians left to fight, was moving with
a speed that dazzled and surprised a world that had
been at comparative peace since the unfortunate
Franco-Prussian affair of the '70s.

Less than a month after Dawn reached home on
Nob Hill, Americans were in action against the rope-
soled infantry trying to hold Cuba for the Spanish
Crown. Remembering the long, dragging campaigns of
the Civil War, Dawn was filled with mixed feelings of
pride and horror at the speed with which her country

had launched the first blitzkrieg of history—although, of course, she'd never hear it called that.

In all, from the declaration of war to the surrender of the badly frightened Spanish government, it was over in less than four months, and some bloody-minded reporter was calling it "our splendid little war!"

But it was not a splendid little war to the people of Spain and America who died in the short, mechanized nightmare. For the Spanish-American War would be the first of the new kind of wars. Wars in which the telegraph, telephone, and rapid transit moved weaponry and human flesh about like quicksilver pawns in the form of chess too swift for the human mind to fully grasp. Orders were flashed halfway around the world with the speed of light, to be acted on within moments. New weapons such as the armored battleship were unleashed to face victory or defeat with a speed no admiral of the past had ever dreamed of. Two Spanish fleets were hammered into destruction on opposite sides of the globe, and the *San Francisco Examiner* had the news in banner headlines before the poor, bewildered Spanish admiralty knew about it. For their part, the Spanish unveiled a mysterious smokeless gunpowder that struck men down on the Cuban fields of glory, with no indication of where the attack was coming from. In turn, the Americans swept the crest of San Juan Hill free of living flesh with devastating hose-streams of automatic fire as a young lieutenant colonel named Roosevelt strode to the crest behind a regiment of Negro regulars with the dismounted volunteers that would go down in history as his Rough Riders.

Dawn waited until the war was over and the last casualty lists had been published before she had herself driven over to Brian Junior's house on Hyde Street.

On her arrival she'd sent word to him she was back in town, but he'd ignored her olive branch, whether in anger or shame.

Her daughter-in-law, Mary, met Dawn at the door as she marched up the steps with a determined expression. Dawn said, "I came as soon as I was sure. I don't have to tell you how I feel, dear. How are Brian and the other children taking it?"

Mary started to say something, faltered, and suddenly the two women were in each others' arms as Dawn patted the younger woman, saying, "There, there, Mother understands."

They found Brian Junior in the drawing room, staring into the unlit empty fireplace until he turned at the sound of their footsteps. Poor Junior had lost a few pounds in the last few days, but it really wasn't much of an improvement. He got to his feet and blushed awkwardly, not knowing what to say.

Dawn said, "Sit down, dear. We've got to be sure there's no mistake about the boy, and if worse comes to worst . . ."

"He's dead, Mom," said Junior, bleakly. Then he sank back in his overstuffed chair and muttered, "I can't believe it. He was only fifteen! How on earth did he ever talk them into letting him enlist?"

Dawn took a seat on the hassock near his knees and sighed, "My, was little Brian III that old? It seems only yesterday I saw you children off on your honeymoon."

"They said it was the Yellow Jack," Junior muttered, half to himself. "His outfit never got into action. The kid never reached the front, but . . . damn them, couldn't they see he was only a little boy?"

Dawn started to say she'd heard the U.S. Army had

lost more men in Cuba to yellow fever than to Spanish bullets, but she realized how inane she'd sound and asked, instead, "How is Mavis taking it? I know she and the boy were very close, and somehow I was hoping she'd be here."

Junior didn't answer, but his wife murmured, "Mavis hasn't been well since giving birth to her daughter, Mother."

Dawn frowned with surprise, then remembered she had heard Mavis and her new young husband had been expecting when she'd left for Europe. She nodded and said, "Yes, I've been meaning to send something for the christening. I'm afraid I've neglected this branch of my family a bit for the past few years, haven't I?"

Mary looked away, but Junior blurted, "Mom, for God's sake."

"Is something wrong, dear?"

"Mom, you know what I'm trying to say. I mean, I thought I was doing the right thing, even if nobody believes me. I mean . . . aw, *Jesus*, Mom!"

And then she was holding him in her arms as he sobbed against her breast in mingled shame and grief as Mary, suddenly overcome, ran out of the room. Dawn held her pudgy son to her for a long time, uttering meaningless nothings as he cried like the baby he'd been and as she somehow felt he always would be. After a time, he recovered enough to ask in a little boy voice, "Am I forgiven, Mom?"

"There's nothing to forgive, silly. Sometimes your old mother thinks she's getting a little dotty, too."

They both laughed, shyly, then Junior drew away with a sigh. "Jesus, I'm glad to have you back. You know what I told Mary when we found out little Brian had run off to join up? I told her he'd have never gotten away with it if you'd been around. Remember the time Gus wanted to run off and fight Indians?"

"I remember, dear. Mothers had more time to think in those days. Heavens, my poor little grandson was in Cuba in less time than Gus could have taken getting up to Captain Jack's lava flats, just a few years ago. Have you seen those new horseless carriages? The Hopkinses have one, up the hill from our place. Terrible noisy thing goes up and down Nob Hill licketysplit, and the Hopkins boy swears it can go twenty miles an hour on the flat!"

They both knew she was just making sounds to fill the void left by the senseless death of her grandson. But what was she to say—that Changing Woman had been kind in letting her see all her children and grandchildren, up to now, alive and healthy in a world growing more unsafe by the minute?

Mary came back in, looking wan but with her face freshly scrubbed. "I'm sorry, Mother. I don't know what came over me."

Dawn sniffed and said, "What came over you was grief, dear. If we were Indian women, we'd be keening and lamenting in a healthier manner, but we're stuck with this civilization business, so it hurts more to lose someone we love. Remember, though, you haven't lost your other children, and speaking of children, where are my grandchildren? Shouldn't they be home from school about now?"

"They'll be here any minute, and of course you'll be staying for supper, won't you, Ginga?"

"Of course, and tomorrow we're all going to drive over to see Mavis and her new baby. By the way, what's my great-granddaughter to be called?"

Brian Junior and his wife exchanged glances, then

Mary said, shyly, 'They named the baby after you, Ginga. She's to be christened Dawn the Second."

Dawn the First felt her eyes misting as she looked away.

"My God, that's a fool name for anyone to give a baby."

Mary looked away, too, as she murmured, "Oh, I don't know. Somehow I've always liked the name."

Dawn had never heard the term "grandparent's revenge," but as the century wore down she would have understood it. Her early sixties, while lonely, were enlivened by her growing swarm of adoring grandchildren and alarmingly sudden great-grandchildren. Few of the latter would be walking by the time the twentieth century arrived, but her teenaged and newly wedded grandchildren made "Ginga" their pet as the aging house on Nob Hill formed the headquarters of their close-knit conspiracy against their somewhat stuffy parents.

Aside from Junior's lapse, Gus, Rose, Junior, and their spouses were all a proud mother could ask for, and Dawn often felt the Great Spirit had been more than kind. Yet her own offspring had often seemed in little ways to be a strange new breed of Californian with their nose-to-the-grindstone ways and sometimes chauvinistic pride in their town and social position. Even Gus, the most like her in so many ways, often looked pained when Dawn repeated one of her tales of the Indians and the Gold Rush era. For although he'd been conceived in shame on a dark night in the mother lode, he'd grown up a city boy whose head was filled with engineering facts and figures. Gus had never written the music he'd dreamed of as a child, for Carlyle and Sons had grown into a complex enterprise, since his estrangement from his half-brother, running it seemed to take all his time and much of his patience.

His son Freddy, however, was growing into a lad after Dawn's own heart. He loved to hear her tell stories of the legendary early days and shook his head with wonder when she told him she'd seen Joaquín Murrietta in the flesh. At fourteen, Freddy bought a Panard horseless carriage with his grandmother's help and conspiracy, and together they sped madly over the peninsula at nearly twenty miles an hour. It was true the Panard could make it up Nob Hill only by taking the gentler incline up Geary, from the west, but it was a lovely toy—and Dawn felt timid about learning to ride one of those new safety bikes, despite the rage for them that was sweeping the country.

The thing that made her feel closest to Freddy, however, was that, unlike his father, Freddy really did seem to be going on with his music. Gus, despite his reservations about the motorcar, was an indulgent father who, perhaps half-mindful of another young man's dreams, indulged the boy's talents by affording the best musical education San Francisco had to offer. One of Dawn's proudest moments came just as the new century dawned: in 1900, Frederick Carlyle conducted the orchestra she'd hired—in the hall she'd hired—for the presentation of his "Gold-Rush Memories."

Few people came of their own free will to hear a rather obtuse symphony by a teenaged composer. Yet the audience filled the orchestra seats, for when Dawn Carlyle issued invitations people jolly well came. The Hopkins family made up for what Dawn considered their rather grisly taste in Steamboat gothic by attending in force, as did Governor Stanford and contingents from the Huntingtons, the Collinses, and the other Nob Hill clans. Together with the Carlyles, they sat through Freddy's medley of old frontier ballads, Indian chants she'd taught him, and a bit of plagiarized Wagner with mixed reactions. Dawn was quite sure he'd improve with time, and considering his age, it wasn't half bad.

Her other grandchildren and their young friends amused Ginga; turning as children always seem to against the values of their own parents, they joined Dawn in her old age by proclaiming views much more like her own than ever her own children had.

Despite the churchbells and fireworks that rang the new century in, despite the speeches and proclamations of a brave new world, Dawn had misgivings for the future of her abused and overexploited state. Hydraulic mining in the overworked gold fields had filled the once clear rivers with fish-killing silt. While one still ate the once famous oysters of the bay with relish, the bay was becoming rather tired. An occasional oyster tasted of petroleum or other substance one would prefer not to think about. San Francisco, crowded into about forty square miles including its suburbs out by the new Golden Gate Park, had become the busiest port on the Pacific Coast. Her bay as well as her streets were overcrowded with people who seemed to put money above all else. Constant winds on clear days now blew trash the length of Market Street, while the still nights when fog held sway were filled with a noisome odor of coal smoke, roasting coffee, horse manure, and the wet rot of produce from a thousand ports piled on the docks or in jerry-built warehouses along the waterfront. The city had grown too fast for anything resembling proper zoning regulations. When the wind was from the east, even the nabobs of Nob Hill complained of the terrible stench of mingled God-knew-what.

The Chinese were blamed, of course. The Chinese Exclusion Act passed back in 1882 had done little to stem the flow of Orientals to California. It was said these days that Chinese often got through to melt into the slums of Chinatown by passing as Filipinos, who could still legally enter the state.

Dawn knew the Chinese had little to do with the stench from the mudflats or the garbage and sewage washed in from the bay. Perversely, she delighted in being nice to them. Her grandchildren joined her in this scandalous behavior, and despite tales of white children being dropped through hidden trapdoors into the secret Chinese passages under Grant Avenue, they joined her on expeditions to Chinatown, where they were delighted with the forbidden taste of lo mein or mu gu gai pan and somewhat awed by the reception Ginga always seemed to get in Chinese shops and restaurants.

Her experience with Brian Junior had made Dawn cautiously aware of her seeming overattention to business, and she now spent less time clipping coupons and more on spending. She didn't really spoil her grandchildren, she told herself and their somewhat concerned parents. What was money for if one couldn't give a granddaughter a wedding fit for a young duchess—or a grandson a new car, if he was old enough to drive and that was what he wanted for his birthday? Heavens, it was her money, wasn't it?

However, Dawn didn't spend all her money, or even the greater part of it, on her grandchildren. Though vigorous and keen of mind as ever, some part of her seemed to revert to her Indian upbringing as she passed the age Hungry Moon had been when they'd first met. The new administration under the somewhat flamboyant Theodore Roosevelt seemed intent on a

policy called conservation, and Dawn gave generously
to such efforts as saving a few of the last buffalo and
the remaining redwood groves. Dawn purchased a
stand of sequoia from the lumber company owning it
and presented it to the government. Her grandchildren,
and even Gus, joined her in sending a blizzard of let-
ters to Washington urging extension of the National
Park System to areas she remembered from her girlhood. While those well-meaning fools in Washington
seemed to see the value of Yosemite and the Grand
Canyon, there were smaller secret treasures to be
guarded, too.

Dawn never forgot herself so far as to vote for the
Democrats, but she scandalized her Nob Hill neighbors when she sided with the budding labor unions
and even took the side of the Salinas small-holders in
their battle for equitable rates from railroads whose
stock she held. She built a model village for the Mexicans who picked her oranges down in Riverside. When
the city of Los Angeles began to clamor for the water
of the Owens valley hundreds of miles to their north,
Dawn was outraged. She enlisted her young allies in
what promised to be a grand fight to save Owens valley
farmers from the ruin she knew would follow diversion
of their irrigation water to the spreading blob in the
Los Angeles basin. Given her support and considerable
power, there was a chance the Owens valley farmers
might have won.

But this was not to be. In the fall of 1903, girding
for what promised to be a grand crusade and perhaps
pushing herself a bit for a woman her age, Dawn was
getting down from her carriage in front of Gump's,
intending to buy a formidable hat, when she suddenly
found herself staring up at an electric bulb set in a
cracked white ceiling.

For a long time Dawn lay there, wondering who she was and where she was and something about water. She tried to sit up, but her left side seemed glued to the bed for some reason. She frowned and tried tó cry out, but all she managed was a feeble croak.

The sound was enough, however, to bring a stern-looking young woman in a starched white uniform. The nurse said something to her in a language Dawn didn't understand. When she answered the young woman in Ho, the nurse muttered, "Oh, dear," and went away.

Dawn lay there, wondering what Changing Woman had done to her, and after a time the nurse returned with a middle-aged White Eyes. The doctor leaned over Dawn and asked, "How do you feel, Mrs. Carlyle?"

There was something about the name that seemed familiar, and this time Dawn was able to answer in English, even as she wondered what language they were speaking. Was it French, perhaps? No, she remembered enough French to know it wasn't. Perhaps they were speaking Spanish. How odd she now understood Spanish so well. Runs Down Antelope had only told her a few trade words.

When Dawn licked her lips her tongue felt oddly thick. "Where am I?" she trembled. "I was going for water—no, a hat. I was going for a hat."

"Speech center's intact, thank God," muttered the doctor, smiling at Dawn. "You're in Saint Francis Hospital, Mrs. Carlyle. You seem to have had a slight, ah, stroke."

"Did someone hit me? There were Bannock on the rimrock a few days ago and . . . No, I remember, we got away from them, that time."

"What's your name, ma'am? Tell me your name."

"I am called Dawn. I am of the Sage Grouse . . . No, my name is Dawn Purvis."

"Purvis was her first husband, Doctor," the nurse whispered, glancing at the clipboard in her hands.

"Some regression's to be expected." The doctor nodded, adding to Dawn, "Where do you live, Dawn? Can you remember where you live?"

"Oh, me and Nevada have a claim up the wash a piece . . . Wait, Nevada got kilt and . . . Let's see, I used to live in Sacramento, but I live on a hill now."

"Nob Hill?"

"Yes, I 'spect that's what we call it. Did I get my hat before they hit me on the head? I was aiming to wear that hat to . . . to somewhere I had to go."

"You're doing fine, Dawn. Just rest easy, now. Your family knows you're here and out of danger. You'll be able to have visitors in a few days. But right now, I want you to take this medicine."

Dawn sipped obediently at the glass straw of the vessel the nurse held to her chin. When she'd drained the glass of sedative, she asked, "Family? Do I have a family? Hungry Moon said they likely got lost in the desert."

The doctor shook his head at the nurse and muttered, "No visitors until I say so. She's fading in and out, and it'll only be distressing to all concerned."

"Do you think she'll recover her mind, Doctor?" asked the nurse, as Dawn bridled. What were they talking about? Of course she'd recover her mind. She felt just fine. Perhaps a little tired, but . . .

And then Dawn was walking barefoot through the summer grass with Nevada, and this time in the dream he was holding her hand. They walked in silence, for it was a lovely gloaming afternoon and they were in love and lovers had no reason to speak the joy in their hearts at times like these. A monarch rose from a clump of cowslip as they approached and Nevada squeezed her hand as her breath caught at the sudden beauty of its black and sunset wings in the gentle Sierra dusk. My, it was getting dark suddenlike this evening, but it didn't fret her none. Soon the stars would be out and they'd make love in the grass, her eyes on the Milky Way as Nevada pounded her rough, but gentle, till they fell into the Long Sleep in each other's arms.

And then she was back in the hospital and some men were looking at her some more and saying things in French, or maybe Spanish. It purely wasn't Ho.

For weeks, then months, Dawn wavered back and forth between her lucid moments and the longer spells of Almost Over. Then one day she woke up to see a young white woman sitting near her bed with a little girl in her lap. The woman asked, "How are you feeling, Ginga?" and this time Dawn's tongue felt better as she croaked, "Hello, Mavis. What are you doing at Gump's? Is that my little namesake? My heavens, Little Dawn, you're growing like a weed. How old are you now, child?"

"I'm five years old and I can spell cat and I love you, Ginga. Are you all better?"

"I think so, dear heart. What's a cat?"

"Oh, Ginga, don't make fun of me."

Dawn's granddaughter shushed the child. "The doctors say you're doing fine, Ginga. When you're ready to go home, remember I asked you to come and stay with my family, first!"

"Piffle, what would an old bag of bones like me do in a house full of growing children? You've enough on your plate as it is, dear heart. As soon as they let me out of this awful place I'm going home to my own house to see what those lazy servants have done to my Boston fern and goldfish. You know how they over-water my ferns and overfeed my poor old fish if I don't watch them every minute."

Mavis started to object. Then, since they'd warned her not to excite the poor old dear, she merely nodded in agreement. No doubt her Uncle Gus could make her behave when the time came to move her. Even Dad was afraid of Uncle Gus. If Uncle Gus couldn't get her to see reason, nobody on this earth could.

In the end, as always, Dawn was to have her own way. Despite the pleadings and near threats of the clan assembled, Dawn left the hospital the day a pair of brothers named Wright flew their impossible machine off the dunes of Kitty Hawk. She insisted on being driven home in a motorcar. This was the twentieth century, damn it, and she had things to do!

But Dawn did little in the next three years except gather her strength and tattered thoughts together. People kept pestering her to sign things and telling her she needed to rest, but every time they pestered her, Dawn sicked Lawyer Sloane on them and they let her be.

Her children and grandchildren still came to call from time to time, but she tired easily these days, and was given to often uncontrollable fits of peevishness. The night she insisted Freddy was trying to steal her car from her, her grandson left it parked in the carriage house and caught the cable car home. After that, his visits were less frequent and Dawn missed him. She wondered why he never brought the girl he was spark-ing to the house like she asked.

The farmers of the Owens Valley lost their fight with the water barons of Los Angeles, but somehow it didn't seem to matter anymore. Nothing in the fright-

ening outside world held Dawn's attention long. She
spent much of her time half dozing in her bay window.
Sometimes, when she dropped off, people came to see
her. Nevada brought flowers once, and an oddly youthful Brian sat at the piano and sang about wild mountain thyme when she requested it. At times she'd chat
with Hungry Moon about her baskets. Some men from
the university had asked her for her baskets, but she
told Hungry Moon they'd only put them in a glass
case and never really understand them, and Hungry
Moon agreed.

Outside, though Dawn watched from her window,
the world didn't seem to be doing much. There'd been
another war someplace, and Dawn wondered, when
she read in the *Examiner* about the Japanese Navy,
how those quaint little men in kimonos had managed
to sink the Russian battleships like that. President
Roosevelt apparently wondered, too, for when he told
them they couldn't have a war, they stopped. It was
just as well for them they did, for her grandson, Brian
Carlyle III, was a Rough Rider, and it wouldn't do to
have both Teddy Roosevelt and a Carlyle mad at you!

Slowly, Dawn recovered most of her strength and
began to spend a bit less time with her ghosts and
more with the newspapers. She was planning to have
Freddy drive her over to see that newfangled motion
picture on Market Street, and one of these days she
was going for a ride in one of those new flying machines everyone was talking about.

But she was still unwell and more confused than she
imagined when, in the early hours of the morning of
Wednesday, April 18, 1906, the San Andreas Fault
slipped a full twenty feet, cutting the city in two.

Dawn was upstairs in bed when the quake hit. It

lasted thirty seconds, and it seemed as if some mad god were trying to drive the western half of the city north with a giant croquet mallet. Dawn's bed hopped across the room in a series of sickening lurches and slammed against the wall as the plaster ceiling came down.

The awakened woman was more puzzled than frightened as she sat up and reached for the electric light switch by her bed, to discover she and the bed were somewhere else. Someone was shouting out in the street, and Dawn got up to go to the window. Her bare feet grated on the fallen plaster, and in the dim gray light she could see that everything in the room was filmed with a ghostly coat of plaster dust. She muttered, "Really, this is very annoying!" and opened the window.

The homes on Nob Hill had been solidly built, and while a chimney had fallen here and there and the cable cars were stalled on Powell Street, there was really little of note to be seen outside. The streetlamps were out, but it was nearly light and Dawn failed to grasp, at the time, that the water, sewer, telephone, and electric power lines had all been cut in scores of places. A handful of people, some only half-dressed, had rushed out into the street and were either staring about curiously or discussing the odd series of shocks. Dawn felt chilled by the morning air and decided to go back to bed. Old Felicidad would doubtless be coming up soon with her coffee and toast. They'd discuss dusting the mess then.

Clucking in annoyance, Dawn shook the coverlet free of fallen plaster and stripped off her gritty nightgown. Then, nude, she got back between the clean linen sheets. The bed was still warm and she snuggled into it with a sigh of comfort. So they'd finally had the earthquake poor Brian had worried about all those years, had they? Well, it hadn't been all that exciting, and heavens, it was too early to get up. The wall clock across the room was hanging at a crazy angle, but it read 5:12. She had at least two hours of sleep ahead of her before Felicidad arrived with breakfast.

In other parts of town, people awakened early by the quake were getting up to go to work, if not as usual, a little early. A drowsy housewife would flip a light switch and frown as the lights refused to go on, but the newfangled Edison bulbs were always burning out just as you needed them, and most homes still had oil lamps and candles for such occasions. In isolated composure, people started to discover that phones were out and that there was only a trickle of water, or no water at all, when they turned the taps.

The only neighborhoods really hard hit, at first, were the jerry-built slums along the filled land near the waterfront. Here the land had subsided, cracking open the paving and bringing down already tottering tenements like houses of cards. But even in the areas hardest hit, fatalities caused by the quake itself numbered fewer than three hundred. Far more serious were accidents from oil lamps and dismembered coal stoves. As the sun peeked over the horizon, fire engines were racing along Market Street and the Embarcadero, and many companies of the Volunteer Fire Department were discovering to their dismay that there was no pressure in the water mains. As Dawn lay sleeping on the west slope of Nob Hill, early risers on the east slope were staring down in wonder at columns of smoke rising from the Barbary Coast, Chinatown, North Beach, and the shantytowns south of Rincon Hill.

Yet many a man left for work that morning with

lunch bucket or Gladstone bag in hand. It took a while for it to sink in that the cable cars weren't running this morning, for some reason. But historic San Francisco was not a large town, and many decided the walk would do them good.

So as homeless slum dwellers struggled up the slopes with hastily salvaged possessions, they were met with incredulous stares by well-dressed men and stylish typists going the other way.

Some few workers turned back. Those who reached their offices or shops along Market or Montgomery Street stared in wonder at the chaos.

Some buildings stood solidly in place, while others had simply fallen into the streets, blocking traffic with windrows of brick and broken glass. Harassed policemen, aided by soldiers sent from the Presidio, were trying to restore order as with every hour the scene grew more confused. On one block, workmen and volunteer passersby would be trying to dig victims out of a heap of ruin. On another block, a band of shabby opportunists would be cleaning out a shattered store.

By now, the scattered fires had begun to form a solid wall of flames in several neighborhoods. Hardest hit was the so-called Butchertown south of Market. As the homes on Rincon Hill were outlined in eerie illumination against a crimson wall of rising smoke, a young man named Amadeo Giannini reached his cubbyhole loan office on Montgomery Street. He'd been in America two years and his proudly named Bank of Italy consisted of two employees and eighty thousand dollars in assets. Giannini was no fool. He knew if the fire didn't reach the business district, the looters would. So he borrowed two wagons from a neighboring firm and hid his books and assets under orange crates and sacking. It would take him all day and a full night to reach the safety of his suburban home in San Mateo, but he'd make it and start all over when the ashes cooled. The produce company who loaned him the wagons would be only one of the many customers Giannini and his renamed Bank of America would help rebuild in the future.

As the young banker was trying to reach San Mateo, Gus Carlyle was trying to reach San Francisco from the opposite direction. The shock had been less severe in San Mateo, and Gus and Ruth had had breakfast before he began to worry. The phone lines were out, and Gus was unable to reach any member of the family as news of the seriousness of the situation spread. Gus started north in his Baker electric, found the road clogged with a solid stream of refugees, and wisely went back to borrow a horse.

Gus knew the seventeen miles would take him the greater part of the day, even avoiding the clogged roads by riding over fences and through yards or fields. He could only hope as he set out that Junior, or Howard, or Freddy, or for God's sake, *somebody*, had checked to see if Mom was all right.

Young Fred couldn't drive from Russian to Nob Hill with the paving cracked up so badly, but it wasn't such a long walk along the saddle between the hills. So he set out on foot, staring down Broadway as he crossed it to mutter "Jesus!" at the solid wall of smoke blocking his view of the bay. By the time he reached his grandmother's house a steady stream of people from the flats below were streaming over the ridge with bundles and occasional pushcarts. Fred stopped a worried-looking Chinese and asked, "Where's everybody going?"

"Plesidio," answered the Chinatown refugee, adding,

"Chinatown allee same gonna burn, my word. Army fella he say evlybody go Plesidio chop-chop!"

Fred walked on up to the Carlyle mansion, took the steps two at a time, and pounded on the door. There was no answer, and when he tried the knob, it was locked. Fred pounded some more, aware his grandmother was an early riser and that Felicidad should have answered by this time if they were still inside. As he stood on the veranda, undecided, a band of young toughs hove into view down the block. They were armed with sticks, and one of them carried a large banjo clock with a look of triumph on his unwashed face. Fred decided it was time he left. One of the toughs shouted something after him as he rounded the corner and started running downhill toward the Presidio. When he met his uncle Brian there, Fred reassured him that he'd made certain the two old women were not up on Nob Hill.

Meanwhile, Dawn dozed in bed, wondering what all the noise was about outside. She glanced over at the wall clock, saw it was only 5:12, and tried to go back to sleep. But sleep refused to come, and heavens, it was broad daylight. Where on earth was that lazy good-for-nothing Felicidad with her coffee?

Dawn got up and dressed, muttering to herself. She'd only kept the old Mexican woman on for company. Felicidad was older and even dottier than herself, for heaven's sake, and Dawn was worried about the old retainer's health. Felicidad had been complaining of being short of breath the last few years, but would she see a doctor about it? She would not. All she did was sit in her room with those blasted candles and her blasted plaster saints!

Dawn went out into the hall and gasped in dismay. Like everything in her room, the hall was filmed with dust. Several pictures had fallen from the wall of the stairwell, and at the bottom of the steps, the grandfather clock lay face down in its own shattered glass. Now how on earth were she and Felicidad going to pick the damned thing up?

Dawn groped her way back to Felicidad's room near the kitchen. She knocked on the door, and receiving no answer, she walked in. Felicidad lay on the bed, eyes staring at the ceiling and both hands clasped in an attitude of prayer. Dawn said, "Are you all right, dear?" Getting no reply, she went to the kitchen to fetch a glass of water. There was no water. There seemed to be something wrong with the tap today.

Dawn returned for a closer look. Then she felt the side of the Mexican woman's neck and sighed, "Oh, damn, what an inconsiderate time to die on me. Felicidad, I 'spect you just did that to get out of dusting this frightful mess!"

Out in the street, a male voice shouted, "I see you, you rascal!" and Dawn flinched as the sound of a gunshot echoed through the house. Leaving the dead woman where she lay, Dawn went to the front windows, but she saw nothing as in the distance a police whistle shrilled.

"Barbary Coasters," she muttered, with a grim little nod. Then she went back upstairs to get the house gun from her dresser drawer. It was loaded, but the effort had tired her, so she sat down on the bed to sort her thoughts out. She must have dozed a bit sitting up, for when she went to the window, it was getting on toward evening. Damn, she thought, as she made her way back downstairs, she'd wasted nearly the whole day doing absolutely nothing and the house was still a mess.

In the gathering dusk, the old woman gathered up

her Indian baskets and wiped them clean, placing them in neat rows. It was a large collection, and by the time she'd finished she was tired again. She went to the bay window and sat down. After a time it seemed quite dark and the street lamps weren't coming on. Dawn tried the lamp switch, found it useless, and made her way to the kitchen in the gloom to rummage for a candle.

The kitchen range still worked, as did the old oil lamp she'd been meaning to throw away. There was something yet to be said for wood-burning stoves and John D. Rockefeller's lamp oil, she chuckled, as she made a light supper. She wondered if Felicidad would enjoy some chicken soup. Then she remembered, and as the full horror reached her for the first time, Dawn began to cry, soundlessly.

She cried through supper at the kitchen table and might have cried some more, had not someone started pounding on the front door. Taking her candle, and the pistol, Dawn went to the door, saying, "I'm coming, damn it!" as the pounding grew louder. As she entered the hall, she saw her visitors were not knocking on the door at all. Heavens, they seemed to be breaking it in!

"Go away!" Dawn shouted, even as an ax blade appeared through an upper panel. The pounding stopped as a whispered consultation seemed to be held on the far side of the heavy oak door. Then a young voice snorted, "Hell, it's just the crazy old widder-woman or her Mex. Give her another lick, Mike."

Dawn raised the pistol, pointed it at the door, and pulled the trigger. The sound was deafening in the confined space and the gun kicked harder than she remembered from the last time she'd fired it, but some-

one in the night yipped like a kicked dog, and as the
running footsteps faded in the distance, Dawn sighed.
"That'll learn you!"

Taking gun and candle, Dawn retreated to her
upstairs room as night fell on the city. It was an oddly
ruddy night, she noted, glancing out the window again.
A ceiling of smoke now hung over the entire city,
illuminated by the still invisible flames on the other
side of the ridge. Dawn didn't know it as she lay on
the bed fully dressed, but everything on the other side
of Nob Hill was now fully ablaze. The flames were
across Columbus and moving toward her.

One day a monument to the Volunteer Firemen
would rise like a fairy tower above Telegraph Hill,
but the Volunteers had already lost Telegraph and
Rincon hills as they fought desperately to save Nob
and Russian. The fire front reached Grant Street and
leaped it on soaring embers as exhausted firemen and
military personnel fought side by side with Chinese
merchants, hatchet men, and a mixed bag of heroes
from every walk of life. Without hose water, there
was little they could do but beat at the flames with
shovels and sacking, or try without much success to
remove inflammables from the path of the wildfire.
Their task was hopeless and they knew it, for the city
was built of wood and solidly massed. But they fought,
and cursed, and some of them died as all of them—
white, black, yellow, richman, poorman, beggerman,
and some thieves—united in a gallant effort to save
the only thing they had in common, the city itself.

Martial law had been declared, and every road in
or out of the city was choked with two-way traffic.
As panic-stricken or simply homeless refugees streamed
out to the suburbs or to the hastily improvised tent

cities at the Presidio or in Golden Gate Park, others cursed and bulled their way in toward the disaster. Coast Artillerymen from Fort Baker, across the Golden Gate, had been patrolling with their Presidio comrades for hours, but other troops were coming up the coast from Fort Ord to the south, marching the last leg of their juorney as rail traffic backed up south of San Mateo.

The mayor's office in the fallen city hall no longer existed, but His Honor ordered looters shot on sight from his new headquarters in an army tent. Only three actual drumhead courtmartials were held, but an uncounted number of looters were added to the three men officially executed as hard-eyed police and military took to shooting first and discussing just what you were doing in that jewelry store afterward. Probably more than one innocent man lost his life that way, while the greater number of looters, as always, would never be brought to justice. Word of the executions may have played some part in the falling off of looting as the night wore on. It's as likely the looting stopped because by then the banks and expensive shops at the foot of Market no longer existed.

As the firefighters retreated up the slopes of Nob and Russian hills, the Army Engineers were arguing with the city fathers about a firebreak. It was obvious that demolition was the answer, but where was one to draw the line? It was too late to blow up Chinatown. The army wanted to clear the ridge of Nob and Russian hills by knocking everything flat a block each way from Powell Street. But these were serious blocks to be talking of so glibly. The homes along Millionaire's Row were worth incredible fortunes, and the people who owned them were incredibly powerful. It was all very well for a supercilious army officer to

speak of firebreaks and dynamite, but an elected public official had to think things over before he faced a
Huntington, a Stanford, a Collins, or a Coit with the
fact that he'd ordered such a mansion destroyed because it seemed like a good idea at the time!

And so as Dawn slept and the politicos dithered,
the flames ate San Francisco, block by block, through
the night. By Thursday morning it was obvious the
hills were going to go, and as obviously too late to
use Powell Street for the firebreak. New lines were
drawn along the wide expanse of Van Ness Avenue,
between the hills and the Presidio district. And this
time there was little argument.

Dawn was awakened by someone pounding on her
door again. It was very dark and she was frightened,
so she didn't answer. She merely sat on the bed, gripping her pistol in the darkness as someone shouted,
"This is the police! Everyone out! Everyone's to move
west of Van Ness at once!"

After a time, the sounds of hammering fists and
shouting strangers faded off down the street and Dawn
got up. She struck a match to see what time it was.
The wall clock said 5:12, but she'd begun to lose faith
in that clock by now.

Dry-mouthed, Dawn went downstairs and tiptoed
into Felicidad's room, as if to make sure the servant
was still there. Felicidad's face was an odd color in
the flickering candlelight, so Dawn drew the sheet
over her dust-filmed eyes and went up front to think
about what she was going to do about the girl.

From the bay window it seemed as if the sun was
rising, or possibly setting. An orange glow painted the
smoke clouds from the east. Dawn had no idea what
time it was, and since she wasn't at all hungry, she

sat and alternately dozed and worried with the pistol in her lap.

If the old woman had lost track of time and space, others were only a little less confused that terrible Thursday. Out at the Presidio a smoke-stained tenor named Caruso was entertaining the crowd by singing to them from atop an army wagon. He sang an aria from *Aida* because Major Dewitt had asked him to entertain and because the opera had been written for the opening of the Suez Canal a generation ago and Enrico Caruso thought this might be as important an occasion, whatever it was. He hadn't managed to find anyone who could explain just what was going on. They'd told him his appearance at the San Francisco Opera was cancelled—and then someone had handed him a shovel.

In the crowd, eight-year-old Dawn II tugged at the sleeve of a tall handsome man who seemed very self-assured and on top of the situation. The man turned with a puzzled little smile as Dawn II asked, "Please, sir, are you someone important?"

The man laughed and said, "I like to think I am, sis. Who are you looking for—a detective, an official, someone like that?"

"Yessir. It's about my Ginga. Uncle Gus found my mommy and daddy and Uncle Brian and Cousin Fred and just everybody, but nobody knows where Ginga is."

"Well, don't tell anyone I told you, sis, but a lot of people are supposed to be over in Golden Gate Park, wherever the devil that might be."

"Oh, don't tease, sir. Everybody knows where Golden Gate Park is!"

"I'm not everybody. I'm Jack Barrymore, and I'm a

stranger in town, sis. Right now, I'm supposed to be appearing in a play, but alas, we seem to be undone, methinks. Look, kid, you'd better go back to your folks before they catch you talking to an actor. This place is terribly crowded, and a wee thing like you could get lost in someone's shoe."

"I never get lost. I know my way all over town, and I have to find my Ginga."

"That sounds reasonable, sis. What, may I ask, is a Ginga? Unless you wear it, it sounds fattening."

"Oh, Ginga is my great-grandmother, and she lives on Nob Hill."

The young John Barrymore nodded and turned his breathtaking profile to the child as he stared over the heads about them in the direction of the hills. Even a stranger in town knew where Nob Hill was, and the actor could see it from where he stood on the parade ground. He could see the flickering flames rising along the crest of the hill, too, as he searched for a clever line.

But what could one say when a city was aflame and a little girl had lost her Ginga? Gently, Barrymore looked down at the girl and said, "I'm sure she's been taken to another camp, sis. You run along to your folks, and I'll tell you what, I'll ask the soldiers if they've seen her."

Dawn ate a bit at what might have been suppertime and went back to her window seat to await the end. She knew, now, that Changing Woman would be coming for her soon, but somehow she wasn't afraid.

Everything changed, for better or worse, in the end. What was it poor Coyote Singer had said about the seas becoming land and the land becoming seas? Nob Hill had been a windswept hill of poppies when she'd met Brian on it, not far from here, so long ago. Heavens, hadn't he ever been handsome in those days! But Nob Hill was now covered with houses and Brian had died a stupid, fat old man. Well, never mind, soon the hill would be cleared of houses and she . . . she'd be dead, too. It would be interesting to see whether she met Brian somewhere in the Great Beyond and what he'd say to Nevada, if he was there, too. She somehow doubted her first husband, Ace, would have made it to any Beyond in a well-run universe. But Nevada . . . No, Nevada wouldn't be in the sort of heaven Christians imagined. Maybe, if the Indians were right, her Nevada would be roaming free in the Happy Hunting Ground, a spotted pony under him and that funny puzzled smile on his lips. Yes, that would be where she'd ask Changing Woman to take her. To Nevada, and Hungry Moon, and Runs Down Antelope, and all her old friends.

Something had moved out in the garden. The old woman slid a manicured finger inside the trigger guard of her revolver and tried to remember what she'd seen and where it had been when she first became aware of it.

It had been over by the carriage house. The door of the carriage house was open and the twin brass headlamps of the Panard touring car still stared out at her from the inky blackness and . . . had the headlamps been *lit* all this time?

The intruder stepped into view, coming around the corner of the carriage house with a red metal cannister. It was a little girl, dressed in a smoke-stained white shift and wearing her sooty blonde hair in braids. What in the world could a girl that young be doing alone out there at a time like this? And what, in God's name, did she think she was up to?

The old woman watched as the child came out of the carriage house and started up the walk to the side entrance. The girl saw the weirdly illumined face staring out at her and waved before vanishing around a corner of the house. The sassy young thing seemed intent on coming in!

The old woman rose, spilling lap robe and pistol on the plaster-dusted carpet as she managed, with some effort, to turn her chair to face the newest threat of this very confusing day. The effort exhausted her, and she sank weakly down to stare dully into the dusty darkness as young footsteps approached.

The girl materialized in the dim light and her voice seemed too loud for her insubstantial outline as she said, "I found some gasoline for Cousin Fred's car, Ginga. If I can just get the darned old thing to start . . ."

"Who the devil are you?" the old woman cut in.

The girl said, "I'm Dawn, Ginga. I sort of thought you might be here and I came to . . ."

"Are you just crazy or is this your idea of a joke, young miss? You know damned well that I am Dawn Carlyle!"

The girl came over and placed a gentle hand on the old woman's shoulder as she murmured, "I know. I was named after you. Don't you remember me at all, Ginga?"

The old woman stared up into the oddly familiar young face and for a moment she seemed to be gazing into a flawed mirror time had overlooked as she asked, cautiously, "Are you one of my children?"

"I'm your great-granddaughter, Ginga. My mother was your granddaughter, Mavis. When I was little, you used to let me play on your piano, over there. Don't you remember me at all?"

The old woman stared into the dark shadows, picturing the room the way it had been a few hours ago and for many years before. Then she brightened and said, "Oh, you were the one who scratched my piano stool with those awful baby shoes little Mavis bought you. I made you play in your stocking feet in my house, remember?"

"Yes, Ginga, I remember. I remember how sweet you always were to all of us, and how stubborn you can be, too. When I didn't see you at the refugee camp over on the Presidio Parade Ground I thought I'd better dash over here and make sure you'd been evacuated with the others. The army's given up trying to save the buildings on this side of Van Ness Avenue, Ginga. We've got to get to the Presidio before they start to dynamite that firebreak I heard them talking about."

"I won't leave. I can't. Everything I have is in this house, and if those Sidney Ducks from the Barbary Coast find my home deserted . . ."

"Ginga, the Barbary Coast was cleaned up years ago, and there's been hardly any looting. The soldiers shot a man for looting on Market Street this morning, and anyway, we'll put some of your best things in the rear seat of Cousin Fred's car and . . ."

"There's too much! I wouldn't know where to start! Why, my Indian baskets alone would fill that little Panard and . . . You know about my baskets, don't you? The museum has been trying to get some of those baskets for years, but I told them they'll just have to wait until I'm dead and gone. Why, I started collecting those baskets up in the mother lode when Nevada and me were panning the Lost Chinaman wash, and some of those tribes don't even exist anymore."

"Ginga, I know about you and the Indians. Everyone knows you were raised by Paiutes after you wandered away from that wagon train as a baby. I know about the silver railroad spike Leland Stanford gave to Great-Grandfather, and we'll take that, too. Only . . ."

"They called them diggers and said they were only half human, but I want you to look at my Yana acorn basket and tell me how a half human ever wove such a lovely thing. I got it from a girl named Humming Bird's Laugh, up near Angel's Camp, and I mind how she cried for joy when I spoke to her in Ute. 'Course, the Yana didn't rightly understand the Great Basin dialects all that well, but the white men laughed at Humming Bird's Laugh when she tried to speak English, and . . ."

"Ginga, we've got to get out of here! The wind is sweeping sparks down from the crest of the hill, and if the garage catches fire before I can crank up the car . . ."

"You go along then, child. I'm too old and set in my ways to start all over in a new house. When you see your father, tell him my will and other papers are at Lawyer Sloane's, hear?"

"Ginga, this darned old house is going to burn to the ground in less than an hour!"

"I know that, child. I'm not as dotty as you think I am. I'm just old. Old and tired. It's something you'll have to live a while, yet, to understand."

The girl considered trying to carry the old woman outside by force, but she knew she wasn't strong enough. It was going to take all her strength to crank the darned old car, if, indeed, she'd be able to do that. She'd never cranked a car, but she'd watched Daddy do it. "We've got to go, Ginga," she suddenly said, as a burning branch fell into a flowerbed outside.

The old woman shook her head and said, "I can't. I won't. Goddammit, girl, this is the *Carlyle House!*"

The girl stepped over to the window and perched on the windowsill with a defeated little smile. After a time her great-grandmother asked, "Don't you think you'd best be going, young miss?"

The girl shook her head and said, "Not if you won't come with me, Ginga. Goldurnit, I'll . . . I'll just *carry* you if you won't come with me!"

"You mustn't swear, child. You'll not carry me, either. I'm going to be very cross with you if you don't mind me like a good girl."

"You can spank me when we get to the Presidio, Ginga."

"Don't be silly. It's too far. These old legs have carried me just about as far as I want them to, child. You just run along and let your Ginga be."

For a time the girl didn't reply. Then she wiped a grimy hand across her eyes and asked, "Don't you love me anymore, Ginga?"

"Of course I love you, dear heart. What a silly question to ask."

"If you love me, you'll come with me, Ginga. We'll take Freddy's car and—"

"Come now, you silly goose, that poor old car hasn't run in years."

"The carbide lamps still work."

"Well, miracles happen, I suppose, but I'm sure the engine's rusted solid and I know the tires are flat. I noticed that just the other day."

Pressing her advantage, the girl said, "At least let's try and start it, Ginga. I'll bet you anything I can start it."

With a slyness to match any eight-year-old's, Dawn asked, "If I show you the car won't start, will you run off to the Presidio like a good girl?"

Young Dawn started to object. Then she nodded. "I promise, but you've got to prove the car won't start, Ginga."

To humor the child, Dawn rose wearily and followed her out to the carriage house, muttering under her breath at the foolishness of their errand. But her great-granddaughter had gotten her out of the house, and outside, the heat from the flames along the crest of Nob Hill and the winds they sucked to their rising plumes of woodsmoke whipped at their skirts.

Dawn was right about the car, of course. Her great-granddaughter tried to turn the crank and couldn't budge it. To keep the fool child from breaking her little arm, Dawn herself bent to give the crank a try. She couldn't budge it, either.

Straightening up, she smiled down at her namesake. "You see? I'm not just a crazy old woman, am I? I told you Freddy's car was rusted solid!"

She felt tired after the effort and decided to rest on the runningboard of the car before going back to the house. As she sat down, the earth tingled and a distant whump filled the air. The soldiers were dynamiting again, she supposed. It seemed terribly perverse of them to knock down houses after the quake had spared so many, but it was turning out to be a most annoyingly perverse day.

Everything was acting crazy. A cool wind from the west was fanning her on one side even as she could feel the furnace-door radiation of the approaching fire front on the other cheek. The firestorm was hurling ash thousands of feet into the atmosphere to spread in a vast cloud lid over the entire bay area. The cooling ash fell like gray snow, far to the east and west, and the winds sweeping along the ground toward the fire powdered everything as if in preview of its inevitable fiery fate. Dawn wondered dully if it were better to wait it out here in the open or whether she'd last a bit longer inside. It didn't seem to matter. By this time tomorrow, she'd only be a memory no matter what she did.

The child tugged at her sleeve, pleading, "Please, Ginga. I'm scared."

"Well, of course you're scared, as well you should be, child. You run along, now. Just leave your Ginga be."

"You can't stay here, Ginga. You'll get burned up!"

"I 'spect I will, dear heart, but you see, I'm old and finished with it all, anyway. Everything I have is over there in that poor old house, and I'm just too old and sick to start all over."

"Ginga, won't you *try*? I can't leave you here, but I'm getting so scared and it's getting so hot!"

Something surfaced in the old woman's memory. How odd, she mused. I remember being on the other end of this conversation, one time, when the Bannock were coming and Hungry Moon wouldn't run with me. Why, I know just how she must have felt, and how you must be feeling. Heavens, Changing Woman certainly does move the world about in circles, doesn't she?

"Ginga, please, we've got to go. We can't stay here another minute."

Dawn started to explain how she knew the little girl would run off and leave her, in the end. But it seemed cruel and she kept the thought to herself, remembering how her fear of the Bannock had overcome her love for Hungry Moon, and how heartsick she'd felt for so many months afterward. She wanted to tell her little namesake not to feel guilty about it, but she couldn't find the words. She knew she'd never really felt right about deserting Hungry Moon until, perhaps, just now. How curious that it had taken her all these years to understand how Hungry Moon had really felt. Dawn II would remember her as a stubborn, foolish old woman, no doubt.

A burning shingle fluttered down nearby and the child flinched. For a moment it looked as though she was going to run away as her great-grandmother expected. Then little Dawn stamped on the smoldering wood in a pathetic attempt to stop the approaching fire front, and the old woman sighed and said, "My, you truly are a willful, tiresome child."

"We forgot to bring the gun," replied her namesake, with a resigned little sigh.

"Oh, for God's sake," Dawn muttered, getting to her feet and holding out her hand. "This whole thing is becoming very trying, young lady. If you're too silly to simply walk away from those flames, I'll just have to take you by the hand and lead you to your mother. I swear, she'd have a fit if she knew you were playing up here on Nob Hill right now!"

The girl grasped her great-grandmother's hand with a happy sigh and started tugging her toward the gate. Dawn protested. "Not so fast, damn it. I'm too old to run."

They went out to the street and headed for the corner as something exploded on the crest above them. Dawn turned at the corner and looked back, frowning, "Felicidad. She's still in the house with all my things. Can't you just run on alone from here? It's all downhill, you know."

"We have to hurry, Ginga. The soldiers are blow-ing up the houses on Van Ness Avenue and we have to get through before the dynamite goes off!"

"Heavens, you really don't know much, do you? You can't go through the houses at the foot of the hill that are still standing, you little goose. You should move along the firebreak until you see a place they blew down already. I'd work my way north toward the bay, if I were you."

"You'll have to show me how, Ginga. If you leave me now, I might get dynamited."

Dawn sighed and led the girl down the steep incline to the next street running along the side of the hill. She pointed and said, "That way's north and everybody knows which way is downhill, damn it!"

"You have to come, too. I'm afraid I'll get lost."

Dawn took a few more steps to the next corner and sat on the curb, knees up against her chest, as she shook her head. "You're not fooling me, young miss! If you ran all the way up to my house from the Presidio, you damn well know the way back!"

The girl tried to lift Dawn by the shoulders, gave up, and stamped her foot, sobbing, "Gosh darn you, Ginga, you're really making me mad!"

Then she spotted movement down the street and cried out, "Help! Oh, please, sir, over here!"

The distant youths froze at the sound of the little girl's voice. Then they approached in a ragged line of five or six. Dawn II viewed them warily, as she saw they were Chinese. Her Daddy said to stay away from Chinese, although he'd never explained why.

The leader of the looting gang stared impassively as he drew close enough to recognize the old white woman and her small companion. One of his followers made a grim suggestion in Cantonese, but the leader suddenly gasped and said, in English, "What is Dawn

Lady doing up here so close to the flames? Where are your men, Dawn Lady?"

Dawn looked up with a puzzled smile. "Oh, do I know you?"

The youth said, "I am Wong Fang. You do not know me, but I know you. How is it I find you in such danger this day, Honorable Dawn Lady?"

The little girl said, "She's tired and I can't make her come with me, sir. Will you help me get her to the Presidio?"

Wong Fang smiled and said, "We were just about to leave for there." He barked a singsong series of orders in Cantonese, and with a little grumbling, two of the youths threw aside the clock and silver candlesticks they'd been carrying and got on either side of Dawn. As they bent to lift her, Dawn protested, "I can't leave my things. Everything I own is back at my house."

"It's her baskets and Great Grandpa's railroad spike and all," explained the girl.

Wong Fang nodded and said, "We shall see to her treasures, little one. You and your grandmother must go with my three friends. The others and I shall see about rescuing such as we can manage from the house. Now, go! We'll try and catch up with you."

"You don't know where my house is," Dawn protested as the two young Chinese, grinning now, picked her up bodily by forming a seat for her on their linked forearms. As a third youth scooped Dawn II up for a piggyback ride, Wong Fang said, "We know your house, Honorable Dawn Lady. Ong Leong marked it for protection many years ago."

And then conversation was cut short as the oriental party split in two, one half moving gingerly uphill toward the flames while the trio in charge of Dawn and the child jogged rapidly down toward Van Ness Avenue. As the slope grew less, Dawn protested loudly that she could walk, goddammit, but the Chinese pretended not to understand and only chuckled at her struggles. She started to warn them about the dynamite, but they were streetwise, too, and she saw they were making for a two-block-wide tangle of flattened brick and debris still smoldering under the acrid fumes of high explosives.

As they picked their way carefully over tangled beams and broken glass, a voice shouted and a squad of blue-clad soldiers challenged them from the shadows of some remaining walls beyond the firebreak. Then the corporal in charge motioned to the three unmoving Chinese and shouted, "Well, for God's sake, bring them women over on this side, you crazy chinks!"

The boys who'd rescued Dawn and her namesake approached cautiously and set the two of them on their feet near the suspicious soldiers. One of them snapped, "All right, China Boy, what were you all doing over there in the cleared area? Looting, was you?"

"No savvy," said the youth who'd carried the child.

Before anyone could say anything further, another soldier pointed and said, "Here comes some more, Sarge! Jehoshaphat, they're packing their loot in plain sight! Do we shoot 'em here or wait for the captain to hang 'em?"

Dawn suddenly blinked another cobweb from her brain as she turned to see Wong Fang and his comrades approaching, loaded with bundles. "Don't be an ass, young man! Those are my things they're bringing with me—and where were *you* when I needed help with my baskets?"

Abashed, the sergeant and his squad fell silent as

Wong Fang, taking in the situation, bowed to Dawn and said, "We had to leave the body of the Mexican woman and your furniture, Brave and Honorable Lady. I am sure we got all your jewelry as well as your mementos."

One of the soldiers asked, "You let these thieving Chinee go through your belongings, lady?"

"They're not thieving Chinee, young man, they're my friends."

"By Tao, this is true," added Wong Fang, feelingly.

The sergeant in charge of the demolition team shrugged. "Well, you'd all best get yourselves over to the Presidio, whoever you are. They've set up tents and soup kitchens for the refugees, but you'd best hurry if you expect to get anything to eat. Half the town seems to be eating on Uncle Sam today, and there's no telling how long we can provide for all of yez."

"We'll take Chestnut to the Presidio," Wong Fang told Dawn, but the old woman protested. "I don't like Chestnut Street. I used to know a dreadful woman who lived on Chestnut. Can't we go along the marina tracks?"

"If you say so, Honorable Dawn Lady."

The little party started to move north, toward the tracks running between Fort Mason at the end of Van Ness and the freight yards of the military reservation below the Presidio bluffs, still carrying Dawn and her little namesake despite their protests that they wanted to walk.

A few blocks north, their way was barred by a police barricade. A burly police captain waved west and shouted, "Make your way along Chestnut, folks. The marina ways are barred to all but military traffic."

Wong Fang bowed and said, "This lady does not wish to go down Chestnut Street, sir. She says we are to use the trackway."

The police captain laughed incredulously. "Does she, now? And who might you be carrying, the Queen of Sheba? Sweet Jesus, China Boy, we're fighting to save San Francisco!"

Wong Fang sighed and said, "Just so, sir, and Chestnut would be the shorter route, but this is Dawn Carlyle of Nob Hill, a much more honored personage than the Queen of Sheba."

The captain blinked and asked, "Not Herself of Carlyle and Sons? Sweet Jesus, Harrigan, get me carriage and take Mother Carlyle and these paple wherever she says!"

Patrolman Harrigan protested, "We're forbidden by the army to use the bayside street, Captain."

"Och, shut your face and do as your told, man! This darling woman outranks the damned auld army!"

He stepped up to Dawn, who was now once more on her feet, and doffed his cap with a gallant bow. "It's Captain O'Bannion, S.F.P.D., at your service, mum. Harrigan's fetching the carriage and is there any other thing I could be doing for yez this terrible day?"

Dawn smiled wanly and asked, "Oh, are you one of Gavin O'Bannion's children, young man?"

"It's proud I am to say I am, mum, and prouder still to be able to pay me respects to a great lady. You don't remember me, do you, mum?"

"Oh, I think I do. Didn't we meet at your mother's funeral? Oh, dear—I hope I haven't offended you!"

"Offend me, mum? Nothing yourself could ever do could offend the house of O'Bannion, for though you may have forgotten the favors you showed us in the

past . . . Och, here's the carriage, and I'll say no
more."

And so Dawn, her great-granddaughter, and her
young Chinese friends arrived in state at the refugee
camp set up on the clifftop parade of the San Francisco
Presidio. They were, it's true, covered with a film of
light gray ash, but the Chinese were walking like re-
tainers on either side, so Dawn attracted not a little
notice as her police escort drove her grandly into the
tent city.

A voice called out, "Mom! For God's sake, we've
been looking all over for you!"

It was Gus. With Brian Junior and the rest of the
family in tow he bulled his way through the crowd
to lift her bodily down from the carriage as Dawn II
explained shyly, "I found her at the house."

And then there was only a babble of confused
voices, asking questions and shouting worried endearments so a body couldn't think. Dawn felt thoroughly
confused and, taking Gus by the arm, murmured,
"Let's go over to the cliff, dear heart. I need some air
and a moment of peace to sort my thoughts!"

Gus frowned a warning at the others as he nodded
and led his mother between the tents to the open space
facing north across the bay. Dawn sat down on the
tail of a cannon mounted there to salute ships entering
the nearby Golden Gate. Gus remained silent for a
time, waiting.

Finally, Dawn sighed and said, "It's been a very
tiring day, hasn't it?"

"Yes, but it's almost over, Mom. The fire's burning
itself out on the far side of Van Ness, and they figure
they've saved two-thirds of the suburbs at least. We
may have to stay here overnight, but the army has set

up soup kitchens and a tent city. As soon as I can find transportation we'll all go to my place in San Mateo, and this time I'll hear no argument about it. You're coming home with us!"

"If you say so, dear. You're the man of the family now. I hope they didn't dynamite your office on Van Ness?"

Gus shrugged and said, "It was half off its foundations from the quake, anyway. We saved the files. We'll worry about new quarters for the firm after I figure out a way to get us all to San Mateo."

As they were speaking, a young officer came over and saluted Dawn. He said, "Major Hodges, California State Guard, mum. That sergeant over there was kind enough to point you out for me."

"Really? What could the state militia want with me, of all people?"

"Orders, mum. State Senator Lopez wired instructions from Sacramento as soon as he heard the flames had reached Nob Hill."

"Oh, my, how sweet of him to remember me after all these years. You'll tell him I'm all right, won't you?"

"Yes, mum. My orders are to place my battalion at your disposal. If you'll forgive me, mum, I only have a company to spare right now, but if you can find any use for them at all . . ."

"Oh, heavens, I hardly need a whole company. In fact, I can't think of a thing to do with a squad! Do you need any soldiers, Gus, dear?"

Gus grinned at the bemused young officer. "Hardly. You don't have a wagon and team I could borrow, do you, Major?"

"For Dawn Carlyle, sir? How many wagons do you need and may I ask where you want to go?"

"San Mateo. Transportation for about twenty people and my mother's luggage? I know it's asking a lot, but—"

"Consider it done, sir! If you'll just wait here, I'll attend to it directly!"

As he paraded away, Gus laughed and threw up his hands. "I don't know, Mom. Sometimes I think Athair was right. You really are a fairy princess, aren't you?"

"Pooh, I'm just your dotty old mother. But if I promise to be good and come with you to San Mateo, how soon will I be able to get back to our house on Nob Hill?"

"Mom," he sighed, "the house is gone. Nob Hill is gone. A third of the city has been burned to the ground. There's nothing there to go home to."

But Dawn's eyes were those of a girl as she smiled, feeling better than she had in years. "Don't be silly, dear heart," she said. "There was nothing there when I first *saw* Nob Hill. We'll be starting with the streets laid out and the water pipes in."

She took her son's arm, and staring at the rising smoke clouds to the east, she added, "Oh, my, aren't we going to have a *grand* time doing it all over again?"